Leviathan

GORDON JOHN THOMSON

ISBN-10: 1500722596
ISBN-13: 978-1500722593

DEDICATION

For my wife, Nobuyo.

Leviathan

Autumn of 1857, and the East End of London is preparing for the launch of Isambard Kingdom Brunel's giant iron steamship, the *Leviathan* - at 32000 tons, the greatest ship the world has ever seen...

In Newgate prison, an innocent surgeon, Dr Jonathan Silver, is waiting in the condemned cell to be hanged for the murder of his wife, Marianne. Fate intervenes in the unlikely shape of a nineteen-year old thief, Elisa Saltash, who, in trying to break her burglar father free from Newgate on the eve of his execution, ends up freeing Dr Silver instead.

Silver and Elisa end up in the riverside world of Wapping, among the seething and dangerous world of the London docks. Silver has only one clue to the identity of his wife's real killer - with her dying breath she had said to him the word "Leviathan"...

Set against the romantic and thrilling backdrop of London of the 1850s - the bustling centre of the greatest empire in the world, with its music halls and brothels and bare knuckle fighting - this thriller is an historical crime story full of mystery, murder, suspense and romance...

CONTENTS

PROLOGUE

Thursday, 8th October 1857

Midnight had passed and, for Jonathan Silver, time had become a precious and fast dwindling resource, draining away into the night like the blood pulsing from a ruptured artery.

Silver was stretched out uncomfortably on a stone bench at one end of his cell, with only a thin horsehair blanket wrapped around him as protection from the cold. But he hardly noticed the cold in his present mood, his mind filled instead with morbid reflections about the nature of time and human mortality. Yet here was the irony! – he no longer had the time left to ponder such deep and unfathomable mysteries, or hope to make any sense of them.

It would have been better for him simply to drink himself senseless on his last night, he decided, rather than wasting his last few hours indulging in such foolish metaphysical speculation. If you had the money, it was easy enough to obtain anything from the venal gaolers and turnkeys in this cursed prison – gin, laudanum – reputedly even whores could be smuggled in, if you wanted them, although that might be a harder thing to arrange in the condemned ward of the prison. But, though lack of money was not one of his problems, Silver had spurned the chance to spend his last night on Earth in semi-conscious inebriation.

Yet he had no religious convictions to turn to in compensation, and – despite the prayer book and bible left in the cell for his spiritual welfare - had forced himself to face his last few hours without the comfort of friend, lover or Supreme Being.

Even at this late hour, there were constant distractions to jolt his wounded mind back into wakefulness whenever he did occasionally retreat into a troubled half-sleep. He could hear a carpenter or joiner still working in the press-yard outside his cell, but that familiar sound of chisel and maul on wood – a sound he'd grown up with, as his father had been a cabinet

1

maker in Dorchester - was scarcely any reassurance to him tonight, given that the man had to be making last minute adjustments to the portable scaffold. Through the tiny barred aperture high up in the outside wall that served as his remaining view of the world, other sounds intruded to disturb his heightened sensibility: a suspicious guard dog barking repeatedly in the distance; the creaking springs and iron shod wheels of a late coach, grinding on the granite setts of Newgate Street as it turned the corner into Old Bailey and made its slow way up Ludgate Hill. From somewhere deep inside the condemned ward of Newgate, a wailing man was competing for attention at this darkest moment of the night with a frightened woman whose fluted and despairing voice was like a call from beyond the grave.

And from beyond Silver's immediate environment - sensed rather than heard - came all the other myriad, restless and muted sounds of a great city stirring fitfully in the dead of night. This seething mass of humanity, with its catalogue of evils and joys, its passions and pleasures, its perversions and dreams – all sublimated by the shroud of night into an uneasy weary stalemate.

Despite a fierce self-belief and determination of character, Silver had found it impossible to remain entirely detached and philosophical about his cruel fate. As the evidence of witnesses had built up relentlessly against him during his trial, he had retreated into a sullen stinging disbelief that this gross miscarriage of justice could be happening to him. His dismissive and imperious attitude had only made him appear even guiltier to the juggernaut of English justice, but Silver had still not felt the necessity of playing at looking innocent, sure in his own mind that the truth would come out in the end.

Yet it hadn't, and now he found himself ruing his contemptuous dismissal of his lawyer's advice on how to behave in court.

Throughout the ordeal of his imprisonment and trial, his mind had wandered constantly, reliving the various episodes of his life. He'd remembered sentimental details of his Dorset childhood as if they were yesterday, and more boisterous memories of his rowdy days as a medical student in "Auld Reekie". For obvious reasons, those pleasanter memories from his youth had exerted a greater hold on him in his despair than more recent experiences. Yet he'd also inevitably recalled darker episodes in his life too that he couldn't block entirely from his troubled mind: his more recent experiences as a surgeon in the Royal Navy, and then his later service during the Crimean War - seeing again particularly those traumatic scenes of madness and despair played out at the base hospital in Turkey where he'd won his spurs as a surgeon, and witnessed the full depth of lunacy that men at war can bring to the world. Yet out of that mayhem, it was sobering to remember that it had been at Scutari of all places – that foul and pestilential place! - that he'd caught his first sight of the lovely Marianne, a startling vision in a halo of lamplight, like a visiting seraphim.

Who would ever have thought that she of all people would have led him ultimately from Scutari to another equally hellish place like this...?

Sometimes, especially during these last few days, his mind had flown high with moments of even greater fancy, and improbable thoughts of escape. How little physical space separated him from the freedom of those teeming London streets just outside his basement cell! A few feet, that was all, even if they were occupied by massive sandstone walls and barred iron gates...

But that street outside might have been at the farthest reaches of the Solar System, for all the means he had of ever reaching it.

There is a point in human existence far beyond despair, and Jonathan Silver, incarcerated in one of the condemned cells in Newgate Prison, and with midnight long gone, finally reached that plateau of dull and wounded acceptance where nothing matters to a man any more. Not life, not love, not desire, not greed - certainly not fear.

Yet, with the hardness of his bench and the inadequate protection of his blanket against the cold, sleep would still not take him and smooth the passage of his last few hours. On this chill October night, moonlight continued to caress the hunched rooftops and the sleeping buildings of the old city; did its best to penetrate the swirls of fog on the still, black river and the soot-laden air clinging to the quiet streets. At least the stinking smells of summer were diminished at this late season in the year, but tonight Silver felt a certain nostalgic longing even for that familiar London stench. Edinburgh, where Silver had studied medicine at the Royal College, was supposed to reek to high heaven, but he'd found that London, his later adopted home, was in a class of its own when it came to repellent noxious air...

Silver was suddenly startled from this introspection on the stinks of a great city by a disembodied voice, emanating with a restrained yawn apparently from nowhere. 'I could murder a pint of porter and a plate of oysters, couldn't you, Dr Silver...?'

CHAPTER 1

Silver had almost forgotten that there was someone else in the cell to share his last night – another man scheduled for that doleful walk to the scaffold tomorrow. His companion was a man of fifty summers or so, but that was all Silver knew of him. The man had been brought into the same condemned cell at ten last evening and been manacled to the opposite wall, but had said nothing at all in response to Silver's token nod of acknowledgement. Silver had thought that having the man in here with him must be a temporary arrangement - for a few minutes at most. The turnkey who had manacled the new prisoner to the wall – a bloated and elderly gaoler called Gardiner - had however soon left the cell and his charges, and hadn't returned since.

Silver had vaguely recognized this to be unusual behaviour: it should have been the turnkey occupying that spare straw mattress on the floor and keeping a close watch on him during his last night, certainly not another condemned man. This cell was clearly never intended for more than one prisoner - barely ten feet by eight, furnished with only one stone bench, one chamber pot, and one iron candlestick, fixed to the wall.

Silver's new cellmate had soon fallen asleep, or, if not, then at least feigning it. And Silver, not wanting a tiresome exchange of views with some unredeemable and possibly mentally deranged murderer, had been reluctant to speak with him anyway, so had quickly dismissed the man's existence from his mind. For a man with so little time left to him, though, Silver had wondered, as he'd listened to his companion's persistent snores, how any man could lose himself so soundly in sleep when standing on the edge of the final abyss, and about to face his maker...

But now something in the man's voice intrigued Silver and provoked him into a reaction. 'Sir, I couldn't agree more,' Silver finally concurred, 'although I might prefer wine with my oysters, and perhaps a little cheese to follow.'

Silver couldn't make out the man's face in the darkness - the turnkey having snuffed out the solitary candle on his departure, and the interior of the cell being lit only by dim filtered moonlight that was sufficient to enable a vague indication of shape and form to be made out, but nothing more. Yet Silver could nonetheless feel a pair of shrewd eyes quietly assessing him in the dark.

The man sat up against the wall and instantly proved himself a person of some resource by unexpectedly finding a match from somewhere, striking it against the brick wall, and reaching up to light the candle in the solitary iron candlestick above his head. *Where had he got that Lucifer from?* Silver wondered.

The light revealed to him that his cellmate had a face as interesting as his voice. This was a younger man than Silver had first imagined from his glimpse of him before midnight, perhaps only forty or so. The reddened skin and curling, greying hair of a middle-aged farmer were conjoined with the lean and wiry build of a labouring man. But the man also had a well-shaped head on broad shoulders and a high, almost intellectual, forehead, which truly did not seem to belong in a prison cell. His face even suggested perhaps an old acquaintanceship for a moment, until Silver belatedly realized why: the man's face had a distinct resemblance to that of the younger John Milton on the frontispiece of Silver's well-thumbed copy of *Paradise Lost*.

Silver suddenly felt the need to talk and unburden himself to this surrogate John Milton. One last contact with the human race. One last chance to redeem a life gone so badly awry.

And Silver's unknown cellmate too seemed ready to talk by now - perhaps prompted by the knowledge that, outside in the press-yard, the scaffold had already been made ready for tomorrow's spectacle. At least their short excursion together into Newgate Street for their encounter with fate would be a welcome escape from the lice and the rats inside the prison, Silver told himself.

Tomorrow was certainly going to be a grand occasion in the annals of Newgate, it seemed: a triple hanging that might bring fifty thousand sightseers or more to Newgate Street – together, no doubt, with vendors of eels and pea soup, stall keepers selling sheep's trotters and adulterated coffee, jugglers, entertainers, pickpockets, whores - all come to ply their trade and enjoy the spectacle. Hence the concern of the turnkeys in ensuring that no prisoner cheated the crowd by topping himself early. That would make the prison governor and his men *very* unpopular with the locals, who regarded a hanging with as much anticipation and excitement as a feast day or fair.

Silver wondered fearfully if he would really be able to die stoically like a man tomorrow, in front of that baying mob. No one could possibly know, though, until the actual moment came, how they would cope with dying in this brutal fashion.

There was an expression commonly used on the streets of London for something filthy beyond description – "black as Newgate's knocker", they said. Silver had wondered during his time here why it should just be the knocker of Newgate Prison that was the symbol of unredeemed filth and despair. This whole stinking place was the smokiest, blackest, foulest place he'd ever been – a place without light or warmth or hope of redemption.

*

The man, who by now had given his name as Jonas Saltash, told Silver his diverting story.

'I'm a Pershore man, Dr Silver – Worcestershire born and bred. And although you might not credit this, I never did a wrong thing in my life until I was thirty years old. I was God fearing and docile – a true innocent. I was a locksmith with my own shop in the main high street of the town, a pillar of the community.'

'So what happened to change you from a pillar of the community?'

Saltash let out a long sigh. 'First thing was that my wife died of the smallpox. A sweet woman who had always kept me on the straight and narrow up to then. But by dying so improvidently, she left me with three young children to feed and take care of by myself. Then my business collapsed in the farming depression of the hungry forties.' He shrugged philosophically. 'No one needs new locks on their doors when they have no food in their bellies. My two younger children soon died of the ague: the sweetest pair of nippers you ever saw. So I gave up faith in prayer after that and went a little mad, I suppose. Then I decided it was time to help myself. I came to London with my surviving child, a girl of eight. My first job was a rich man's house in Highgate. My little girl acted as my lookout; cool as a cucumber, she was. I told myself it would just be the once – I would steal only enough to get me a start in London. But they were such damnably easy pickings! Who would want to do an honest day's work after that? Rich men cheat and steal from the rest of us all the time and get away with it, while the poor have to live off their scraps. So I thought: why shouldn't I redress the balance and restore some natural justice to the world?'

Silver grunted cynically. 'Why not indeed? So you're a philosopher as well as a burglar, Mr Saltash.'

Saltash nodded without embarrassment. 'I am indeed. But not just any burglar, Doctor. The best.'

Silver grimaced wryly. 'And yet you got caught.'

'A police detective called Charlie Sparrow was my undoing. A relentless and inhuman devil for pursuing a man is Sergeant Sparrow. As smart as paint too, although you'd never guess it by studying him. The man looks like some timid little bank clerk who lives with his old widowed mother.'

'But what are you doing here in the condemned cells? Burglary is no longer a hanging offence,' Silver reminded Saltash.

'It is if someone dies during the job.' Saltash shook his head ruefully. 'It was an unholy accident that brought me to this pretty pass. A house out in the country near the village of Finchley. The family was supposed to be away with their servants, but a manservant came back early that night – a big old ex-soldier with an evil temper – who would have killed me if I hadn't fought back. In the fight, he accidentally fell down some steps and broke his neck.'

'So you were merely saving yourself?' Silver said caustically.

Saltash ignored the hint of sarcasm in Silver's voice. 'I was. But the judge didn't quite see it that way.'

'Not very understanding of him.'

'No, not compassionate at all.' Saltash cocked an inquisitive eye in Silver's direction. 'I suppose you're innocent too, Dr Silver.'

Silver frowned at that remark, wondering what Saltash's interesting definition of "innocent" might be, if he truly considered a rogue such as himself to be so. 'What makes you say that? And how do you know my name anyway, Mr Saltash, or so much about me?'

'Oh, everyone has heard of a gentleman like you, sir...'

'I'm no gentleman,' Silver denied brusquely.

Saltash barely paused to catch breath. 'I'm sure you are, sir, even though the papers was full of how you brutally stabbed your wife at your home in Russell Square in Bloomsbury. And yet you don't look like a man who would do such a wicked and uncharitable thing, if you don't mind me saying so.'

Silver didn't stir on his stone bench. 'It's of no concern now whether I did or not. The law decided in its infinite wisdom that I did do it.'

Saltash squinted across the cell at him. 'Well, perhaps it might be still a concern. Lots of people have escaped from here, you know, Doctor. For example, the famous highwayman Jack Sheppard got out of here three times in all...'

'Yes...before they finally hanged him at Tyburn,' Silver interrupted harshly. Yet he was still interested enough in what his companion was saying to lift his head and look directly across the cell at the man. 'And I have to break the unpalatable news to you that the prison Jack Sheppard escaped from was an entirely different and ramshackle Newgate from this modern one. No one has escaped from here recently, as far as I am aware. This building was designed to keep men in permanently.'

Saltash's mind seemed to be dwelling in a world of its own. 'Perhaps that's true,' he conceded airily. 'But that doesn't mean there's no hope of getting out of here.'

'It *is* true. And it's far too late for hope – you would be better employed making your peace with your maker, if you believe in such a thing,' Silver snapped irately. This was not the kind of talk he'd wanted to hear from this man. He'd wanted the comfort of another human being facing the same fate, not the raising of tantalizing and imaginary hopes in his mind at this stage.

Saltash moved closer to the sputtering candlestick above his head. 'Perhaps for you, Dr Silver. But not for me. I'm not going to be hanged tomorrow. Not if I can help it anyway...'

*

After a long silence, Silver wrapped his horsehair blanket more tightly around him again, and then asked, 'How can you avoid it?'

Saltash blinked slowly. 'Perhaps because I might have a guardian angel watching over me.'

'An angel?' Silver studied the man's face again. *Was he talking literally?* Was the man mad, as well as being a rogue?

'My daughter, Elisa – God bless her! - has been cultivating one of the turnkeys here. He will help me escape tonight.' Saltash hesitated shyly. 'You too, if you wish, Doctor.'

Silver was curious, despite all his doubts. 'Which turnkey do you mean?'

'The one who brought me here tonight. Gardiner, the old 'un. You must have realized that's not normal procedure – for two men to be left in a condemned cell together on their last night.'

Silver frowned. 'Yes, why did he do that? And why is he not here watching us, as he's supposed to?'

'Because Gardiner has other things to do – to arrange my escape route, and also to give sleeping draughts to as many of the other turnkeys as possible. He'll do anything for my Elisa, you see. It's that porcelain white skin of hers. He truly is putty in her hands, so she tells me. And there's no fool like an old 'un, is there?'

'You would let your daughter do something like that on your behalf? Trade her virtue to save you? And to a man even older than yourself?' Silver couldn't quite keep the note of disgust out of his voice.

'It was her own idea, Doctor. And anyway, I'm sure it's not her body she's selling to Gardiner, but the promise of permanent financial security. She has promised him more money than he's ever had in his life.'

Silver sniffed. 'Are you sure that's all she's promised him?'

'Well, for all I know, she might also have promised to marry him and sail off with him to the shores of Araby,' he admitted. 'But she'll not keep any of those promises, even if she has made them.' Saltash was becoming defensive now, not entirely immune to Silver's barbed criticism. 'She can well afford to pay Gardiner off - and that promise of a comfortable retirement will have to satisfy the man.'

'How can she afford enough to pay off a man like Gardiner? If he's really doing this for money, then I doubt his help will come cheap.'

Saltash stirred on his straw mattress and said expansively, 'Oh, Elisa has learned everything of my illicit trade from me, and made herself mightily rich in the process. She started helping me on jobs at the age of eight, as I said, and then began working on her own with a little mug-hunting and yack-snatching...'

Silver had not the slightest idea what he was talking about.

Saltash was still in full flow, '...Before moving on to cutting purses. Then she took to a little breaking and entering in her own right. She could have been in the circus, my girl, the things she can climb, and the tiny spaces she can get through. Almost supernatural, it is. Now she usually works alone and applies herself to only the grandest houses – places I would be afraid to go near - and knows exactly what fine works of art and jewellery to take from them. And all that knowledge and skill at barely nineteen years of age! It warms my heart to see how well my girl's done for herself.'

Silver nodded knowingly. 'I see. You mean she's a thief and a burglar too.'

Saltash swelled with fatherly pride. 'The best.'

'You said *you* were the best, if I recall,' Silver reminded him coolly.

'Then I was exaggerating. But certainly not about Elisa. There's nowhere that girl cannot break into, or out of – not even Newgate. And with Gardiner's help, she will not fail me tonight.'

Silver shook his head ruefully. 'It's still a foolish notion. One turnkey cannot get you out of here, no matter how much you pay him. You would need every uniformed man in the place to open their gates and look the other way.'

'One man can open this cell door at least. And free my hands and unlock my leg irons.'

'And then what? Even if you get out of this damned condemned ward, you're still enclosed within the main prison block. There are four or five other locked iron gates after that between you and the main gate to Old Bailey.' Silver had discovered this much about the layout of the prison earlier in his own captivity - a time when he himself had still entertained some vague hopes of escape. The main block of the prison was arranged in a bleak quadrangle of soot-covered brick, six stories high, around a square stone-flagged exercise yard where little light penetrated, and certainly no hope.

Saltash wasn't discouraged by Silver's scepticism. 'Don't worry. My little beauty has a head on her shoulders – taught herself to read and write from the age of eight, she did, and has filled her own head since with all sorts of wondrous knowledge. And it's because of that learning of hers, and all those books she reads, that she happened on an ancient plan of Newgate and the city that shows a disused and forgotten Roman sewer running close to where the main exercise yard of the prison now sits. And perhaps a way to get into it...'

Silver hummed in disbelief. *'Perhaps a way...?'*

'...She believes the Roman sewer leads out under the old city wall to the Fleet and thence to the river. She has given me precise instructions how to gain entrance into the sewer and follow the route. If we go that way, we can avoid going through the main block of the prison altogether.' He paused, a bubble of saliva forming on his lips in his excitement. 'Are you willing to give it a try with me, Doctor? I could use your help.'

'The Fleet was bricked over many years ago,' Silver argued. 'It's a stinking pestilential sewer that runs under Farringdon Street now, not a river at all.'

'I know that already. What are you afraid of? A few turds? A few rats? You! - a doctor who served in the blood and gore of the Crimea! Would you prefer instead to feel your neck being stretched tomorrow until it snaps?'

'And how do we get to the exercise yard? We still have to go through several gates to get even that far, don't we?'

Saltash was almost triumphant. *'Two* gates, that's all, Doctor, and a passageway below ground level. That's where Gardiner comes in handy: he has the keys that will get us through those gates.'

Silver sniffed doubtfully, but inside, his excitement was growing. *Could there be a way out of here after all, or was this man a lunatic, clinging to some demented and impossible dream?* 'There won't be anyone else guarding that passageway tonight?'

Saltash was dismissive. 'It's nearly two in the morning, Dr Silver. And that passage only gives access to the exercise yard. Why would anyone be watching it at this ungodly hour – an underground passage that leads nowhere?'

Silver still half-suspected the man was mad, but even the slimmest of chances was a golden lifeline when all other hopes had been extinguished. 'Why do you want me to come? You look fit enough to make it on your own.'

'There may be some heavy work required along the way to break into that old sewer, and I might not be able to make it alone. I'm not as strong as I used to be – I believe my lungs have become tainted with the consumption while I've been rotting in here these three months - while you are still clearly in the full prime of your youthful vigour.' He smiled heartily, not looking in the least like a consumptive, as far as Silver could see. 'Come, Doctor, don't give up hope of a long life for yourself yet. My Elisa is waiting with a boat on the river to spirit us away if we can find our way through the sewers. This time tomorrow you could be on a clipper heading to the East Indies, or on a steamship to New York...'

CHAPTER 2

Silver had only a few moments to get his mind in order while contemplating the heady possibility of escape, before an iron key rattled in the lock and the heavy oak door of the cell creaked open.

Silver recognized the grey-haired overweight figure standing in the open doorway as the missing gaoler Gardiner. Yet, although the absent turnkey had finally returned to see to his charges, he seemed to Silver to be a man in a less than certain mood about what to do next, as he checked the contents of a canvas bag he had brought with him.

Someone was standing behind Gardiner's heavily perspiring form and soon pulled the hesitant gaoler aside into the passageway in order to enter the condemned cell himself. The arrival of this second person - a slender youth in ragged greatcoat, heavy breeches and cap - was clearly something Jonas Saltash had not been expecting. That much was obvious to Silver from the way his cellmate sucked in his breath explosively in surprise when the boy strode confidently through the doorway.

Yet Saltash's puzzlement soon turned to boiling anger. He sprang energetically to his feet to challenge the boy, despite the heavy shackles and leg irons restraining him. 'What the blazes are *you* doing here? You're not supposed to be *here*! That wasn't the plan we agreed!' he complained to the newcomer, all of his earlier amiable and eccentric behaviour vanished at a stroke, and turned into unexpected vitriol. Moreover, that anger and exertion soon brought on a violent fit of coughing that almost doubled Saltash up with pain, and made him sink back again onto his dirty straw mattress in despair. Silver looked at him in alarm, then climbed down from his stone bench as far as the travel of his leg irons would allow, to get a better look at the man. From the violence of that reaction, it seemed that Saltash had not been exaggerating his morbid worries about his health after all. That blood-flecked coughing fit did indeed display all of the signs of quite advanced consumption, despite the still healthy size of the man, and the broadness of his shoulders.

Silver's slight confusion over the boy's identity was soon resolved by what Saltash said next. 'You were supposed to be waiting down by the river with a boat, not risking your neck in here, Lizzie,' he commented bitterly to the newcomer. Then a thought apparently occurred to Saltash, and his voice took on a note of extreme curiosity. 'How did you get in here anyway, my girl? Did I father a phantom creature that can move freely through solid walls?'

Listening in on this conversation, Silver realized instantly that the "boy" had in fact to be Saltash's daughter Elisa, although, given the weak and flickering light of the solitary candle in this dismal cell, his error was understandable enough.

Even now that he understood who she was, she still made quite a convincing imitation of a young man as she moved further into the cell with an almost masculine swagger and self-confidence. She dropped to her knees beside her father's mattress while the aged turnkey Gardiner, still breathing and sweating heavily, continued to keep an uneasy watch in the narrow passageway outside. 'I know I was meant to wait on the river for you, father. But I couldn't take the risk of something going awry.' Her voice – quite a refined voice given her background - dropped to a whisper. 'John has been getting cold feet these last few days,' she said *sotto voce* to her father. 'So I came dressed like this as a visitor to the prison this afternoon, to reassure John and make last minute preparations for the escape. But when I saw the distraught state of mind that he was in, and realized that he might go back on his promise to me, I decided I couldn't leave things to chance. I had to stay to ensure John kept his word. I've been here in the prison ever since...'

'How did you manage that?' her father asked, still in slight awe of his daughter's almost supernatural skills.

'Never mind about that now,' she said curtly, 'we've got to get moving.'

Silver decided it was time to say something. 'Are you sure this so-called Roman sewer even exists?' he interrupted tartly.

Elisa turned her head from her kneeling position and gave him a long cool look. 'And who is this knucklehead, may I ask?' she demanded peremptorily of her father, as if she'd not noticed Silver's presence until now, although Silver knew fine well that was impossible.

Saltash, still coughing in painful fits, struggled to his feet again with his daughter's help. 'That's the famous Dr Silver. Show some respect, girl.'

Elisa stirred in an even more hostile manner as she supported her father's weight with her shoulder. 'Ah, you mean the infamous *wife* murderer.'

Saltash was amused by his daughter's brazenness. 'The very same.'

'He doesn't look as evil as I expected,' Elisa claimed dismissively. 'In fact, he seems rather ordinary...'

'Why, what were you expecting?' Silver asked her sharply. 'Horns?'

Gardiner now forced his way into the cramped cell and pulled Elisa roughly aside from her father, before nodding belligerently in Silver's direction. 'Silver has to go with you too, Lizzie. Otherwise he'll tell what he's seen before he goes to the gallows tomorrow.'

'Then why did you put my father in the same cell with him, you numbskull, so that he would see everything?' she remonstrated, puzzled. 'There was no reason for it.'

Gardiner frowned resentfully. 'There's no need to use such language to me, Lizzie.' Gardiner was clearly as slow-witted a fellow as he seemed at first glance. 'Maybe I wasn't thinking straight, Lizzie. But Silver has seen me helping you now, so he has to go too.'

Saltash pushed himself in front of his daughter – not easy in the confines of the narrow cell, and with his feet cruelly encased in iron. 'It's all right, Mr Gardiner. You need have no concerns on that point. Dr Silver will be coming with me and Elisa.'

Silver objected to the man's assumption of his docile acquiescence. 'I don't remember yet agreeing to join you in this foolish venture, Mr Saltash. What if I don't care to go and die inside some filthy pipe? Perhaps I'd rather hang in the open tomorrow, breathing air - of a sort at least - than suffocate underground tonight.'

Elisa was furious, and grabbed the front of Silver's prison uniform. 'Have you no spirit, Dr Silver? I've risked everything coming here tonight to save my wretched father. And now a low murderous individual like you will destroy his only chance? If my father wants you to come with us, you *will* join us! Is that clear?'

Silver could feel the surprising strength in this girl's fingers as she twisted the cheap worsted cloth of his coarse overall into a tight knot. Perhaps a girl like this really could find a way out of this labyrinthine hellhole...

*

Silver quickly allowed himself to be persuaded, but only begrudgingly.

In truth, though, he did prefer to die trying to escape rather than being wheeled out helplessly to the scaffold tomorrow, head covered in ignominy, to face the jeers and insults of a baying mob...

After Gardiner had unlocked the manacles on his hands, and the leg irons tying his ankles together, Silver felt rejuvenated, the blood surging through his limbs again and bringing him fresh hope and energy. Losing that weight of iron from his body was exhilarating, and the unfamiliar ease of movement made him feel incredibly free, almost as if he could fly. *How long had it been since he'd been allowed to walk unencumbered like this?*

Within seconds they were on their way, Gardiner taking the lead with a lantern held high. The three others followed the bulky perspiring figure of the gaoler as he led the way down a steep flight of steps, then along a dim stone passageway lit by oil lamps, where the joints between the masonry blocks were oozing with slime and moisture. These old stone walls below ground level were clearly older than seventy years, and therefore, Silver surmised, probably part of the underground cells of the earlier Newgate on which the present building had been built.

'Soon be out of here, Doctor,' Saltash declared optimistically with a backward glance at Silver. Saltash's coughing had by now abated, but that temporary improvement in his health hardly seemed to justify his optimism in Silver's view.

Eventually Gardiner reached a second flight of stone steps that brought them higher again, and a further passageway at ground level with a metal studded oak doorway at its end. So far Saltash had been right about there being no one on duty in this isolated part of the condemned ward.

Elisa bringing up the rear, raised her own lantern, and then moved forward past Silver and her father to inspect the door with Gardiner. It didn't look to Silver like it had been opened for many a long year, the rusted metal plate of the escutcheon covered by a thick skein of cobwebs. 'This is not the way we agreed, John,' she commented to Gardiner suspiciously.

'Yes, I know that, Lizzie,' Gardiner snapped in return. 'But I believe someone may be on the prowl tonight in that passageway leading directly to the exercise yard – a new young turnkey called Minshall, who I think may be a spy or snitch for the governor. He seemed very suspicious of me today...' - he shushed Elisa's attempted further protest with an admonitory finger – '...so I have thought of a safer way of reaching the yard.'

Gardiner opened the creaking door to reveal a spiral iron staircase. Silver had been expecting Gardiner to take the downwards flight at this point, but instead the gaoler surprisingly took the steps leading upwards. This choice surprised Elisa too, Silver could tell, and she whispered again to remonstrate with him.

'Why are you going up, John? You can't hope to reach the exercise yard this way. We surely have to go *down* from here, if we are to get to the exercise yard.'

'I've told you already, Lizzie: we have to change the original plan and go *this* way. That new man Minshall refused my offer of a drink tonight so he will certainly not be sleeping soundly like the rest of the turnkeys. And the cells he is responsible for are located close to the passageway that leads to the exercise yard. If Minshall catches me there with you, I'm finished. They would hang me too, or transport me at the very least, for what I'm doing.' Gardiner was working himself up into a fine nervous lather, sweat pouring off his round ham-like face and balding head, despite the chill and the damp in these old passageways. But he still felt the need to justify himself further to the girl. 'If we go this way, there is no risk of running into Minshall at all. Using these stairs, I can get you onto the main roof of the prison. From there, you should be able to lower yourselves down to the exercise yard while I return to the cells and pretend to be drugged too, like the other turnkeys.' He indicated the rough canvas bag he had draped over his shoulder. 'See, Lizzie,' he added encouragingly, 'I have brought enough rope for you to climb down from the roof, and a pickaxe and other tools to enable you to expose the drain you're looking for.'

Elisa reacted with cold fury, though, to this nervous and hesitant explanation. 'That's not what you promised, John. You said we would be able to walk into the exercise yard. My father has been languishing in this prison for many months, and is sick with the consumption. He doesn't have the strength to climb down eighty feet of rope...'

'It may not be what I promised, yet it will have to d...do,' Gardiner began to stutter in his distress, his face shining with sweat, and his breath palpitating alarmingly with the fear of discovery. 'Please try and understand, Lizzie...'

Silver could sense that, despite his fear, the old turnkey's infatuation with this young girl was driving him on to help her, even when every fibre in his body was screaming for him to say no. It was deeply uncomfortable to watch this degree of anguish, guilt and confusion – *passion* even - tearing this elderly man apart.

Elisa was still simmering, but she nevertheless squeezed herself against the stonework to allow Gardiner to go ahead of her up the iron stairs. Silver suspected she had lost her bearings anyway in Gardiner's convoluted escape route, so had no other choice now but to follow her accomplice wherever he led them.

Silver took the stairs immediately behind Elisa, leaving her father to take up the rear of the party now. 'Does that man really believe you care for him?' he asked her coolly. 'Is he that much of a fool?'

She didn't even turn her head in response, but Silver could hear the derision in her voice. 'Yes, of course he is.' She stopped briefly to glance down at him. 'But then all men are gullible fools, aren't they, Dr Silver? And some are wicked too - you of all people should know that,' she added malevolently.

At the top of the stairs, after six or seven spiral turns, with similar dismal and gloomy passageways leading off at each level, the three of them emerged into what looked like the highest level - a dusty and seldom used chamber, it seemed, with blank brick walls and what appeared like a solid wooden roof above their heads.

Elisa was in a cold fury by now with the old turnkey. 'What is this place, John? How can we hope to get onto the roof from here?'

Actually it looked to Silver as if this was *exactly* the use the architect and builder of Newgate had intended for this mysterious staircase and empty chamber – as an essential access to the roof, in order to maintain or repair it. As if to confirm that, he saw stacks of builder's material and tools lying around the edge of the room – slate tiles, lead piping, timber joists, mauls and saws and hammers.

But Gardiner failed to respond to Elisa's question. Instead he suddenly dropped his lantern and his canvas bag with a crash, then began to gurgle and froth at the mouth, making strange unearthly sounds...

*

Those inhuman sounds made the hairs on the back of Silver's neck stand up in protest, but he still had the presence of mind to quickly right the fallen lantern before it set fire to the place. By this time, Gardiner had sunk to the timber floor in clear distress, like a scuttled East Indiaman settling sedately to the seabed.

Elisa leant down to him, holding her own lantern near his face and whispering urgently in his ear. 'What's wrong, John? What ails you?'

Silver knelt down rapidly beside her and put his hand to Gardiner's chest. 'He can't answer you; he's having a heart seizure,' he explained rapidly. 'I have seen this many times before in older men where the blood vessels are constricted with fats and other obstructions, or the valves are malformed by age and disease.'

Elisa regarded Silver worriedly. 'Then do something for him! He looks to be dying.'

Silver ignored the curtness of her command, and put his ear close to the man's breast. 'His heart has stopped completely now. The effects of exertion and worry on an already overloaded heart, no doubt.' He didn't pause further, but wrenched the turnkey's voluminous uniform and shirt open and listened intently to his chest one further time, before beginning to pummel and pound the ribcage with his fists.

Elisa, crouched by his side, was startled by his performance. 'What the devil are you doing? Trying to bring a dead man back to life by cruelty?' Even her father seemed amazed by Silver's strange and violent actions, his jaw dropping as he stood watching behind his daughter.

Silver continued pummelling with his fists without pause. 'This is a technique I have seen used by physicians in the Ottoman Empire,' he explained breathlessly to Elisa and her father. 'The Muslim doctors I encountered in Constantinople can often restart a heart by violent massage, provided the length of the stoppage is not excessive.'

Silver paused briefly, his own chest heaving with the unfamiliar effort, before trying again. But a further five minutes of desperate massage achieved no sign of life in the waxen face of the gaoler, no ghostly flutter of his heart, or a return of any trace of breath.

Finally he gave up, wiping the cold sweat from his brow. 'It's no use,' he apologized. 'Perhaps it's my lack of skill in the technique, or it may be that the man's heart is simply diseased beyond human help.' He cursed softly under his breath. 'I'm sorry. I have done this successfully before, I promise you, but I have obviously not had much opportunity to practise the method of late.'

He climbed to his feet, leaving the old gaoler's vast corpse stretched out on the dusty floorboards like a beached whale.

Elisa bit her lip, but her anger had subsided by now. 'I'm sure you did your best.' The girl was surprisingly tender with the old gaoler. Leaning forward, she closed his staring eyes gently with her fingers. Then she took off her greatcoat and covered his body with it.

'You really liked the man?' Silver observed with surprise.

'I did.' She lifted her chin determinedly. 'And what is so wrong with that? He was a nice old man, despite working in this terrible place.'

Her father stepped forward out of the shadows, seemingly unconcerned about this odd display of sentiment by his young daughter for one of his gaolers. 'How do we go from here, my girl? I've looked around. There seems no way out of this chamber up to the roof.'

Elisa stood up slowly, her eyes still lingering on the body at her feet, covered with her own greatcoat. 'John brought us here for a reason. So there must be a way to get to the roof. An access ladder or hatch, or something.'

Silver agreed with her so took the turnkey's discarded lantern and moved quickly around the room, examining every corner and feature, before finding what looked like a narrow recessed stone chimneypiece in the middle of the wall at one end of the chamber.

'This is no normal chimney,' he announced, as he bent down and prodded the lantern up into the space above. 'There never was any need for a fire up here, in an unoccupied windowless chamber like this. So this has to be the way up to the roof.' He stuck his head further into the space. 'There are step irons set in the side of the stonework, but the space looks damned tight.' He lowered himself down again and reappeared in the chamber. 'Gardiner would certainly never have made it up there,' he announced, 'but we three just might.'

'Then I'll go first, being the slimmest,' Elisa said tartly, moving smartly over to the chimney. 'We'll have to douse the lanterns for the present, because we daren't show a light above,' she warned, 'but there is a moon tonight so we should be able to see well enough.'

Unlike her overweight turnkey accomplice, this girl seemed no more than a wraith, Silver decided, as she disappeared up the stone shaft with ease, like a coil of smoke vanishing into thin air. In a few seconds Silver heard her voice call down softly, but with clear satisfaction, from above. 'John was right. It is easy enough to get up here. But we still have a difficult way to go. Pass the rope and the tools from John's bag up to me first,' she ordered.

Silver didn't waste time wondering what she meant by that remark about a difficult way to go, but recovered the coil of rope and the pickaxe from the turnkey's canvas bag, and passed them up to her. Without pausing for breath, he helped Jonas crawl into the bottom of the shaft and then, when he seemed to be making heavy weather of the climb, heaved him up the shaft by his arse – a backside still surprisingly muscular and sturdy, considering his wasted lungs.

It was a tighter squeeze for himself up the shaft, though, especially carrying a lantern, and Jonas, by now wedged on the roof above, had to return the favour by giving him a hand to heave himself out into the night air.

The sudden feeling of cold and gusting air on his face was as intoxicating as nectar to Silver. Even the smoky and tainted air of London tasted like the breath of Mount Olympus, after weeks buried in the bowels of Newgate Gaol. The sooty dome of St Paul's loomed vast and mountainous in the near distance, dominating the huddled rooftops in all directions. With a rush of breath, Silver vowed silently to himself that no power on earth was ever going to get him back into that cell below. He preferred to jump off this roof, and dash his brains out on the hard flagstones below, rather than be taken alive again...

CHAPTER 3

Thursday, 8th October 1857

In the moonlight, Silver could make out the outline of the roofs that formed the other three sides of the main quadrangle around Newgate's central exercise yard. He and his two fugitive companions had found themselves unfortunately on the most visible side of the quadrangle nearest Newgate Street, although that might have been expected, since this was the side adjacent to the condemned ward and the outer press-yard where the gallows was now presumably ready to be wheeled out into the street tomorrow at first light. The press-yard itself was well lit with flickering oil lamps, and still displayed occasional sounds of activity even at two in the morning, so that there was a real risk that someone in the yard below might see them crouching on the roof above, if they happened to look up.

By contrast, the exercise yard on the interior of Newgate's tall quadrangle of soot-covered brick was a good fifty yards across and completely unlit at ground level; also as silent as the grave, and with the bottom concealed in such deep shadows that from roof level it resembled a square and bottomless lake filled with the blackest pitch. Now that they had managed to gain access to the roof, that exercise yard seemed to Silver to be the worst possible place to climb down into, on the miserably small chance that this slip of a girl might actually be able to find her way into some supposed ancient Roman sewer that would magically lead them to freedom. *Surely the best way was simply to climb down directly into the press-yard – that is, on the* outside *of the prison - and try to make a direct escape from there...?*

He suggested this to the girl but she dismissed it with a morose sniff. 'You would not get ten yards that way, Doctor, before you would walk into the grateful arms of a whole gang of gaolers. But please feel free to go that way if you like, provided that you first wait an hour or so until my father and I have had the chance to make good our escape.'

Silver quickly reviewed his options in the light of that cutting remark. The fact was that the girl was probably right in her assessment of the situation: there were too many guards and watchful hangers-on lingering on that side of the prison, waiting patiently for their following morning's entertainment. So although this probably fictitious Roman sewer might offer no more than the slimmest of hopes, at least it was some slight chance of salvation. On the positive side, there was enough moonlight for Silver and his companions to discern their situation on the roof without the need to light their lanterns again. Yet that helpful old moon, showing intermittently through slow moving banks of silvered cumulus cloud, was a double-edged sword, of course, because it also enabled them to be clearly seen, hiding on this roof, should anyone happen to be awake in one of the cells or rooms opposite, and casting an eye in their direction.

The geometry and condition of the roof also presented a more pressing problem of its own – it sloped at a dangerous thirty degrees from a central ridge to the eaves. Nor were there any convenient lead gutters or drainpipes to catch the flow of rainwater at the edges of the roof, just a featureless roof and a sheer drop into the stone-flagged exercise yard below.

Jonas smiled grimly at Silver, showing gaps in his front teeth. 'I think this roof is something of a nightmare, isn't it, Dr Silver?'

'That it certainly is,' agreed Silver, running his hands along the surface. The slate felt so greasy and slippery to the touch, with a green scum of decay coating its surface, that it seemed quite impossible to even stand up on such a roof except by precariously straddling the ridge. And even there, it felt to Silver like one wrong step would be enough to send him and his companions sliding helplessly down the incline to their deaths. But here at least was one advantage of being condemned to hang in the morning – the threat of physical danger no longer meant much to a man in his position...

'Let's tie the rope to the chimney piece,' Silver suggested to Jonas. Although built of flimsy brickwork, that tiny projecting chimney appeared to present the only feature on the roof that might conceivably be strong enough to take one end of the rope. The rest of the roof was a steep and slick expanse of slate tiles, apparently devoid of a single nail or projection. 'I hope your late gaoler friend knew how to calculate,' Silver observed ironically to Elisa, 'and that his rope is therefore going to be long enough.'

Elisa looked apologetic for once as she began coiling the rope over her neck and shoulder. 'Even if it is long enough, I'm afraid it won't be quite that easy, Dr Silver. We first need to get over to that other part of the roof over there.' She indicated a further section of the roof to the east, which looked similar in all respects to the one they presently occupied, except that it appeared to be separated from it by a yawning seven-foot gap.

'Why do we have to go over there, Lizzie?' her father whispered irately. 'Why can't we just climb straight down from here into the yard?'

Elisa sighed softly. 'Because the exercise yard below is divided into several distinct areas, that's why. From my precise measurements of the line of the Roman sewer, which I checked from the street outside using a railway engineer's theodolite, I believe the sewer passes close to that far corner of the exercise yard...' - she indicated vaguely in the distance with her arm – 'which is unfortunately separated from the yard below us by a wall. If we had gone the way John originally promised, then we could have walked into that far corner of the exercise yard directly. As it is, we will have to get across that gap in the roof somehow, in order to reach it.'

Silver interrupted brusquely at this point, while wondering how and where this girl could possibly have learned to use a railway engineer's theodolite. 'We could still lower ourselves down from here, and then climb the wall in the exercise yard to reach the corner you're talking about.'

Elisa laughed humourlessly. 'I wish it was that simple! I had a close look today at that dividing wall in the exercise yard. It has a *cheval-de-frise* on top. You know what that is, Doctor, I presume? A devilish barrier of rotating iron spikes that would skewer you like a stuffed pig, if you were to attempt to get over it. No one can climb over such a thing without impaling themselves...not even me.' She hesitated modestly. 'Well, perhaps *I* could, being specially gifted in that direction. But you and my father certainly could not succeed.'

Silver grudgingly accepted her decision – perhaps a seven-foot jump across a gap in the roof was a better alternative than being impaled on a wall by rotating metal spikes. The three of them therefore moved gingerly along the ridgeline of the roof towards the unexpected gap, to assess the extent of the hazard. From above it looked like a veritable chasm, with a small private paved yard lost deep in shadows at the bottom.

Elisa remained positive. 'It's only seven feet across. Anyone can jump that. A child, even.'

'Anyone in good health, anyway, my girl,' Jonas commented bitterly, '...and on a nice dry surface on the flat, and with a good run up available. This is on a slippery wet sloping roof in the depth of night, and in poor light.'

Elisa stood up on the ridge. 'Not *that* poor. Watch, father. I'll show you how easy it is.' With those final few words, and no other preparation at all, she took two steps and launched herself casually into the void, even though still encumbered by her lantern, and the heavy rope carried over her shoulder.

She did indeed make the jump look effortless, Silver had to agree, as she landed daintily on the ridge on the far side with all the agility and skill of a circus performer, and with a clear foot or more to spare. There she put down her lantern carefully on the ridge of the roof, together with that vital coil of rope.

Silver threw his lantern and the pickaxe over for her to catch, not quite so sure that he could make it across encumbered in the same way. Then he followed her over before he could give himself time to worry about the distance required for the leap, and the hard stone yard far below. As he landed on the other side of the chasm with his right foot, though, he failed to meet the very centre of the ridge and consequently his boot began to slide away down the slippery slate incline of the roof. That was, anyway, until he felt a hand like a vice grab his tunic and stop his fall, before pulling him back to safety on the ridge. This girl was extraordinary in her strength and natural agility, he had to admit.

For a moment, as she held him closely to her on the ridge, he could distinctly feel the roundness and firmness of her breasts under that man's poplin shirt, pressing hard against his own heaving chest. Then they separated, while Elisa, ignoring the brief intimate contact as if it had never happened, beckoned her father over to the edge to jump too.

Saltash gulped, then tried to take a mighty leap to emulate his daughter. But his left foot slid backwards on the greasy slate as he did so, and he lost a lot of his forward momentum. Yet even so, his right foot still managed to make contact with the ridge of the roof on the other side, if also leaving him hopelessly unbalanced and scrabbling for safety. Immediately he began to topple backwards into the chasm but Elisa was again lightning-quick in her response. Her right hand shot out to grasp her father's arm and prevent him falling backwards. And she did somehow succeed, after a fashion, in restraining his fall and pulling him over to her side of the gap. Yet the two of them were both dangerously out of equilibrium now, despite Elisa's best efforts to recover, and they collapsed together in a heap on the sloping side of the roof, before sliding away down the slate-covered incline towards the main exercise yard eighty feet below.

Silver immediately began slithering down the roof from his present safe perch astride the ridge to try and intercept them, but was a second too late to prevent Jonas going over the edge with a silent scream and the sound of a violent impact from below. Yet he found Elisa at the overhanging eave, still managing somehow to cling on one-handed to a tiny finger-hold of a projection, her feet dangling helplessly over the black void below.

Even in that situation, she was absolutely fearless. 'I...can't...hold on...much longer. Give...me your...damned hand.' It was more a command than a plea for help.

Silver pressed his body face down to the edge of the roof and extended his left arm out to reach her. Somehow the rough serge of his prison uniform found enough purchase on the oily surface of the slate to stop him sliding further, and he was able to make contact with her searching left arm to jerk her up to safety. Despite her strength she seemed impossibly light to him – certainly no more than seven stones.

For a moment they lay together on the roof, gasping and breathless, before Elisa reluctantly craned her neck over the edge to see what had become of her father.

Silver's stomach turned over when he looked over the edge too. The moonlight penetrated just deep enough into the exercise yard to reveal that Jonas had landed chest down on top of the dividing wall in the yard below and was impaled like a carcase of beef on the *cheval-de-frise*...

*

Silver had to assume that the impalement had killed Jonas outright because the man had made scarcely a sound as the iron spikes sliced through him. Even so, he wondered why the sound hadn't brought every turnkey in the place rushing to the exercise yard to investigate. Yet there was not a sign of a response from anywhere: either the turnkeys were all fast asleep under the effects of Gardiner's sleeping draughts, or else the sounds of tormented screams and tearing flesh were nothing unusual in the night-time routine of Newgate Prison.

Elisa wasted no time in fretting over her father's fate, but rapidly squirmed her way back up to the ridge, then recovered the pickaxe and the coil of rope, and tied the rope to a similar chimney shaft to the one they had used to ascend. In no more than a minute she had played out the rope, tied the handle of the pickaxe to her belt, and descended into the darkness like a sailor sliding down from the main mast of a brig. Silver, after recovering his lantern and tying it to his back with loose twine, followed her down the rope at a more sedate pace, his muscles and the soft skin of his surgeon's palms protesting at this unusual strain. He landed silently on the stone-flagged yard – the rope was indeed long enough! - and moved rapidly over to the wall where Elisa was examining her father's body from below.

Yet, amazingly, it seemed that Jonas Saltash was still clinging to life somehow, even with an iron spike driven straight through his abdomen, and with the contents of his guts leaking down the wall in sickly profusion. Silver knew of course that the man was as good as dead, as

Saltash himself must also clearly know by now.

Yet Silver had to wonder in awe at the man's fortitude in taking that hideous impact, and all this subsequent torture, without uttering a sound. Surely the pain had to be indescribable. Perhaps the man was as iron-willed and self-disciplined as his remarkable daughter.

There were no tears or histrionics from Elisa, who seemed in perfect control of her emotions. Even after only this briefest of acquaintances, Silver already knew enough of her character by now not to expect anything else. Yet even so, she still surprised him with her coolness and lack of normal human reaction when faced with the daunting sight of her father, dying in agony above her head. Perhaps she was simply a callous bitch after all, Silver wondered, a woman who had given up regular human feelings when she took to a life of crime. *Yet, if that were the case, why had she risked her neck tonight in this wild venture to save her father's life?* The only sensible conclusion was that she did truly care for her father, but that she was adept at concealing those feelings for fear of appearing weak.

Jonas could still speak, but only barely. Listening to the dying man's words was a painful thing even for Silver to have to bear, so had to be a thousand times worse for a dutiful daughter to cope with. To Silver, that heartrending voice seemed already to be emanating from somewhere beyond the grave rather than from that bleeding and broken body straddling that wall. 'You have to go now, Lizzie. I'm…done for. We did our best, girl.' He tried to smile, but blood frothed from his mouth instead. 'Live long, sweetheart, and have…plenty of babbies. And…remember your dear mother…always.' He turned his eyes to Silver. 'Get her…out of here, Dr…Silver. They'll…hang her too…if she's…caught here…with you.'

'I can take good care of myself, father,' Elisa declared bleakly.

Then Jonas gasped one last time, and his head lolled to one side, his agony finally over.

Elisa didn't waste further time on her father. Without another word, or even a backward look at him, she took her lantern, lit the candle inside, then proceeded at a run to the far corner of the yard.

'It's over here,' she announced calmly. Silver followed her and saw that there was indeed a cast iron grating cover, hard up against the corner formed by the brick walls, so presumably there was a drain below. It didn't look like the entrance to any extravagantly large Roman sewer, though. With the pickaxe that Gardiner had provided, and making no attempt now to stay quiet, Elisa removed the cover completely, exposing a manhole chamber and a pipe below.

The pipe seemed no more than a two-foot diameter pipe at best to Silver, and disturbingly modern. 'That is no Roman sewer,' he observed worriedly. 'And it also looks hardly big enough for a mouse to get down...'

'We have to squeeze through this small pipe first,' she explained wearily. 'But we will find the Roman brick culvert within a few feet of here. Trust me.' She bristled at his expression. 'But please feel free to stay behind, if you wish, Dr Silver. I'm sure the hangman would greatly appreciate it.'

*

Crawling through that first section of pipe - which proved to be more like fifty feet long rather than the optimistic "few feet" promised by Elisa - was quite as hellish an experience as Silver had imagined. It was like being buried alive in an evil-smelling grave - perhaps worse even than being hanged.

But somehow he squeezed himself through the final stinking few feet, and popped out of the end of the pipe like the cork from a bottle. Clearing the foul mud from his face, Silver discovered to his astonishment that Elisa had been right. Revealed by the lantern that Elisa was still carrying, he saw there was bright red brickwork above his head, definitely the curving arched crown of an ancient culvert...

'How on earth did you get your lantern through that narrow pipe?' Silver asked her in wonder. The lantern was a weighty metal cage with glass panels, and it had never even occurred to Silver to try to bring his through that frighteningly narrow pipe with him.

Elisa stood calmly above him, plastered in so much mud that she resembled a nigger minstrel in a street carnival. 'I dragged it behind me with my feet.' She frowned matter-of-factly. 'How else? And it's just as well I did, otherwise we would be completely blind now.'

Even with all the mud on her face, Silver thought he detected an anguished look in her eyes for the first time. 'I'm sorry about your father. He was a brave man, dying like that without making a sound.'

She shrugged. 'He was.' She sighed explosively. 'But it cannot be helped. Come, we have to hurry. They'll not be far behind us.'

Silver found that he could almost walk upright now in this long straight length of brick culvert. He marvelled at the quality of the Roman brick, and the clean lime mortar joints, still pristine after fifteen hundred years.

From there the journey became fraught and dangerous again, though. Another section of medieval-looking culvert, narrower and less salubrious than the Roman; then the true filth of the former River Fleet - once a free-flowing stream, but now a rat-infested stink hole of a culvert built in old King George's time. They seemed to walk or crawl along this evil-smelling tunnel for hours, until finally Elisa held up the sputtering flame of her lantern to reveal a metal grille, and a distant gleam of moonlight on the sluggish river below.

Knocking out the rusted grille with his feet, Silver slid ten feet out of the end of the culvert and fell face down into evil-smelling mud. Raising his chin, he felt a sinister stirring in the mud bank all around him and saw the heads of a thousand bright red blood-worms emerging eagerly from the toxic soil to taste the flesh of their unexpected visitor...

CHAPTER 4

Sergeant Charlie Sparrow had been a detective with the Metropolitan Police for nearly ten years, which made him one of the longest serving of the Met's plain clothes squad. He knew his secretive profession made him deeply unpopular with the vast majority of the population of the city – people liked to know where they stood with the police, and didn't like the thought of policemen who looked and dressed like everyone else, lurking deviously in their midst, watching and waiting for them to break the law.

But Charlie Sparrow could live with the thought of being unpopular. He earned ten shillings a week more than even a skilled tradesman or factory worker could, a wage which kept his wife Edie happy, and his two growing nippers well fed and shod. In fact, because he didn't have a vast brood of kids like almost everyone else he knew, he and Edie lived very well indeed in a nice terraced house in the better part of Lambeth - even having the wherewithal to keep a maid, if only a lazy Irish girl called Kitty from the wilds of Donegal who had apparently never seen an outdoor water closet until arriving in London last year.

Not that Sparrow liked this city any more than Kitty, if truth be told, being himself a country boy originally, from the Medway area of Kent. Even after so many years in the "Great Wen", London was still sometimes hard for him to take – its stinks and smells, its rag-gatherers, dust heaps and knackers' yards, its gin palaces and tenements and squalor. Ten years ago, the Metropolitan Police commissioner had wisely decided not to recruit his new detective force from among his existing blue-coated peelers, nor even from the lower middle or working classes of London (whose loyalties might be divided when push came to shove.) Instead he had decided to take his recruits mainly from intelligent hardworking young men from the country – impoverished yeoman farmers and tradesmen and the like – men wishing to escape rural poverty and looking for a new direction in life. Charlie Sparrow had been one of those first tradesmen recruits; he had originally been a carpenter back in Kent, as his father had been before him. And although he still missed the simpler life he'd known as a boy, he had never truly regretted his decision to join the Metropolitan Police force.

At ten o'clock in the morning, Sparrow stood in a well-appointed and upholstered office on the second floor at 4 Whitehall Place, warming his backside at the brightly burning coal fire, waiting for his superior to appear. Through the sash window he caught sight out of the corner of his eye of a line of newly recruited constables being drilled in the cobbled yard below. In those far-off days when this street had been part of the Palace of Whitehall, that yard behind this building had been where Royal visitors to the court from Scotland had supposedly been lodged, hence the name Great Scotland Yard. Or that was one version that Charlie Sparrow had heard, anyway, to account for the name.

In the watery sunshine lighting up the cobbled yard, Sparrow had to admit that the new recruits did look surprisingly smart in their blue frock coats. And those rabbit-skin stovepipe hats made them look all of seven feet tall, turning even an ordinary-looking bloke into someone of standing in the community. Yet the uniformed peelers remained nearly as unpopular with the general public as their plainclothes detective colleagues (even though they had been around in the city for thirty years now, so you had to wonder how long it would take for London's populace to warm to their police force and begin to trust them.) Everyone knew the real truth however: peelers – bobbies – or whatever you called them - were there to enforce unfair laws on behalf of the property owning classes. They were snoops, spies, snitches, not protectors of the poor and worthy. Such was the popular opinion anyway, and Sparrow often suspected himself that the general consensus wasn't all that wide of the mark.

Sparrow's reflections on the trials and tribulations of being a policeman in this city were brought to an abrupt halt by the sudden arrival of his superior. Metropolitan Police Assistant Commissioner Robert Grindrod bustled into the room like a whirlwind, carrying with him his usual accompanying maelstrom of energy, and dumped his top hat on the leather-covered desk. 'Well, this is a fine how-do-you-do. I've just had my arse kicked black and blue by the Commissioner over this embarrassing escape from Newgate, so beware. In my present mood, I might feel like passing on the compliment to you, Charlie.'

'He's not happy, then?' Sparrow couldn't always curb his sarcastic asides to his superiors, even though his relationship with Grindrod in particular had often been a troubled and difficult one.

Grindrod was not a man gifted with much of a sense of humour. He was forty-seven years old now but looked at least a decade older than that, his face sagging from the long disappointments and frustrations he'd suffered in trying to get higher up the slippery rungs of the Met's promotion ladder. He had been Sparrow's immediate superior in the small detective force based at Shadwell Police Station in East London until a few months before, when his promotion to assistant commissioner had finally brought him what he'd always yearned for - to be the head of the detective force in the main headquarters in Whitehall. If truth be told, though, it was his assistant Charlie Sparrow's impressive arrest record at Shadwell and Wapping that had led to Grindrod's enhanced status within the force and his eventual promotion. And both he and Sparrow knew it...

Even now, Grindrod needed only the slightest excuse to consult his former sergeant or use his direct services. 'Not exactly happy,' he said. 'A man escaped from the condemned ward in Newgate yesterday for the first time ever that I can remember. That doesn't make the Commissioner look good. These days we only hang fifteen or twenty villains a year at Newgate so you can understand why the mob feels cheated over yesterday when they were promised a triple hanging. The mob are like me – they can probably still remember the good old days when there was a hanging every week.'

Grindrod slumped into the hard leather chair behind his desk, while Sparrow reluctantly moved away from the fire. 'They still had one left to hang yesterday, didn't they?' Sparrow commented dryly. 'Wasn't that enough blood for the mob?'

Grindrod glanced down at the papers on his desk and ran a weary hand through what was left of his hair. The new Assistant Commissioner didn't have much hair left on top of his head now, Sparrow couldn't help noticing from his standing position – and even those few remaining thin reddish straggles he still possessed looked ready to depart soon to join their fallen comrades. Grindrod's mutton chop side-whiskers were more luxuriant than ever, though, as if he was growing them deliberately as compensation for his advancing baldness on top. His belly had expanded of late too, Sparrow noted, and was now straining to escape from that ill-buttoned broadcloth jacket. And his fingers were stained even brighter yellow than previously, with the nicotine of those endless cheap cigarettes he smoked. Unlike his boss, Charlie Sparrow preferred to save his money to wasting it on drink and smokes, and couldn't completely hide the complacent superiority of a non-smoker and teetotaller over the weaknesses of his fellow men.

'Hardly enough blood for the mob at all,' Grindrod went on morosely. 'A common little Irishman from the bogs. No fun in hanging the likes of him. It was the arrogant Dr Silver they wanted to see twitching at the end of the rope, that's who.'

'Not Saltash? Wasn't he a big enough name for the mob to see swing?'

'No, he certainly wasn't. And the mob was cheated of that pleasure too, I might remind you. Anyway, despite his high opinion of himself, Saltash was no master criminal - he was never more than a petty thief who didn't realize when he'd overreached himself.' Grindrod's eyes narrowed. 'It was you who caught Saltash after that Finchley job, wasn't it?'

'It was - I nabbed him as he was boarding the steam packet to Rotterdam at Gravesend Pier. But I was sorry for it. Especially now, with what's happened.'

Grindrod grunted. 'Rank sentimentality for a devious villain.'

'Maybe. But I had a soft spot for him anyway. And he was never really a killer, so it wasn't nice seeing him skewered like that to the top of a wall, poor devil. Worse than being hanged, that was.'

Grindrod didn't look interested in the possible suffering of one of his old criminal adversaries, but he did seem pleased to learn that his old sergeant was already on the case. 'So you did find time to go to the gaol yesterday as I asked, and have a good nose around? How did Silver and Saltash get out, then?'

'They apparently got onto the roof of the prison, then down a rope into the exercise yard. That's when Saltash must have fallen and skewered himself, poor devil. As for Silver, he must have slid out through a drainage pipe in the corner of the yard. Eighteen inch diameter at most. I found a pickaxe and a lantern there, that he must have left behind.'

Grindrod coughed in disbelief. 'I wouldn't have thought it possible to get through a pipe that small.'

'It did look impossibly tight for a big man to squeeze through. And I certainly didn't feel tempted to try it myself, what with all the – excuse me! - *shit* in there. But there was no other way he could have got out of the exercise yard, and I expect the pipe soon became bigger on its way down to the river.' Sparrow tugged at his thick black moustache. 'I don't know how Silver knew there was a pipe there to try for, though – from the surface it hardly looked big enough for a rat to get down, never mind a big man like him. And there's no record of that drain on any of the building plans that I've had a look at, so it makes you wonder how he knew that it might be a plausible way out.'

'You're sure Silver ended up in the river, and that he isn't still buried down there in the pipe somewhere, are you?' Grindrod asked hopefully.

'I put some red dye down the hole, then checked later down by

Blackfriars Bridge. There was a nice red patch on the water by the time I got down there.'

'There's always red patches on the river,' Grindrod declared sourly. 'What with all the suicides down there slashing their own throats, or jumping off London Bridge. And anyway, there are dye works all along the river dumping their filthy waste into the water.'

Sparrow held his temper with difficulty. 'This dye was definitely mine, sir, and it was also clearly coming out of a pipe near Blackfriars Bridge. Also, the iron grill on the end of the pipe was loose and hanging off. If you want my honest opinion, sir, I think Silver probably did make it as far as the river, so he could be anywhere by now...'

'No footprints you could follow?'

'Not by the river. There were a lot of footprints on the mud banks, but the riverside there is so busy with mudlarks grubbing in the water for the odd lump of coal or copper nail, or any bit of rusted iron, that, by the time I got there, it was all too trodden over to make any sense of it. There could have been a herd of elephants grazing down there yesterday at Blackfriars, by the looks of it.'

Grindrod wasn't content to leave the subject there, though, and returned to what had happened earlier in the escape. 'Yet to get to the prison exercise yard in the first place, Silver and Saltash must have had inside help, don't you think?'

'Oh, for certain. The dead turnkey who was found in an attic room in the prison, a man called John Gardiner, was definitely in on the escape. Otherwise I don't see how Silver and Saltash could have got out of the condemned cells in the first place, or could have got hold of the rope and the tools.'

'So did the two of them turn on Gardiner and strangle him in that attic room, after he let them out of the cells?'

'No, the turnkey's death looked entirely natural to me. A long overdue heart attack, I would say, from the look of him. Someone had even put a greatcoat over his body, which shows a deal of respect and affection for the dead man rather than hatred.' Sparrow paused heavily before coolly dropping his bombshell. 'But there was also a *fourth* person involved in the escape.'

'A fourth?' Grindrod whistled in surprise. 'Are you sure of that?'

'Absolutely sure! I might not have been able to track any footprints by the river, but I had a little more luck inside the prison. There were definitely two distinct sets of fresh footprints in the layer of slick mud in the corner of the exercise yard where they disappeared into the drain. One was almost certainly Silver's; the other belonged to someone smaller and lighter.'

Grindrod grunted suspiciously. 'Could this have been another corrupt turnkey helping Silver?'

'No, I don't think so. Judging by the footprints, this other person – whoever he was – must have escaped through the sewers with Silver, and then emerged into the river with him.'

Grindrod frowned heavily. 'So they both got away by boat?'

'Almost certainly. It seems the likeliest way.'

Grindrod sat back in his chair and stretched expressively. 'Someone had worked this plan out well, Charlie. Someone with brains. Perhaps this fourth person you mentioned…?'

'The plan didn't go all that well as far as Jonas Saltash and John Gardiner were concerned,' Sparrow pointed out dryly, before adding a begrudging "sir" again for convention's sake. 'But for Silver, I suppose it worked out well enough. But did he organize the escape himself, though? Or was this fourth person possibly a friend of Saltash who arranged it all, and Silver merely profited from it by accident?' Sparrow was thinking out loud now, almost ignoring his old chief. 'Yet, whoever this other person was, he can't have been someone else on the inside - there was no one else missing from the prison, you see, either among the gaolers or the inmates. So, at the moment, I really have no idea who this mysterious fourth man might be.'

Grindrod nodded grimly. 'The identity of this supposed fourth person does puzzle me greatly too. But it seems a certain gentleman has called here this morning and expressed a wish to speak to me personally about this case so perhaps he might help enlighten us in that direction.'

'And how can he do that, sir? Who is this visitor?' Sparrow asked curiously.

Grindrod consulted the notebook in front of him. 'Name of James Minshall. It seems this Minshall is a turnkey at Newgate. He told the sergeant on the desk below that he has come here in his own free time because he has useful "private information" about the escape and is anxious to be of service.'

'Very public-spirited of him, I'm sure.' Sparrow frowned before consulting his own notebook. 'But yesterday I talked to all the turnkeys who were on duty in the condemned ward on Wednesday night. And I don't remember anyone called Minshall being among them. Nor did any of the turnkeys I spoke to offer me any "private information". Quite the opposite – they had all clammed up tight as a drum to protect themselves.'

'Perhaps that's why this man Minshall has come here – it might be easier for him to talk here in private, if he has some snitching on his colleagues to do. Or perhaps he just prefers to talk to someone of higher rank than a sergeant.'

Sparrow hoped Grindrod was being ironic with that last comment, but wasn't entirely convinced. Grindrod could be a pompous bastard when he wanted to be, and his promotion to Assistant Commissioner had only made him ten times worse.

Grindrod stirred uncomfortably in his leather chair at the sour expression on Sparrow's face, before clearing his throat abruptly. 'Well, let's see if this gentleman really can be of some help to us,' he said, ringing the small bell on his desk to summon the duty sergeant from down the corridor.

*

When James Minshall was eventually ushered into Grindrod's room by the downstairs sergeant, Sparrow took an instant dislike to this dapper and effeminate young fellow in his fancy dark brown weskit, black cravat, top hat and moleskin trousers. Perhaps it was the man's blonde eyelashes that disturbed him in particular – Sparrow had always had a horror of men with white eyelashes, because they seemed so unnatural. Or it could have been any number of other things about this man that he found objectionable: his glossy straw-coloured hair, his watery blue eyes or - most annoying of all - his shifty, ingratiating manner.

Sparrow stood aside by the fireplace to listen, while the visitor halted hesitantly in front of Grindrod, clutching his tall felt hat nervously between his fingers. Grindrod didn't choose to put the man at his ease and invite him to sit down, but instead coughed brusquely. 'Well, Mr Minshall, what do you have to tell me about this escape from Newgate...?'

Despite his slight hesitancy of manner, Minshall spoke up confidently and confirmed that he was indeed a turnkey at Newgate and that he had been on duty on Wednesday. It was soon explained to Sparrow why this man had not been on his list of people to see yesterday at Newgate: it seemed Minshall hadn't been officially named on the duty roster for the condemned ward on Wednesday night, and had been there on the night shift only as a late volunteer replacement for an elderly turnkey called Job who had been concussed in an accidental fall at his home the same day. And yesterday afternoon, when Sparrow had been nosing around the condemned ward of the prison, Minshall had been off duty again and catching up on his sleep at his own home in Limehouse.

'So how come no one heard all this commotion going on?' Grindrod demanded irately of Minshall, after he'd listened to this introductory explanation by his young visitor. 'Several people crawling around on the roof of Newgate Gaol; one even falls off the roof onto a wall and drives a spike through his guts in the process. And you gentlemen warders of Newgate manage to sleep through the whole damned thing!'

'I was deep underground in the cells, sir, at the time this happened, and looking after my own charges, so wouldn't have heard anything from there. Anyway, sir, the prison at night is always noisy with moans and screams – half of the prisoners should really be in Bedlam, except there is no room for them there.' Minshall had still managed to retain his insinuating manner after this diatribe from Grindrod, even raising a slightly superior smile at this point. 'And I believe that Gardiner had also doctored the porter of several of his colleagues with a sleeping draught, so they can hardly be blamed either for not hearing anything unusual.'

'So why are you here?' Grindrod asked bluntly. He didn't add, '...*and wasting my time*,' but that was the clear unspoken thought behind his question.

Minshall faltered for one instant under Grindrod's harsh stare before recovering gamely. '...Because... to be honest, sir...I did have some earlier suspicions about this man Gardiner. He was behaving very strangely on Wednesday during the day shift. All that day he looked in a state of high excitement, sir, sweating a lot and even redder in the face than usual. And once during the day, I saw him in deep conversation with a visitor to the gaol - a fair and pretty youth of fifteen or sixteen. In fact I had seen that young man in the prison a few times before, so my interest in him was naturally aroused...'

Sparrow guessed that there might have been more than just mental arousal involved, noting Minshall's own delicate features and effeminate mincing manners.

'If you were suspicious of Gardiner, why did you not report it to the governor?' Grindrod demanded.

'I have only been a turnkey at Newgate for a matter of weeks, sir. And Gardiner had been there for twenty years or more, so I had to be cautious in making accusations against someone so senior without any real evidence.'

Grindrod sniffed coldly. 'No guts, eh? Pity! Then what can you do for us now, Mr Minshall? Come to bolt the stable door?'

The man's eyes flickered with annoyance for the first time, but he controlled himself. 'No, sir, but perhaps I can still help you find the runaway horse.'

'How?'

'In this way. On one occasion – eight days ago, I believe - as I was leaving duty at the gaol, I happened to see this particular youth outside, the one who I later saw talking to Gardiner on the day of the escape. I live in Limehouse and I couldn't help noticing that this youth walked home through the city in almost the same direction as myself...'

Grindrod inhaled sharply. 'Ah! So you followed him?'

'I did,' Minshall admitted. 'I was curious about his reasons for visiting the prison so often, that's all.'

'So where does this *pretty* youth of yours live?' Grindrod pronounced the word "pretty" with a deliberately salacious emphasis.

Minshall gulped. 'He lives in Wapping, sir, but that's all I can say for the present.'

'You *lost* him?'

'Regretfully, sir, yes. But I do know the general neighbourhood in which he must live – in the sailor's area on the waterfront, east of the London Dock. I believe I could find him again if I were to devote some time to the matter...'

'This youth could be entirely innocent – a genuine visitor to the prison, unconnected to Silver's escape,' Sparrow finally butted in, unable to stay silent any longer.

Minshall turned his watery eyes on Sparrow, standing by the crackling coal fire. 'That could of course be true, sir...but then I did hear tell that there might have been a fourth person involved in the escape on Wednesday night who got away with Silver.'

Grindrod resumed the questioning, after giving Sparrow an irate look that clearly demanded to know why this young whippersnapper of a turnkey had heard about the existence of this fourth man even before he had – and he the head of London's detective force! 'And you think this "pretty" youth might be the fourth man? Is that your assertion, Mr Minshall? And he might, or might not, live in Wapping?'

'Err...yes, sir, that's it exactly. At least I believe it to be possible, based on this young man's behaviour, and his meeting in the prison with Gardiner on the day of the escape.'

'Well, that could possibly be of interest to us,' Grindrod finally conceded. 'Are you confident you could find this youth again?'

'Err...yes, sir...that is to say...probably...given enough time.'

'Then when you do, please let me know.' Grindrod stood up with his hand outstretched to show Minshall that the interview was at an end.

Minshall didn't take the proffered hand and the heavy hint immediately, but stood his ground. 'If I find this person, would there be a...*reward*...sir?' he asked slyly, a delicate framing of a delicate question.

Grindrod gave Sparrow a knowing look out of the corner of his eye, as Minshall finally accepted his handshake. 'If this youth of yours leads us to Dr Silver, then yes, Mr Minshall, there will indeed be a substantial reward...'

*

After Minshall had left, looking smug and pleased with himself, Grindrod smiled grimly at Sparrow. 'Well, Charlie, what did you think of our Mr Minshall? He obviously doesn't know that we've already posted a reward of a hundred pounds for the recapture of Dr Silver.'

'I would bet that he does know all about it,' Sparrow stated succinctly. 'He was probably talking about a *further* reward of some sort.' He reflected a little more. 'An odd cove for a turnkey, this Minshall, don't you think?' he asked suspiciously. 'Did you see the fancy way he was dressed? Who'd trust a turnkey who dresses in a waistcoat and cravat like that, or who has such mincing manners?'

'I couldn't agree more. He looks like somebody's bum boy all right. Still, he might turn up something on this mysterious fourth man of yours.' Grindrod eased himself to his feet again and went over by the window, where the new recruits in the yard below had now been replaced by a throng of impressive carriages and bewhiskered visitors in top hats and frock coats.

'Buggery and damnation!' Grindrod swore. 'I forgot there was a deputation of politicians dropping in on us today. I suppose I'll have to go downstairs and meet them, and then kiss their fragrant Whig arses ever so gently.' He drummed his fingers on the windowsill. 'I want Silver caught, Charlie – it's my top priority. I've spoken to Inspector Carew at Shadwell and he has agreed that he will give you any uniformed officers you need to ensure that Silver is quickly nabbed again.' Inspector Carew was the chief uniformed officer at Shadwell Station, and a man who harboured some considerable resentment against the elite detective force in Whitehall, and the privileged treatment they seemed to get from the powers that be. As a result, Carew did usually make life for the small group of Whitehall detectives based at his own station as difficult as possible. Charlie Sparrow suspected that the resentment against him in particular would only be worse now after Grindrod's intervention, so certainly was not expecting anything like cooperation from Carew in the matter of the search for Dr Silver. There was also likely to be a problem with the City of London police too…

'The city boys won't be happy about this,' Sparrow pointed out. 'They'll see Silver's escape as being on their patch,' he observed tersely. The City of London had its own force of police which, for historical reasons, was largely independent of the rest of the Metropolitan Police. And cooperation between the Met and the City force, like cooperation between the detective force and the uniformed branch of the Met itself, wasn't always of the best.

'I don't care about those pompous pricks at the Old Bailey. I want Silver back, and you're the best man to find him, especially if he might be in your neck of the woods, which seems likely. Wapping seems the obvious place to go if you need to flee the country by ship.'

'There must be several hundred vessels from all over the world moored presently in the docks, or on the river, so where am I supposed to start looking, sir?' Sparrow complained pointedly. 'In fact,' he argued, 'Silver is probably already on an East Indiaman heading for Batavia or the Cape - it wouldn't be difficult for him to find passage within a few hours to wherever he wanted to go. He was a well-to-do man with important friends and connections, so I'm sure he could have got hold of any funds he needed to help him pay for his passage.'

Grindrod shook his head ruefully. 'If he has, then we've lost him. But I'm not so sure Silver would run. Not immediately, anyway, not when there must be so many loose ends in his life to sort out.'

Sparrow, hearing that, thought he would stir things up a little. 'Well, Silver did claim consistently throughout his trial to be innocent, as I recall. And for a man actually seen sticking a bloodied knife into his wife's heart, a claim like that does take a certain amount of brazenness. Unless, of course, he *was* actually innocent, and someone was lying. After all, he didn't try to escape when the police finally arrived at his house, did he...?' he added slyly.

Grindrod gave him a sour look. 'You're not another one who fell for his cock-and-bull story about finding his wife dying on the stairs, are you?'

Although Grindrod had not been directly involved in prosecuting Silver, Sparrow knew fine well that the Assistant Commissioner had nevertheless taken a strong personal interest in the case. Therefore Sparrow decided to choose his next words circumspectly. 'I wouldn't put it that strongly, sir. But, without knowing all the facts of the case in detail, I did feel that there was something about the whole story that didn't quite make sense. There was something odd about the murder weapon, wasn't there?'

Grindrod snorted. 'It was a decorative Russian paper knife, that's all.'

'Well, that's unusual in itself. There can't be too many knives like that in London, so where would Silver have got such a thing?'

'You need to check the facts, Charlie. Silver could easily have acquired that knife during the Crimean campaign. He served there only three years ago as a surgeon, and could simply have bought it, or even taken it off the body of a dead Russian.'

Sparrow remained unconvinced. 'Still, it's a strange knife to have used to murder his wife.'

Grindrod sniffed coldly. 'He did it! The wife's own maid saw him do it, for God's sake! Even if you think she was mistaken or lying, there was simply no one else in that house who could possibly have done it. No one else could have gained entry to the house during those few minutes, and Dr Silver was the only person inside with blood on his person. We *proved* it!'

'Yes, you're probably right,' Sparrow agreed hastily, not wishing to rouse the ire of his superior further.

'I *am* right. And I also think Silver will lie low in London for a time before he makes a run for it, so that gives us an opportunity to grab him again and make sure his avoidance of the hangman was only a temporary reprieve for him...'

CHAPTER 5

Friday 9th October 1857

Had he but known, it would have gladdened Assistant Commissioner Grindrod's heart to learn how close to the truth he had been with that speculative statement. Jonathan Silver *was* still in London, and actually no more than five miles away from Whitehall Place as the crow flew.

And at eleven on this chill October morning, lying near naked under a coarse woollen blanket on a makeshift bed – a straw mattress laid on the floor of Elisa Saltash's kitchen - he was still asleep, and dreaming an unsettling nightmare filled with images of thieving mudlarks drowning in toxic mud, and of himself being eaten alive by giant blood worms.

Then, as he felt the bite of one of those bloated worms crawling over his flesh, sucking into his soft skin with their busy mouthparts, he shuddered silently before his eyes opened with a violent start...

The sight that met his eyes immediately woke him up further – and perhaps with even more of a jolt than the thought of being eaten alive by worms...

He saw that Elisa was occupied at the other side of the room in taking a bath. And even though it was a tall swan-shaped zinc bathtub that concealed most of her from his view, he still had a diverting image of her slender neck and face in profile to excite his interest, her skin pale and almost translucent against the rough dark plaster of the wall behind. She was apparently unconscious of his waking presence, though, humming softly to herself as she worked assiduously at her ablutions, cleaning her face and neck with a wet rag, and gently soaping her hair.

Then she proved beyond doubt that she thought him still asleep, as she eased herself discreetly to her feet and doused herself with a pail of steaming water. Silver quickly pretended to be asleep again, while his mind dwelled enjoyably on the memorable if fleeting spectacle he had just witnessed - of water dripping down from pale pink nipples and softly rounded buttocks.

Yet the sight had been such an enticing one that he didn't have sufficient willpower to keep his eyelids tightly closed, and they soon fluttered open again in the hope of a repeat view. Yet the hope of a further secret glimpse was short-lived; instead he found Eliza eyeing him belligerently in return from her standing position in the bath...

'You're awake,' she observed coldly. She did make the small concession of covering her nakedness partially from his sight with the pail, but that only served to accentuate the erotic intensity of the moment in Silver's mind. But there was certainly no squeak of girlish modesty or coy retreat under the water to escape from his probing male eyes, as there would have been with almost every other young woman of his acquaintance caught in this same delicate situation. This girl clearly felt no shame about the way she looked, and had no particular fetish about concealing her body from a man. *And why should she, when she looked like this?*

'Why are you taking your bath here, of all places?' he asked her defensively.

'I always bathe here, and I don't see why your unwelcome presence should make me change my habits. It's warm in the kitchen, and I can heat the water over the range above the fire. And it's hard work carrying the water from the backyard up two flights of stairs to my bedroom.' She glared at him as he continued to inspect her in an unabashed fashion. 'In any case, I thought you were still asleep. This was not done for your amusement, be assured of that. You should have let me know you were awake and spying on me.'

Silver decided not to deny this accusation as this would only prolong a pointless conversation even further. 'Did that man Gardiner ever come here?' he asked, a sudden unsettling suspicion forming in his mind as to how she might have seduced that elderly turnkey into helping her.

She shrugged, the last of the water still trickling down her smooth pink thighs. 'What if he did? I owed my father that much – to trade a little of my womanly modesty in return for my father's life, even if in the end the effort was wasted.' She lifted her chin defiantly, and stared back at him. 'Men are so predictable in their carnal appetites, aren't they? Especially *old* men.'

Silver did feel suddenly ancient, faced with this enigmatic slip of a girl. 'It appears so...'

*

Thirty hours ago, they had shared a rowboat together on a hushed and evil-smelling River Thames, with a dazed Silver ineffectually working the oars as he tried to adjust his mind to his unexpected new situation. A subdued Elisa, as black with mud as an African heathen, had sat moodily in the stern, occasionally directing him with a melancholy word of command.

Silver wasn't finding it easy to cope with the sudden assault on his senses of all this space and sky, or of the disconcerting sense of freedom that came with it. Initially his reactions to finding himself free were – surprisingly - more ones of panic and bleak foreboding than exhilaration. He was in that paradoxical state of mind that can arise when a man has given up all chance of life and is then unexpectedly offered a way back from the brink. In Silver's case this had resulted in a perverse inclination to resent this change in his circumstances, and, more particularly, to resent the person who had brought it about.

Although this river and the city crowding its dirty banks never slept completely, Silver felt that this hesitant and uneasy stillness that hung over the Thames and its environs at three in the morning was probably as near as it would ever get to that perfect soporific state. A heavy viscous quality permeated the greasy surface of the river and seemed to invade the darkened waterside buildings too so that everything on view possessed the attributes of a still life painting, a moment frozen in time: the silent boats and wherries of the watermen stirring uneasily at anchor, wooden skiffs beached on the mud like decaying animal carcasses, the massed lines of moored paddle-steamers at deserted jetties, waiting for morning and the rush of daytime passengers anxious to be taken up and down river.

Under Southwark Iron Bridge they drifted in near silence on the ebb tide, with the regular dip of the oars into the oil-black water almost the only sound. Night mist clung to the heavy water like an insubstantial ghost. Turning his head for a moment, Silver listened to the muted sounds of the slumbering city. Even now there were no noises of pursuit behind them as far as he could tell, which surprised him greatly.

Had they somehow engineered a way out of Newgate without the gaol keepers even realizing that they were gone yet? It seemed almost too much to hope for, to have achieved such a miraculous escape.

The girl had said almost nothing to him since they had crawled out of the final length of sewer and stumbled across the foul riverside mud to the waiting rowboat, half-hidden under the wooden landing stage of an ancient jetty stairs. For his part too, Silver was reluctant to engage her in meaningless conversation. *What could he possibly say now that would compensate her for the death of her father?* He realized his company was now an embarrassment to her at best; and, at worst, a major liability and irritation. He had, after all, only been tolerated by her as part of the escape in order to keep the turnkey Gardiner cooperative and complaisant. Now that the need to protect Gardiner from suspicion of complicity in the escape had been overtaken by events, and her father too was lying dead inside Newgate, impaled cruelly to the top of the exercise yard wall, there was no reason at all for her to continue to help him, apart perhaps from the worry that he might give her away if he should be caught again.

The blackened stone arches of London Bridge appeared ahead, and Elisa made him steer with the oars under the central span, well away from any prying eyes on the banks. Tomorrow those pavements on the bridge above would be echoing with the footsteps of tens of thousands of clerks, shop workers and tradesman on their way to work in the city, while the cobbled roadway would be filled from end to end with the clatter of horse-drawn omnibuses, butchers' carts on their way to Smithfield, drays, wagonettes, and two-wheeler cabs. But tonight, caught up in the witching hour, there was only one curious boy, a ragged street urchin, peering mutely at them through the balusters of the parapet.

This crossing under London Bridge brought them into the Pool of London. Even with all the vast acreage of docks that had been built along these lower reaches of the Thames in the last forty years, the river below the Tower of London was still a concatenation of every sort of sailing ship, a vast fleet that almost filled the entire width of the channel from shore to shore. Tea clippers, schooners, windjammers. Essex barges full of hay and straw for London's countless working horses. Kent barges with grain and building stone. Dirty colliers from Newcastle, as black as the city they came from. Every sort of steamship proliferating too – less beautiful shapes than the sailing vessels, stocky and bulky with paddles and stacks and screws – but still the shape of the future, no doubt. Silver propelled the rowboat onwards, letting the rhythm of the river guide him, not quite sure where the girl was taking him, if anywhere, but reluctant to press the issue with her. Perhaps they would eventually get to some lonely piece of Essex shoreline, or disused jetty or crumbling warehouse, where she would calmly cast him ashore to take his own chances. If she did, then Silver knew that he would accept her decision and go without a hint of protest. Because of his unfortunate and stubborn personal pride, he would never be able to bring himself to beg for further help from someone unwilling to give it, even if, by neglecting to do so, he would be condemning himself to certain recapture. On the run alone on the Essex marshes, or somewhere else equally exposed and inhospitable, he knew that he would hardly last more than a few hours in this muddied desperate state before the law would find him again. His only real hope for the present lay in disappearing somehow into London's vast rabbit warren of mean streets, and among its numberless poor.

On past the countless masts the boat glided, the pull of the ebb tide even stronger now so that Silver only used the oars sparingly, or when necessary to make slight corrections in his course. Imposing brick warehouses stood tall against the northern sky, dwarfing the crumbling hovels and the quayside inns along the shoreline, the lines of which were picked out by the odd gauzy gaslight or smoky oil lamp.

They reached the beginning of the southward bulge of Wapping, with the parish of Shadwell beyond, and Limehouse further to the east, all covered improbably by a miasma of silver mist as fine as gossamer.

The entrance to St Katherine's Dock came and went, then they floated on further past Union Stairs and Gun Dock to the former Execution Dock, the traditional place of hanging in the last century for pirates and sea rovers, whose bodies had apparently been left to rot in chains until covered by at least three tides. Behind the waterfront hovels loomed the walls of London Dock and the vast regimented ranks of quay walls and warehouses dominating present day Wapping, stuffed to their rafters with tea, muslin, calicos, spices and indigo from the East Indies, and rum, sugar, coffee and tobacco from the West.

Between the giant dock basins and the river were the waterside taverns, lodging houses, mean tenements, and washed-up deposits of leaning makeshift homes, which crowded the Wapping waterfront like barnacles on a rotting hull. Here was where the peripatetic seamen of the world spent their London shore time, like albatrosses returning briefly from skimming the waves of the Southern oceans. They came to port after months at sea with money burning holes in their pockets – thirty or forty pounds sometimes - this cosmopolitan breed of thugs and former gentlemen, of one-eyed and one-legged heroes, mutineers, ex-pirates and empire builders - home to the greatest city on Earth. And there to greet them on their return were the more permanent and mostly landlubber residents of Wapping, who ministered to the needs of these wild and untamed visitors from the oceans of the world – the stevedores or lumpers, the watermen who worked the lighters, the suppliers of rope and tackle and nautical instruments, the ships' bakers and laundresses, the landlords and inn keepers and storekeepers - and, not least, the whores and their Flash Men.

Elisa glanced at the forest of masts projecting in the distance above the dominating wall of London Dock and finally said something of note to break the long silence between them. 'They say these new Aberdeen-built clippers can beat even the Boston clippers to China now. Sixteen ships sailed from Foochow in July and around the Cape of Good Hope, and three of them - all Aberdeen-built - arrived here two days ago, after being at sea for only ninety-nine days. Imagine that! Less than a hundred days to sail from China, right across the Indian Ocean, then around Africa and up the whole length of the Atlantic. The captain of the first ship to dock won a prize of a hundred guineas for being the quickest to return - well worth it to the tea merchants, I suppose, now the new season's tea harvest can sell at ten shillings a ton.'

Silver listened to this knowledgeable speech with surprise, and wondered if she had made it only to distract herself from thoughts of her dead father. 'It sounds like you know all about the tea business.'

'Oh, I do. I fully intend to own my own clipper one day – or even a *fleet* of clippers, maybe.'

Silver's mood was changing by now, with the full exultancy of freedom finally beginning to take hold of him. Yet he was still consumed by doubt and uncertainty too, unsure what to do next to try and hold on to this precious state that he'd formerly taken so much for granted.

Elisa solved his dilemma by standing up in the stern of the boat. 'You'd better let me handle the oars now, Doctor.'

Considering her background and her current profession, Silver was still finding himself continually surprised by her ladylike manners and language. He glanced at the darkened Wapping shore. 'Is this where we're going, then?' he felt encouraged enough to ask.

'It's where I'm going...and I can hardly just leave you here to fend for yourself, can I? Even I am not that much of a witch!'

Silver didn't argue with her severe judgement of herself and quickly changed places in the boat with her. When she had taken over the rowing, he sat watching her in the moonlight, amazed at this girl's fortitude and powers of recovery after having to watch her own father die tonight in such a violent and sordid fashion. There had been no sign of any tears at all from her - although, under all that caked mud on her face, it would perhaps have been difficult to see them anyway. Yet, despite the lack of obvious emotion, she did exhibit a certain dignified and brooding melancholy that clung to her every gesture and expression, a melancholy which Silver assumed had to be the result of her father's brutal demise. *But who could really say what was going on inside the head of such an unpredictable creature as this?*

She brought the boat skilfully into the landing stage of the Wapping New Stairs, then, casting the boat aside to drift away into the thick scum of sludge and sewage along the shore, led him from there past the silent headquarters of the River Police, up Old Gravel Lane. He followed her through the darkened cobbled streets, wondering at their distinctive names – Gun Alley, Dung Wharf, Hangman's Gains. Fortunately they encountered no patrolling peelers or river policemen on the way, nor even a yawning parish night watchman at the end of his rounds.

In Pear Tree Alley, Silver espied through a break in the surrounding buildings where the distant river turned south beyond the Surrey side to encompass its huge loop around the Isle of Dogs. This "isle" was no true island though, as he knew well, but instead a lonely and ugly peninsula of flat marshland, pockmarked with windswept stunted limes and poplars, criss-crossed by ditches, and protected along its shoreline by high earth dykes and the skeletal remnants of old windmills. People did live on the Isle of Dogs, but they were a race apart from other Londoners, a semi-aquatic race like the Dutch, whose watery and leaning hovels, settling in the mud, seemed more like the beached boats of a marine-living species than true land dwellings.

But Silver was attracted in particular by the sight of something unfamiliar - a long black wall rising like a cliff face against the moonlit marshes.

'What is that wall?' he asked Elisa curiously, having no idea what it might be. Certainly he'd never seen or heard tell of any cliff of any sort on the low-lying marshes of the Isle of Dogs.

She paused and turned her head to follow the direction of his pointed finger. 'That's no wall,' she corrected him under her breath. 'There's no wall in the world that size except maybe in China! That's the Great Ship - the *Leviathan*. The engineer Brunel – the man who built the Wapping tunnel, and then the Great Western Railway to Bristol - has gone mad, so they say, and is building his own Ark. The largest ship ever built, seven hundred feet long and higher than the Tower of Pisa. Is he waiting for the next Flood? That seems like the only way he will ever get that iron monster to float off its marshy birthplace.' She turned her eyes to his, and Silver detected for the first time a hint of tears in those unblinking eyes and the genuine hurt in her voice at losing her father. 'Sometimes I wish a great flood really would come and wash away this whole filthy world, and all the people in it...'

*

Elisa finally reached her destination, the back entrance to a chandler's store, located in the hugger-mugger of lanes and alleyways to the east of London Dock. As she opened the back gate for him, Silver did not query this odd choice of destination, grateful simply to be off these dangerously empty streets.

The backyard through which they passed to get to the shop turned out to be a mean cobbled space equipped with an earth closet and a water pump, and with dirty blades of grass sprouting between the rough uneven stones. The family accommodation at the back of the shop was no hovel, though, despite the way it looked from the outside, but a clean and well-kept home with modern gas lighting on the ground floor, bright chintz curtains on the windows, well-made furniture, and wax-polished wooden floors. On arrival Elisa immediately lit a gas burner in the entrance, spreading just enough light for Silver to see his way around.

While Elisa was outside in the yard locking up, Silver made a quick illicit exploration of her living quarters. There was a large workmanlike kitchen at ground level, a neat if cluttered parlour on the first floor, and a tiny bedroom in the attic above the parlour that could only be hers from its unexpectedly feminine ambience. He had only just returned rapidly to the kitchen when she came in from the yard, a look of deep suspicion on her mud-caked face. 'You'd better wash some of that mud off before you sleep. I don't want my kitchen filthy.' She saw his doubtful expression. 'Don't worry. The water from the pump is good, even for drinking; it comes from a deep well, not from the river, so there's no chance of catching cholera in this house.'

After taking her advice and hosing himself down under the pump in the backyard, Silver had been ordered curtly to sleep on the mattress laid out for him in the kitchen. He had blinked in surprise at this fresh order, but mostly because it came from someone he hadn't recognised at all, until he realized that this pretty dark-haired girl with the sharp voice was none other than a startlingly cleaner and more conventionally dressed version of Elisa Saltash. Where she had cleaned herself so thoroughly, while he had been hosing himself down in the yard, he had no idea. The character of this clean female version of Elisa was no warmer or more amiable than the mud-caked male version, though, as, with one last resentful glance in his direction, she had retreated coldly up the crooked wooden stairs to the sanctuary of her bedroom two floors above.

And in that kitchen Silver had stayed for the last thirty hours, apart from occasional trips to the privy in the cobbled backyard outside. On those essential excursions he had noted that the chandler's shop in front was presently closed for business. Yet it looked like a going concern to him when he went down the connecting stone passageway briefly to investigate, with new stock filling dust free shelves. This set Silver to wondering whom the shop belonged to, and who worked there when it was open.

He hardly saw much of Elisa at all during this first day, Thursday, since she kept mostly to herself, apart from bringing him a bowl of thick pea soup and three chunks of black rye bread at six in the evening. She did leave her private quarters several times during that first day, though – he knew that much from the sound of her footsteps - doing something in the shop in front, or in the backyard. In the afternoon she had gone off into the dirty back lanes of Wapping on some longer errand that took several hours. Silver hadn't asked her where she'd been or what she'd been doing, and she certainly hadn't volunteered any information on her return.

Silver was curious about Elisa's life and daily routine, but clearly wasn't going to get any easy answers from her, so spent his time instead mostly occupied in sleeping or pondering his uncertain future. Yet he found it hard to think clearly in his present state. The fatigue and stress of his imprisonment, and his subsequent escape, had finally caught up with him, it seemed, provoking a reaction of extreme lassitude and languor.

Until this moment, anyway, on this chill Friday morning when he had woken abruptly and caught her in the midst of her bath...

A few minutes later she came back down to the kitchen from her bedroom, now fully dressed, and with her manner giving no indication that anything untoward had occurred between them earlier. The kitchen was cosily warm as she'd kept a coal fire burning cheerfully in the cast iron range the whole of Thursday night and all this morning. Outside, the estuary weather was turning foul and autumnal, with a fierce cold rain rattling the windowpanes - unforgiving weather that made Silver doubly glad that he had found such a snug and warm place of refuge. Yet, for several reasons, he knew that he couldn't afford to stay here too long, and that he would therefore soon need to find a more permanent place to hide. *But where...?*

Elisa went over to the range, added more coal from the scuttle to the fire, then prodded it back into life with an iron poker, before coming back and facing him. She was dressed in better fashion than he'd seen her on the previous day, now wearing a high-necked lacework bodice and bottle green skirt. With her hair tied up prettily too, she didn't much resemble the intrepid youth who had broken into Newgate in a desperate bid to save her father, and then made her escape across dangerous rooftops and through filthy sewers. Her dark hair was glossy and had hints of russet in it, he noticed, and her features were similarly striking, particularly her large emerald eyes and determined mouth. Her father's boast had not been an idle one, Silver had to agree: dressed as herself she was an undoubted beauty, and could have easily passed for a lady's maid or a young governess rather than a professional thief. Or, with even more stylish clothes, perhaps even a lady herself...

Her dress and her pleasant fragrance reminded Silver that he was naked under this coarse blanket apart from his drawers, and that, despite hosing himself down in the yard the day before, he still smelled rank and disgusting.

Elisa seemed to read his mind. 'If you would like to draw some water from the yard, then you can use the bath too. Don't worry: no one can see into my backyard from the neighbouring houses, and the shop in front is presently closed for business for a few days. You can even heat the water on the range, if you wish. It might be more comfortable for you.'

He stirred with an unfair resentment, uncomfortable with such consideration from her. 'Don't put yourself out for me, Miss Saltash. You've done more than enough for me already.'

'Yes, I believe I probably have,' she said tartly. 'But I'm afraid you stink, Dr Silver, so, if you want to stay here any longer in my kitchen, then I insist that you wash yourself.'

He smiled faintly at being addressed quite so directly. 'Do you have any men's clothes that might fit me? Or can you obtain some? I don't want to be a burden to you but I can hardly put my prison clothes on again, even if they are washed.'

'You can't in any case, Doctor, because I have disposed of them - burned them in the backyard yesterday while you were sleeping,' she announced primly. 'But perhaps I *can* find something else suitable for you to wear, without having to go out and buy something new from a men's tailor, which might attract attention. My father was a similar height and build to you, and I have some of his old suits and shirts and undergarments here in the house...'

*

She returned an hour later when he was still luxuriating in the warmth of his bath, and, standing by the kitchen table, inspected his exposed chest and arms casually with an apparently disinterested eye. Silver did wonder if that casual attitude might not be an affectation on her part, but he was glad that the soapsuds had at least added a degree of opacity to the water to conceal his manhood and reduce the embarrassment of the situation.

Despite her apparent lack of interest in his naked masculine form – be that feigned or otherwise – Silver guessed that she was still nevertheless enjoying a little light revenge on him for what had happened earlier in the day. She held up a selection of clothes for him to peruse later when he had finished his bath: workman's overalls and jacket, a good quality tweed suit, a bowler hat, working man's cap, striped cotton shirts, a flannel vest and buttoned drawers, a black waistcoat. Even polished black boots, size eleven, almost new.

As she laid out the various garments on the table, she regarded each of them with a dry and unsentimental eye, despite her intimate knowledge of their previous owner. 'I suppose my father will have no further use of these now, so they would only go to the rag-and-bone man,' was all she said on the subject.

At this point Silver expected her to leave and allow him to complete his bath in privacy. But instead she produced a newspaper from a voluminous handbag. 'I bought this morning's *Times* for you, Dr Silver, because I thought it might be of interest to you to read about your bold exploits in escaping from Newgate...'

Silver was forced by her bantering tone into a sharp reply. 'Are you sure it wasn't your own pride you were gratifying by buying that newspaper, Miss Saltash? Were they not more *your* bold exploits than mine?'

She partly conceded that point with a cool nod. 'Shall we say *our* bold exploits, then? They didn't quite make the first page of news inside, what with the mutiny in India, and business panic continuing in America. But you'll be pleased to know that we are featured on the second page, and have two full columns.' She opened up the newspaper with a flourish and showed him the columns in question. 'My late father's name hardly rates a mention in the story, though, while yours is featured heavily. The newspapers do seem to hate you in particular, Dr Silver, although I don't know why.'

'I would have thought that obvious,' Silver growled at her.

She shrugged, indifferent to his ill temper. '...Though, to be frank, they seem to object more to your temerity in escaping from prison than to the horrid fact of you murdering your wife. It seems you should just have taken the punishment for your evil act like a man, and not done such a cowardly thing as fleeing justice.'

'Yes, it was unforgivable of me,' Silver muttered sarcastically. 'Do they know anything about you, though, Miss Saltash, and your participation in the escape?'

'Apparently not, which is hopeful.' She laid the newspaper out on the breakfast table, then stared at him again in the bathtub, with rather more deliberate interest than before. 'You will need to change your appearance, Dr Silver,' she warned him, 'otherwise you will be easily caught.'

Silver was disconcerted. 'Why?'

Elisa now produced another large folded sheet of paper from her bag, which she also unfolded carefully for his inspection. 'These billboard posters have been put up all over London this morning, offering a large reward for your recapture, and come complete with this police artist's drawing of you which, while hardly a work of art, is reasonably lifelike. You still look enough like this drawing to have to worry, Doctor, despite losing so much weight in prison. But I can trim your hair and beard, if you like, and perhaps make you look like a different man.'

Silver glanced at the newspaper on the table and its main headline story, and was diverted momentarily into wondering about the progress of the ongoing mutiny in India. Sepoys had mutinied against their English masters in May and since then had cut a swathe of murder and destruction through British India, perpetrating massacres of women and children at Meerut and Cawnpore, and besieging the British garrison at Lucknow. Silver had mostly lost track of events in India since July, though, since he'd been caught up in the personal tragedy of Marianne's murder, and of his subsequent arrest and trial. But now his interest in these distant events had been stirred again. 'Is Lucknow still under siege, then?' he asked Elisa curiously.

'Yes, it is. And I for one hope the sepoys continue to give our troops a bloody nose. What right do we English have to be there, lording it over another race?'

Silver was annoyed in turn. 'And what right do you have to break into people's houses and take whatever you wish?'

Elisa sniffed coldly. 'My father obviously said far too much to you in prison about my private affairs, Doctor. I don't believe I have to answer you, but I will try and explain my motivations anyway. I learned when young what it was like to be poor and hungry, and I promised myself then that I would do whatever was necessary to make sure I was never caught in that predicament again. The rich have done very little to earn their wealth and comfort, so I don't feel too guilty about relieving them of a little of it. I am merely practising the art of Christian charity, without the need to ask, that's all. And I am certainly using their money in a much more sensible and productive way than *they* ever would.'

Silver raised an ironic eyebrow. 'That's an interesting moral perspective on thieving.'

'I'm the last person you should be provoking in your desperate situation, Dr Silver, especially now that my natural hospitality is wearing thin. In fact, not to put too fine a point on it, is there no one else you can turn to for help now?' she continued bluntly. 'Someone who can provide you with money or a more permanent hiding place until the chase dies down?'

Silver didn't much like the sudden threatening tone in the girl's voice. *Was she intending to throw him out of here as soon as he finished his bath?* 'I suppose the law will be watching all my friends, so it would be unwise of me to go looking for help from any of them. And anyway, I have no wish to make trouble or aggravation for them.' Silver had left his lawyer, Nathanial Walker of the Inner Temple, with the power of attorney for his financial affairs, but contacting Nathanial would be even riskier than going to Sophie or Edward for help...

Elisa adopted a thoughtful look. 'How about relatives? Do you have none that might help you?'

'My parents are both dead, and I have no brothers or sisters still living to turn to.'

Elisa narrowed her eyes. 'How about your sister-in-law, Mrs Sophie Rolfe? Would she not help you?'

Silver was startled. 'And how the devil do you know about her?'

Elisa was clearly pleased with the reaction she had provoked.

'Because I did a little research into your family relations, and then went to see the delightful Mrs Rolfe at her home in Took's Court near Chancery Lane yesterday afternoon.'

Silver was even more astonished. 'Why? To betray me?'

'Well, it is true that the reward for information leading to your capture is a full one hundred pounds, Dr Silver, and that is no trifle to be spurned without some thought. But in fact I wanted to meet your sister-in-law and find out her opinion of you. Luckily she is currently interviewing girls for the position of parlour maid, so I availed myself of that opportunity and put myself forward for the position.'

Silver held his breath. 'And...did you give me away to her?'

A smile played across Elisa's lips. 'I can't say I wasn't tempted. But no - in this case the risks outweighed the reward.'

'In what way?'

'Because if you do get caught, Dr Silver, there is a fair chance you would implicate me accidentally, even if you didn't mean to. And I'm sure you would do so willingly if you ever suspected me of betraying you. I don't know how much my father told you about my own...err...*business activities*, but I do know he was sometimes loose with his tongue. So it seems we will need to trust each other if we both want to stay out of the hands of the law.'

'I will not give you away, even if I do get caught,' Silver promised her caustically. 'I am not that mean-spirited. Or that stupid.'

Elisa nodded sagely as if the point had never genuinely been in question. 'Well, let's not put your intelligence to the test, shall we? Getting back to the subject of your sister-in-law, I was struck by one inescapable conclusion about her. The fact that she apparently believes you innocent of her sister's murder.'

'How would you possibly know that? And why would Sophie discuss such a thing with someone applying for the post of parlour maid? Did she really believe you were an ordinary girl applying for the position of maidservant? You hardly sound like one – your voice is far too educated and ladylike.'

She smiled faintly, liking the compliment, Silver could tell, if reluctant to admit it. 'Ah, but I am an accomplished actress with many voices, from skivvy to gentlewoman. I have to be in my line of work.' She adopted a convincing low class Southern Irish accent. 'Yesterday I was Annie Riley, a hard-workin' girl from the town of Cork, newly arrived in England.' Reverting to her own voice, she added complacently, 'As it happens, your pretty sister-in-law must have been impressed by Annie's demeanour and sweet Irish voice because she did kindly offer her the position of parlour maid...'

Silver was aghast. 'You're not seriously thinking of taking her job, are you?'

'No, of course not, although she does have many beautiful *objets d'art* that would interest me professionally, so it would have been a perfect opportunity to inveigle myself into her fine house...'

Silver was tempted to get angrily to his feet in the bathtub at this point but his natural modesty ultimately prevented him. 'Sophie is not rich,' he protested.

'She seems like it to me,' Elisa observed tartly.

'That's only because she recently married a young man of means...Edward Rolfe.'

'So I was led to believe. And the handsome young couple do have many distinguished paintings on their walls by well-known contemporary artists like William Frith and John Ritchie,' Elisa carried on relentlessly, 'one of which in particular drew my attention.'

'Why?' Silver demanded morosely.

'Because it was a portrait of *you*, Dr Silver, by the young artist John Finnie, and on full display in Sophie's own drawing room. Now, for the life of me, I cannot believe that Mrs Rolfe would do such a thing – keep your portrait hanging there in full view of herself and all her visitors - if she really thought you were the man responsible for the death of her beloved sister. Of course she *could* be wrong about that,' she added doubtfully. 'Women have been known to err badly in their judgement of men.'

'But you don't think so?' Silver asked hopefully.

'Let's just say I'm not sure what to make of you yet,' she admitted reluctantly, after a long reflective pause. Finally Silver noticed a faint pink flush in her cheeks, a slight reaction to his own long and challenging stare.

'Then will you continue to help me?' he pressed her. 'At least for a few more days until I work out what to do for the best.'

She nodded reluctantly. 'Yes. You can stay here for a few more days until you're ready to go. I was planning to bring my father here anyway until the chase died down so I have enough food and coal in the house.'

Silver murmured his gratitude, before asking another question. 'Who owns the shop in front, Miss Saltash?'

Her green eyes flickered. 'I do, along with several other businesses in this area. A young man called Liam Flintham works for me in the store Monday to Saturday, but he is presently away attending to his sick sister in Essex. Be warned in case you meet him accidentally: Liam knows nothing of my other life as a...'

'As a thief?' Silver said bluntly.

'Yes, all right...*as a thief*,' she repeated calmly. 'I am known to him, and generally in this area, as Miss Elisa *Smith*, the respectable daughter of the deceased owner of this shop.'

'*Smith*? Not a very original soubriquet.'

'Perhaps not. But you will need to change your name too, as well as your appearance, Doctor, if you want to stay out of the hands of the law,' she advised him acidly.

Silver reflected for a moment, before agreeing with her. 'Then I'd better use the name Wade.'

'Any particular reason for choosing that name?'

'Wade was my mother's maiden name.'

She laughed mockingly. 'Not very original either. You're really not much of a criminal, are you, Mr *Wade*...'

Silver glowered in response. 'So do you really trust me, Miss Saltash...?'

'Call me Miss *Smith* from now on,' she chided him. 'Or better still, Elisa. Then you will not make any mistake if anyone should overhear any of our future conversations.'

Silver thought it was a hopeful sign that she should believe there might be any future conversations between them at all. 'Your father, and Mr Gardiner for that matter, called you "Lizzie", did they not?' Silver remembered, being deliberately provocative.

'I think I prefer "Elisa" from you, *Mr Wade*,' she declared primly.

'Then do you really believe that I am an innocent victim of a miscarriage of justice...*Elisa*.'

'I told you - I'm hardly as confident in my opinion of you as that, Mr...*Wade*. Your sister-in-law might well be the one who has misjudged you, rather than the law.'

'And yet you are still helping me.'

Elisa became agitated at that, her face growing darker. 'It's not because of any personal regard for you. It's because I despise the peelers, that's why. Especially a certain *Sergeant Sparrow* –' she almost spat the name out – 'who apprehended my father. I intend to get even with this Sergeant Sparrow in due course for what happened to my father.'

Silver regarded her suddenly bitter expression with concern. 'Tell me something. From your own experience as a professional criminal trying to evade the law, where do you think I should go from here...*Elisa*? Where's the best place for a man on the run like me to hide?'

Elisa considered that for a moment, then gave a wry shrug. 'I don't know, to be honest. Nowhere in England will be safe for you any longer, I fear. Once your face is well known to the law, you will always be in trouble. Luckily mine is quite unknown to the peelers, so I am not in your unenviable position. If I were you, frankly, I would take immediate passage on a ship as far away from England as I could get.

Make a different life for yourself in the New World or Australia - that's my advice, Mr Wade.' She glanced at him shrewdly. 'But I sense you're not ready to run yet, are you?'

'No, I'm not. There are other things I need to do here in England first.'

'What other things? Clear your name, perhaps?' she mocked. 'You have an absurd idea of English justice if you believe it ever capable of changing its inflexible judgements.'

His eyes went automatically to the kitchen window and to the distant view of tall masts on the river, rising above the waterfront rooftops. 'No, nothing as naïve as that. What I do want, though, is a job working on that Great Ship...'

CHAPTER 6

Monday 12th October 1857

Monday 12th October 1857

Three days later, Jonathan Silver felt transported to a different world, ridiculously content amid the raucous noise, thick tobacco smoke and clink of glasses and tankards.

The Ship Inn was a public house at Millwall on the Isle of Dogs where the men from the Napier and Russell shipyards came after their twelve-hour shifts to wet their whistles and remove the dry taste from their throats of sawdust, raw smoke and red-hot iron. Yet the main saloon of The Ship Inn was probably even smokier than the adjacent shipyard, if truth be told, and perhaps even noisier too.

'Can I buy you another glass of ale?' Silver asked his first companion. Liam Flintham was Elisa Saltash's principal employee in her chandler's store, and the man who had brought Silver here tonight. And although Liam worked for Elisa, a greater contrast in humankind between him and the enigmatic Miss Saltash would have been hard to imagine. Liam was a very upright and proper young man who'd grown up in the town of Maldon on the Blackwater estuary in Essex, and his accent still made him stand out here on the Isle of Dogs as much as a Scotsman or a Hindu. He was thin and bony, and so erect in his posture even when sitting, that he gave the impression of a man with a substantial length of rigid whalebone shoved up his back passage.

'I could probably manage another one, Jonathan, if you insist,' Liam said with a wide smile. Silver was already becoming well acquainted with that broad toothy grin of Liam's, which erupted under his thick thatch of carrot hair like a sudden ray of sunshine on a gloomy day, and transformed his plain freckled face into something almost beautiful. Liam had taken immediately to Silver when Elisa had introduced him on Saturday as a casual acquaintance of hers, and he had shown no doubt in her story that Silver was an itinerant workman called Jonathan Wade

56

looking for gainful employment in the Napier shipyard.

As for Elisa, she had shown commendable restraint in not pressing Silver for the reasons why he wanted so badly to find work in the shipyard, even though her curiosity had clearly been piqued. But, given that she would be getting Silver off her hands, she seemed prepared to do anything within reason to expedite the matter, even if she didn't yet understand the motivation behind it.

Liam was still unmarried, and Silver had soon become aware from his continual talk of Elisa that he worshipped the very ground that she walked on. Yet this object of Liam's lovesick adoration was not precisely the same Miss Elisa Saltash whom Silver had encountered so memorably over the last few days, but a paler, politer version of her called Miss Elisa *Smith*. Butter would not melt in the mouth of the saintly and reserved "Miss Smith", Silver had decided with amusement, as he had watched how very different her behaviour and accent was when in company with the gentle Liam. That was until he remembered soberly that she was still mourning her father and therefore perhaps deserved a little more respect and understanding from him for her sad situation, even if her late departed father had been a rogue and a thief at best.

It seemed to Silver that Liam was so badly smitten with Miss Elisa Smith that he would have probably worked for her for nothing if she had asked him to. Young Mr Flintham would also no doubt be even more willing to throw his hat into the ring for Miss Smith's pretty little hand one day, assuming he could ever work up the courage to ask such a thing anyway. Being an impossibly shy man with women, though, Silver doubted that Liam would ever be able to work up that much courage, which was perhaps just as well, given that the object of his dreams really was just a chimera of the most deceiving kind...

The Ship Inn was an old timber tavern of three stories that backed directly onto the river near the terminal of the Greenwich paddle steamer ferry, on the very southern tip of the Isle of Dogs. It was a rickety building whose oak floors sloped unevenly and deflected and creaked alarmingly underfoot, and whose rear bay windows seemed to be suspended an impossible distance out over the water by some miracle of structural mechanics that even the great Sir Isaac Newton could never have explained. But, regardless of how these windows were standing without any apparent support, the view of the *Leviathan* from them was truly astounding...

The vast shape of the hull of the great ship in the adjacent shipyard – virtually complete to deck level now - almost obscured the sky to the north like some great towering cathedral to modern Victorian enterprise and commerce. Iron staging towers and gangways ran up the vertical sides of the hull to dizzying heights, which were swarmed over even at night by armies of teeming workers as thick as ants. Close up, the scale of the undertaking was truly extraordinary, and Silver had almost forgotten all his own troubles for a moment, when he first glimpsed the size of this riveted iron monster up close, soaring high and wide almost to the heavens...

'And how about you, Mr Crabtree? Can I offer you another drink too?' Silver continued as he made a beckoning signal to the serving girl in the saloon bar. Silver had profited from the fact that Liam, as part of his trade at the chandler's store, supplied goods directly to local shipyards, so was on first name terms with many of the people who were building the *Leviathan*. In particular he was very well acquainted with a senior foreman at the Napier yard, and had been very willing (for his secret love Elisa's sake, Silver guessed) to make this introduction tonight between "Jonathan Wade" and his foreman friend, Mr Crabtree.

Jude Crabtree was also an Essex man, but unlike Liam he was a dour and grizzled individual of forty-five, so was old enough by rights to be Liam's father. In fact it turned out that he'd worked in his youth for Liam's barge captain father on the River Blackwater, which explained to Silver why his relationship with Liam seemed so much more intimate and fatherly than that of mere casual acquaintances.

The pretty blonde serving girl swiftly brought three more tankards of frothing Essex ale, and Crabtree gave her ample bottom a healthy squeeze through her mass of petticoats before setting her down briskly on his knee. 'Alice is always black and blue by the end of her night's work – even with all these layers of petticoats she wears,' he said with a leer.

'Thanks to you mainly, Jude.' Alice was however too busy eying Silver with interest, though, to do more than half-heartedly fend off Crabtree's wandering hands. 'Who's your new friend, Jude? I haven't seen 'im in 'ere before.'

Silver did feel surprisingly safe from discovery and arrest here, partly because there was almost no established law on the Isle of Dogs, and even more because he felt himself virtually unrecognizable in his guise of labouring man Jonathan Wade. He'd lost nearly twenty pounds during his sojourn in prison, and as a result there were hollows in his cheeks and stringy muscle in his belly and arms that hadn't been there in the prosperous self-satisfied doctor ministering only a few short months ago to the wealthy of Bloomsbury, Piccadilly and Mayfair. And with his hair newly shorn and his beard trimmed neatly by Elisa's expert hand, and dressed in rough serge and canvas working men's clothes, the transformation was complete. Only his accent might let him down, he'd realized, but he had soon reverted naturally to the West Country patter of his youth, the accent he'd had before he'd been gentrified by medical school and the years of doctoring abroad in the Navy.

'This is Mr Wade – Jonathan Wade, Alice,' Crabtree informed her. 'But my, those titties of yours are fine and firm today,' he added, cupping the girl's breast with his right hand.

Alice smacked his roving hand reprovingly. 'Never mind my titties, Jude.' She bounded nimbly to her feet and away from his outstretched hands. 'I bet a gentleman like Mr Wade there would never do such a thing,' she said as she flounced away, with a last lingering look in Silver's direction.

Liam nudged him in the ribs. 'It looks like you've won the admiration of fair Alice there, Jonathan,' he enthused.

Silver was about to make a suitably modest response to that until Crabtree suddenly took firm hold of Silver's hands by the wrists and began examining the palms closely. 'You say you're a carpenter, Wade, and that you'd like a job inside the yard?' Crabtree's voice was filled with sudden suspicion as he felt Silver's palms. 'These don't look much like carpenter's hands to me, although they have done a bit of rough work recently, I admit.'

Silver was deeply uncomfortable with the situation, but didn't try and prise his hands away, reluctant to make a scene that would bring more attention to him. 'I was a carpenter for several years, Mr Crabtree,' he claimed softly. 'But later I went to the Working Men's College in Red Lion Square and studied a bit of book learning in my free time, in order to become a clerk. After that, I took work in St Barts Hospital in the city as a medical clerk. But now I'm sick and tired of it - I want to get back to doing some real manual work, and to earning some real money.'

Crabtree finally released Silver's hands. 'Married, Wade?'

Silver deliberately left his hands on the table, in full view. 'No.'

'Why not?'

'Never had the inclination so far, Mr Crabtree. There are too many Alice's in this world to enjoy, aren't there?'

Crabtree laughed heartily at that, as he lit up a pipe of tobacco. 'That's true enough. But I would prefer it, Wade, if you would leave this particular Alice alone. I'm working hard on her at the moment, and can feel her resistance to my own manly charms beginning to crumble.' For a man like Crabtree, with a wife and five grown-up children at home, that seemed a ridiculously optimistic assessment of his chances of seducing the buxom young Alice, but Silver decided wisely not to argue. And definitely not to smile at the man's presumption.

'Now, with regard to this matter,' Crabtree went on, puffing at his pipe, 'what sort of work did you have in mind to do?'

'Carpentry, of course, if possible. But anything manual would be all right, within reason.'

Crabtree weighed him up carefully, a note of suspicion returning to his rasping smoke-laden voice. 'You sound like a man trying to escape from something.'

'Or *someone*,' suggested Liam eagerly. 'Woman trouble, is it, Jonathan?'

'You could say that,' a relieved Silver murmured.

Crabtree belched loudly. 'Well, Liam vouches for you, Wade, and you do look strong enough, so I will help you find something in the shipyard if I can. But the problem is most of the remaining timber work on the great ship already has a full complement of carpenters and joiners assigned to it. And we are only a few weeks away from launching the ship...'

'Won't that finishing work still have to go on even after the ship is launched?' Silver asked.

'Yes, that's true enough. Once it's launched, the ship will be moved over to the Deptford side for fitting out, and for the engines to be completed. But it will still be hard getting you into one of the gangs of carpenters doing that fitting-out work. They're all Irish for one thing, and as close and clannish as only a tribe of real Paddies can be.'

Silver was getting desperate. 'If they're launching soon, won't they need extra hands in the yard to build the timber slipways for the launch?'

Crabtree studied him shrewdly through the thick wreathes of smoke from his pipe. 'Yes, that's a good point. They probably will. Certainly the slipways are well behind schedule. My own gang of riveters is only working on completing the remaining unfinished bits of the hull before the launch, which isn't work that would suit a carpenter. But I can check for you with the foreman building the slipways, if you like. That work won't last for more than a few weeks, though,' he warned, 'so it won't provide you with long term employment.'

Silver smiled reassuringly. 'Doesn't matter, Mr Crabtree. I'll take anything for now, to see me through the autumn.'

'All right, then,' Crabtree agreed, after pausing with his pipe to take a long swig of ale. 'I'll have a word with Matthew Spurrell – he's the main foreman for the slipway work.' Crabtree squinted at Silver, as if trying to peer through a fog. 'Do you know much about the history of our ship, Mr Wade?'

Silver guessed that, despite the promise of help from this man, he was still on trial of a sort, so had better show some enthusiasm for this epic project. 'I have heard that there has been some argument between the contractor and the engineer about who is the real force behind the creation of this ship.'

Liam butted in, another obvious enthusiast for this grand engineering work. 'Doesn't matter what this man Mr Russell says, there is no doubt who is really the father of this great ship. And that man is the famous Mr Brunel himself. He has designed it to be the greatest ship in the world, nearly ten times the size of any other vessel afloat. Imagine that – *ten times*!'

'Why is it so big?' Silver asked with genuine interest. 'Is there any sensible point to making a ship this fantastical size?'

Crabtree interrupted gruffly. 'Yes, there is - because it's being built for the Eastern Steam Navigation Company to carry trade directly to Australia. Mr Brunel already built two great ships for the Atlantic trade ten or twenty years ago, but this new vessel is a different scale altogether from the *Great Western* and the *Great Britain*. Some people want to call this new ship the *Great Eastern,* for obvious reasons, but everyone in the Napier yard calls it the *Leviathan,* and I for one hope it stays that way. The plan is for the *Leviathan* to steam from London to Australia without the need to take on coal. Saves building and supplying a coaling station at the Cape, you see. That's what Brunel realized – that to be able to carry enough coal to reach Australia, a ship must be scaled up in size massively from all present day ships. But of course that creates problems too.'

'Like the hull design?' Silver suggested.

Crabtree nodded and appraised Silver with a shrewd inspection. 'I can see you understand a little about the subtleties of designing ships, Wade. Yes, it is a challenge making a hull of this vast size strong enough, but Mr Brunel knows exactly what he's doing. I've seen ships built for thirty years now and never seen anything like this one. Mr Brunel has designed a double hull of one-inch thick plate with longitudinal stiffeners running the whole length, and with almost the full height of the hull divided up by great stiffened bulkheads. This ship will be unsinkable in my opinion...' - he hesitated before giving a wry smile - 'provided we ever get it to float in the first place, that is.'

Silver remembered what he'd read about the earlier stages of this troubled project. 'I heard there were big financial problems in getting even this far.'

At his point Alice came back to reclaim some pewter tankards, and her impressive bust, as she leaned provocatively across the table in Silver's direction, distracted the men's conversation for a moment. Extricating herself from Crabtree's surprisingly fast hands, she soon retreated with a laugh and an exuberant shake of her firm young hips.

Crabtree waited to admire her retreating figure before he went on, puffing again at his clay pipe. 'They couldn't find a single yard on the Thames big enough to build the *Leviathan*. But John Scott Russell, who owns the yard at Millwall here, bid for the work because he knew he could lease the adjacent empty Napier yard too. Napier had just sold up – he thinks the Thames is no place to build the larger steamships of the future so he'd moved back to Scotland to set up a new yard on the Clyde. I hope he's wrong, or my livelihood on the Thames will soon be gone. And I don't want to have to go up there and live with the Jocks.'

'Me neither,' agreed Liam with a shy smile.

'Then Russell went broke after a year or so into the contract,' Crabtree continued, 'and dropped the Eastern Steam Navigation Company in it good and proper. Work stopped for a year while the financial mess was sorted out. Eventually the company themselves took over the building of the ship directly – hiring the Napier Yard themselves, and many of Russell's old workforce, including myself. It has been hard work making up for lost time, but we have nearly completed the hull now. But the company has had Russell's creditors on their backs the whole time, bleeding them dry, while Russell's engineers, who are still mostly loyal to their old employer, have made Brunel's life a hell. Yet he's now almost there, despite all the pain and aggravation they've put him through.'

'Why are Russell's creditors involved?' Silver wanted to know. 'What claim do they have on the company building the ship?'

Crabtree tapped the side of his nose knowingly. 'Ah, there's the rub. You see, while most of the ship is in the Napier yard, the bows happen to hang over into the Russell yard, and the company is therefore having to pay Russell's creditors through the nose for the privilege. So the Eastern Steam Navigation Company directors – and you can hardly blame them, when they're seeing their money bleeding away into the river - are putting their engineer under great pressure to launch before he's really ready.'

'Sounds like a difficult situation for Mr Brunel,' Silver surmised.

'It certainly is, and it's taking its toll on the man,' Liam interjected again. 'I saw him in the yard the other week when I was delivering supplies from Miss Smith's store to the yard, and the man has aged twenty years in the last twelve months.'

Crabtree slammed his empty tankard down heavily on the rough-hewn table top and nodded through the window at the towering hull of the *Leviathan*. 'How much do you think that ship weighs in its present situation, Wade?'

Silver hazarded a guess. 'I don't know. Ten thousand tons, mebbe?'

Crabtree looked impressed. 'Not a bad guess. Actually *twelve* thousand tons, and most of that riveted iron plates and angles. So it will be a difficult task to move that much deadweight, that's for certain.'

'Can't they just tip her into the water, Jude?' Liam asked.

Crabtree grunted. 'They could, of course. But Mr Brunel thinks that would be a disaster to have that much mass sliding out of control into the river. Therefore he's insisting on a controlled launch, even though this will be the heaviest object that man has ever tried to move on the face of God's earth. There are many people, though, who will be only too happy if he fails, particularly among the press and the Eastern Steam Company's commercial rivals. But then, great men of vision have always found plenty of enemies among all the lesser men and weasels around them,' he added sagely, with a further puff on his pipe.

'How will the ship be launched then?' Silver was so caught up in this drama of the great ship that he had almost forgotten his own perilous situation as a fugitive.

'As you can see, the ship has been built sideways on to the river, as Brunel insisted. Now that the hull is nearly complete, we are building two massive iron cradles to support her amidships, and then two giant sloping slipways under each cradle. Those are the slipways you could be working on, Mr Wade, if you play your cards right. They are made up of timber piles supporting a deep concrete bed. On top of the bed will be a lacing of timber baulks on which a series of iron rails will be laid. The cradles too are shod with iron, so that all the contacts between the cradles and the rails will be iron on iron.'

'Will iron slide on iron?' Silver wondered doubtfully.

Crabtree shrugged. 'If the Engineer says it will, then I believe him. I'm sure he's done smaller scale tests to prove this will work.'

A tall middle-aged man squeezed past their table at this point, and Crabtree made a respectful nod of his head as the man passed. If Crabtree had had any forelock left to tug, then Silver guessed he would have gladly tugged it, which meant the man had to be someone important. Silver consequently paid the man some close attention as he walked away, noting the fine stovepipe top hat and black frock coat, and the other clear marks of him being a gentleman of sorts, which made him an unlikely visitor to a raucous and common place like The Ship Inn.

Silver nodded at the retreating dark-haired figure. 'Who was that gentleman? He didn't look much like someone who belongs in a tavern like this.'

Crabtree sniffed. 'No, I'm not sure what he's doing in here either. That was Mr Daniel Strode. He was formerly one of Mr Russell's chief design engineers and latterly his business partner too, so has become one of the worst thorns in Mr Brunel's side since Russell was kicked off the job. Strode's a clever man and a gifted mechanical engineer, there's no doubt, so Russell had made him responsible for the design of the paddle engines of the Great Ship – although to Mr Brunel's specification, of course. A wealthy man too, is Mr Strode, with a grand house in Blackfriars, so they say, and a fine carriage to bring him to work every day. After Russell declared for bankruptcy, Brunel was forced to employ Strode directly to supervise the completion of the paddle engines because he himself is not by rights a mechanical engineer...' – Crabtree laughed ironically – 'even though I dare say Mr Brunel understands the general workings of steam engines as well as any man alive. But the ship has to have both paddle engines and a screw, so Brunel and the company have had no other option but to use Strode's services, despite their reservations about employing a man so blatantly loyal to Russell.'

Silver frowned. 'Why both paddle engines and a screw for the Great Ship? I thought that ship designers had long demonstrated the superiority of the propeller over the paddle as a means of ship propulsion?'

Crabtree fixed Silver with a curious stare. 'Yes, Wade, that's true. But that's the trouble with Mr Brunel being a man fifty years ahead of his time. Mechanical engineers haven't been able to keep up with him. They cannot yet harness enough power and torque to drive a single shaft on a ship of this size, so the *Leviathan* has to have paddles as well as a propeller...'

*

The wind was building ominously, with great thunderheads of cloud rolling in from the west, as Silver took the West Ferry Road that led north from the southern tip of the Isle of Dogs back towards Limehouse and Wapping. The wind flattened the grass along the tops of the dykes like a scythe, and the gnarled old lime trees in the occasional dips and hollows seemed to be leaning complacently into the force of the gathering storm like seasoned old salts in a fearsome sou'wester.

As he struggled to make progress against the fierce wind, Silver marvelled at the chance encounter with that gentleman in The Ship Inn - marvelled because Daniel Strode was in fact the *very* reason why he had chosen to seek employment at the Napier shipyard.

Silver had never met this man Daniel Strode before, but for several reasons – all of them tenuous at present – he had become quietly convinced during his time in gaol that Strode might be the very man who had murdered his wife Marianne...

Yet, to be frank, he had no more concrete evidence of those suspicions than of there being men on the Moon, which was why he hadn't confided his reasons for wanting a job in the Napier shipyard to Elisa Saltash. She no doubt would have mercilessly mocked his hopes of proving his innocence - and particularly with so little evidence against Strode to go on. All he really had against Strode, in truth, was the fact that he had been a former jealous suitor of Marianne's, and that she had once expressed her deep-seated fear and dislike of the man...

Hence Silver's decision to come to Millwall, to try and learn what he could of the man, and his habits. It was a desperate throw of the dice to come here, but he had no one else to suspect even remotely so had pinned all his hopes on Strode being the guilty man. Yet Daniel Strode, on first inspection, hadn't turned out to be quite what Silver had been expecting. From Marianne's brief description of the man, and of her reasons for turning down his offer of marriage, Silver had expected someone rather older, more dissolute and sinister perhaps, certainly not that surprisingly impressive and handsome figure anyway...

Before he was halfway to his destination, the rain began to fall in solid sheets from the raging sky, smiting his face with evil force, so that Silver was forced to stop and hold up the lantern he had borrowed from Liam, and squint painfully into the raw wind to see the way ahead. He clamped his seaman's cap tighter on his head and buttoned up his greatcoat to the collar, grateful to Elisa as he did so for both of these useful gifts, as well as for the ten gold sovereigns she had lent him to survive. Her father's clothes had proved to be an extraordinarily good fit for him in his current leaner situation, although Silver still didn't feel entirely comfortable walking around in the clothes and boots of a dead man...

A few minutes further on, and the darkness became even more impenetrable, leaving Silver to stumble on almost blindly, aware only of the untamed power of nature roaring like a wild beast above his head. He began to wish that he had stayed behind with Liam at The Ship and accepted that offer of a lift back to Wapping later in the evening in Liam's snug delivery cart.

No point in turning back now, though - he was already soaked through. And so, hurrying on as fast as he could, he kept his head low and his back bent, emulating the flattened grass and the stunted trees all around him. The road – barely more than a muddy track – became even more squalid as he progressed northwards, a miserable and pot-holed road wedged between the foaming river on the one side, and the desolate marshes on the other. On that landward side, despite the direction of the wind, the evil smell of stagnant ditches filled the air with the taint of a slaughterhouse.

Silver was relieved when he saw occasional lights ahead, and realized the long low wall to the right must be the line of the West India Dock rising above the marshes. Crossing the series of bridges over the entrance channels to the dock basins, he saw the welcoming if sparse gaslights of Limehouse ahead, and the sparks and puffing steam and oil-lit carriages of a locomotive on the Blackwall Line, heading up the slight incline towards Fenchurch Street Station in the city. Though how the driver was holding his engine on the tracks with the wind roaring and gusting with such savagery was beyond Silver's comprehension.

London already had a ring of new railway terminuses on its outskirts, built in the boom railway years of the 'forties - London Bridge, Fenchurch Street, Euston, Waterloo Bridge Station, Kings Cross, and now Brunel's new station to the west, Paddington – yet there were many more planned. In his lifetime of thirty-four years, Silver had seen the country he loved transformed beyond recognition by the coming of the railways and by industry, blackening the countryside and filling the air and water with filth and noise. It was a high price that was being paid for progress, seeing all these green English fields disappearing under brick and stone and soot...

He passed through the mean streets of Limehouse - once a little riverside settlement called Limehurst because of its lime kilns, before being ultimately overwhelmed by the bricks and mortar of the invading city from the west. Then as the distant bells of St George's-in-the-East struck ten o'clock, he took Ratcliffe Highway through the parish of St Paul's, Shadwell heading west. The power of the storm was now diminished by the protection of the hovels and brick walls lining the cobbled road, and he could walk at a steadier pace here. Silver snuffed out his lantern, which he didn't need any longer given the regular street lamps along this section of Ratcliffe Highway. Approaching the parish boundary with Wapping on the east side of the London Dock, he saw two rough seamen arguing with a young woman on the opposite side of the road under a gaslight, and hurried on, not wanting to get caught up in some domestic disturbance between a gin-soaked street girl and some even drunker and more violent ruffians.

But his conscience wouldn't quite allow him to pass on without investigating, so he reversed his steps a little only to discover that the young woman actually appeared to be the innocent victim of a couple of nasty pestering sailors.

'I bet there's a pretty little arse under those petticoats of yours, isn't there, my beauty?' the taller of the two villains was saying to the girl as Silver reluctantly crossed the road and approached the group.

Neither the girl nor the two men seemed to notice his approach as he sidled closer, waiting for an opportunity to intervene if he had to. Judging by her dress and her quiet demeanour, the girl was certainly no street girl, he observed, and therefore seemed worthy of his protection at the cost of a punch or two thrown in return, provided it was no more than that. In his precarious situation as a fugitive, Silver did not much feel like taking on the threat of a knife-wielding opponent. And these two middle-aged wharf rats certainly looked just the types to be carrying weapons, Silver thought, so he hung back for as long as he could, hoping the men would somehow come to their senses of their own accord and leave the girl alone.

But that proved a forlorn hope: the men had clearly had far too much to drink at the local public house along the way, The White Rose Tavern, and had chosen to vent their resulting drunken sexual frustrations on this poor girl. The girl herself didn't seem that scared by her predicament, though - more bemused by it if anything. She looked to Silver like a respectable maidservant or shop worker, dressed in heavy serge skirt, high-necked cotton blouse and thick blue crocheted shawl. But walking around on her own at ten in the evening probably wasn't the wisest thing for her to do in a place as notoriously lawless as Wapping.

'Please leave me alone, sirs,' the girl said in a quietly dignified manner. 'You're makin' a mistake. I ain't no street girl. I'm sure you can find women like that around here if you wish. Now please, let me pass, will yer.'

The shorter wharf rat mocked her politeness. 'Oh, please let me pass, is it?'

The taller, a burly and pockmarked man with bad teeth and wiry hair, pushed her a little. 'I'll let you pass all right, dearie. But just show us a bit of your firm young arse first, and then we'll be on our way. Isn't that right, Jack? That's all we want. Just a glimpse.'

'That's right, Joey, me mate,' the shorter Jack agreed, grabbing the hem of the girl's skirt to reveal her stockings and petticoats. 'Oh, this is fine. She smells like a lady.'

'And how would you know, Jack?' Silver finally intervened, when there was nothing else he could do.

'Fuck off, pilgrim,' the taller Joey said bluntly, without even turning his head to acknowledge the newcomer, 'unless you want trouble.'

Silver was wary of peelers but couldn't leave these two to have their sordid way with the girl. They wouldn't be able to stop at just taking her drawers down, he knew that well enough.

He turned partially away as if conceding defeat, then hit tall Joey a savage blow with the swing of his lantern. Blood exploded from the man's nose and jaw as he collapsed against a brick wall and slid to the ground.

'Why, you nasty fucker...' Jack began before Silver, without another word, head-butted him savagely on the bridge of his nose, after which the foul-mouthed Jack Tar sank against a wall into a bloodstained heap.

'Wot did you do that for?' The girl didn't seem particularly grateful for his help. 'It weren't necessary.'

'Perhaps not, girl, but I am in a hurry.' Then Silver became aware of a patrolling bobby in the distance along Ratcliffe Highway to the east, and decided it really was time to leave. 'Excuse me now. I have to be off.'

Silver ran off west, taking his lantern with him, then became aware that the girl was following him, at a run too.

'Why are you following me?' he asked her peevishly. 'That copper will look after you.'

The girl could run surprisingly fast, even in her heavy skirt, and double petticoat. 'I ain't got no love for the bobbies. Nor 'ave you, it seems,' she added shrewdly.

Finally they turned off Ratcliffe Highway into New Gravel Lane, the boundary between the parishes of St George's-in-the-East, and St Paul's, Shadwell, where Silver felt safe enough from pursuit now to slow to a regular walk. 'What's your name, girl?'

The girl was scarcely out of breath, whereas Silver himself felt as if his lungs were about to explode out of his chest in protest at the violent exercise. 'Amy. Amy McLennan.'

Silver nodded to her. 'My name is Wade.'

She bobbed a little curtsey in return like a kitchen maid come to clean the grate. 'Then thank you kindly, Mr Wade, for your 'elp. I didn't mean to sound ungrateful back there.'

He eyed her coolly. 'You should stay away from these streets, late at night.'

'It's not that late; it's only just gone ten,' the girl countered. 'Hanyway, most seamen are all right if they're sober. Better than gentlemen, if you wants to know,' she added dismissively, with a sidelong look at him.

'What's wrong with gentlemen?' Silver asked her warily.

'Gentlemen is much bigger blackguards than wot blackguards is, in my opinion,' the girl announced sternly.

Silver laughed. 'You don't take me for a gentleman, do you?'

'Not exactly. But then you don't sound like you come from around here either,' Amy suggested curiously.

'I'm a Devon man. From the pretty town of Sidmouth. And you? Are you local, Amy?'

'Yeah, close. I was born in Bermondsey south of the river. But I lives and works in Wapping now. I was on an errand, on my way to buy some fresh fruit and vegetables from a storekeeper who stays open until midnight. But I'll probably not bovver now, after that trouble.'

Silver couldn't help noticing, as he walked beside Amy, what a tall well-built figure of a girl she was. About twenty, Silver would have said, with her dark hair bare and unadorned, and tossed about appealingly by the wind and the rain, and with an almost Latin-looking face. Her olive skin was complemented by long eyelashes, dimples in her cheeks and flashing white teeth. A face like hers seemed to belong more to a sun-baked Italian port like Genoa or Naples; Silver could easily imagine a girl like this sunning herself with friends and beaus in a quayside piazza on a hot summer evening to the sounds of mandolins and water crickets. So her beauty was somehow alien and out of place on a stormy autumn night in a dismal sailor's haunt on the River Thames like Wapping. Silver wondered if she knew how close she'd nearly come to being raped and beaten because of her striking beauty. Not at all, though, judging by the still luminous look in those dark eyes and the secret smile hiding in her voice.

'Where do you live, Amy? Can I walk you home? I live in Wapping too – in Gun Alley, to be precise.' Silver had moved out of Elisa's place yesterday, and taken a room in a seaman's lodging house in Gun Alley, just off Old Gravel Lane.

'Then we're close neighbours. I lives in a 'ostel for women here on New Gravel Lane. We takes in women in trouble there. Saves 'em from the workhouse, anyway, and gives 'em shelter and useful employment, to keep 'em from panderin' to the vices of seamen.'

The rain was becoming heavier again, and the wind stronger, so they both increased their pace. 'So, fallen women, are they?' Silver suggested tactlessly.

Amy wrapped her blue shawl around her head, although her hair was already soaked through by now. 'You might call 'em "fallen". Personally I'd say they was not so much fallen as knocked to the ground by evil men.' She frowned at him, the rain flattening her dark curls to her forehead. 'And what do you do, Mr Wade? Are you a seaman?'

'I have been to sea,' he said. 'But I'm really a carpenter.'

She stopped walking, despite the pouring rain, and wrinkled her brow. 'A carpenter who don't want ter talk to the police.'

'Well, to be honest, I have had a little trouble with the law in the past. I have the debtors after me. But you wouldn't split on me to them, would you?'

'I certainly wouldn't, not when you risked your neck savin' me tonight. That would be plain unchristian of me, especially when you're a carpenter too, just like our sweet Lord.' She began walking again, and pointed to a building thirty yards further down the street, a substantial three-storey affair built around a central courtyard, like a coaching inn. 'That's the 'ostel for women where I live and work.'

'Looks like an old inn.'

'It were, I think. Some rich do-gooder woman bought it, and, like I say, now runs it as a refuge for local women in trouble to stay as long as they want.'

Silver raised an eyebrow. 'Free of charge?'

'Yeah, but they 'ave to do their share of chores. There's no men allowed in, so don't expect to be able to come in after me,' she warned him cheekily.

'Sounds like a nunnery,' Silver suggested maliciously.

'Yeah, except there ain't no nuns inside. Only girls like me…'

Silver smiled at her. 'And what exactly do you do there, Amy?'

'I 'elp around. Keep the place clean and see the kitchen is stocked.'

'You're not a fallen woman yourself, then?' Silver teased her.

'No, I've learned to stay well away from men.'

'A wise head on young shoulders.'

Amy didn't seem interested in acknowledging the compliment. 'And 'ave you a job as a carpenter around 'ere, Mr Wade?'

'Yes, I just got a job working on the Great Ship on the Isle of Dogs. I hope so, anyway. They're getting ready to launch in a few weeks so they're hiring extra men to speed up the work.'

Her eyes shone with pleasure as they reached the main gateway into her home. She didn't seem in a hurry to enter despite the rain falling in torrents, splashing the cobbles at her feet. 'Then you're a lucky young man to get such an opportunity.'

'I'm not so lucky…or so young,' he denied.

She inspected him carefully under the flicker of a nearby oil street lamp. 'You're not so old either. I wish I could work on somethin' like that. Imagine! – workin' on the biggest ship in the world. Girls never get the chance to do wonderful things like that.'

'Oh, you might get the chance to do wonderful things too in time, Amy. I wouldn't be at all surprised,' Silver said, doffing his cap to her, as he headed at a run down the windswept empty street towards the river and his own lodging house.

CHAPTER 7

Monday 12th October 1857

At midnight Charlotte Livingstone sat at a bay window, listening to the raging of the storm outside. Storms had always attracted her for some unfathomable reason, perhaps because of their primordial violence and unpredictable power and fury...

'Come back to bed, Charlotte,' the man said, lifting his head off the pillow. 'You'll catch a chill sitting there at an open window.'

Charlotte turned her head for a moment and smiled reassuringly at him. 'I will come back in a minute, Daniel. But the room is very close, and I need a little fresh air to clear my head.'

The man threw off the covers, then eased himself out of bed and came slowly towards her. The sight of his naked body still aroused her powerfully again, even only a bare few minutes after making love. Although he was twenty years older than her, his body was still as powerfully muscled as a youth's, with a pronounced masculine chest and a sculpted narrow waist. He moved like a Greek athlete too; with that natural suppleness and grace and beauty, he seemed to her to belong to a different time and place. She could easily imagine him at the legendary gymnasium of Olympia, wrestling in oiled and naked splendour under the intense glare of the Peloponnesian sun, by the fair waters of the River Alpheus. That seemed a far more fitting home for a man like Daniel Strode than this modern city of London with all its dirt and squalor.

Charlotte sighed inwardly. Men were so fortunate, weren't they, not having to endure the rigors and physical humilities of endless pregnancies in their lives. Her own mother was only two years older than Daniel, and yet she was a dried-out shell of a woman with all her vigour and youth gone forever. And yet this man of the same age still looked like a God, come down from Mount Olympus...

She pulled his borrowed dressing gown around her naked shoulders to ward off the chill of the wind whistling through the open windowpane. From here in Pennington Street, she could see the whole of the London Dock and its infinite lines of warehouses arrayed before her, and, immediately below, the twenty-foot-high brick wall protecting it like a prison. Beyond the dock basins were the lights of the riverside taverns, and the numberless riding lights of storm-tossed vessels thronging the river. Yet Charlotte didn't like this part of London, for all its excitement and its hints of distant and exotic faraway places that she dreamed of one day visiting with Daniel. She wondered with slight peevishness why he couldn't arrange for a more convenient and salubrious rendezvous for their assignations than this old run-down house near the docks.

Yet, of course, she understood the reasons for avoiding the more fashionable areas of town. He didn't want to run the risk of his semi-invalid wife or her querulous relatives discovering them by accident, so it was certainly better to meet somewhere far removed from Daniel's family home in Bridge Street in Blackfriars. This location did perhaps suit Daniel more than her, though, because it was scarcely a convenient distance from her own home in Islington. But that was perhaps no bad thing either, she decided, when any premature exposure of their affair would destroy her reputation permanently. It was not really the remoteness of Wapping that she resented, more its insalubrious air and dangerous streets...

He came up slowly behind her, and seemed less concerned about her catching a chill than he'd said, because he gently eased the dressing gown back from her shoulders to bare her breasts to his inspection.

She quivered at his touch as he cupped her breasts from behind and nuzzled the soft skin at the nape of her neck.

'Did you know,' he murmured into her ear, 'that an infamous series of murders took place here not fifty years ago – the Ratcliffe Highway murders? A whole family was murdered brutally not more than a hundred yards from where you are sitting right now.'

She shivered. 'Don't say things like that, Daniel. It frightens me.'

He laughed faintly. 'Sorry, my sweet. That was thoughtless of me,' he added as he squeezed her breasts with more force and breathed heavily into her hair.

She got slowly to her feet, still with her back to him, and let him remove the dressing gown completely, feeling his eyes moving down from her neck to her slowly stirring buttocks.

His hands moved down in front to her swelling belly and she wondered if he would know by the plumper feel of her these days that she was already eight weeks gone. Tonight, she had resolved finally to tell him the truth. The baby would change everything, she felt sure. Force him to confront the realities of his unhappy marriage and finally leave that wretched and clinging wife who could never love him as she loved him.

Suddenly desperate to please him, she arched her back with deliberate provocation, knowing what the more carnal side of his nature liked. Yet she still almost jumped with shock as she felt him penetrate her immediately from behind, huge and engorged like a stallion. His wife could never give herself to him like this, she thought exultantly, knowing that after tonight her future would be secure forever...

*

Jonathan Silver's present living quarters in Gun Alley were noticeably less salubrious than Elisa Saltash's warm and comfortable kitchen, even if only a hundred yards or so away. Yet, once Liam Flintham had returned to work in the chandler's store, Silver knew it would have been dangerous for Elisa's position in the community for him to stay there, so he had selflessly elected to go and find another place of refuge. Elisa's local reputation as the virtuous and virginal Miss Smith would have been hard to maintain if Liam had discovered, or even suspected, that the mysterious Jonathan Wade was apparently living under the same roof.

Not that Elisa herself had pressed him to go immediately. In fact, after her initial coolness towards him, she did seem to warm to his presence in her home a little, even thawing out to the point of smiling at him occasionally. When he had suggested that it was time for him to leave, she had even tried to talk him out of it and offered to let him stay upstairs in the parlour away from Liam's - and the shop customers' - prying eyes. But Silver thought she really had done enough for him by this time – more than enough, in truth. Despite his own natural modesty when it came to assessing a woman's feelings for him, Silver sensed that Elisa was becoming quietly attracted to him, even with the vast difference in their ages and backgrounds. And he in return had been forced to acknowledge his own growing interest in her, which was a dangerous and probably self-indulgent emotion to give into in his desperate situation, so was an extra valid reason for him leaving the protection of her home as soon as he could.

It was a ridiculous thought anyway – to imagine a liaison between someone like him – a man on the run - and a girl as unpredictable and hard to fathom as Elisa Saltash. Still, he couldn't help thinking about her now, particularly remembering her rising from that zinc bath like Venus being born, and certainly bearing no resemblance to any common thief he had ever encountered before...

He groaned with frustration at the thought and tried to sleep, as the fierce wind rattled a loose windowpane, and the old roof above his head creaked and sighed with the strain of fighting the forces of nature. But it was difficult to sleep at the best of times in this mean attic room at the very top of this old lodging house in Gun Alley. He had taken the room on his own at ten shillings a week, rather than share with four or five others as most seamen in this lodging house did. Yet, even so, the accommodation was hardly luxurious. The lodging house was owned by one Thomas Steams, a retired seaman, and Silver had found it by the simple expedient of walking around Old Gravel Lane on the previous Saturday looking for "vacant room" signs. Mr Steams, though, as Silver soon discovered, seemed to be inebriated on rum to the point of incapacity most of the time, so that the day-to-day running of the lodging house fell naturally to Fanny, his bulky and hard-faced wife of forty. She however ran the place with a rod of iron, which was probably just as well given the quality of the clientele who came through her doors, some of whom would have even made the egregious Joey and Jack from tonight's encounter appear quite gentlemanly by comparison. Silver could only hope that those two didn't in fact lodge here, or there might be evil repercussions should he bump into them accidentally on the stairs...

Reflecting on that encounter with those two wharf rats tonight, Silver knew that he had been taking a fearsome risk in helping that girl Amy. Yet, even as a hunted fugitive, he'd found he couldn't just switch off his conscience and pass on the other side.

Elisa, as a parting gift to him before his departure from her home, had gone around the immediate neighbourhood on Sunday, discreetly taking down any wanted bills for his capture that she could find. Despite his notoriety in this city, she had only found a half-dozen to remove so it seemed unlikely that many of the people of Wapping would yet be likely to recognize him as the fugitive in question. Silver suspected that half the population of Wapping were themselves fugitives of one sort or another anyway, and therefore only too happy to keep their curiosity about their fellow residents to a minimum in return for the same consideration. So, all in all, he had probably found the perfect place to hide, among the numberless and nameless seamen of Wapping.

He was however increasing his risk of discovery greatly by venturing outside the area to seek work at the Napier shipyard on the Isle of Dogs. There were a lot more professional and skilled men working in that yard who would no doubt read newspapers and penny dreadfuls, and even see billboards too, who might then spot a resemblance between the new carpenter in the yard, and the fugitive and infamous wife murderer, Dr Jonathan Silver...

God Almighty! The bedbugs in this straw mattress were eating him alive tonight, while the whole mean little room stank of shit and urine. In fact the whole room smelled so vile that there could have been a dozen rotting corpses in here with him for all he knew. Silver determined that he would complain to Mrs Steams first thing tomorrow and get her cleaning girl Daisy to buy a new mattress for this room, and air the whole place, at the very least, before he was eaten to the bone. He would have to keep his complaints discreet and restrained, though, to avoid drawing too much attention to himself. "Anonymity" had to be his middle name from now on...

In the flickering candlelight, Silver observed that there was a painting of the Virgin Mary, and a decorative wooden cross, on the opposite wall to his bed, as if Mrs Steams seemed desirous to bring a little religious contemplation to even her, mostly Godless, clientele. Yet, on second thoughts, the wallpaper behind these religious symbols was so blackened and peeling with age that Silver suspected that the painting and cross had more probably been there since long before Mrs Steams' time – perhaps they even dated back to old Farmer George's time. Silver concentrated his thoughts on the face of the Virgin as he tried to drift off into sleep. The Virgin of that picture – a naive copy of a Renaissance masterpiece - did have an unsettling resemblance to his own angel, Marianne, the woman who had entered his life so mysteriously, then burnt like a powerful candle within it for a short time, before being finally extinguished with equal mystery and abruptness...

Marianne had been a difficult woman to fathom, there was no denying it, and Silver, although loving her wholeheartedly, had never really felt that he understood her. In fact he'd never really comprehended fully what she had been doing at Scutari, the base hospital in Turkey, where he'd first met her during the Crimean campaign, when she came to his ward to visit her friend Captain Caitlin, a badly wounded survivor of Balaklava. Ostensibly she was working there as a volunteer nurse, yet Silver had soon suspected that the truth wasn't quite as straightforward as that. She had been noticeably secretive with him from the start and, after their first few chance encounters in his ward, had only agreed to meet him later outside the hospital grounds, and in private. Her slightly odd behaviour had prompted Silver into asking his close medical colleagues discreetly what they knew of her, which turned out surprisingly to be almost nothing. Soon Marianne had become almost a ghostlike figure to him, appearing at odd times from nowhere like a spirit, yet impossible to find at others. In fact, during all those three months that Marianne was at Scutari, he was never able to find out - from her or from anyone else - in which part of the hospital she actually worked, or exactly what she did there. It was true that Scutari was a vast hospital, and one in constant turmoil from the influx of wounded and dying men from the battlefield, yet it was still hard for Silver to believe that no one else in this place knew such a striking looking nurse as this...

In the end Silver had decided that she had probably volunteered for nursing duties at Scutari only to be near her friend and lover Captain Caitlin, and that her secretive behaviour was designed to conceal from Caitlin her growing attachment to her lover's own surgeon. This behaviour had hardly encouraged Silver to trust her, yet soon he was too far gone with love to care. Regardless of his doubts and suspicions about her, he had become intoxicated by her beauty, and also by her wit and luminous intelligence, which seemed to shine despite all the death and disease around her. Within two months of knowing her, he had proposed, and – most mysteriously of all for such an enigmatic creature - she had accepted him at once. Then, just as abruptly, she had disappeared from his life for another six months, before reappearing again like a vision to greet him on the quayside at Southampton when he finally landed back home after his long tour of duty.

Had theirs really been a happy married life, though? A perplexing question to try and answer. On the surface, the answer was an equivocal yes. She had certainly tried her best to make him happy in those two short years, and endeavoured, when back in London, to settle down to the subordinate duties of wife to a busy doctor and surgeon at St Bartholomew's Hospital. Yet Silver had always been conscious that she was restless and perhaps unfulfilled by the staid domestic life he had imposed on her. Despite her overwhelming femininity, there was a side to Marianne that seemed disturbingly masculine – full of ambition, energy, fearlessness. She was one of those rare women who would have made a great man, Silver thought, but for that accident of birth that had given her a womb and breasts.

Yet she *had* feared one man, he remembered, and that man ironically a close friend and confidante of her recently deceased engineer father, George Lovelock. That man was the engineer and businessman Daniel Strode, a violent and irrational man who had wanted to marry Marianne himself several years ago and who had apparently deeply resented her refusal of his offer...

In his slow uneasy drift into sleep, with the wind howling outside, Silver relived Marianne's terrible final day...

It had started badly enough, with him having to remove the gangrenous leg of a seven-year-old boy called Arthur Blake. Arthur, the son of a greengrocer in Hackney, had broken his leg a week before when falling under the wheels of an omnibus in the Grays Inn Road, and Silver had set the multiple fracture with high expectations that his recovery would be complete.

Yet, despite Silver's best attempts to keep the leg clean and free from infection, young Arthur's leg had soon yielded to a terrifying plague that threatened to rage through his entire body like a forest fire unless they amputated the leg quickly. Silver had remembered a conversation he'd had two years ago with an impressive young Hungarian doctor he'd met in Vienna – Semmelweis by name – and wondered if he could have done more to reduce infection at his own hospital by the application of chlorinated lime, as this Dr Semmelweis had recommended. Other doctors in St Barts, however, had always refused to believe that the hospital could be full of the agents of disease, because it appeared so well-scrubbed and clean. Silver had soon made himself deeply unpopular with his colleagues because of his assertion that the surgeons of St Barts might actually be killing far more of their patients, as a result of their own unsanitary working habits, than they ever saved. As a result, they had fought Silver's proposal to use chlorinated lime to clean the floors and walls of the hospital at every turn, with the consequence that patients like little Arthur Blake were still being routinely condemned to unnecessary early deaths by their own doctors' wilful refusal to face facts...

Silver had taken a cab home to Russell Square in early evening in a miserably depressed mood, unable to erase from his mind the memory of removing Arthur's tiny pathetic leg, and of the distraught look on his mother's face in the green-tiled corridor afterwards. Thank God for ether and chloroform at least! Ten years ago he would have had to take off that boy's leg without even the benefit of anaesthesia – at least that sort of agony was now a thing of the past.

Even the sunshine and warmth of a long English summer evening, with greenfinches and blackbirds singing euphoniously in the green leafy square, couldn't dispel from his mind the horror of this day, though. He'd seen much worse at Scutari, of course, but not to a seven-year-old boy, thank God...

He let himself in at the front door rather than waiting for the parlour maid to come. Their Scots maid Jeanie always took such a long time responding to his rings that now he seldom bothered her, unless he'd forgotten his own front door key.

He glanced at the silver gilt tray on the entrance table where today's mail was kept for his inspection, but his attention was drawn immediately to the stairs as he heard a slow gasp.

But was it a gasp of pain or pleasure...?

Marianne was sitting on the stairs, her face just visible above the balustrade, and for one moment Silver thought she was playing some sort of silly game with him, waiting to pounce on him as he went up to the first floor. For a well brought up lady, Marianne did have a whimsical side that would have made her an entertaining comedy actress or music hall turn if she'd so desired.

He smiled at her from the foot of the stairs, wondering what this strange game might be, until he realized with dismay that her return smile was in reality a grimace of pain, and that she was holding her left side tightly. Then, as he moved around the balustrade at the bottom of the stairs and she came fully into his view, he saw with shock the burgeoning rosette of blood on her white and green day dress, and climbed the stairs to her side in two swift bounds.

'Quickly, let me see,' he ordered.

She moved her blood-stained hands with difficulty and he saw the terrible truth, a knife plunged straight through the fabric of her bodice into her heart, with blood pulsing horribly through the open wound. The knife looked an innocuous thing – no more than a decorative paper knife - but the blade was buried in her chest up to the handle. Even in his frenzied state of distress, Silver couldn't help noticing the fine scrollwork on the silver handle and an extravagant monogrammed design that looked like the Cyrillic version of the letter T. As a surgeon he knew that a knife thrust through a heart chamber would not necessarily stop the heart beating immediately. But the bleeding from the wound must be filling up her body cavities with blood, drowning everything, and that was what would bring the heart rapidly to a halt unless he could stop the haemorrhaging somehow. As if to warn him of the urgency, Marianne's eyelids began to flutter wildly and her eyes to roll back in their sockets.

His own heart thudding madly, he eased the knife out of her chest simply so he could remove her bodice and corset and see whether there was any way to halt the awful bleeding. There was just a small possibility that the knife had missed all the major blood vessels and the more vital parts of the heart itself, and might have been lodged in some relatively harmless place, although it would require an extraordinary miracle for that to be the case.

Still, he clung on to that hope because that is what he'd been trained to do as a physician. And rather than unbutton the back of her bodice, he decided to save time by taking the sharp blade of the paper knife to the material in front and drawing it down violently to expose her corset.

But he stopped the progress of the knife through her dress as he realized that she was trying desperately to catch her breath and get a word out to him. He put his ear close to her mouth for a second, trying to discern her last tortured words.

It was at this point that he became aware of Marianne's maid, Jeanie, at the top of the stairs, watching him with the bloodied knife in his hands, with unalloyed horror...

*

With the storm still raging outside, Silver woke up with a start to find himself weeping uncontrollably into his dirty straw pillow...

CHAPTER 8

Sergeant Sparrow was doing his best not to be impressed this morning, but it was a difficult task, given the testing circumstances.

Not least of these circumstances was the elegant house in Took's Court in which he presently sat, a house whose front door had been accessed by a flight of brilliant sandstone steps scrubbed to a honey-coloured cleanliness that his wife Edie and her lazy Irish skivvie Kitty could only dream of...

Edie's attitude to house cleaning was, to say the least, tolerant and easy-going – *why should I kill myself scrubbing everything white, Charlie, when it'll only get dirty again?* Her logic could not be faulted but Sparrow's late mother Margaret could never have lived comfortably with such an attitude, and had to be turning over in her grave at the thought of the lackadaisical girl that Charlie had married.

Certainly this neat Queen Anne house, as perfect from the outside as a doll's house, made Sparrow's own meaner thirty-year-old terraced house in Lambeth – of which until this moment he had been inordinately proud – look run down and dirty by comparison. The iron railings in front of this house in Took's Court were painted jet black with nary a trace of rust (which couldn't be said of his own railings in Lambeth, which had much more than a trace, in truth), and the sash windows of the three prosperous stories above gleamed diamond bright in the October morning sunlight. Perhaps last night's storm, which had blown itself out by now, explained the pristine condition of everything, he wondered hopefully, yet rainstorms didn't seem to work like that in Lambeth. Lambeth – and his home in particular - usually looked a lot worse after a storm, if anything, with clogged drains and dirt-streaked windows.

The drawing room into which Sergeant Sparrow had been shown

also presented a different level of ambience to any room he was used to. The best room in his own house was the dim and musty back parlour where he read his evening paper after dinner, with his collar removed, and his braces left dangling free for his kids to trip over. This room was four times the size of that parlour, and, unlike that room, light and airy and elegant, and with walls sumptuously decorated with thick silk embossed wallpaper and fine oil paintings.

And yet perhaps it was less the house and its surroundings that had truly impressed Charlie Sparrow this morning, and more the qualities of the young mistress of the house. Here, Edie, for all her womanly charms, also fared badly by comparison with Mrs Sophie Rolfe. But then most women would fare badly in such a competition, Sparrow decided complacently, so Edie needn't feel too badly about it. Charlie Sparrow was not a man in the habit of using the word "angelic" to describe people, but if he had, then Mrs Rolfe would probably have been the first recipient of this unusual largesse on his part.

Mrs Rolfe was only twenty or so, blonde and dainty in appearance, with the flawless skin of a child. Seated in formal fashion on an ottoman, she blushed a little under his steady gaze. 'Do you think I should report it, Sergeant?' she asked.

Sparrow had been admiring her peach-coloured cheeks and cornflower blue eyes so attentively that he'd lost the thread of what she was saying.

'Report what, ma'am?' he responded, puzzled.

'About this Irish girl, Annie Riley, who came here last week and accepted my offer of the position of parlour maid.'

'What about her, ma'am?'

Sophie blinked appealingly. 'Well, she never came yesterday to start work as she said she would. Do you think some harm might have befallen her?'

'I doubt it, ma'am. More likely she changed her mind and found a better paid job somewhere else. The Irish are untrustworthy people at the best of times.' Sparrow chose tactfully to ignore all the Irish blood coursing through his own veins, from his grandfather on his mother's side. 'What I would like to discuss with you, though, is your brother-in-law Jonathan Silver.'

Sophie became immediately wary. 'I supposed that was the reason why a policeman would come to my door so early in the day.'

Sparrow added a sterner note to his voice. 'Well, my apologies, but your supposition was perfectly correct, ma'am. Have you seen Dr Silver since he escaped from prison?'

Sophie pursed her lips severely. 'I have not.'

And would you really tell me if you had? wondered Sparrow, fixing his eyes on hers again. It already seemed clear enough to him that Mrs Rolfe considered her brother-in-law innocent of the murder of her sister, despite the judgement of the legal system to the contrary. 'How well did you actually know the good doctor?' Sparrow was being rather more abrasive in his tone with this girl than he truly intended, perhaps as a perverse reaction to the angelic way she looked.

Sophie straightened her back stiffly. 'We had become close friends during the near two years that he was married to my sister. He became a true brother to me in that time - the brother I never had before.'

Sparrow sniffed indulgently. 'Then tell me something about his background – this *brother* of yours.'

Sophie did not appear putout by Sparrow's obvious cynicism, apart from a hint of puzzlement in those startling blue eyes. 'Jonathan was born in Dorchester in the West Country. His mother and his two siblings all died when he was young, I believe, so Jonathan was mostly brought up by his father and various female servants.'

'He was well-to-do? The father, I mean.'

'I think so. He was only a cabinetmaker originally, but forty years ago – before Jonathan was even born – the father started up a factory in Dorchester for the mass production of quality furniture. He became well known for the manufacture of furniture in the Sheraton and Hepplewhite style, for a fraction of the cost of hand-made items. This caused him severe trouble with the local Luddites who burned his factory down several times, or so Jonathan told me. But the father eventually prospered, sufficiently in the end to send Jonathan to medical school in Edinburgh. He wanted his son to have the advantages of education and society that he had never had, although he must have also hoped that Jonathan would one day take over the family business. Yet Jonathan appears not to have been suited to running a factory, and the father eventually sold the business not long before he died. As for Jonathan, he subsequently became a surgeon in the Royal Navy for several years, before coming home and starting a private practise in Southsea in Hampshire. Later he volunteered to work at the army hospital at Scutari in Turkey during the recent war in the Crimea, before returning to England yet again to take up private practise in Bloomsbury, combined with a surgical resident post at St Bart's in the city.'

Sparrow reflected on that intriguing personal history. 'So the son became a gentleman of sorts, with aspirations to marry into a well-bred family such as yours?'

Sophie smiled wanly. 'Appearances can be deceptive, Sergeant. To be frank, my own grandfather was only a simple miner from the Nottinghamshire coalfields, a man of no education at all...'

'Hard to believe, ma'am,' Sparrow couldn't help interjecting.

'...But true nonetheless. It was my father, George Lovelock, who raised himself up from his humble origins, and entirely by his own efforts. He learned the basics of steam locomotive design when he was young and, even though he left school at twelve, went on to become one of the great railway engineers of the last twenty years. He built many of the new railway lines in the Midlands and the industrial Northwest.'

'Your father was another Brunel, then?'

Sophie flushed slightly. 'Perhaps he never quite achieved such an exalted status as that gentleman. Papa was always too modest to compare himself with Mr Brunel, whose exploits are indeed legendary. Yet, to my mind, Papa was still an exceptional man in his own right.'

Sparrow tugged thoughtfully at the ends of his moustache, seeking inspiration. 'Your father is dead, I believe, ma'am?'

Sophie's eyes flickered with momentary sadness. 'Yes, a heart attack in June. He was only three years past fifty, and had seemed in perfect health until then. So it was a shock to us all.'

'I'm sorry to hear that, ma'am. This year has obviously been a troubled one for you.'

'Yes. But at least Papa was spared enough time to see me well married...'

Sparrow interrupted her. 'And that was when...?'

'I married Edward in May, Sergeant – on May the ninth, to be precise. Papa's early death at the beginning of June was a great tragedy for us all, and particularly for Edward...'

'Why so, ma'am?'

'Because he was alone with Papa in Papa's study when it happened. Edward still blames himself for not being able to save him.'

'But then your husband is not a physician, is he, like Dr Silver?'

Sophie sighed visibly. 'No, he is not. Yet he still feels he should have been able to do more to save Papa's life.' She lifted her chin and regarded Sparrow again with those startling blue eyes. 'But my poor papa's early death did at least save him the horror of seeing his other daughter horribly murdered. Marianne died less than a month after my father, on the second of July. Thankfully, relations between him and Marianne were fully restored again by the time of his death. That is one thing I am particularly grateful for.'

Sparrow jumped on that admission. 'So their relations weren't always cordial?'

'Regretfully, no.' Sophie hesitated. 'There are things you should perhaps know about my sister Marianne...'

'Please go on,' Sparrow encouraged her.

Sophie collected her thoughts. 'She was eight years older than me,

Sergeant, so we were never quite as close as sisters of similar age would be. Seven years ago, when she was only three and twenty, she was actively pursued by the son of a business associate of my father's – an older man called Daniel Strode. Papa was experiencing business difficulties at the time – he'd lost so much money in the railway fever and speculation of the late forties - and had strong reasons for wanting to cement an alliance with this man Strode, whose own father was a major manufacturer of paddle steam engines for ships. But Marianne proved unwilling to support Papa's business needs, and turned Daniel Strode down. She fell out badly with our father as a result, and became estranged from him for some years.'

Sparrow was curious about this piece of old family history. 'What happened afterwards?'

'Marianne had a small inheritance of her own from a maternal aunt, and she chose to leave the family home. She travelled for several years in Europe, and even further afield. As a girl I secretly received letters from her from all sorts of exotic places – from Cairo and Calcutta, from St Petersburg and Athens. She became fluent in several different languages – French, German, even Russian...'

'She sounds like quite an adventurous young lady.'

'Yes, indeed she was. Eventually she turned up in Turkey as a volunteer nurse during the war in the Crimea.'

'You mean at the same base hospital where Dr Silver worked – the one attended by Miss Florence Nightingale and her volunteer nurses.'

'Yes, indeed, at Scutari. That was where she and Jonathan met. But I believe Marianne was there even before Miss Nightingale and the other volunteer nurses ever arrived. In fact, Marianne herself was one of the first people to bring the government's attention to the disgraceful conditions in which our heroic wounded troops were being kept.'

'When exactly did she meet Dr Silver?'

'She met Jonathan late in November of 'fifty-four, I believe – when they were both working at Scutari - and married him back in England in October of 'fifty-five.'

Charlie Sparrow asked the obvious question. 'Was their marriage a happy one, would you say?'

There was a hint of a tear in Sophie's blue eyes now. 'I thought so. But at the trial, one of their servants – a rather indiscreet parlour maid called Jeanie - reported that there'd been frequent arguments between husband and wife.'

'Do you know the reason for these arguments? Was Dr Silver seeing other ladies, do you think?' Sparrow demanded abruptly. 'If he was, there was no mention of it at the trial, as I recall.'

She flushed at his abrasive tone. 'You really expect *me* to know such intimate things about my brother-in-law, Sergeant?' She relaxed again onto her ottoman seat with a visible effort. 'But if you are asking me, then I suspect not. Jonathan loved my sister, I'm sure of it, and had no other women in his life. His only mistress, if I can put it that way...' - here Sophie coloured even more prettily – 'was his career, especially his determination to find a solution to the scourge of infectious diseases that afflict this city so terribly - typhoid, typhus and cholera. Jonathan really had no time for other women, Sergeant. His only sin – if it can be considered such - might have been neglect of the woman he loved.'

Silver sounded a rather dull and pompous prig to Sparrow, on this evidence. 'Then did your sister have other gentlemen friends? Could that have been the reason for the arguments?'

'*Alleged* arguments,' Sophie pointed out curtly. 'I never saw or heard any of these rows, myself. I might agree with others that my sister was unconventional and not always entirely proper in her dealings with gentlemen. But, as for taking lovers after she was married, I think not. I believe she took her vows of marriage to Jonathan very seriously. Yet...'

'Yes,' Sparrow said encouragingly, 'go on.'

Sophie did continue, but with seeming reluctance at talking about her sister in this fashion. 'Men certainly continued to pursue Marianne. She was an attractive flame to many moths. She was very beautiful, of course, which made the attention somewhat predictable.'

'More beautiful even than you, ma'am?'

She went bright red this time at such an improper question. 'Yes, of course,' she responded in a puzzled voice, as if the thought of equalling her sister in beauty had never occurred to her even remotely.

Sparrow probed further. 'Do you know the names of any of these gentlemen? These *moths* fluttering around your sister.'

'What is the purpose now of such a question? I thought you were only trying to recapture Dr Silver?'

'Yes, that's true, ma'am,' Sparrow admitted, 'but I am also interested in his case as a whole.'

She grasped at that straw eagerly. 'Then you believe he might have been convicted unfairly?'

Sergeant Sparrow was too old a hand to be drawn as easily as that. '*You* obviously do, ma'am. I see you still keep Dr Silver's portrait on your wall.'

Sophie turned her head to look at the painting in question, directly above the fireplace. 'Yes, I do. All the paintings in this house are my husband's, apart from that one, which is now mine. A talented young artist called John Finnie painted that portrait a year ago at my parents' request, together with one of Marianne herself. I brought the portrait of Jonathan here from Mama's house after Marianne's death. Mama wasn't sure about keeping it, but I didn't want to see it destroyed on a whim.'

Did that perhaps suggest that the mother wasn't as sure of Dr Silver's innocence as the sister, Sparrow wondered. 'You don't have any picture of your dead sister, I see?' he inquired artfully.

'My mother still keeps Mr Finnie's companion portrait of my sister in her own house,' Sophie answered primly, as she continued to study the portrait of Silver with a look of melancholic pleasure.

Noticing the glow of pleasure in her eyes, Sergeant Sparrow finally worked up the courage to ask the young Mrs Rolfe a more intimate question. 'Excuse me asking this, ma'am. But did you have any personal feelings for Dr Silver?'

She stared coldly at him in response . 'Yes, I did. But only those of a loyal and devoted sister, as I told you before.'

Sparrow's policeman's nose told him that this might not be entirely the truth. That specially regarded portrait, in pride of place on her wall, seemed to suggest a closer attachment than that of a mere brother-in-law. But perhaps this devotion was either something she was hardly aware of herself, or something she deliberately chose to deny to herself. 'I would like to talk to some of these gentlemen friends of your sister,' he said, returning to his earlier point, before slyly adding some tempting bait to his line, '...and – you never know - it might possibly turn up something helpful to Dr Silver's case.'

Sophie finally gave in after that last inducement. 'There are two particular individuals I can think of whom you might profit from talking to. Please understand I make no accusations against these two gentlemen, but it would be interesting to know where they were on the night my sister died last July. One gentleman is a Mr Martin Tyrell. Tyrell is a railway speculator who pursued Marianne relentlessly, even after she was married, although I'm sure the attention was never returned voluntarily.'

'And where does this Mr Tyrell live? Do you know?'

'In Westminster, I believe. Fourteen Vincent Square. His dinner parties there are famed for their lavishness, and for the social standing of his guests.'

Sparrow scribbled quickly in his notebook, acknowledging guiltily that he was now grossly exceeding the brief that Grindrod had given him to carry out, yet driven on by a certain curiosity to explore more of the background of this interesting case. 'And the other gentleman you mentioned?'

'Robert Caitlin, a captain in the Thirteenth Light Dragoons. Caitlin served at Balaklava and survived the famous Charge of the Light Brigade. I believe, from her letters, that there was some strong attachment between him and Marianne in Turkey - until she met

Jonathan anyway.'

Sparrow coughed. 'She preferred a mere sawbones to a hero of the Light Brigade?'

Sophie would not be drawn into giving away any further details. 'Apparently. But is that so hard to believe?'

Sparrow let that pass for the moment. 'Where is Caitlin now, ma'am? Have you any idea?'

'A friend told me recently that he is on leave on half-pay in England, and presently staying with a relative in Kensington Gore beyond Hyde Park. At Colby House, I was told, which is opposite Kensington Palace.'

'Then his relative must be extremely well to do.' Sparrow remembered something else. 'What about the first man you mentioned to me, ma'am? Daniel Strode? Was there any contact between him and Marianne after her return to England?'

'I wouldn't know, Sergeant. I doubt it, though. I do know Marianne was afraid of the man and his violent temper, so certainly wouldn't have gone looking to renew the acquaintance.'

Sparrow couldn't help murmuring, 'Interesting...'

Sophie stood up abruptly at this point, and Sergeant Sparrow was forced to copy her and to climb rapidly to his feet as well. 'Will you really be able to recapture Jonathan?' she asked him moodily. 'He is obviously a man of considerable resource who will not easily be caught again. His escape was quite remarkable, don't you think?'

'Remarkable, indeed. He must have had some help from someone, though.' He directed an accusatory look towards Mrs Rolfe, more to test her reaction than for any other reason.

Sophie almost smiled in response. '*Me*, Sergeant? I wish I did have the resolve and courage to have helped Jonathan because he is surely a victim of intemperate and misguided justice. Imagine what he has gone through these last months! To not only lose the wife he loved, but then to be accused of her murder. It's a wonder it didn't drive him insane.'

'But who else could have had the opportunity to kill your sister? There was no evidence of anyone breaking into the house that day, or of any stranger calling, so whoever did it must have opened the front door himself. That seems to rule out these gentlemen who were infatuated with your sister. I imagine very few people had access to the house in Russell Square where it happened, apart from Dr and Mrs Silver themselves, and their servants.'

'Not entirely correct. Marianne had given me a front door key for her house, for use in case she and the servants were ever away. And she probably did the same for her closest acquaintances. She was very trusting and open with her friends.'

That latter notion seemed unlikely to Sparrow; people didn't usually hand out copies of their front door keys indiscriminately, even to trusted friends. 'You didn't speak at the trial in Dr Silver's defence, ma'am,' he pointed out. 'If you were so convinced of his innocence, why didn't you try to sway the jury in his favour a little?'

'Later I wished I had. Yet the fact is I had no real evidence to give, apart from an endorsement of his good character. I did write a note to Jonathan in prison offering him my support. But he wrote back telling me it was better not to create enmities with the rest of my family by openly siding with him. He said it would only awake unfounded suspicions of...of...'

She coloured yet again and Sparrow could only stand back and admire such womanly perfection. She was quite possibly the loveliest woman Charlie Sparrow had ever seen in the flesh – outside of the stage or music hall anyway - although that didn't mean she couldn't also be a conniving bitch who'd killed her own sister out of jealousy. He decided he would check the police statements taken before the trial to see where Sophie herself had been on the evening her sister was killed...

Yet, he told himself, she had found a husband of her own not long before the murder of her sister, so it didn't seem likely that she would be harbouring murderous and jealous thoughts towards Marianne at the same time...

Sparrow was just wondering what sort of husband Sophie might have found for herself when, as if on cue, there came a brief knock at the open door of the drawing room, and a man entered. He was a handsome well-made man of about thirty-five years, but – if this was her husband - not nearly good enough for a girl like Sophie in Charlie Sparrow's honest judgement.

Sophie confirmed that this was indeed her husband by introducing him, but in a slightly flustered voice as if she hadn't realized he was in the house. 'This is Detective Sergeant Sparrow of the Metropolitan Police, Edward,' she went on. 'He has been given the task of recapturing Jonathan, it seems.'

Rolfe sniffed coldly. 'Then I can't say I wish you well, Sergeant, in hounding an innocent man.'

Annoyed by his belligerent tone, an irritated Charlie Sparrow inspected Mr Edward Rolfe in more detail, looking for things to dislike about the man in return. He was soon gratified to discover several objectionable traits in this handsome young dandy. Sparrow had never had much time for the idle rich (not unless they looked like Mrs Sophie Rolfe anyway.) And from the way her husband was dressed, in frock coat, gaiters and silk cravat, Edward Rolfe did seem to belong naturally to that fortunate category of humankind. Sparrow did wonder sourly at this point about the unfairness of life in general, and, in particular, about the pampered lives of such parasitic young gentlemen of leisure as Edward Rolfe appeared to be. It had to be an extremely agreeable way of life to be married to a beautiful young wife like Sophie, while also presumably having a substantial portfolio of property and investments to insulate you from all the usual financial concerns that plagued the rest of mankind. Yet it also seemed to Charlie Sparrow to be an affront to natural justice that such useless and overindulged people should be tolerated in a sane society.

In retaliation for the man's patronizing look, Sparrow deliberately turned his back on Rolfe and walked over to the portrait of Silver, which he then proceeded to examine ostentatiously. 'Is this really a good likeness of Dr Silver, ma'am?' he asked Sophie. 'It makes him look very different from the image on the billposter we put up at the weekend. According to this, he's a remarkably handsome man.'

Sophie joined him to look up at the portrait in more detail. She was taller than he expected from her dainty appearance when seated, in fact only two or three inches shorter than his own five feet seven. Charlie Sparrow could also not help noticing that her corseted waist was tiny – perhaps no more than seventeen inches - and made even more appealing by contrast with her impressive swelling bosom. As a man who sometimes had to lace and shoehorn his wife Edie's bulging bits into her stays, Sparrow could appreciate the magic of a perfect slender female figure in all sorts of unexpected ways.

'Yes, it's a very good likeness. I believe Mr Finnie captured him perfectly,' Sophie concluded.

Looking up at the image, Sparrow almost felt himself under scrutiny from the stern eyes in the portrait. The painting was so lifelike that this encounter did feel unsettlingly real - like staring into the soul of a real human being and feeling his interrogating presence in return.

And where are you hiding right now, Doctor? Sparrow wondered moodily to himself.

Edward Rolfe spoke up behind them. 'Sergeant, there seems to be a uniformed police officer in the street gesticulating and making strange faces through the window at you.'

Sparrow turned reluctantly away from Mrs Rolfe and saw Constable Frank Remmert pressing his face to the glass in a most distracting fashion.

'Sorry about my young colleague's lack of manners,' he apologized to them both. 'But in fact he's not pulling a strange face, sir,' he added dryly. 'That's how Constable Remmert always looks.' He sighed. 'I'd better go and see what he wants, otherwise he may spend the whole morning gurning through your window.'

Sophie smiled charmingly at his little joke, and Charlie Sparrow's heart did a little somersault in response. Given Edie's unromantic nature and her distressing tendency to snore in bed, it had been quite a few years since any woman had provoked Charlie Sparrow's heart to do anything like that.

Edward Rolfe showed Sparrow personally to the front door and made his farewells with a sardonic and insincere smile playing across his handsome features. Sergeant Sparrow didn't much care to be dismissed in this offensive way so deliberately lingered on the threshold for a moment, trying to annoy the man in return. He soon found an excuse for doing so as his eyes alighted on a striking work of art in the hall, a gilded portrait of the Virgin Mary as the main trunk of a stylised tree, whose branches were filled with the colourful medallions of saints.

Rolfe followed the direction of his eyes. 'Do you like Russian art, Sergeant?'

Sparrow sniffed. 'Is that what that is?'

'Yes, indeed – it's a seventeenth century work by Simon Ushakov called *Planting the Tree of the Russian Realm*. I bought it in St Petersburg a few weeks ago, on a visit there. In my spare time from business, I am a connoisseur of the arts…'

Despite an almost total disinterest in art, Sparrow found himself captivated for some reason by the brilliant colours of this odd religious painting. 'It looks expensive.'

Rolfe shrugged. 'They say that only a fool knows the price of everything, but the value of nothing, Sergeant. Whatever I paid for that painting, you can take it from me that it wasn't nearly enough.'

Sparrow believed he had just been subtly insulted, but wasn't entirely sure when the man continued to smile at him in that enigmatic way as he shook his hand in farewell.

Outside, in the cool autumn sun, the gawky and spud-faced Frank Remmert marched up breathlessly to Sparrow.

'That man Minshall…' he began.

Sparrow groaned. 'What about him?' Then a hopeful thought occurred to him. 'Has he found Silver then?'

'No. But he has found something else. Back in Shadwell. The body of a woman…'

*

'A very pretty girl,' Constable Remmert observed.

'Yes.' Charlie Sparrow was too busy crouching to inspect the body to pay much attention to what young Frank Remmert was saying. Compared to Frank Remmert's own potato-shaped face, anyone would look attractive, of course, but this dead girl genuinely had been pretty. Not quite a beauty to match Mrs Sophie Rolfe, of course, but still a girl with fine features, fair silken hair and a skin with a peachy bloom that hadn't yet yielded to the decay of death.

But then she hadn't been dead for long; that much was certain. The woman was in her early twenties, Sparrow guessed, and fully dressed. *Well* dressed actually, in velveteen skirt and lace bodice, and a fine brocade overcoat. A surreptitious check under her layers of petticoats showed she was wearing thick winter drawers too. So what was a woman this well dressed doing stretched out in this ugly bit of wasteland on the boundary between the parishes of Shadwell and Wapping? Dead bodies were not an uncommon occurrence on the dirty streets of these parishes, but to find the body of a young and comely maid here was rather shocking...

'Who owns this land, Frank?' Sparrow asked Remmert, as he eased himself to his feet. 'Any ideas?' Remmert was the only one of the constables at Shadwell whom Charlie Sparrow ever addressed by his first name, but then they had worked together in the force for five years, off and on, even though Remmert was still only twenty-two years old. Although Sparrow was actually a member of the elite Whitehall detective force, in practice he spent most of his working time based at the Shadwell and Wapping Station, therefore, unlike many of his other detective colleagues, had formed a close working relationship with the uniformed officers at that station – the junior ones anyway. Constables like Remmert certainly did Sparrow's bidding quickly enough, even though he technically belonged to a different branch of the service and was not strictly speaking their direct superior officer. Sergeant Sparrow certainly thought of these uniformed constables as "his" men, and gave them direct orders accordingly, although the senior uniformed officer at Shadwell, Inspector Carew, was not always happy with this situation, which he saw as undermining his own authority.

'Probably belongs to the London Dock Company now,' Remmert guessed. 'I think they are planning to extend the London Dock here in the future, according to what I've heard.'

It seemed a sensible surmise to Sparrow. The mean houses and hovels that had been here formerly had been cleared in the last two years and the rubble and cobbles that had been left behind had now been taken over by a luxuriant growth of weeds, the remnants of last summer's ragwort, willowherb and fat hen. The area around the body was clear of vegetation, though, Sparrow observed, and the reason was obvious. Sparrow could see from the marks in the mud that the local people from New Gravel Lane had clearly been using this little open area for games, probably for the popular Bumble-puppy, which was a local variant of skittles.

The police surgeon hadn't yet turned up to look at the body, but Sparrow could see without being told that rigor mortis hadn't taken hold yet and that the girl was still slightly warm to the touch. And she was dry too, while the ground beneath her was sopping wet, so she certainly hadn't been out in last night's storm. Dead less than three hours, he would have said. It was now eleven o'clock, so that meant she'd died after eight this morning.

This patch of wasteland was only forty yards or so off New Gravel Lane, which was a busy thoroughfare of public houses and small businesses, so there was a good chance somebody might have seen something useful. Sparrow guessed from the footprints that the girl had been murdered at this very spot this morning so must have walked here, either of her own volition, or under threat. *But what was a ladylike person like this doing in the first place in such a rough neighbourhood?* It didn't make much sense.

Sparrow's other companion now spoke up hesitantly. 'Strangled, was she?' James Minshall asked.

Charlie Sparrow grunted in response. 'Looks like it from the bruise marks on her neck. How did *you* happen to be the one to find her, Mr Minshall? You don't even live around New Gravel Lane, do you?'

Minshall was dressed less well today than Sparrow had seen him in Whitehall last Friday. These were either his normal workday clothes – a smock, stained moleskin trousers, and loose flapping greatcoat – or else he was trying to blend in with the other residents of Wapping and Shadwell. Wearing a greasy flat cap instead of a top hat, he seemed a foot shorter. Charlie Sparrow liked him a little better dressed this way, but not by much.

'No, as I told you, Sergeant, I live in Limehouse,' Minshall answered. 'But I've been keeping my eyes and ears open around Wapping and Shadwell in my off-duty time.'

'Doing what?' Sparrow asked offensively, as if he'd entirely forgotten their conversation in Whitehall Place four days ago.

Minshall looked down at his boots and lowered his voice to an uneasy whisper. 'Looking for Silver, as I promised. And trying to find some trace of that boy I saw visiting Newgate several times over the last few weeks.'

'Ah yes, the *pretty* youth.' Sparrow said pointedly. 'And have you heard or seen anything of him?'

'Err...no, not yet. But I was onto something concerning Silver himself.' Minshall glanced across at Constable Remmert's uncompromising features, before returning his eyes to Sergeant Sparrow. 'I got into conversation early this morning with another one of your constables from Shadwell Station, Sergeant – Kennally by name – and he told me that he saw a commotion near the White Rose Public House in Ratcliffe Highway last night about ten. A girl in a blue shawl was being molested by a couple of sailors, and this tall man – six feet two or more - came to her rescue.'

'Kennally never mentioned this to me,' Sparrow complained. 'And you thought this rescuer of the girl might have been Silver?' he guessed.

Minshall blanched slightly under Sparrow's critical inspection. 'He *could* have been; that's all I'm saying. The height matched. Silver is well over six feet tall so stands out in a crowd.'

'And the description? Did that match too?'

'Not exactly. This man was dressed as a workman, and had his hair and beard cropped short. Silver's hair and beard were long when he escaped, although it would have been easy enough for him to have had his hair cut short in the meantime to avoid recognition.'

Sparrow frowned. 'But would a man on the run really risk discovery in this way? The man who rescued that girl was more likely a genuine workman. What exactly did he do to help her anyway?'

'According to Kennally, he quickly flattened the two sailors. Then both he and the girl ran off together.'

'*Ran off together*, do you say?' That sounded more interesting to Sparrow. 'Why would the girl run off too, though, if she was the supposed victim?'

'I don't know,' admitted Minshall. 'But I thought it was still worthwhile for me to nose around the area today and see if anybody else saw anything of this incident. I am on night duty this week so I have my days free to roam. In particular I was hoping to find this girl in the blue shawl who was being molested last night, to see if she could tell us anything about her rescuer. Kennally gave me a good description of her; he thinks he has seen this girl around the area a few times before, although he doesn't know her name or where she lives exactly.'

Sparrow rolled his eyes, and said dismissively, 'Not too much to go on, then,' even though in fact he was quietly impressed by Minshall's guile and persistence.

'Kennally said I should try down New Gravel Lane as he had a feeling that the girl in the blue shawl lives down here somewhere. So I did. I was walking past this bit of wasteland behind the Black Horse tavern when I caught sight of the bright colour of this woman's dress on the ground. So, after I checked that she was dead, I ran back to Shadwell Station and alerted Constable Remmert here.'

If Minshall was expecting congratulation from Sergeant Sparrow at this point, he was doomed to disappointment because all he did get was another suspicious and dour shrug. 'This isn't the girl who was being accosted by the sailors, then?' Sparrow asked.

Minshall shook his head emphatically. 'No, the girl from last night was a serving girl of some sort. This woman is obviously a well-to-do lady, I would say.'

At this point, two of Sparrow's other constables reappeared – Waddle and Rankine – who he'd instructed to comb the area of rubble and weeds looking for anything noteworthy. Rankine was holding up a woman's pigskin bag. 'Found this, Sergeant, under a bush,' he declared excitedly.

'Anything in it?' Sparrow asked dubiously.

'Nothing at all - except for this letter anyway...' Rankine triumphantly handed the object in question to Charlie Sparrow with a flourish, as if he was expecting an accompanying fanfare.

Sparrow inspected the fine copperplate writing on the outside. 'Hmm. Sent to a Miss Charlotte Livingstone, forty-three Pentonville Road, Islington.' He unfolded the letter and read the contents. 'It seems that this young lady – assuming this is Miss Livingstone anyway - had a lover, or at least an admirer. This letter is dated a few weeks ago - September the twenty-fifth - and is a brief note inviting her to meet for a tryst in Regents Park.'

'Who is the writer?' Minshall asked eagerly.

'Ah, unfortunately, her lover was a little coy about giving his full name or address, although he has signed it "Daniel".'

'That was helpful of him, at least,' Constable Remmert observed.

'Yes, indeed,' agreed Sparrow. 'A damned sight too convenient, though, finding that bag so easily, and with a letter inside it. Almost as if the murderer *wanted* us to find it...'

CHAPTER 9

An icy rain was blowing in off the river, numbing fingers and faces with its raw embrace, as Silver deftly notched the end of yet another timber baulk with his ripping chisel. These baulks were made on a gigantic scale, like everything else to do with this project – eighteen inches square, best quality Baltic pine, and twelve to fifteen feet in length. The top layer of these massive timbers was designed to carry the closely packed lines of Great Western Railway bridge rails, laid parallel to the keel of the great ship, down which the *Leviathan* would hopefully slide on its cradles on launch day, right to the water's edge.

Working under the shadow of that great towering hull, Silver felt sometimes dwarfed by the scale and majesty of this undertaking, which seemed on a par with creating one of the Ancient Wonders of the World. Regarding the immense size of this vessel, it was difficult to imagine it ever moving at all, an object seemingly as vast and immovable as the Pyramids or the Great Wall of China. If that great iron hull did eventually move, then here was a feat of engineering and human imagination to tell his grandchildren about, Silver thought, should he ever live that long. In a strange way, the exhilaration and inhuman demands of this enterprise had helped to diminish the pain of his own personal problems, which did seem miniscule and unimportant when compared with this grand assault of Man on nature.

The amount of timber going into these giant slipways was truly phenomenal, but then each one was 120 feet wide and 240 feet in length, sloping down at a gradient of one in twelve from the raised construction bed on which the flat keel of the giant ship presently sat, to the edge of the water at low tide.

After three days working in this yard at Millwall, Silver was still trying to adjust to the frantic pace of the hard manual work, and struggling

physically to cope with the numbing fatigue of twelve-hour shifts. He
had expected to manage more easily than this, after his punishing time
in prison. Until his final confinement in the condemned ward in
Newgate gaol, he had spent the previous weeks in gaol breaking rocks,
driving a treadmill or picking oakum – the loose fibre picked apart from
old unravelled ropes to be used as plugging material in wooden ship
planking. None of these activities had been a pleasure, yet the treadmill
had been the worst since the more vindictive of the turnkeys were apt to
screw the ratchet on the cylinder tighter to make it almost impossible to
keep the treadmill turning. The prisoners called those sadistic turnkeys
"screws" in retaliation but it was small consolation.

But for sheer physical effort, the hewing and sawing of these giant
timber beams for the slipways of the *Leviathan* was something beyond
even the Newgate treadmills, and therefore far outside his experience.
As a boy he had worked in his father's factory in Dorchester and learned
the skills of carpentry and cabinet making to a reasonably professional
degree, so he had complacently expected that he could cope with this
less-skilled work easily. But for all the lesser skill involved here, the
sheer amount of manual labour required almost supernatural strength
and endurance.

The work was not helped by the physical conditions. Bleak October
weather held the Thames in its dismal iron-grey grip, as it had ever since
Silver had turned up for work three days before. The sun never seemed
to shine on the Isle of Dogs, apart from odd watery glimpses through
banks of weeping cloud and mist. Behind the shipyard, the hovels of
Millwall seemed to be huddled hopefully against the rear wall of the yard
as if seeking shelter from the relentless wind. Out on the marshes
beyond, the wind continued to whistle and wail constantly like a
vengeful spirit.

Silver blew into his fingernail and smiled at his two companions,
despite the irritation of the icy rain blowing straight into his eyes. Jimmy
Flynn was a polite hardworking young man from Deptford just across
the river, while Billy Faber, an apprentice joiner with a shock of fair hair
and a cherubic face, was no more than a boy. Billy was from Wapping
so Silver had already fallen into the habit of walking home with him
after their long shifts together.

Billy was so slightly built that he had to be struggling even more than
Silver with the physical demands of this work. But he was a game boy
and never complained of the blisters on his fingers or the cuts on his
skin.

Silver began again with chiselling the recess for the joint at this end
of his baulk, before realizing that his foreman had returned to check on
the progress of their little gang. Matthew Spurrell was a local man from

Rotherhithe, about thirty-five, with a widow's peak of black hair, and muscular forearms like piston rods. Being short of skilled carpenters he had gratefully accepted Jude Crabtree's recommendation of "Mr Wade" and offered him a job at once working on the slipways. And now that he'd seen "Mr Wade's" proficiency with chisel and maul, Spurrell seemed doubly glad to have taken him on.

Jude Crabtree was with Spurrell now, also eyeing Silver's recent handiwork with the complacent pride of someone who realized he had stumbled onto a first class worker by complete chance.

Spurrell said a few complimentary things about Silver's skill and work rate before clearing his throat uncomfortably. 'Wade, Jude here tells me that you've had some book learning and the like.'

Silver looked up hesitantly, wondering what was coming. 'Yes, Mr Spurrell, I have.'

'How come?'

Silver stood up and straightened his weary back. 'I suppose I wanted to improve myself a little. But it was nothing grand, you understand. I only went to evening classes at the Working Men's College in Red Lion Square, and studied a bit of mathematics and accounting in my free time in order to work myself up to a clerk. And later I worked at St Barts Hospital in the city as a medical clerk, so picked up a bit about medicines too.' Silver had not invented this believable past for himself with this tale, but had instead simply taken over the real past of a genuine clerk called Ricketts whom he had known at the hospital. Clearly Crabtree and Spurrell believed this personal history absolutely, which proved to Silver the virtue of taking over the details of a real person's background as his cover story whenever possible.

Spurrell appraised him thoughtfully. 'It's not your knowledge of medicines I'm interested in, Wade, but that bit of mathematical know how might possibly come in handy. The engineering assistant for the slipways, Mr John Harkness, is saying there's something wrong with our...err...*my*...setting out of the slipway. I've been called up to the design office to answer some tough questions about it, so I need a bit of support. Can you join me and Mr Crabtree for a few minutes?'

This clearly was not a request but an order. Silver could understand why Spurrell might need some moral support if he was about to be interrogated over possible mistakes he'd made. Spurrell was a poorly educated man, Silver guessed, who normally relied heavily on his natural intuition to make things fit on site, and was therefore struggling to cope with the demands of such a complex task as the present one. Silver already knew that the triple latticework of timber baulks for these two slipways was supposed to be set out precisely to dimensions and levels defined by Mr Brunel himself, and with little room for error. But something had obviously gone wrong somewhere with Spurrell's intuitive setting out, so Silver hoped the mistake was a small enough one to be rectified.

The situation wasn't hopeful, though, if the error was a major one. The bottom layer of baulks was already firmly bolted to the timber foundation piles driven deep into the Thames mud and London Clay, and removing and replacing them would be impossible in the time they had left to complete the slipways...

*

The drawing office was near the entrance gate to the Napier yard, a long and ugly two-storey brick shed with rusting iron roof and flaking black paint. The upper floor was where the engineers and draughtsmen worked, and was reached from the main yard by an external iron staircase, constantly dripping rust and filthy water in this damp autumnal weather.

Almost the first person Silver saw when he entered the gas-lit drawing office was the man he had come here expressly to find, Marianne's one-time suitor, Daniel Strode. Strode was seated at the desk of his own private office, directly opposite the main entrance to the drawing office, looking through a thick raft of drawings. Silver had made no contact at all with the man so far – in fact had not even got near him - although that was hardly surprising given their very different stations in the yard. And what with the backbreaking nature of his work, and the long punishing hours, there'd been no chance for Silver to do anything else but work anyway, much less keep a man like Strode under surveillance. In fact Silver had soon begun to wonder how he could ever hope to investigate the man's life and activities given his personal circumstances. On reflection, the whole enterprise now seemed a foolish and an ill thought-out one. He realized now that he should have taken Elisa's advice and simply cut and run for a foreign refuge somewhere. What he had been hoping for was essentially a miracle - to somehow stumble on some incontrovertible evidence against Strode of complicity in his wife's murder that he could send to the authorities.

Whereas, in actuality, all he presently had against the man were the facts that Strode had wanted to marry Marianne seven years ago and that she had turned him down for her own private reasons. That thin thread of a connection between Strode and his murdered wife scarcely seemed sufficient grounds by itself for suspecting Strode of murder after such a long time.

And yet...

And yet Silver could not forget that final tantalising word that Marianne had breathed in his ear as she'd expired in his arms...

Her eyes fluttering, breath tortured, she had forced herself to utter a few last choking words Yet the only one that Silver had been able to decipher with any certainty had been the word...*Leviathan...*

That was what she had said, Silver was convinced.

And he had driven himself mad since then trying to decide what Marianne's purpose could have been in saying that enigmatic word. *Or had he simply misheard or misunderstood her last dying utterance?*

Regardless, he had told his own barrister what he'd heard, but Mr Walker had not chosen to raise this dubious point in court during the trial. But then Nathanial did at heart privately believe him to be guilty, Silver was sure, which probably explained his lackadaisical conduct of his defence.

It was only later, after the trial, that a plausible reason for Marianne saying that word had finally occurred to Silver. A few weeks before her death, Marianne had been reading the *Illustrated London News* after dinner, and had mentioned Daniel Strode's name to him in passing. It was the only time that Silver ever heard her mention Strode's name, yet he had not forgotten it because of her obvious dislike of the man. Her first remark about him had been innocuous enough - she had simply remarked that his career as a marine engineer appeared to be on the rise as he was named in an article as the chief designer of the paddle engines for the great ship being built on the Isle of Dogs.

And then she had looked at Silver across the room, slightly shamefaced if anything, and admitted with rare frankness, 'You know, Jonathan, Daniel Strode is the only man who ever truly scared me. *Such a wild and unpredictable man, and one with no moral compass at all, I fear...*'

The sight of the man now stopped Silver in his tracks for a moment. But Strode took no notice of the visitors to the drawing office as they passed the door of his private room, his impressive beak of a nose glued instead to the task of poring over minutiae on his drawings. Silver even had a moment to glance inside without the man apparently noticing. His worktable was strewn with engineering drawings of the giant paddle engines that were of staggering complexity and scale, so Strode clearly was as gifted an engineer as Jude Crabtree had suggested. Only a man of true genius could come up with paddle engines of such size and ingenuity as this.

Everyone in the yard knew that Strode and his engine fitters were under particular pressure, as there were still key tasks that needed to be carried out to the paddle engines before the launch could take place - namely completing the main crankshafts and engine bearings. Presently it was an extremely tight race between the men building the slipways, and those installing the engines and boilers, to avoid the ignominy of being the ones responsible for the ship missing the next suitable launch date on the 3rd of November. Certainly, no one wanted to incur the

Engineer's legendary bloodcurdling wrath over this, a wrath which, according to Spurrell, had been known to make grown men weep piteously.

Silver and the two foremen continued down the long length of the main drawing office, past the massed ranks of designers and draughtsmen scratching with their quill pens on paper, and with their gas burners turned up to maximum to dispel the October gloom. Judging by the drawings on their boards, these men appeared to be preparing the drawings and specifications for the upper superstructure and deck works that would be completed at Deptford after the launch. Silver had heard that the saloons and state rooms on the ship were planned to be the most luxurious in the world - should the ship ever finally make it into the water anyway...

The activity was equally as feverish at the far end of the drawing office where the launch design team was concentrated. A group of intelligent-looking young men were gathered at a meeting table in an alcove of the main drawing office, deep in discussion. For a moment, Silver and his two companions looked around uncertainly, not wishing to interrupt.

Eventually a man stood up from the group and came forward to speak to them. Silver recognized him as John Harkness, the engineering assistant responsible for the construction of the slipways. Silver had not spoken personally to him as yet but the man had been pointed out to him several times in the yard over the last three days. Harkness was recognized generally in the yard as a pleasant and affable man, unlike most of the other engineers and foremen. His fair hair was receding rapidly but the man still had a youthful and amiable face despite that thinning crown and was clearly still a few years short of forty.

He smiled a welcome now as he approached the three of them. 'Thank you for coming promptly, Spurrell. Let's see how we can resolve this little problem of ours.'

Silver liked the man instantly. Not many engineers or foremen in this yard were still capable of smiling at this tense stage of the project, but this man seemed to be one of the few not losing his perspective or his good temper. Most of the project workforce seemed almost overwhelmed by the impossible burden of their work, and the whole yard – from labourers up to craftsmen, and up to the Engineer himself – were buckling under the strain, and generally always in a foul and argumentative mood as a result. Irritations and resentments simmered between workmates and colleagues, and routine discussions often ended in verbal abuse or fights. Silver had only been here three days so had to wonder what it must have been like to have worked at this mad pace for the last two years or more.

Harkness moved over to a drawing board where a general arrangement drawing of the stern slipway was laid out for inspection. Silver, moving diffidently behind the two foremen, couldn't help but admire the artistry of the drawing, the beautiful calligraphy, and the hand colouring. 'I've been to check the levels this morning,' Harkness began almost apologetically, 'and I'm sorry to say that the lowest level of timber baulks on the slipway has been placed incorrectly. They're a full twelve inches too high at the bottom end of the slipway, compared to my drawing here. That may not sound much, but the ship will never make it down the slipway unless the gradient is exactly one in twelve. The slope has been calculated precisely to suit the Engineer's wishes.' Harkness clearly knew this mistake was Spurrell's fault, but he was being as gentle with the man as possible. 'There isn't time to take those beams up again and re-level them. Therefore we need to make some ad hoc adjustments to the upper layers to bring the final angle of the slipway back to one in twelve. Is this something you can resolve yourself, Spurrell, or will I have to work the changes out for you?'

Matthew Spurrell was lost for words for a moment, with a brick-red countenance to reflect his embarrassment. 'I...err...I...that is...'

Silver reluctantly came to his rescue, and stepped forward. 'It shouldn't be too difficult, sir. If I could have some calculation paper, I'm sure I could work out how the dimensions and levels of the upper beams need to be changed to suit.'

Harkness was surprised by the unexpected intervention. 'You understand geometry and trigonometry, do you...err...?'

'Wade, sir. Yes, I know enough trigonometry to do this, sir, if you have the mathematical tables.'

Harkness briefly turned his gaze to Crabtree and Spurrell before returning to Silver. 'And can you maintain the programme on the slipway, even if you have to make these corrections to the upper beams?'

Silver thought rapidly out loud. 'We'll have to re-cut some of the baulks already finished, sir, but not too many, I believe. So we should be able to catch up again within a couple of days, sir.'

Harkness clapped a firm hand on Silver's back. 'That's the sort of talk I like to hear.' He turned to Spurrell again. 'This man of yours could be a Godsend, Spurrell. Where did you find him?'

Crabtree pushed himself forward. 'That was me who found him, sir. Wade is an old friend of mine and was looking for work.'

Harkness inspected Silver again with a shrewd eye. 'So, Wade, how much do you understand of the planned launch? Do you know how we intend to get the *Leviathan* into the water?'

Silver kept his voice down, aware that draughtsmen at nearby drawing boards were looking at him curiously. 'Mr Spurrell has told me enough, sir. There'll be tackles rigged at stern and stem of the ship, and chains from these tackles will pass around sheaves secured to barges moored in the river and then back to steam winches on the shore.'

Harkness smiled boyishly. 'And? What else?'

'Amidships, four eighty-ton manually-operated crabs or winches mounted on moored barges.' Silver paused, watching Harkness's lingering smile. 'Plus hydraulic rams at bow and stern.'

'Yes, absolutely right. That's over two thousand tons of propelling force to move the ship, including a thousand tons courtesy of gravity down the slipway.' Harkness let his smile finally die away.

'But will it be enough? - that's the question,' a new voice added.

Silver became aware from this that a man in a dusty black suit and muddied boots had joined their small party and was listening in on the discussion intently, a huge cigar clenched in his mouth. The man was tiny, balding, with a drawn white face. 'And how do we stop her if she begins to slide too fast?' the newcomer asked Silver. 'Do you know that too?'

'Yes, sir. There's a huge checking drum fitted with brakes at the top of each slipway to halt her slide, if necessary.'

The man smiled at Harkness. 'You're right, John. This man is a Godsend. Perhaps I should let him take charge of the launch: he understands it better than I do.'

Silver had already realized the identity of the newcomer, of course. This was the man of the hour – Isambard Kingdom Brunel himself - the most famous engineer in Britain, without doubt, and most probably in the entire world. The man who had built the Thames Tunnel with his father when he was no more than a boy, then went on to build both the Great Western Railway, and the world's most advanced ships.

Silver became aware that even more people in the drawing office were now listening in on this surprising conversation and showing some unwelcome interest in him, so he did his best to step back out of the limelight. 'I doubt that very much, sir.'

Yet Silver had his own personal reasons for being grateful to this man, so, despite his discomfort at being picked out in this way, nevertheless felt gratified to be in his presence...

Even after Silver's time at the field hospital at Scutari in Turkcy, the high death rate and suffering had continued for the British wounded of the Crimean campaign, despite the arrival of Miss Florence Nightingale and her radical improvements to nursing standards in the hospital. The appalling conditions in the hospital became a matter of national disgrace which no one seemed able to solve, least of all the dithering and ancient Prime Minister, Lord Palmerston, and his fellow Whig politicians in

Westminster. In the end, tiring of political inaction, the engineer Brunel had taken up the cudgel directly. Entirely at his own instigation, Brunel had designed a prefabricated hospital, complete with water closets and running water, which had eventually been shipped out and built at Renkioi in Turkey last year to replace the now infamous base hospital at Scutari in which so many good and brave men of the war in the Crimea had perished unnecessarily. It hadn't been Brunel's fault that, despite his best efforts, the new hospital had come into operation too late to save all the many lives that it could have. Yet even so, Brunel had still undoubtedly saved hundreds of wounded British servicemen from succumbing to the same infections that had killed their comrades, so that Jonathan Silver did feel a great personal debt to this man...

'Your name, Mr...?' Brunel inquired.

'Wade, sir.'

'Well, you seem to have a fine grasp of what we're trying to do next month, Mr Wade. I wish all of the men in the yard understood the difficulties half so well.' With that Brunel stumped off down the length of the drawing office, his hobnailed boots clattering noisily on the floorboards. He seemed even smaller and more insignificant as he walked away – almost comically small, in fact, like a child dressed in man's clothes.

But as little and insignificant as that man might be physically, Silver thought, he was blessed with a powerful will and a giant imagination...

*

'Do you want to see anything of the engines?' Harkness asked Silver eagerly, basking still in the glow of Brunel's praise. 'I could take you inside the hull to have a look at them, if you wish. They're impressive beasts – the cylinders and crankshafts are some of the largest iron castings ever made. The paddle engines are an oscillating design with four cylinders of six feet diameter and a fourteen feet stroke. Imagine it - fifty-six feet diameter paddles! Yet the screw engines are the real innovation: they're James Watt horizontal direct acting engines, and far more revolutionary in concept than the paddle engines...'

Crabtree and Spurrell had returned to the yard below, but Harkness had requested Silver to stay behind for a little, although Silver wasn't sure why. Clearly, though, Harkness was a man who loved what he was doing.

'I think I'd better get to working out those new dimensions for the beams, and then get straight back to the slipway, don't you, sir?' Silver suggested diffidently.

Harkness seemed almost disappointed. 'Yes, that's probably wise in the circumstances. You can use that table over there. I'll see someone brings you writing paper and the mathematical tables you need. I will check your working out personally,' he warned, 'but something tells me it won't really be necessary.' He prepared to walk off, but came back for a second and said quietly in Silver's ear, 'Speaking frankly, Wade, I fear for Mr Brunel. They are going to turn this launch into a circus, you know - even selling tickets to the public to watch.'

'Who are, sir?'

'Why, the directors of the company. One can hardly blame them for doing it, of course, trying to recoup some of their huge financial loss. The *Leviathan* is already three times over budget, and not yet launched, and the directors are still facing punitive charges from Russell's creditors for the part use of their yard.' He sighed. 'But the company is nevertheless risking disaster by forcing Mr Brunel to launch before he's truly ready. And now the Press are hounding poor Brunel too, driving him to distraction. He is regularly lampooned in *Punch* as an egotistical madman. The gross unfairness of such an accusation is what staggers the mind. Mr Brunel is the sanest and kindest man I've ever met, despite his occasional lapses of temper.'

Silver was about to make some token reply when he became aware that another man had joined them. He had to hide his surprise when he realized the newcomer was none other than Daniel Strode...

'Well, John,' Strode greeted Harkness belligerently. 'And will your slipways be ready for the next spring tide on the third?'

Harkness glanced at Silver before answering. 'If God wills.'

Strode grunted dangerously. 'I doubt very much whether God will have much say in the outcome.'

'Perhaps not.' Harkness was still amiable on the surface but Silver could detect a serious undercurrent of antagonism between these two professional engineers. Strode and Harkness obviously knew each other of old, but didn't much care for each other, judging from the dangerous glint in both their eyes and the wary tone in their voices.

For his part Strode appeared completely uninterested in the tall carpenter standing with Harkness, so Silver was able to take the opportunity of studying his wife's former suitor at close proximity without any fear of his curiosity being returned.

Strode was over forty, Silver surmised, but a handsome and muscular man for all that, still having all his own hair, and most of his own teeth by the look of it. Unlike Brunel, this man somehow managed to retain some sartorial elegance even in a place as dusty and dirty as this Millwall shipyard. His black frock coat looked remarkably unwrinkled and dust-free, and his boots were still polished to a hard waxy shine. Above that great beak of a nose were penetrating blue eyes, thick arched eyebrows and a mane of jet black hair.

Silver could appreciate why Marianne had never felt entirely comfortable with the man. Strode was a man with a predatory air, and Marianne hadn't cared to be prey for anyone.

Harkness also wanted to get away from the man, it seemed. 'Excuse me now, Daniel. I really must get back to work, and so must Mr Wade here.'

Strode finally distinguished Silver with a look, but his eyes didn't linger for long. 'Yes, of course,' he agreed coldly, before turning away haughtily.

Harkness watched his retreating back with distaste. 'That's a difficult man to deal with, Wade. I would suggest you avoid anything to do with him, if you can possibly help it. It might ruin your life otherwise.' For an amiable man like Harkness, those words were surprising and seemed tainted with the bitterness of personal experience...

CHAPTER 10

Thursday 15th October 1857

At eight o'clock that evening Silver was back in New Gravel Lane in Wapping, after walking home from the Isle of Dogs with Billy Faber. Silver knew that Billy lived somewhere down by the Wapping waterfront but he hadn't discovered exactly where so far because until now they had previously parted ways on the way home at the top of New Gravel Lane. But this time Silver was minded to walk back to Gun Alley a different and less direct way, and so accompanied Billy further.

Although he hardly admitted the truth to himself, Jonathan Silver did have an ulterior motive for taking this particular way home tonight: this route would also take him past the Hostel for Women where sweet young Amy McLennan worked. Silver hadn't run into Amy since their initial encounter three days ago, but this was unsurprising considering all his daylight hours since then had been spent at the shipyard out on the Isle of Dogs. Yet there had been something intriguing about that pretty maid that had made him want to renew the acquaintance, despite the severe position he was in.

As a reward for his vaguely formed plan, he found that she was indeed there tonight, standing complacently under the flickering oil lamp at the entrance to the women's home. She was taking the evening air apparently, but wisely had her blue woollen shawl wrapped tightly around her against the cold. For once, though, it was a dry evening on the banks of the Thames, today's rainstorm having finally blown itself out, and the overcast sky now breaking up to reveal patches of bright starlight.

Surprisingly it was to Billy that Amy spoke first, giving him a cheery greeting as he approached. It seemed an odd coincidence to Silver that Amy already knew young Billy, but there was no doubt of it from his reaction. Billy went as red as a beetroot when Amy smiled invitingly at him and could only manage a half-strangled and embarrassed reply in return.

Amy then turned her attention to Silver, who managed not to blush equally in response. 'And you, Mr Wade, 'ow are you tonight?'

'Tired out,' he admitted ruefully, 'as you can probably tell from my weary face.'

Amy didn't choose to disagree, but then Silver had learned by now that East End women always said exactly what they meant to their men folk, and never sugar coated anything. 'Yeah, you do look worn out. They're workin' you and Billy 'ard on the Great Ship, then.'

'That they certainly are.' Silver hesitated, not sure whether to say more, or walk on immediately with Billy. He would in truth have liked to talk to this pretty girl longer, but he'd noticed a lot of peelers around on the streets tonight for some reason, which made him nervous of staying too long in one public place.

Amy became sombre for a moment. 'Mr Wade, did you 'ear that they found a girl – a young woman - murdered at the back of the 'ouses 'ere?'

Silver shook his head. 'No. I hadn't heard. When was this? Not one of the women from your hostel, I hope?'

'No, thank the Lord, she weren't one of ours. Nobody seems to know who this woman was, but the rumour on the streets is that she was some kind of a lady, not a local street girl. It was Tuesday mornin' when the peelers found 'er, and they're obviously worried it might 'appen again. That's the reason for all the bobbies on the streets tonight.' She flashed him a shrewd look and her voice dropped to a whisper. 'If you don't want to get stopped by a peeler, you'd better get off 'ome quickly, Mr Wade.'

That sounded like good advice to Jonathan Silver. The increased police presence on the streets of Wapping as a result of this unfortunate woman's death was an unsettling development for Silver. It would be even more dangerous for him to stay here in Wapping if the police were now stopping people on the streets at random to check on their identity.

Silver quickly doffed his cap to Amy, said a polite good night, then he and Billy quickly walked on.

'How come you know Amy, Mr Wade?' Billy asked with a backward glance at her, a slight note of jealousy in his voice. 'I thought you was new 'ere in Wapping.'

Silver gave Billy a reassuring pat on the shoulder. 'I don't know her really. I only met her by accident when she was waylaid in the street by a couple of ruffians a few days ago...'

'So you helped her?' Billy didn't sound reassured by the story.

'Yes, I helped her get away from those two bilge rats, as I'm sure any man would have. How come you know Amy anyway? She hasn't lived in

Wapping long, or so she told me.'

Billy wrinkled his smooth child's brow. 'Oh, my mum works at the same 'ostel as Amy. Thick as thieves, they are, 'er and my mum. Although, for some reason, my mum keeps telling me not to bovver her. I dunno why.'

'She is few years older than you, Billy,' Silver pointed out with a straight face.

'I s'pose,' Billy agreed taciturnly, then nodded down a dirty side alley. 'This is my gaff 'ere, Mr Wade. See you termorrow, then. Quarter to six at the top of the road, as usual?'

With that, Billy ducked down the side alley to the backyard of his own mean terraced house, while Silver headed off in the opposite direction, down Cinnamon Street towards Old Gravel Lane. Before reaching his lodging house in Gun Alley, though, he decided to take a further short detour down the alleyway that led past the back entrance to Elisa Saltash's chandler's store. Because of his chosen route home tonight, Elisa's home happened to be almost on his way too, so he was naturally drawn to this now familiar place.

He was only halfway down her alleyway, though, when he saw the figure of a man in a cap step cautiously out of the darkened gate to her backyard. Instinctively, as the fugitive he was, Silver stepped back into the shadows of a wall and held his breath. He was curious to know who this person leaving Elisa's place so secretively might be. It was difficult to see much in the pervading gloom of the alley but the figure seemed too short to be Liam Flintham. And anyway, Liam would normally leave the premises by the main shop entrance in front. It seemed more likely to Silver that this was Elisa herself, despite the male costume. The figure turned and headed in the opposite direction to him, so, inevitably, he followed, despite his earlier intention to go straight back to his lodgings in Gun Alley.

Soon the figure drew near the end of the alleyway where an oil lamp provided some flickering and insubstantial yellow light, and Silver saw that he had been right in his supposition. Once again, it appeared Elisa had given in to her predilection for dressing up as a boy – in fact she was dressed tonight in much the same way as she had been a week ago when she'd broken into Newgate to save her father, if a little smarter, and certainly less ragged. Most girls could not make a convincing man by merely dressing in jacket and trousers and a cap, yet Elisa seemed to be able to project herself into the part with the accomplishment of an actress, even walking exactly like a young man.

From her behaviour and her dress, it seemed she might be up to her old tricks again and off on a night time burglary expedition – a thought that seemed hardly credible to Silver given that her father had died only a few days previously, and that she had escaped the law herself only by the skin of her teeth. This was a girl clearly addicted to living dangerously. Because of her obviously suspicious behaviour, and her male disguise, Silver didn't make himself known to her, but decided to follow her for a while at a discreet distance - this despite his real desire to get back to the relative safety of his lodging house and to the comfort of his bed after a long hard day at work. Yet, with all these peelers on the streets of Wapping tonight, Silver was still tempted for a moment to give up his pursuit of Elisa and leave her to her own devices, such was the depth of his fatigue, and his pressing need to lay his head on a pillow for the night. Though his lodging room was still far from clean, Mrs Steams had fumigated the place yesterday after his complaints, so the bed bugs at least were now much more muted in their hunger, if the straw mattress was still as hard and lumpy. Yet, even with the thought of his nearby bed, Silver found he couldn't abandon Elisa – something told him that she might be heading for serious trouble tonight.

He was soon glad that he had chosen to ignore his own fatigue and follow Elisa, because in Old Gravel Lane he spotted a man drinking a glass of gin at the doorway of a public house ahead, who on seeing Elisa on the other side of the road, suddenly dropped his drink in surprise and set off after her too. The man had bright yellow hair and was a smartly dressed young fellow who didn't much resemble the typical Wapping street ruffian or wharf rat.

Elisa walked on quickly, apparently unaware of the yellow-haired man in close pursuit, and Silver found he had trouble keeping up with the two of them after his long day at the shipyard. His joints and muscles were aching, and his hands sore and chafed from the long use today of saw and chisel. Elisa was clearly suffering no similar physical disabilities, though, as she rapidly traversed the whole length of Old Gravel Lane, then turned west along Ratcliffe Highway, before eventually taking a further turn northwards towards Cable Street. Silver had fallen a good hundred yards behind by this time and was struggling even to keep Elisa and her yellow-haired shadow in sight. In Cable Street, after more than half-a-mile of vigorous walking from her home, Elisa hailed a passing horse-bus, pulled by two sturdy greys, the driver of which stopped for her with alacrity and allowed her to squeeze into the last place inside. The yellow-haired man managed, with a sudden energetic turn of pace, to get on the same bus, by shinning up the back ladder just as the vehicle began to move away again, and finding the last precarious berth up on the roof. Silver was too far behind to get on the same bus and could only watch in frustration as it pulled away at high speed, the pair of greys apparently fresh and full of vigour. From the sign on the back, it seemed the omnibus was destined to cross the whole of London to the new Paddington Station on the northwest side of town.

Silver searched around desperately, wondering how he could possibly catch Elisa and warn her that there was someone on her pretty tail. That yellow-haired man didn't seem to be following her for any innocent reason – from his behaviour outside the public house he had seemed to recognise instantly who the "boy" might be, so Silver guessed that he could be a detective or off-duty policeman on her trail. Silver's searching eyes soon gratefully spotted a second horse bus coming down Cable Street, which turned out to be heading for Bayswater, which was close enough to Paddington for Silver's purpose. But the conductor, hanging precariously on the back of the bus, refused to let the driver stop his horses to let Silver board. 'Out of the way, squire,' he yelled. 'We're full up. Twelve already inside and eight on top! That's our lot.'

Silver was almost contemplating giving up at this point and letting Elisa take her own chances. But he kept remembering what she had done for him – the risks she'd taken, the money she'd lent him - so the thought of tamely allowing her to be taken by the peelers rankled with him.

He would have to do something desperate, though, if he wanted to help her. He was an escaped fugitive, he reminded himself, therefore it was gross stupidity to make himself even more visible than he need be. *Yet what was the alternative...?*

Ignoring his own inner protests, he ran west along Cable Street after Elisa's departing omnibus, looking for a hackney cab, or for any other vehicle for hire. Cabs were few and far between in the East End, though, where the mass of people simply couldn't afford them, so Silver had to run a long way before eventually striking lucky. Outside a raucous pub at the corner of Christian Street he found one, but with the driver, a sad-eyed man with a greying walrus moustache, just dismounting and tying the reins of his two-wheeler to a hitching post.

Silver ran up to him. 'I need a cab, driver. It's an emergency.'

The cabby looked him up and down, inspecting his poor clothes and his workman's boots with an expression of clear suspicion. 'Sorry, matey. I'm finished for tonight, and I'm about to wet my whistle after a long day.' His horse seemed to concur with that sentiment and took a long drink of its own from the stone drinking-trough located conveniently outside the pub. The driver went inside without another word, to a blast of noise and tobacco smoke and heat from within.

Silver waited thirty seconds, then rapidly untied the reins of the horse, eased himself up onto the driver's box at the back, and cracked the whip to get the reluctant horse moving again.

*

Even though the elderly chestnut mare didn't like being roused from her welcome refreshment at the stone trough, she did soon close the gap with the heavily loaded omnibus ahead of them as Silver drove his stolen cab north up Leman Street and past Goodman's Fields. Now well into the parish of Whitechapel, Silver and his reluctant horse soon reached the old turnpike gate where four main roads from the East converged to enter the city together at Aldgate. Then on through the city he kept up a steady clip-clop pace behind the horse bus – Leadenhall Street, Cornhill, Cheapside...

The fact that Elisa's bus was being pulled by a pair of greys made it relatively easy for Silver to recognize it and keep it in sight, even after entering the city's congested streets with their crush of vehicles and pedestrians. The overloaded bus was having a particularly rough ride, though, it seemed, lurching and rolling on the rough cobbles. Omnibuses were never a comfortable ride at the best of times with their iron-shod wheels grinding and rumbling on granite setts, but this particular omnibus seemed to have deficient springs too.

Then Elisa's horse-bus reached Newgate...

Silver couldn't avoid a shudder of apprehension as he in turn passed the high stonewalls of the prison in which he had languished for the last few months, and particularly at the grim gateway of the press-yard where he should have been hanged a week ago. The night was cold enough already, but the sudden thought of being dragged out to the scaffold to have his neck stretched permanently chilled him even more than the rush of autumn air on his face.

On they went, Silver having to dawdle deliberately now that they had left the more crowded roads of the city behind, in order to avoid passing the frequently stopping omnibus. He'd seen no sign of Elisa leaving the bus so far, so it seemed her destination was somewhere among the rich pickings of the West End, as might be expected.

Perhaps she wasn't on a job at all, he thought hopefully at one point, but merely travelling incognito, dressed as a man for her own protection. The only women who would normally travel on their own to the West End at this time of night would be the high-priced painted whores of Leicester Square or the Haymarket.

It became increasingly certain to Silver, though, that Elisa had to be engaged in one of her burglaries tonight, as the omnibus chugged on through Holborn with her still on board, and showing no signs of wishing to disembark. The two greys pulling the bus were tiring now and making particularly heavy weather of the steep climb up Holborn Hill after the equally steep descent from Snow Hill, so that Silver had to slow his cab to a similar crawl. By the time the omnibus got to the top of Holborn Hill, Silver and his two-wheeler were only a few yards behind. Then they passed together through the slums of High Holborn and Silver had a moment of sombre reflection as he realized he was only a quarter of a mile from his own home in Russell Square, now shuttered and dark and empty, with dust sheets over the furniture...

The horse-bus eventually reached Oxford Street with its shops and dazzling gaslights, seemingly a hundred times brighter than the sparse and flickering oil lamps of Wapping and Shadwell. Standing on the box of his two-wheeler, Silver felt acutely uncomfortable in this place, seemingly as exposed to view by the bright gaslight as if he was spot lit on the stage of the Theatre Royal. He was suddenly aware that he wasn't dressed like a normal cabby, and that his appearance was already drawing some curious glances from the well-dressed passers-by.

Finally, at a few minutes after nine o'clock, Silver was relieved to see Elisa eventually. dismount from the omnibus in Oxford Street. She did not seem too putout by the rough bouncing ride she had suffered across the breadth of London because she gave the driver a cheery boyish wave, before heading purposefully south towards Piccadilly. The yellow-haired man also got off and followed her, of course - after a discreet interval anyway - but Elisa still seemed not to have noticed his presence.

Silver chose not to abandon his stolen hackney cab at this point, not sure if he mightn't need it to help Elisa make a quick getaway. Instead he followed the two of them at a snail's pace through the quieter streets of Mayfair, keeping far enough behind them now not to arouse suspicion. His heart was beating faster and his muscles were tightening with stress as the night went on, yet he was frankly enjoying the frisson of excitement that tonight's adventure had brought, if anything. Certainly his earlier fatigue had vanished for the moment as he became caught up in this intriguing cat-and-mouse game between Elisa and her pursuer.

Eventually he lost sight of Elisa and her follower somewhere at the northern end of Berkeley Square, so guessed that Elisa's target had to be one of the grand houses on the square. A large 18th century neo-classical mansion occupied the northwest corner plot on the square and seemed the likeliest residence to interest a thief with Elisa's purportedly high tastes.

What could she be after, though? Nothing heavy, that much was certain. Tonight she wasn't equipped to carry anything bulky so had to be in search of something light and portable...*and valuable, of course.* Jewellery therefore seemed the likeliest target tonight for Elisa's acquisitive tendencies.

Silver wondered what to do now. Eventually, for want of anything better, he parked the cab by the iron railings in the centre of the square where the old chestnut mare could resume her interrupted drinking at a stone trough. Stretching his legs on the pavement, Silver turned sharply to look up at the darkened windows of the corner mansion, and accidentally bumped into a well-dressed young lady in flowing crinoline, accompanied by a top-hatted gentleman companion. For a second Silver's eyes met hers as he made his apology, only to feel the blood draining from his face as he realized who the young lady was.

It was Marianne's sister, Sophie...

Yet she hadn't recognised him in return, though - for which he was duly thankful – because she moved on immediately with only a slight formal acknowledgement of his muttered apology. Silver wondered in perplexity at the chances of such an unfortunate meeting when she didn't live anywhere near Berkeley Square. Yet perhaps the coincidence was less unlikely that he thought - she might be some miles away from her married home near Chancery Lane, but she still had to be a regular visitor to Mayfair, he realized, because her mother had continued to live nearby in the Lovelock family home on Piccadilly even after the death of her husband.

Silver watched Sophie and her companion walking away with a touch of regret, wondering if he should now avail himself of this unexpected opportunity to speak to her. He hadn't seen the face of the man with her but was sure from his build that it had to be her husband Edward. He was half-tempted for a moment to run wildly after them and make himself known to them, longing for the thought of some civilised human company and warmth again. But his head sensibly restrained his heart from what would have been a potentially disastrous course of action. If he made himself known to Sophie and Edward, he would be putting them in a very difficult situation. And although Elisa had told him, after her visit to Took's Court in the disguise of an Irish serving girl, that Sophie still clearly believed in his innocence, Silver wasn't completely convinced of that. Nor did he have any real idea what her husband Edward thought about the notion of his guilt, or innocence. Silver had not had time to get to know Edward Rolfe well after his recent marriage to Sophie, and, although he and Rolfe had got on well enough together, Silver had no reason to believe that he would merit any special consideration or loyalty from Sophie's husband.

Yet the sight of Sophie tonight had left a dull ache in his heart, as he remembered all the happier times he'd spent with her and her family...

*

Still struggling to regain his composure, Silver climbed up onto the back of the cab and prodded his protesting horse into life again. Circling the square, he found a side road that he thought might lead to the rear of the corner mansion, which proved to be the case. He ended up parked under a spreading plane tree at the end of a cobbled mews lane where he could get a good view of the rear wall and garden of the mansion.

Yet from what he could see from the back of the cab, the corner house appeared more like a neo-classical palace than a suburban villa, with tall windows, elegant proportions and fine butter-coloured stonework. A very different environment from the Steams' dilapidated lodging house in Wapping where he currently resided, although the smells from the drains at the back of this house were remarkably similar. The West End might be the haunt of the rich and privileged, but it did at least suffer from the same sanitary problems as the poorer parts of the metropolis - blocked sewers, overflowing cesspits, and streets full of horse manure and dead dogs.

Minutes went by – perhaps even a full hour - it was difficult to be sure since he had no timepiece - and Silver eventually found himself overwhelmed by fatigue again and falling unresistingly into a deep dreamless sleep.

Then he was woken abruptly by the thunderous sound of a shot, followed by a scream.

A woman's scream...

CHAPTER 11

Thursday 15th October 1857

At three o'clock that same day, Sergeant Sparrow had been forced to conduct an exceedingly difficult conversation with a woman on the edge of an emotional abyss. The whole experience had felt to him more like a séance with a spirit, rather than a meeting with a live flesh-and-blood person.

Mrs Adelie Livingstone was a thin, drawn woman of forty-five, with a ramrod straight back, bloodless lips and a bony countenance. Black bombazine, however, suited her severe looks, Sergeant Sparrow was prepared to concede, and her mourning dress did give her an undoubted aura of quiet dignity.

She had already been to the police mortuary this morning to identify the body of her daughter, and Sparrow had allowed her time to return home afterwards to compose herself, before following her to Islington later to ask a few pertinent questions. So far Sparrow had spared her the pathologist's discovery that her daughter had been with child.

The house at 43 Pentonville Road was also as well suited to Mrs Livingstone's severe appearance and qualities as her mourning costume: rather run-down externally, certainly past its prime, and with little ornamental value left. Yet the house must have been a handsome, and even happy, place in better days, as Mrs Livingstone herself may once have been, Sparrow told himself. Despite the lines of strain on her face, and the metronome tick of a nerve in her cheek, Sparrow could detect a residual resemblance to that unfortunate and beautiful girl stretched out on the marble slab in the Whitechapel mortuary.

'You are a widow, ma'am, I believe?' Sparrow began, trying to ignore his discomfort at being perched precariously on the end of his armchair rather than in the middle of the seat as would be customary. The significant sag in the middle of the worn brocade upholstery suggested that he might sink through the armchair completely should he dare to place his buttocks there.

Her mouth quivered, followed by a gulp of pain, before she got out a strangulated reply. 'I am.'

'And your husband is long dead, is he?'

She nodded sombrely. 'Yes. He didn't unfortunately leave his family well provided for, as you can see.' She traced the outline of the room with her eyes – the bare plaster walls, the old worn Turkey carpet, the shabby and scuffed provincial furniture.

Sparrow took a deep breath. 'Why was that, ma'am?'

Mrs Livingstone sighed in return. 'Perhaps he was unfortunate, or perhaps he became over-ambitious. He was a reasonably wealthy and successful man at one point, and we lived in a certain degree of luxury for a time. Yet it wasn't enough for him and he began to invest in riskier undertakings. Regrettably he lost his entire fortune in the railway speculation crash of the forties and shot himself on New Years Day ten years ago.'

'Oh dear, that's terrible,' Sparrow sympathised. 'Did you and he have other children apart from Charlotte?'

'Two sons. The eldest, Jack, died in the Crimea. I wish I could say he had done something heroic in giving up his life for his country, but in fact he died of dysentery. Ultimately he was as foolish and ill-prepared for life as his father. My other son, Arthur, went to California to make his fortune in the Gold Rush, but I haven't heard anything from him in three years or more.' She put her hand to her brow at this point, as if wondering at the perverse and wicked hand of fate.

It felt like time for another "Oh, dear" but Sparrow decided not to venture a second one too quickly since dispensing sympathy in a sincere manner had never been his strongest suit. 'It must have been difficult for Miss Charlotte, bearing so much family heartache.'

'It was, but she made the best of it, as I did. She had to find work as a governess on reaching the age of sixteen.'

'Was she currently in employment?' Sparrow inquired.

'No, but she had recently left a post with a respectable family in Hampstead.'

'Who were...?'

'The family of a Mr George Harkness, I believe, of Downshire Hill. She'd been with them for three years, until only last summer in fact.'

Sparrow's curiosity was aroused. 'Why did she leave, if it was such a good position?'

'She gave notice for personal reasons.'

'Which were?' Sparrow persisted.

Mrs Livingstone looked up in surprise at his crass bluntness. 'By "personal", I mean the reasons were *private* to my daughter, Sergeant. She would not say anything about her reasons even to me, except to say that she found it impossible to continue in that particular post. Consequently she was busy looking for a new position.'

That sounded to Sparrow as if the father of the house, or someone else in Downshire Hill, might have been pressing their unwelcome attentions on Miss Livingstone too far, which might explain the girl's pregnant condition. 'Could that be why she was in Wapping on Monday? Seeking a new post?'

Mrs Livingstone responded to that question with a withering and dismissive stare that almost penetrated Sparrow's shoulder blades. 'That's hardly likely, Sergeant. I doubt that many families in Wapping employ governesses for their children, do they?'

Sparrow had to agree that was true. The numberless, shoeless, ill-fed children of Wapping looked far more in need of a square meal than the services of a governess.

This woman was having to fight now to keep control of herself, Sparrow could see, and was having real difficulty maintaining a stiff upper lip while she answered his questions. Sparrow could sense that the floodgates of grief were about to open soon, so pressed on with his questions while he still had the opportunity. 'When was the last time you saw Miss Livingstone?'

Her lips quivered. 'Four days ago. As I told one of your officers previously, she said she was going to Ramsgate to stay with an old friend from school, Lucy Swithers, who'd invited her to spend a few days taking the sea air. However, I have since learned that wasn't apparently the case.'

Sparrow had already had a colleague from Ramsgate check with Miss Swithers and his return telegram had indeed established that no such invitation had ever been issued. Mrs Livingstone did not seem as surprised at this revelation about her daughter's untruthfulness as she might have been, so Sparrow surmised that she'd already suspected that her pretty daughter might have been meeting a gentleman instead of Miss Swithers. Perhaps, though, the mother was resigned to giving Charlotte a certain amount of social latitude if she thought that, by doing so, her penniless daughter might attract a viable husband.

Sparrow wondered how to raise an even more difficult question than merely the possibility of Charlotte having had a recent liaison with one particular gentleman. Had Charlotte perhaps moved on in the last month or so from the respectable profession of being a governess to a profession rather older and less respectable? Could that be why she had been in a place like Wapping? If she was misleading her mother about her private life, then it had to be a possibility, if a small one. Even if she had taken to the oldest profession, though, it seemed unlikely that a girl with her breeding and looks would be plying that trade in Wapping or Shadwell. Girls from good families who ended up selling their bodies would more likely frequent the fashionable *poules de luxe* of the Haymarket or the Strand, or gaming rooms like the Argyll Rooms, where the best girls reputedly cost between two and three guineas for the night. A pretty well-mannered girl like Charlotte could even aim to end up ultimately as one of the *grandes horizontales* of the West End, if she played her cards right.

Not that Sergeant Sparrow had ever personally come across one of these *grandes horizontales*, of course, yet he had heard tell of these legendary creatures...

So, while poor East End street girls were only too happy to migrate westwards in search of better rewards and better-heeled clients, it was unheard of for a West End girl to want to move in the opposite direction. Girls only worked the streets of Wapping and Shadwell, flirting with the wharf rats and dregs of the waterfront, if they had no other alternative.

Not that the lives of ordinary street girls in the West End were exactly uplifting. Sparrow had walked down the Haymarket only a few nights ago and seen mothers blatantly bringing their little daughters there to do business. A pretty blue-eyed girl of about twelve had taken him by the hand and invited him to follow her. Fortunately for her, Sparrow was not one of those policemen who felt carnally tempted by these sylphlike girls, instead feeling only intense sympathy for them and for their desperate situation...

Returning his attention to Charlotte's mother, Sparrow decided to be circumspect in his approach because he sensed that just one overly direct remark about her daughter's private life might send this already distraught woman completely over the edge. Taking another deep breath, Sparrow finally plucked up the courage to ask his difficult question. 'Could it have been a *gentleman* that Miss Livingstone was actually visiting this week, rather than Miss Swithers, ma'am?' he said in almost a whisper.

Mrs Livingstone's lips were beginning to quiver uncontrollably. 'No, I don't believe so. Charlotte had been melancholy of late, it's true. But I don't think that her mood was the result of meeting any gentleman. It was probably because of having to leave that home in Hampstead where she had been well settled and happy until recently.'

That answer seemed less than convincing, Sergeant Sparrow thought, as if Mrs Livingstone was trying to persuade herself of her daughter's fidelity.

'...In any case, as a governess to a pair of young girls in Hampstead, she had few opportunities to meet gentlemen of any sort on equal terms.'

That was a rather more convincing argument, Sparrow had to agree. And, even if Charlotte had come across gentlemen in the course of her work, very few of them would be interested in marrying an impecunious governess, Sparrow knew, although they might well have an interest in deflowering a pretty one of her virtue, given the slightest opportunity.

'You may be wrong about Miss Livingstone not having a gentleman friend, ma'am,' Sparrow warned her, finally taking out the important piece of evidence found at the scene near New Gravel Lane. 'In her bag we found this letter dated September the twenty-fifth, and written to her by someone called Daniel, inviting her to meet and walk in Regents Park on the following Sunday.'

Mrs Livingstone jerked upright in her chair. 'It doesn't mean that she would have accepted such an invitation, unchaperoned. My daughter was a person of sense and decorum, unlike both her brothers.'

It still sounded to Sparrow as if the woman was trying to convince herself, rather than him, of her daughter's good sense. 'Then you know nothing of any man called Daniel whom your daughter might have been seeing?'

Mrs Livingstone added some steel to her voice, dredged from one last secret reserve of strength. 'I do not, Sergeant. Nor do I believe she would have been seeing a gentleman without telling me about it.'

Sparrow nodded but wasn't persuaded by her answer. Regardless of what the mother thought - or said anyway - Sparrow was now quietly convinced that Charlotte had been in Wapping on Monday for an assignation with a man. And that man, whether called Daniel or not, had probably killed her.

Yet , for the moment anyway, he decided to keep the truth from Mrs Livingstone about her daughter's delicate condition – there would be nothing gained by her knowing at present, and the woman already had more than enough sorrow to bear as it was.

Poor bitch, he thought, watching the woman's steely resolve finally crumble and melt into tears in front of his eyes. But whether it was more for the mother, or for her dead daughter, that he felt the greatest pity, Charlie Sparrow couldn't say for sure...

*

At ten that same evening, Sparrow was settling down for the night in his room at Shadwell police station. When working a long shift like today and finishing duty too late to get home before the early hours, he frequently didn't bother going home to Lambeth at all, but chose instead to sleep on a makeshift camp bed in his room.

Frank Remmert appeared at the door just as Sparrow was loosening his braces and about to take his boots off.

'Better keep those boots on, Sarge,' Remmert recommended. 'There's a cab just arrived outside. The cabby says a man called Minshall asked him to come here at top speed, and take you back to Berkeley Square toot sweet. I suppose it must be the same Minshall who works at Newgate, and who found Miss Livingstone's body on Tuesday.'

Sparrow's thoughts were more taken with the bizarreness of the destination, though, than with the identity of the man who had dispatched the cabby to fetch them. '*Berkeley Square*? In the West End?' he demanded incredulously.

'No, Berkeley Square in Spitalfields,' Remmert said sarcastically.

Sparrow gave him a sharp look in return and decided peevishly that he'd let Frank Remmert get far too uppity and familiar with him recently. It was probably now high time to curb some of this boy's natural cheek...

'Did Minshall give any reason for wanting us to tear over to Mayfair at this time of night?' Sparrow demanded. 'He hasn't found another body, has he?' he added with heavy sarcasm.

Remmert either didn't notice Sparrow's reproachful look or else it just bounced off him like a wooden skittle off a brick wall. 'I don't think so. According to what he told the cabby, Minshall says he's spotted that boy who he suspects helped Silver break out of Newgate, and has been following him this evening. And he's now convinced that this boy is in the middle of breaking and entering a house in Berkeley Square tonight. So Minshall says we need to get over there and nab this scallywag before he's off again.'

Sparrow leapt to his feet at the news. 'Then what are we waiting for?' He hesitated at the door. 'But we'd better do this properly and take our own growler. Tell that cabby we'll follow him...'

*

By a little after ten-thirty, Sparrow and Remmert had made the three-mile dash across town in the police growler and were secreted with James Minshall in a secluded corner of the back garden of a vast house on the corner of fashionable Berkeley Square. Inspector Carew had already gone off duty at Shadwell Station for the evening, but his uniformed night duty sergeant had at least allowed Sparrow to take Remmert with him as support despite thinking the exercise was likely to be a waste of police time. Sparrow would have liked to take one more Shadwell constable along too in case the tip was a good one and he might have a burglar to apprehend tonight, but the duty sergeant had dug his heels in at that point, and refused to allow any more of his men to leave their own beat on what might be a wild goose chase. There'd been no time to warn the owner of the house in Berkeley Square, or his servants, discreetly about what was going on, but that would probably have defeated the object of the exercise anyway - of hopefully taking this mysterious youthful burglar by surprise. That was assuming the burglar was already inside the house, of course, which Sparrow was far from convinced of...

'So you followed this youth all the way over here from Wapping, did you, Mr Minshall?' Sparrow whispered to the man at his side.

'Yes. I spotted him walking up Old Gravel Lane from the river, so thought I'd see what he was up to. As soon as I started following him, I realised from his furtive manner that he had to be up to no good.' Minshall took out his pocket watch from his waistcoat and tried to make out the time in the dim light. He looked worried by what he saw. 'I think I must be late for work on the night shift by now.'

'Never mind about that, Mr Minshall,' Sparrow reassured him. 'If you're right about this, I'll put in a good word for you with the governor of Newgate. You are sure the boy broke into *this* house, are you?' Sparrow eyed the man's bright yellow hair with disfavour – hair that colour was damned easy to spot even in this weak half-light, like a shaft of limelight in a theatre. Sparrow did wonder peevishly why the man wasn't wearing a hat tonight like any normal man.

For some reason Minshall seemed in a more equivocal mood than usual. 'I *think* this must be this house. It was near here where I last caught a glimpse of the boy.' He frowned uneasily. 'But that boy must have the devil on his side, Sergeant – he can disappear, then reappear, almost like a ghost. One moment he was there right in front of me in the street, the next he'd simply vanished into thin air. But he must have got into this back garden somehow; there was no other place he could have gone. Not unless he truly is a spirit anyway.'

'Don't worry, he's no spirit. Although he might be one by the time I finish with him.' Sparrow turned grimly to Remmert on his other side. In their hurry to get here from Shadwell, there'd been no opportunity to call on any further police reinforcements on the way to Mayfair. And even if there had been time, Sparrow would have been highly reluctant to stop at the local police station in Piccadilly and ask for the station commander's help because he'd had a long and uneasy rivalry with the uniformed inspector there, a sarcastic and obdurate Irishman called Pierce Murphy. Inspector Murphy hated him personally even more than did Inspector Carew at Shadwell Station, which was saying something. But Sparrow complacently cast aside any doubts about the wisdom of going it alone tonight. *Surely the three of them could catch one pimply youth?* 'Frank, do you have any idea who owns this house?'

Remmert had been seconded for a while at Murphy's station in Piccadilly so knew some of the housemaids and servants in the area quite intimately, and could even recognize some of their well-heeled masters and mistresses, if only to salute in passing. 'If I remember rightly, this pile belongs to a baronet and Whig Member of Parliament, Sir Digby Carfax and his second wife, Lady Susan. He's about eighty, and she's about thirty so she always looked a little "hungry" for company whenever I saw her...' - Remmert tapped his nose and leered – 'if you know what I mean.'

Sparrow sniffed coldly. 'She'd have to be bloody *starving* to be interested in a man with a mug like yours, Frank. These Whig gentlemen live well enough, though, don't they? But I thought they were all "liberals" now, men of the people?' he complained facetiously, mostly to himself.

Before Remmert could make some kind of a response, there came the sound of a shot from inside the house – a thunderous blast like a twelve-bore shotgun - followed by a woman's scream...

'Do we go in, Sarge?' Remmert asked breathlessly.

Sparrow didn't answer, but placed his hand roughly over Remmert's stupid mouth, while gesticulating with his other hand in the direction of the second floor, where a window had been slid open and a slender figure was rapidly descending a drainpipe to the ground.

Remmert and Sparrow split up at once and converged on the wraithlike figure as it melted into the inky blackness at garden level. Sparrow felt someone or something run into him at breakneck speed, sending him sprawling into a thorny bush and winding him badly. But he still had enough possession of mind to make a despairing grab with his right hand, which did briefly make contact with something soft and flesh-like.

That was until a massive bony fist pulled him to his feet and struck him full in the face. A satisfied voice said, 'Gotcha, you little bugger.'

Sparrow practically spat into the face of his attacker with fury. 'That's me you bloody well clocked, Frank, you bone-headed idiot! The boy's gone for the back wall. Quick, get after him!'

'That wall's fourteen feet high and topped with broken glass. He won't get over that in a hurry,' Frank announced confidently, but nevertheless used his rattle and shouted for whoever it was to stop in the name of the police.

But after feeling their way down the dimly lit path, they found no fugitive crouched cowering in hiding at the base of the wall, and certainly no one speared painfully on the shards of glass on top.

'Don't you ever get sick of always being right, Frank?' Sparrow asked him balefully, as he pulled out a handkerchief and tried to stem the flow of blood dripping copiously from his battered nose...

CHAPTER 12

Thursday 15th October 1857

A minute after hearing the woman's hair-raising scream, Jonathan Silver was still waiting in his hackney cab, unsure of what action to take. *Could that scream have come from Elisa?* Somehow he thought not; she wasn't the type of girl to ever scream like that, not even if her life depended on it.

Finally he urged his horse forward from its shadowed place of concealment and out into the gaslit mews lane at the back of the house. He could hear the sounds of severe commotion coming from the other side of the wall: curses and blows and rapid footsteps, then the sound of a police rattle and a warning to stop. There was a padlocked wooden door in the middle of the wall, and the brick wall itself was a good fourteen feet high and topped viciously with broken bottle glass cemented in mortar, so Silver couldn't imagine anyone coming out of the house that way.

Yet he was soon proved entirely wrong. A figure appeared from nowhere at the top of the high garden wall, and, somehow avoiding the broken glass, casually vaulted over the wall into the quiet mews lane beyond, before rolling over several times on the muddy cobbles and then magically regaining its feet.

Silver quickly urged the old chestnut mare further forward and shouted at the crouched figure. 'Get in before the police arrive!'

For the first time in their acquaintanceship, Silver thought he'd taken Elisa Saltash completely by surprise.

Her jaw dropped a little at least. 'What are *you* doing here?'

'Shut up and get in!' Silver commanded her rudely.

In a few seconds they were out of the other end of the alley and back in Berkeley Square, heading south at a brisk trot towards Piccadilly and Green Park.

*

Passengers could speak to their drivers if they wished through the small sliding passenger hatch at the back of the typical London Hackney cab, yet Elisa Saltash seemed strangely reluctant at first to make any use of this convenient means of communication. In fact, they had almost reached Leicester Square before she finally slid down the hatch and turned her head to say reluctantly, 'So, tell me. How did you happen to be there in Berkeley Square tonight? And how did the police know I would be there?'

Silver had to concentrate on his driving for a moment so didn't answer her immediately. Leicester Square was not the easiest place to negotiate with a cab at the best of times – a run down square set within an insalubrious and densely packed neighbourhood of slums and shabby tenements, and, reputedly, even opium dens. Perhaps, though, Leicester Square was destined to turn into a more genteel area in time because of the new music hall, the Alhambra, recently built on the east side of the square, which was now attracting rather wealthier patrons to the area. Tonight the square was engulfed by a vast throng of these well-dressed theatregoers - soldiers, top-hatted gentlemen and their crinolined escorts – who were just leaving the auditorium after the evening performance. Spilling out onto the streets, the crowd swirled and broke like an incoming wave around Wyld's Monster Globe, a giant iron structure dominating the centre of the square. The globe had been there since the Great Exhibition in '51, and Silver, with a sudden melancholy thought, remembered visiting it with Marianne only a month before she died. From the viewing platforms and galleries inside, the oceans and continents of the world were revealed in startling detail, and he and Marianne had been interested in particular to see the topography of the Crimea and the Black Sea, that exotic and little-known part of the world where they had first met...

Silver let Elisa's curiosity about his unexpected appearance tonight remain unsatisfied for a few seconds more as he guided his unsettled horse through the confusion in Leicester Square. Finally, though, he answered her question, 'I followed you from Wapping.'

She turned her head sharply so that he could see her profile under that boy's cap. 'What! You followed me? In this cab? How did you get hold of a cab?'

'I stole it from outside a pub in Cable Street.' Silver couldn't quite keep a note of shame out of his voice. *Or was it perhaps pride?*

She bubbled with laughter at that as Silver finally found a break in the crowds and managed to squeeze through the exit from the square and turn right into St Martins Lane. 'I don't believe you,' she added slyly. 'The upright Jonathan Silver stealing a hackney cab?'

He tapped the lacquered woodwork of the cab with the stock of his whip. 'Believe your eyes, then.'

She coughed disbelievingly, before lapsing into silence again.

There were plenty of peelers on the streets here, Silver noticed worriedly, so he was nervous about being held up by the traffic. It wouldn't take much idle curiosity on the part of one of these bobbies to wonder why a man dressed like a labourer was driving a cab, and why his passenger appeared to be some street urchin...

Entering Trafalgar Square, Silver picked up pace past St Martins-in-the Fields, before turning left after the imposing bulk of Morley's Hotel into the Strand. 'You're fortunate that I did follow you, Elisa,' he said through the hatch. 'Another man was following you tonight – a young man with straw-coloured hair – and I think it must have been him who summoned the police.'

'Who was he? This man you claim to have seen.' She didn't seem ready to believe that she'd been followed by two people tonight, a note of derision in her voice.

'I don't know who he is; I've never seen him before. But Yellow Hair recognised you all right as you were walking up Old Gravel Lane – even dressed as you are, as a man - and went after you like a gun dog.'

Silver could see that Elisa was worried, despite her practised air of insouciance. 'Then he hopefully doesn't know my real identity, or where I live.'

'Perhaps not,' Silver conceded. 'But even so, they're closing in on you, Elisa, just like they're closing in on me. What made you do such a reckless thing tonight as breaking into that house? It's only eight days since you tried to break your father out of Newgate. I thought you would sensibly lie low for a while after an experience like that.'

She craned her neck around to look at him again through the hatch. 'I had been planning this robbery for months, even before my father was taken by that cursed policeman Sparrow. So I saw no reason to change my plans, not when there was so much at stake. You see, a wealthy Whig baronet, Sir Digby Carfax, lives in that house with his young wife, Lady Susan, but they were supposed to be abroad, and with most of their staff away too. That's why I decided to raid their home tonight, before they returned from their European excursion...'

'But it seems they aren't abroad, are they?' Silver interrupted.

She sighed. 'Unfortunately not. They returned a few days early after Sir Digby had experienced a recurrence of gout while in Venice. My inside informant broke the bad news to me yesterday.'

'So you knew the household was back and yet you *still* broke into the house...?' Silver was lost for words for a moment.

Elisa had a dry riposte to that. 'What can I say? I enjoy a challenge. In any event the rewards were too great not to give it a try.'

'And what rewards are those?' Silver sniffed suspiciously.

Even in the dimness of the cab interior, Silver could sense her skin glowing and her eyes brightening as she described the object of her desire. 'It's a famous pink-white pearl necklace called the *Tears of the Prophet,* which once belonged to the Maharajah of Kaipur, and is worth at least ten thousand pounds. They say the pearls were originally a gift from Ali, the son of Abu Bakr, to Ayesha, the wife of the prophet Mohammed himself, hence the name. What is known for sure is that the necklace has a provenance that goes back at least a thousand years to the Abbasid dynasty in Baghdad, before coming into the possession of Mahmud of Ghazni. Eventually it was stolen by the Seljucks after they overran Khorasan and seized Baghdad...'

'You're quite the little Near Eastern scholar, aren't you?' Silver interrupted tartly.

She ignored his sarcastic intervention. '...Then it was in turn possessed by the followers of Osman and found its way to a pasha in Constantinople before the Maharajah of Kaipur obtained it from him twenty years ago by some treachery. After the Maharajah's fortunes too went into decline, Sir Digby bought the necklace from this Indian gentleman as a wedding present for his young wife when they married in Rome three years ago. And I knew from my informant in the house...'

'And who exactly is your snitch?' Silver asked tartly.

Elisa threw him a wary look in return before finally answering. 'My snitch, as you call her, is one of the upstairs maids in the house, with a taste for better things than her wages can presently afford. She warned me yesterday in a hastily delivered note that, although Sir Digby presently keeps the necklace among his wife's other valuables in a Chubb safe in his own bedroom, she had heard Lady Susan mention that Sir Digby intended shortly to put the necklace into a bank for safekeeping. Hence the reason why I had to try tonight... '

'Yes, but what about the risks of breaking into an occupied house?'

Elisa snorted angrily. 'Of course there always has to be some risk! But even though Sir Digby was back in residence, I was still sure I could get into the house and open that safe without waking him: Sir Digby does usually retire early because of his gout, and I've practised enough on that make of safe to be able to open a Chubb in the dark without making any noise. And I was right: Sir Digby must have had a hard day counting his money because I found him fast asleep in his old four-poster and snoring fit to wake the dead. I could have blown the safe with gunpowder and he wouldn't have heard.'

'And what about the servants? And the young wife?'

Elisa smiled knowingly. 'Ah, his young wife, as I suspected, is not so hardened yet to an old man's snores as to want to sleep in the same room. And my well-paid maid informant had agreed to put a small dose of extract of valerian root into the evening meal of mutton to send most of the staff into a deep sleep too...'

Silver had to concentrate on his driving again as people and vehicles crossed at random in front of him. The Strand appeared even more choked with an excess of humanity than Leicester Square had been. It was well after eleven o'clock by now but the pavements were still densely packed with a surging throng of Londoners who enlivened this, the busiest street of the greatest city on earth, with their noisy and unpredictable presence. Silver encouraged his horse to keep moving despite the obstacles and distractions, past the gas-lit entrances to raucous pubs and noisy gin palaces, to beer shops and restaurants. The very air of the Strand smelled of mild and bitter ale, of seafood and oysters, and of less savoury things too. Its crowded pavements seemed populated by an endless cast of memorable London characters. Covent Garden porters with heavy baskets of fruit and vegetables on their heads, even at this late hour. Pink-cheeked delivery boys, moustachioed hotel doormen, shoe-shines, loafers, idlers, pickpockets. The bewildered alien faces of Chinamen and lascars; the pinched faces of waifs and barefoot boys, and of emaciated Bryant and May match sellers, their bodies sagging under the weight of their heavy trays. And every type of beggar too - the representatives of the great hungry and ragged army of the night...

And adding even more colour to the Strand and its environs were the women of London in all their varied profusion. Flower sellers, poor girls from the East End in straw bonnets and tattered skirts, rich women from Belgravia in silks and satins, and statuesque actresses and chorus girls from Drury Lane. Tired, bedraggled, powdered, painted, frazzled, pert, gay, lively, exhausted, elegant, tragic. On the arms of stage door johnnies or regimental sergeant-majors, or clinging in gin-stained abandon to the lowest ebb of humanity.

From the back of his Hackney cab Silver was seeing London tonight in a way he had never seen it before. The eyes of a fugitive inevitably saw the world in a different light, of course, and this deeper insight inspired by his own persecution revealed to him the city's underlying heartlessness and wickedness, but also hinted at its possible redemption too.

Finally, as they reached Temple Bar, with the worst of the West End crowds behind them, he spoke to Elisa again. 'So what happened in the house? Who fired that shot I heard?'

Elisa yawned tiredly. 'That was the gentleman of the house himself. Sir Digby might have been fast asleep, you see, but his young wife certainly wasn't.' She rolled her eyes in annoyance. 'Obviously she doesn't like mutton stew. She happened to come into his room for something as I was opening the safe, and discovered me there. She then woke Sir Digby abruptly, who found a gun somewhere by his bed and, blithering with fright, took a pot shot at me. What sort of knucklehead keeps a loaded shotgun by his bed?'

'Perhaps he's been troubled by burglars,' Silver suggested dryly. 'You weren't frightened yourself, then?' he asked hopefully.

She turned her head to mock him through the back window. 'Hardly.' She half-smiled at his expression. 'You look disappointed, Dr Silver. Ah, I see, you thought it was *me* who screamed tonight? No, that was his own sweet young wife who made that sound, I promise you. In trying to hit me as I ran across the room, Sir Digby nearly gave her a full broadside instead. He missed her by only a whisker.'

'Luckily for you. Because, if he had killed her, they would still have hanged *you* for it,' Silver stated morosely.

*

By midnight they were back in Cable Street in the East End, close to where Silver had taken the cab. Before they got to the corner of Christian Street, he dropped Elisa off on the other side of the road. Then, after a careful check to see that no irate cabby was still lingering in the vicinity, he left the horse and cab tied to the same hitching post as before, where the old mare immediately resumed her interrupted drink in the same trough. Even though it was after midnight now, the pub was still open so there was a good chance the cabby was still inside and hadn't even noticed his loss yet.

Elisa joined him a hundred yards down the road and, pulling her cap low over her eyes, linked arms with his. 'You're much too kind-hearted to be a real villain, Dr Silver,' she informed him condescendingly. 'I'm surprised you didn't leave that cabby a sovereign for the hire of his cab for the evening.'

Silver shrugged. 'Isn't this a bit familiar, you holding on to me like this?' he asked her.

'Not at all. It's after midnight, and we're a couple of pals wending our drunken way home after the pub. What could be more natural?'

She did put on a good imitation of a drunken man's random walk, Silver had to admit.

There were still a lot of people on the streets at this late hour, even in a poor and often dangerous district like Wapping. As they walked down Old Gravel Lane, Silver saw that the public houses were still all open, and doing good business with their seamen and labouring clientele, with a blast through their swing doors of ale fumes and tobacco smoke, laced with the sounds of bad fiddle playing and raucous singing.

Even in their short walk through Wapping, they passed three blue-jacketed policemen on patrol, equipped with truncheons and warning rattles, so it seemed that the increased police presence on the streets would be continuing even through the night. Fortunately none of them took the slightest notice of Silver and Elisa as they made their apparently drunken way home.

Elisa glanced around nervously, though, as they finally turned off Old Gravel Lane into the maze of alleyways in which she lived. 'I suppose the presence of all these peelers on the streets tonight is a consequence of that young woman being murdered in New Gravel Lane a few days ago.'

'I hope that *is* the reason,' Silver muttered, 'and that's it not because they know I'm hiding here in Wapping.'

Elisa smiled faintly. 'I don't think you're that important. But just in case, I think you'd better come back with me tonight, Dr Silver, rather than go directly to your lodgings where your late arrival might be noted. And you do deserve some small reward for the help you gave me tonight.'

Silver blinked at that, not sure what to make of such an enigmatically phrased invitation. But he certainly wasn't minded to turn it down, being a man in desperate need of a reward of some sort, no matter how small. In fact anything approaching even the slightest touch of compassion and understanding from a fellow human being would be welcome in his current miserable state, and particularly from a pretty woman.

Inside her kitchen, there was no cheerful welcoming fire, but the room was still much warmer than outside from the residual embers in the grate.

'Why is it that you don't keep a maid who could keep your house warm for you?' he asked her curiously. 'With all this thieving that you do, you certainly must be able to afford it,' he added with slightly malicious intent.

Elisa returned him a sour look as she poked at the remains of the fire in a desultory manner, trying to prod it back into life. 'I prefer to live on my own and look after myself. In any case, a live-in maid would get to know far too much of my personal business, and I can't afford to take the chance of being betrayed.' She put the poker down with a clang in the coalscuttle. 'Why are you still here in Wapping, Jonathan? And working in that shipyard on the Isle of Dogs? What are you hoping to achieve by it? Absolution of some kind?'

'I believe that the man who killed my wife works there,' he declared bleakly. 'If I can't get justice for myself, then at least I can get some natural justice for her.'

That remark jolted her for a second, he could see, or at least gave her pause for thought. After a long moody silence, she asked calmly, 'Are you planning to kill him, then?'

'It's an option, if all else fails.'

'All else will fail. The law will never help you right any wrongs, you can be sure of that! Are you sure that this man is truly the guilty party?'

Silver shook his head. 'No, far from it. Which is why he is still alive – for the present anyway.'

She came forward and stood in front of him. 'What's his name, this villain of yours?' she asked curiously.

Silver was reluctant for a moment to divulge the name, but it occurred to him now that Elisa might be able to help him investigate the man. 'His name is Daniel Strode,' he said finally, after another long pause.

She frowned. 'You mean *the* Daniel Strode – the well-known engineer - the man who designed the paddle engines for the *Leviathan*? *That* Daniel Strode?'

Silver was surprised. 'You *know* him?'

Her eyes fluttered in a mock show of femininity. 'Let's say that "Miss Elisa Smith" knows Mr Strode slightly, and has even flirted with him on occasion. But he's not the type of man that the real me would ever be attracted to, even though he is a handsome and unsettling brute, I am prepared to concede.'

Silver sniffed suspiciously. 'How do you happen to know him?'

'You forget – I own other local businesses here apart from the chandler's store, including a tanner's yard, a grocery store and a laundry among them. So I supply Napier's yard with many things at present – from candles to soap to clean linen for their directors' boardroom.'

Silver was struggling to understand her situation. 'Then why do you need to thieve? You must be a very wealthy young woman already. Your father told me you were rich, but I never believed him.'

She coughed. 'Rich by Wapping standards, perhaps. But I told you: I want to be *really* rich. I want to own a whole fleet of China clippers that will traverse the world and bring me real power and wealth.'

Silver grunted dismissively. 'I thought you despised the rich?'

'I don't despise their *money*, you can be sure of that! I only despise those who have acquired wealth without working for it, and then use it to exploit the poor.'

'And you call stealing "work", do you?'

She flared even more at that. 'You try it if you think it's so easy. In any case, I will only steal until I have enough capital to succeed in business. After that, I will retire with my ill-gotten gains and ensure that no one ever steals from *me*, you may be sure of that.'

Silver shook his head in bewilderment at this contradictory and obstinate girl. 'But there's more to your stealing than merely getting money, isn't there? Why do you take these insane risks like you did tonight? It's almost as if you want to be caught.'

She smiled faintly. 'Perhaps insanity runs in my blood.'

'Yes, perhaps it does,' Silver agreed acidly. After a moment's reflection, he added more soberly, 'That man Liam Flintham loves you, you know. You've taken him in completely with your demure act. I've only spoken to him a few times, but it's quite clear how much he worships the ground you walk on.'

She looked taken aback for a moment by him making such an intimate pronouncement on her private life, before finding her voice again. 'No, he doesn't,' she denied roughly. 'What Liam loves is the person he *thinks* I am, the sweet virginal Miss Elisa Smith. It's a pity then that she doesn't exist, but you can hardly blame me for that. I must simply be a much better actress than I imagine...'

'Or else, perhaps there is more of your real character in the sweet Miss Smith than you care to acknowledge?' Silver goaded her.

'Hah!' Elisa sneered. 'Believe that at your peril.' Yet her eyes glowed for a moment with secret pleasure at what he'd said. 'I almost wish, though, that I could find a genuine "Miss Elisa" for Liam to cherish and love because he is such a deserving boy. But the real me, should he ever discover it, would be a profound disappointment to him.'

Silver moved closer to her. 'You don't think anyone could love you for yourself, Elisa?'

She shook her head vehemently. 'No, I don't believe so. I would be a difficult person for any man to live with.' She seemed to be struggling with her inner self. 'That is, I don't know if the man exists who could truly love me as I am. I haven't found him so far, that much is certain.'

Silver pressed home his advantage, feeling her bewilderment and sudden vulnerability, and wanting to understand this girl's strange life and even stranger morality. 'Why is it that you wear trousers to do your stealing? Is there some particular reason why you need to turn yourself into a man in order to go thieving?'

She looked down at her outfit, and felt the cap on her head, which still concealed her hair. 'There is no sinister reason for this,' she said. 'Believe me, I have no secret wish to be a man. It's simply the most practical attire for climbing up walls and through windows, that's all. And it's a good disguise.'

'But it's not only that, is it? Part of you does yearn to be a man, I think. Is that your father's doing? Did you always feel a disappointment to him because you weren't the boy that he really wanted? The boy to follow in his footsteps...'

'No, none of that is true,' she argued unconvincingly. 'But I will admit that part of me does want the *freedom* that men have. To be able to roam the world and do as I damn well please!' She lapsed into a more thoughtful mood. 'But, anyway, it seems that I will have to stop wearing trousers for the foreseeable future, now that this yellow-haired devil is on my trail and would recognize me dressed like that. You think he's a policeman?'

Silver nodded. 'It seems likely. Or else an informer for the police.'

'Well, no matter, I shall just have to limit myself to wearing skirts and petticoats and silk stockings for the moment, that's all,' she concluded demurely, after long reflection. 'That's not such a savage penalty to have to face.' She yawned tiredly again. 'But now, it's time to sleep. I'll fetch the straw mattress for you.' She frowned at his response – a look of disappointment had obviously flickered briefly across his face despite his best attempt to remain stoical. 'What is it? You seem put out by something?'

Was she mocking him with that question, or seducing him? Or merely being herself?

'You did mention a *reward* for my help tonight,' he pointed out.

She cocked her head to one side. 'That's true, I did. But I meant only a warm and dry mattress to sleep on in my kitchen for the night. Is that not enough of a reward for you?'

'And if I were to say no,' he said provocatively, moving even closer to her.

She finally took off her boy's cap, untied her luxuriant hair and let it fall to her shoulders. 'Then, please accept this small extra token of thanks.' She stood on tiptoe, and placed her lips sweetly against his, holding them there for ten seconds or more.

To Silver, that soft brush of her lips against his, as gentle as the touch of a butterfly, seemed quite as intimate as making impassioned love to her. *How long had it been since he'd enjoyed the touch of a woman's lips on his own?* It felt like an eternity ago.

She finally stepped away from him. 'Is that enough "reward" for you, then, Dr Silver?' The tone of her voice now certainly sounded to Silver like mockery.

'More than enough.' He didn't know what else to say, and managed to sound to himself both curt and prudish. Around this girl, fifteen years his junior, it was he who somehow felt like the ingénue, the sexually inexperienced and inept one.

She picked up a lighted oil lamp and moved to the narrow staircase at the back of the kitchen.

'Was tonight really worth it, then?' he asked her resentfully, as she put her foot on the first step. 'All that risking your neck, trying to steal some necklace? And what have you got to show for it, apart from

132

bruises?'

She stopped and returned his quizzical look. 'Actually I have *this* to show for it,' she claimed with quiet pride, as she reached into her jacket pocket and drew out for his astonished inspection a glittering pearl necklace of brilliant pink-white perfection.

'I should have shown you this before since you were instrumental in helping me steal it. Allow me to introduce you to the *Tears of the Prophet*. These particular tears will buy me a tea clipper, the first of many, I hope...'

CHAPTER 13

In the falling dusk, a line of white fog was moving up the Thames estuary like an advancing wall, burying everything in its path. In another half hour, Silver doubted that he would be able to see his hand in front of his face.

He had just driven the directors' carriage from the shipyard to the terminal of the Greenwich Ferry at John Harkness's personal request, taking a pair of visiting dignitaries – a Tory member of parliament and a director of the Eastern Steam Navigation Company - back to meet the paddle steamer for their return journey up river to Westminster and Little Chelsea respectively.

Because of the good work he'd done over the last two days in resolving the problem with the levels on the slipway, Silver was aware that Harkness now treated him almost as a confidante and personal assistant. It was flattering in one sense, yet Silver was increasingly uncomfortable with the close attention of the assistant engineer, because it was naturally making him stand out among the rest of the slipway gang. In addition, this sudden elevation in his standing was also souring his relationship with his foreman, Matthew Spurrell, because Harkness now addressed any technical issues about the construction of the slipway directly to him, rather than to Spurrell as he should.

Silver realized now that he should never have spoken up so freely when in the drawing office on Thursday. He had now marked himself out conspicuously as someone out of the ordinary run of labouring men, so it would be difficult for him to simply become invisible again and merge back into the background. Yet he would have to try, perhaps by playing the dullard until Harkness tired of his company and found someone more appropriate to be his confidante...

Silver was in no hurry to return to the yard, and stood watching the gaily painted paddle steamer as it reversed away from the jetty landing, then turned to pull away forward into the murk, its paddles churning the greasy grey water into cream-brown froth that resembled the head on a pint of porter. Retracing his steps down the length of the jetty to his waiting horses and carriage, he became aware that the jetty was now completely deserted on this Saturday evening apart from one young woman who had apparently got off that same steamer, and was now looking around her uncertainly as if lost.

The young woman – not much more than a girl actually – seemed an unlikely visitor to the Isle of Dogs. From her distracted behaviour, Silver wondered if she had got off here by mistake, instead of at Greenwich on the south side of the river, which seemed a more likely destination for her. If she had got off here by mistake, then she was in a little trouble because there would be no other steamers calling here until tomorrow morning, while the options for getting off the Isle of Dogs by road on a Saturday night were limited, to say the least.

He went over to her with reluctance. Common sense told him that in his situation he should mind his own business, but then common sense was not always defensible: he could hardly abandon this genteel-looking girl possibly to a miserable night alone on this near-deserted jetty.

He doffed his workman's cap to her. 'Beg pardon, miss. But are you waiting for someone?'

Up close, she was certainly a pretty little thing - barely twenty years old, Silver would have said, with flaxen hair and a sweet child's face. Under her white-trimmed bonnet, her blue eyes opened wide with alarm. 'No, not exactly, sir. I...err...need to get to the...err...Napier shipyard,' she stammered nervously. 'I thought it was...very close to this ferry.'

So it seemed she was in the right place after all, although it was perhaps even more intriguing that a girl like this would have some genuine business at the shipyard on a Saturday night, rather than merely being lost. Dressed in a fine burgundy dress with several layers of petticoats beneath, she appeared far too well attired and well-spoken to be a mere maid or serving girl. Yet ladies in such fine apparel were rare visitors to the Napier shipyard except on launch days.

'The entrance gate is only a few hundred yards from here,' Silver reassured her.

The girl blanched a little when she saw the deserted track leading to the jetty. 'There are no cabs for hire here?'

'I'm afraid not. Not much call for cabs on the Isle of Dogs.'

She raised her chin determinedly. 'Then I shall walk.'

'The way there along Ferry Road is very muddy.' Silver glanced down at her burgundy skirt and silver-buckled shoes. 'And it would be a pity to ruin your fine clothes, miss. I work at the yard and have the directors' carriage here. I'm sure the directors wouldn't mind me offering you the use of it for a short time. Please let me drive you to the main gate.'

She was still slightly suspicious of him, but Silver's encouraging smile reassured her sufficiently, and she allowed herself to be persuaded and led to the snug brougham.

'This isn't putting you to any trouble, sir?' she asked him, as he helped her inside into the back seat, which proved a troublesome business because of the many layers of thick petticoats she was wearing. Silver couldn't help noticing that her outer petticoat was scarlet rather than plain cream or white, which gaudy note was an interesting new twist to female fashion as far as he was concerned.

'Not at all, miss. I am finishing work for the day soon, and then I shall be taking myself off home.'

He took the muddied road at a gentle pace so as not to splash too much mud on the fine lacquered woodwork of the carriage. It was still before six but the autumn dusk was descending rapidly now, while the river fog continued to roll in across the flat marshes so that it felt as if the horizon was closing in relentlessly all the time.

In five minutes they had reached the cleaner cobbled road in front of the shipyard gates, where he pulled the brougham to a halt. He got down from the driver's seat to speak to her, and found her snuggled up against the cold in the passenger compartment. 'Do you want to go inside the shipyard, miss, or would you prefer to wait outside?'

She glanced up in trepidation at the vast looming bulk of the *Leviathan*, dominating the miserable grey scene like some giant ancient megalith, and shivered. 'No, I don't need to go inside. Is there an inn nearby, perhaps, where I can wait for my...acquaintance...to arrive?'

Silver was intrigued as to whom she might be meeting. 'There is a tavern down Moss Lane called The Ship, but I fear it's not a suitable place for a lady on her own.'

'You're probably right, sir.' She sighed. 'Then I shall simply have to wait here in the street for a few minutes. Please don't bother yourself about me further, sir. You've been more than kind enough already.'

Silver decided that he had probably done as much as he could for this independent-minded young woman, and took her at her word despite his doubts about leaving her here alone. In the gathering gloom, he did however make one last effort as he helped her out of the back of the carriage. 'Can I perhaps call someone from the yard for you, miss? Is there a particular person you wish to see?'

'Please don't trouble yourself, sir. I shall be perfectly all right waiting here.'

She didn't appear all right, though - in fact rather lost and sweetly forlorn, standing under a solitary gaslight with droplets of moisture from the thickening river fog collecting on her velvet bonnet and her smooth pink cheeks.

But Silver left her anyway, his help apparently no longer required. Climbing up onto the driver's seat again, he drove the brougham in through the main gates and into the cobbled stable yard behind the drawing office where the horses and other company carriages were kept.

Liam's delivery cart was still there, he saw – he was visiting the yard today with deliveries from "Miss Smith's" chandler's store - and Liam himself soon appeared from the back of a nearby brick shed as Silver began unhitching the two elderly horses from the directors' carriage.

Liam's thick carrot-coloured hair was much darker than usual when slicked down with rain, Silver noticed, which gave him a more restrained and mature look than usual, although it hardly made him any more handsome. His smile was as broad and toothy as ever, though, disarming all criticism. 'Jonathan,' he greeted Silver. 'I didn't know you dealt with the horses.'

'Only for today.' Silver explained the situation that had called for him to deputise for the coachman who normally drove the brougham. 'It seems that Jack the driver is laid up in the shipyard infirmary with a badly bruised leg; he took a bad kick on the shins this afternoon from one of the more bad tempered mares in the stables. So Mr Harkness, the engineer for the slipways, asked me to stand in for him and deliver two important visitors safely back to the ferry.'

Liam came over, putting on his tall felt hat. 'Are you about finished for today, then?'

'I am, Liam, as soon as I finish putting these horses in their stalls for the night.'

Liam smiled again. 'Well, I've finished my deliveries to the yard and I'm planning to drive the cart back to Wapping at six, so I'll be very glad to give you a lift home and save you the long walk back to your lodgings.'

In the next ten minutes, Silver had time to sluice himself down at the pump in the entrance yard and change into a fresh shirt, before returning to the stable yard and joining the patient Liam on the front of his rickety old cart. As they rattled over the cobbles leading back to the main gate, Silver couldn't help noticing a fine barouche carriage standing outside the yard under the streetlamp opposite, close to where he had dropped off that determined young lady earlier, although she herself was nowhere to be seen. The driver of the gleaming black barouche was a fierce–looking individual with a rampant black beard and a stovepipe hat wedged tightly on his uncompromising head.

As Liam prodded his old nag through the open gates of the shipyard,

John Harkness appeared from the gatehouse, dressed in frock coat and top hat, and looking the very model of an English gentleman. Liam obligingly stopped the cart as it was clear that Harkness wanted a word. 'Ah, there you are, Wade. Thank you for taking those visitors back to the ferry for me at such short notice. I know it's not your job but you looked to me like someone who could probably handle a carriage without turning it over. And it probably wouldn't have been a good idea killing our illustrious visitors, especially that MP Mr Wilkinson.' He laughed appealingly at the thought. 'At the moment the Eastern Steam Navigation Company needs all the friends in Parliament it can get.'

Silver nodded in the direction of the fine barouche on the other side of the road. 'That's an expensive-looking coach, sir, for such a place as this – much finer even than the directors' brougham.'

Harkness's smile faded. 'Yes, indeed. But then Mr Strode doesn't appear constrained by lack of money like the rest of his colleagues.' With that sour note in his voice, he wished them good night and stood back to let Liam drive through the gates.

On the way past the barouche, Silver did his best to peer discreetly inside the back of that fine carriage. But all he managed to see in the lamp lit interior was the silhouette of a man sitting on the far side of the barouche, and what looked like a woman sitting just out of sight of the near window, her presence given away, though, by her pale hand placed casually on the window rest. The sleeve of her dress might have been burgundy but then, in the gathering darkness of a misty October evening, it could in truth have been any colour at all. Yet Silver had little doubt that this was the young lady he had helped earlier. Apparently the acquaintance she had been looking for was none other than Mr Daniel Strode...

*

'Do you find Miss Smith pretty, Jonathan?' Liam asked innocently.

Silver was unsure how to answer this charged question as the cart trundled along the riverside track back to Wapping. The fog lay so thick about them now that they seemed trapped within a small featureless space of mud and rough marsh grass, as remote and forbidding as the surface of another world. The brass oil lamp swinging on its pole behind the driver's seat seemed like the only point of illumination left in this world of impenetrable darkness.

Silver pulled his greatcoat and scarf tighter around him to ward off the chill of the swirling fog. 'Yes, she's very pretty,' he finally admitted. 'And you, Liam, what do you think of her?'

'I think she's the most perfect creature in the world,' Liam said ingenuously, without even a hint of evasion.

Silver studied Liam's huddled figure with deep misgivings. Liam was a gentle and generous soul who didn't deserve to be misled in this slightly cruel way, so Silver thought he should perhaps try and discourage him from wasting too much of his time in imagining a future with the perfect "Miss Smith". 'Have you any hopes in regard to Miss Smith, Liam? Has she given you any encouragement?'

Liam was a little bemused by the question. 'That's hard for me to answer, Jonathan, since I've never had much romantic encouragement from any woman, as far as I know. I'm not even sure I would recognise it if I saw it. But no, Jonathan, I can't work up my hopes there too highly. Miss Smith is after all an attractive young woman of means, and I'm only a storekeeper and clerk who works for her, that's all. It would be foolish of me even to think I stood some chance with her. I'm hardly a young girl's dream.'

After that they both lapsed into thoughtful silence. With the steady clip-clop of the horse's hooves on the track, Silver soon found himself half-dozing after yet another backbreaking day on the slipway. Yet he was still sufficiently awake to give some more thought to the question of Elisa Saltash...

If he was being frank with himself, Silver found Elisa just as much of an attraction now as Liam did, even if he viewed her in an entirely different way from Liam's rose-coloured perspective. His view of Elisa was far more complex and equivocal, yet he still wasn't sure that he understood her true nature any more than Liam did. In truth she seemed to be a dozen different and complex women all bound up in one body. Businesswoman, friend, actress, performer, loyal daughter, brass-faced hypocrite, temptress, thief...*which of them was she, really?* Perhaps all of them...

Two nights ago she had definitely been in seductress mode, he thought, and he had certainly been in a mood to be tempted by her. Yet in the end he had accepted that sweet little kiss she'd given him as complete payment for his help that night, and spent the rest of the night dutifully on the straw mattress in her kitchen, even though he half-suspected that she'd expected him – even *wanted* him - to follow her up those stairs to her own bedroom and make a more physical claim on her. He wondered why he hadn't done exactly that, when he'd been so sorely tempted. Perhaps it was because he resented being played deliberately like a fish on a line, which he also half-suspected she was doing...

Liam dropped him in Ratcliffe Highway near the top of Old Gravel Lane, as he kept the store cart in the muddy stable yard of a warehouse on the north side of the highway, where "Miss Smith" also kept much of her valuable stock of trade goods under strict lock and key. Silver thought that it was ironic that Elisa imagined she had a right to steal from the rich, yet saw no contradiction in ensuring that her own increasing wealth was well protected from the needy behind high brick walls set with broken glass.

As Silver walked along Ratcliffe Highway, the chilling fog continued to thicken, leaving the streetlights as mere hazy globes of light suspended in a world of white, and the granite cobbles as wet and shining as polished metal. Silver didn't mind walking these Wapping streets on nights like this, when the fog felt like a protective blanket. Yet even Liam had felt obliged to warn him that the peelers were out in numbers on the streets of Wapping and Shadwell tonight, and particularly at the bottom end of Old Gravel Lane, where most of the sailors' lodging houses were concentrated. Silver could only hope that their presence here had more to do with the search for the murderer of that girl in New Gravel Lane four days ago, and less to do with him.

He tried to tell himself that the police couldn't possibly have any evidence that he was hiding in Wapping. How could they, when he could have chosen anywhere in London, or even in the rest of the country, to hide out if he'd wished...?

But maybe the peelers were cleverer than people gave them credit for. Silver still wanted to know who that man with the yellow hair had been, and – if he really was a policeman, or police informer, as he suspected - how he could possibly have recognised Elisa in her convincing guise of a man...

He came to the junction of Old Gravel Lane with Pennington Street, which was dominated along its southern side by the north wall of the London Dock – a wall so high that tonight the top disappeared into the clinging white mist and made the whole edifice seem even taller and more imposing than usual. Pennington Street itself was a richer street than most in Wapping, or at least one with wealthier residents than the mean alleyways and dingy lanes down by the river. Most of the buildings on the north side of Pennington Street were either middle class homes or the premises of small family businesses: drapers, chandlers, bakers, laundries. Some of the houses were even more substantial than that - the homes presumably of well-off merchants and ship captains.

Silver couldn't help noticing a fine carriage parked conspicuously a little way down Pennington Street, outside one of the grander houses on the north side, an 18th century U-shaped building arranged around a central cobbled courtyard, like a small coaching inn. He noted the carriage was a fine black-painted barouche, a vehicle of unusual luxury to be seen in Wapping, even on a wealthier street like Pennington Street. Such fine carriages belonged more naturally to the high society world of Mayfair and the West End. Yet Silver was still about to dismiss the presence of this opulent carriage from his mind and pass on down Old

Gravel Lane, until a thought occurred to him that the proportions and look of this carriage seemed very familiar.

He turned and walked the fifteen yards to the carriage to investigate. The horses – a pair of fine black mares - stirred at his approach, and the driver had to restrain them sharply. Silver muffled his face partly with his scarf as he came closer, not wanting to be recognized by the driver. His precaution was justified as he saw that the driver was indeed the same bearded man who had been in the driving seat of Daniel Strode's barouche at the shipyard on the Isle of Dogs earlier. Therefore, unlikely coincidence as it seemed, this had to be the same carriage, and Daniel Strode was therefore likely to be inside this house in Pennington Street.

Yet according to Jude Crabtree, Strode lived in Bridge Street in Blackfriars so this was certainly not his own residence. So what was Strode doing here in Pennington Street in Wapping? He could simply be visiting an acquaintance, of course, but, with Silver's deep suspicions about the man, he was naturally drawn to consider a more sinister explanation for Strode's unexpected presence here.

Silver glanced up at a lighted window above the courtyard entrance and saw someone moving about in the gas-lit room. Lit prominently by a bright gasolier above her head, a pretty young woman dressed in a fine burgundy outfit was smiling at some unseen companion. Her lips were parted in admiration, her blue eyes even more plainly adoring...

If she had glanced outside at that moment, she could not have failed to see Silver in the street below and perhaps been left to wonder what her saviour from the Millwall ferry terminal might be doing here of all places. But fortunately for Silver, she didn't move her head, her attention instead fixed entirely on the person she was talking to, to the exclusion of all else.

Not wishing to venture his luck further, Silver quickly beat a retreat back down the street towards Old Gravel Lane. He continued to keep his face hidden from the surly bearded driver as the man got his horses moving again and manoeuvred the carriage skilfully under the entrance arch and into the inner courtyard of the building. Since he was bothering to take the carriage into the yard, it seemed that Strode's driver was expecting to be here for some time - perhaps even all night...

Judging from the scene he'd just witnessed inside, Silver too suspected that the driver might have a long wait ahead because that young woman visitor did not look like she would be leaving the house in Pennington Street any time soon. Despite everything, Silver was not so far gone in human feelings that he couldn't recognise a woman in love when he saw one...

*

'So what the bloody hell is going on, Charlie?'

Just as he was hoping to finally go home at seven o'clock on this fogbound Saturday evening, Sergeant Sparrow had received an unwelcome visitor in his room at Shadwell Station – none other than Assistant Commissioner Robert Grindrod in person.

Sparrow was soon made abundantly aware that Grindrod was in an irate mood, as his chief paced back and forward angrily. If anything, Grindrod was even more out of sorts than he had been last week in Whitehall, and, with his thinning red hair damp from the thick East End fog and plastered unattractively to his freckled scalp, looked even balder on top than formerly. The pressure of this job that he'd craved so long was obviously having a telling physical effect on him. At this rate, Sparrow thought morosely, the Assistant Commissioner's once plentiful hair wasn't going to last another week, never mind another year.

Given the circumstances, though, Sparrow had some sympathy with Grindrod's foul mood (which might seem justified to some considering the mess that his minion was presently making of his various cases.) Sergeant Sparrow was the first one to admit that he hadn't exactly covered himself in glory over the last few days. Perhaps he was losing his touch as a detective after all these years, and finally revealing his feet of clay...?

Yet Charlie Sparrow was still in no mood to be browbeaten by a man like Grindrod who had profited so much from his record of successful cases at Shadwell over recent years, so he came out fighting in response. 'What exactly are you referring to, sir?' Sparrow asked him coolly, feigning ignorance of what he knew must have brought Grindrod here tonight, hot foot from his own wealthy patch in Whitehall.

'I mean what the bloody hell were you doing in Berkeley Square on Thursday night?' Grindrod barked.

Sparrow nodded resignedly. 'Ah, that. I had a message from that young turnkey James Minshall. That's what took me to Mayfair.'

'What sort of message?'

Sparrow sighed softly. 'He'd spotted that youth he mentioned to us a week ago. The one living in Wapping who he suspected might have helped Dr Silver escape from Newgate last week.'

Grindrod stopped pacing and settled his bulky frame down in the visitor's chair with a long sigh of his own. Despite that sigh of exasperation, Sparrow could see that the Assistant Commissioner's interest had clearly been aroused by this unexpected connection of Thursday night's embarrassing events to the fugitive doctor. 'And...?' Grindrod demanded.

'Minshall had followed this pretty youth from Wapping to Berkeley Square and thought he was planning to break into a house on the corner there, owned by some rich nabob called Sir Digby something or other.'

'Carfax,' Grindrod interrupted through gritted teeth.

Sparrow hadn't really forgotten Sir Digby's name, although he wished he could. 'Minshall proved to be right on the money about this boy he'd followed. But I'm afraid I wasn't able to stop the thieving beggar from getting away with a necklace of some sort.'

Grindrod picked up the copy of today's *Daily Telegraph* that he'd brought with him. Angrily opening the newspaper and rifling through the inside pages, he found the offending article in question. "*Metropolitan Police Outwitted by Bold Thief*" – that's a fine headline for a man to have to wake up to. The newspapers just love turning us into a laughingstock.' Grindrod twisted his face sourly. 'The necklace in question, by the way, is called the "*Tears of the Prophet*", and in my experience only seriously valuable bits of jewellery get to have names at all, never mind names like that. I had to see Sir Digby today at the Houses of Parliament and apologize in person for our incompetence. Actually *your* incompetence, now I think about it. So tell me, Charlie - how did this boy-thief manage to get away from you and your men?'

'It wasn't quite like that, sir. I didn't have an army of constables waiting to grab him when he shinned down that drainpipe,' Sparrow protested. 'There wasn't time to get more men to the scene in time. Inspector Carew had already gone off duty, and his duty sergeant rightfully wouldn't give me any more of his men to go chasing across London on what might have been a fool's errand. We did well to even get there from the East End in time.'

'There were still three of you, at least,' Grindrod reminded him balefully

'If you include Minshall himself,' Sparrow argued weakly. 'But Minshall is not a policeman.'

'You still let a slip of a boy make monkeys of you all,' Grindrod growled.

Sparrow puffed out his cheeks. 'Yes, I'm afraid we did. But that boy can climb in a most unnatural manner, sir, so perhaps there is something to Minshall's theory that this pretty boy helped Silver escape from Newgate. The back wall to that garden was fifteen feet high, if it was an inch, without the slightest toehold or finger hold, and topped, to boot, by broken glass embedded in mortar. I don't know how any normal flesh-and-blood person could have got over it – the boy must have supernatural skills to have managed it! Or else he's a circus performer of some sort. By the time we got hold of the key to the back gate from Sir Digby's manservant, and made our way into the mews lane behind, the thief was long gone.'

'How did you get into the back garden in the first place, then?'

Sparrow made a wry face. 'Through the front garden, of course, and then along the side of the house. That was easier than trying to get in the back way as the thief apparently did.'

Grindrod settled back in his chair again, his anger not so much abated as subsided into grim despair. 'So you now believe that Minshall might be right about this young jewel thief? But why would this pretty boy thief help Silver escape? And how would Silver even know such a person?'

'I don't know, sir, but there is a chance that the boy is still helping Silver by finding him a place to hide in Wapping or Shadwell. You yourself thought that Silver would lie low for a while before he tried to leave the country, and Wapping is certainly the perfect place for that.'

Grindrod frowned. 'Have you had any sightings or reports of Silver on your patch to back this theory up?'

'It's just possible that we have. One of the uniformed constables here at the station – Kennally - saw a man help a local girl fight off a couple of drunken sailors in Ratcliffe Highway last Monday night. The man and the girl both ran off, though, when Kennally got close to the scene. According to Kennally, there's a chance the man might have been Silver – the description matched, particularly the height. At least six feet two inches.'

Grindrod sniffed, unimpressed. 'There could be ten thousand young men of that height in London. Who was the girl?'

'Kennally doesn't know her name, although he thinks she lives down New Gravel Lane somewhere. If we can find her, she might know where Silver is hiding, assuming it was him. The fact that she ran off, though, might suggest that she has something to hide from the law too, so she's unlikely to come forward voluntarily.'

Grindrod grunted dismissively. 'It still doesn't sound much to go on.'

'Perhaps not,' Sparrow admitted. 'But I do agree with you now, sir, that Silver may not have made a quick run for it yet, so could be hiding somewhere in this neck of the woods. I've started sending out a team of my constables to check every lodging house in the neighbourhood to see if any very tall young men have recently taken up residence. You never know, if we find Silver, he may return the compliment and lead us to this pretty youth with the light fingers and a taste for expensive jewellery, rather than vice-versa.' Grindrod was looking a little too hopeful after this optimistic assessment of the situation, so Sparrow thought that he'd better dampen his expectations a little, otherwise the Assistant Commissioner would no doubt be telling his political masters that both cases - the jewel theft, and the recapture of Dr Silver - were already as good as closed. 'Unfortunately, at the moment though, Inspector Carew can't spare any of his men for the job of finding Silver...he has even asked me to concentrate on another matter entirely…'

Grindrod grimaced. 'Ah, yes. You had a nasty murder here last week. The Home Secretary, Sir George Grey, asked me only today if we were making any progress in catching this evil villain. This is a crime that has shocked the whole city, it seems. I have offered Inspector Carew more detective resources if he needs them…'

'I can understand the shock, sir. We're even more shocked about it here, since it took place in our own backyard, so to speak. A nice young lady, Miss Charlotte Livingstone, strangled and her body dumped on waste ground near New Gravel Lane. I don't know what the East End is coming to; it didn't used to be like this. Oh, we've always had our drunken brawls, and our men folk knocking their wives' front teeth out from time to time. But strangling a pretty young woman in broad daylight? I don't see any local man doing a wicked thing like that. This must be an outsider – maybe some jealous lover of the woman acting on an evil impulse.'

Grindrod frowned. 'Couldn't her death be something to do with Silver? If he is hiding out here, then it's quite a coincidence that a young ladylike woman like Miss Livingstone should be horribly murdered within a few days of his escape.'

Sparrow was sceptical. 'I can't see any likely connection with Silver, sir. Even if he did kill his wife, he isn't the sort to go strangling women at random. My money is on Miss Livingstone having been killed by a jealous acquaintance, not by Silver.'

Grindrod shook his head sadly. 'You still give some credence to this nonsensical speculation about Silver being innocent, don't you?'

Sparrow shifted uneasily in his chair. 'I wouldn't put it that strongly, sir. But if he *is* a murderer, he certainly doesn't fit the customary mould...'

*

On his way home, Silver soon turned off Old Gravel Lane and took a circuitous route home in the hope of avoiding the patrolling peelers that Liam had warned him about. His roundabout route therefore brought him presently past the entrance to the Hostel for Women in New Gravel Lane where young Amy McLennan lived and worked.

But if he had been hoping to see her pretty face at the door again, taking the evening air as she had last Thursday, he was doomed to disappointment. Yet with the fog thickening tonight into a dense pea souper that chilled everything to the marrow, it was no real surprise that it had driven most people indoors.

He passed on rapidly and was a hundred yards further down the road, near the Black Horse public house, when he heard footsteps running urgently behind him. Fortunately they didn't sound like a peeler's heavy hobnailed footsteps, so he didn't make a guilty dash for it, but turned as casually as he could to see who it was. He was pleasantly relieved to find that it was Amy running after him at top speed, her skirts flying and her hair in disarray. She clearly wasn't running after him for any casual reason, though, but instead seemed to be in a panic of some sort.

'Mr Wade, thank the Lord I saw you walkin' past! There's been an accident – Ginny has fallen down some stairs and is in a pitiable state. Please come and do what you can for her. If you were a sailor, then p'raps you have some doctorin' skills, do you?' she added hopefully.

'Yes, a little,' Silver agreed cautiously.

That was enough reassurance for Amy and she turned immediately and ran back to the hostel, Silver following closely on her heels.

The hostel was bigger on the inside than Silver had expected - a sizeable three-storey 18th century lodging house of plaster lathe walls and timber columns, built around a cobbled stable yard, with continuous open galleries running around the yard on each level. But Amy led Silver straight across the yard, through a low doorway and along a narrow whitewashed corridor, to the kitchen.

A middle-aged woman was lying groaning with pain on the stone flagged floor, at the foot of a timber staircase. Despite the agony that was twisting her face into ugly expressions, Silver could still detect a resemblance to young Billy Faber from the yard.

'You must be Billy Faber's mother?' he said to her, as he knelt down beside her.

The woman was in too much distress to answer, and screamed again with the pain.

'Yes, this is Ginny, Billy's mum,' Amy confirmed. 'She slipped on the loose plankin' on the stairs. This is my fault. I've been meanin' to get it seen to.'

'Where's the pain, Ginny?' Silver asked the stricken woman gently. 'Show me, if you can't tell me.'

'In my...right arm...at the top. I can't...move it,' Ginny moaned through gritted teeth.

Silver began to feel the arm, looking for breaks, first in the carpals, then the radius and ulna, and finally in the humerus. He turned his face up to Amy. 'I don't think there's anything broken. She's dislocated her shoulder – pulled her upper arm clean out of the socket. We need to pull it back into place as soon as we can. You'll have to help hold her still.'

Silver lifted Ginny up into the best position he could get her for the delicate operation, then showed Amy how to hold her from behind. At her own initiative Amy found a handkerchief for Ginny to bite on, to stop her chewing off her own tongue. Silver was pleasantly surprised at how quickly Amy grasped everything that he told her to do, particularly clamping Ginny into such a tight professional nursing hold.

Then he began to apply tension to the arm while manoeuvring the joint at the top. Ginny screamed loud enough to shake the rafters, then fell into a faint, but only after Silver had heard a satisfying click as the top of her arm returned into its rightful place.

Amy looked at him with undisguised admiration. 'This is gettin' to be a 'abit, Mr Wade. You savin' my neck, I mean.'

Silver returned her look with equal admiration, plus a smile. 'Well, it is a very pretty neck, so it's certainly worth saving...'

CHAPTER 14

Sunday 18th October 1857

Sergeant Sparrow had decided by now that working in a tanner's yard was probably not for him. The stink was indescribable for one thing; and the drudgery and unpleasantness of working in such an evil-smelling place made this appear quite as bad a choice of career as being a night soil collector. Yet, glancing around at the miserable stunted examples of humanity who cleansed the hides in this yard, it seemed likely that they had little choice in the matter of their life's work. No chance of an undemanding 9:30 – 3:30 job in the City as a bank teller or a lawyer's clerk for uneducated wretches like these; no hope of these sons of Hibernia ever making three pounds a week sitting cosily behind a counter, or wearing a neat tweed suit and a clean white collar to work every day.

Fortunately most tanners were based in Bermondsey on the south side of the river, so Sparrow normally had little direct acquaintance with them or their poisonous trade. Yet there were other smaller yards dotted all over the East End too, including this one in Albion Street just north of Ratcliffe Highway. Manufacturing leather was, after all, a profitable business - the fourth biggest industry in England after cotton, wool and iron, so they said. As a consequence, vast numbers of animal skins – goat, seal, buffalo - were imported from all over the world through the London Dock to end up in the tanners' yards of London, so the location of this yard made perfect sense.

This particular business, Warren's Tanners, had two long brick sheds with dirty broken windows, rusted iron truss roofs, and an atmosphere redolent of the outer reaches of Hades. Having this close personal connection to Hell, the owners of Warren's Tanners obviously didn't feel the need to keep the Lord's Day completely sacred since the place still seemed to be working after a fashion, despite the summoning

Sunday morning sound of church bells all over the East End.

The long brick sheds were filled with circular vats and bubbling chemicals and animal hides in the process of being transformed into leather, the whole nausea-inducing operation being manned by weary-looking men in stained aprons with complexions very like the leather they made. Sparrow imagined that if he had worked in a place like this for twenty years, then he too would be similarly complexioned by now. In front of the sheds was a sizeable cobbled yard, awash in greenish-white wastewater and other unmentionable slops.

Sparrow again examined the body that had been recently pulled from the outdoor sunken lime tank located in front of the two main sheds, and had a disturbing feeling of déjà vu. Apart from the fact that this girl and her clothes had been partly bleached to a chalky white by the lime solution in the tank, she nevertheless bore an uneasy resemblance to Miss Charlotte Livingstone.

Frank Remmert's youthful and vapid mind wasn't always the easiest for Charlie Sparrow to read – usually there wasn't much going on in there at all, in Sparrow's honest opinion. But Sparrow could see in this case that his younger colleague was thinking much the same thing as himself. Was some devious person luring pretty young women to Wapping and then murdering them in horrid ways?

If he was, then this individual must have a singularly accomplished silver tongue because Sergeant Sparrow doubted that he could even persuade his own wife Edie to venture anywhere near Wapping any more, even though she'd been born in this very parish. But then Edie was becoming quite the bourgeois lady of late in her little house in Lambeth, and didn't much care to be reminded of her lowly origins as a street trader's daughter from the East End...

Sparrow had been enjoying a Sunday morning lie-in in Lambeth this morning when Edie had rushed upstairs to tell him there was a police growler waiting for him outside and that he was needed urgently back in Wapping. Inspector Carew had asked for him personally to go to the scene of a suspected crime, so Sparrow had realised it must be something important if Carew was prepared to overlook his longstanding resentment against the detective force and ask directly for his help. Sparrow hadn't even had time to shave or wash, and he now felt his bristly chin with a definite residual resentment at his disturbed Sunday. He turned to the tannery manager again, a grizzled moustachioed Yorkshireman called Ernest Harvey.

'Who found the body, Mr Harvey?' Sparrow asked.

'Yon gatekeeper, old Will, at about seven.' The manager pointed out an ancient bent man, bearded like a patriarch, and so small of stature that his beard seemed the most massive thing about him. 'I think he'd fallen asleep in his hut by 't gate,' Harvey went on, 'so anyone could have walked reet past him. I can't blame poor old bugger, though, at his age.'

'And he fished her out?'

Harvey twisted his already twisted face even more. 'He said he did.'

'She was found fully dressed, like this?'

'She was indeed. I thought she might have fallen in't tank by accident, like, but that can't be. Anyway I soon noticed the marks on her neck where she'd been strangled. Must have been a strong man to make marks like that.'

Sparrow agreed privately with that. 'Who owns this yard, Mr Harvey? Is it yours?'

Harvey shifted his feet uneasily. 'No, it's not mine. I wish it were. It belongs to an unmarried business lady who lives nearby.'

Sparrow frowned. 'A rich spinster woman, then?'

Harvey shrugged. 'I think you'd have to say she's nobbut a girl, really. But anyway, she seems to be someone who knows exactly what she's doing. She only bought 't yard from old Mr Warren in't summer, but she has big ideas for improving things.'

A crowd of curious sightseers had gathered at the gate, undeterred by the pervading smell of lime and pures. Pures – dog turds - were an indispensable part of the tanning process, being needed to remove the lime from the skins after they'd been soaked for several weeks to dissolve the hair. As a result tanners paid ninepence a bucket for the pures, which were therefore avidly collected - even fought over - by the street urchins and ragamuffins of London.

This young woman still had her hair at least so could only have been in the pit a matter of minutes at most before she was found. Sparrow imagined that it must have been very nice hair once, probably lustrous flaxen curls rather than these dismal sodden remains.

'Her name is Jane Penfold, Sarge,' Remmert announced confidently, with the air of a conjuror producing a rabbit from a hat. 'In case you're wondering.'

Sparrow snorted in disbelief. 'How the bloody hell do you know that already?'

'I found a label sewn into her outer petticoat. And a red petticoat too, which might tell us something.'

'You're an expert on ladies fashion now, are you, Frank?' Sparrow muttered sarcastically.

Remmert blushed slightly. 'No, but I've never seen a nice respectable girl wearing anything but white or cream petticoats, have you? I mean, red is for tarts or actresses, isn't it?'

Sparrow reserved judgement on that. 'She's fully dressed underneath, is she, like Miss Livingstone?'

Remmert coughed delicately. 'Yes, wearing thick winter woollen drawers. And only been dead for a few hours, I would say, so she couldn't have been killed long before the gatekeeper found her. I'd say she was strangled in the street early this morning, then dumped soon after in the lime tank. There wouldn't be much left of her hair by now, if she'd been in there longer than that.'

Frank was probably right, Sparrow concurred, but that still didn't explain why another nicely dressed young lady like this had been apparently walking on the streets of Wapping on her own, and particularly at such an ungodly hour. Sparrow had spent many years in and around Wapping and Shadwell and couldn't ever remember seeing any ladies promenading here on their own, and certainly not first thing in the morning.

Turning his view towards the crowd who had gathered in ghoulish silence at the gate of the tanner's yard, Sparrow's attention was drawn to a flash of colour among these otherwise colourless spectators. There weren't many individuals with hair that distinctive yellow colour, so he realized that the tall person standing at the back of the five-deep crowd had to be the turnkey James Minshall, despite the man's apparent attempts to conceal himself among the curious spectators. Sparrow sighed. 'What's *he* doing here, do you think?' he asked Remmert.

'Don't know.' Frank Remmert didn't much care either, judging from the flat uninterested tone of his voice.

But Sparrow was more curious about what Minshall was doing here and, finally catching the turnkey's reluctant eye, beckoned him over.

Minshall seemed even more reluctant to come over, though – perhaps because there'd been some harsh words spoken between them on Thursday night after that debacle in Berkeley Square. Minshall had blamed him for allowing the thief to escape, and Sparrow – while accepting some of the truth of the charge – had been angry to hear such complaints from a mincing and effeminate bum boy like Minshall.

But eventually Minshall was persuaded to push his way through the crowd and come into the tanner's yard. Sparrow decided to conceal his resentment of the man for the moment and greeted him politely enough, as the man approached the lime pit uneasily, picking his feet carefully like a woman to avoid the murky greenish puddles filling the yard. Yet Sparrow still couldn't prevent a first sour remark escaping his lips. 'There seems to be dead women wherever you go in Wapping, Mr Minshall.' The remark had been no more than an innocuous one, yet it set Sparrow's own suspicious mind instantly racing. Could this man Minshall have something to with the deaths of these women himself? It was not entirely outside the bounds of possibility, although Minshall certainly didn't look the sort of man who could commit a crime of passion. Not over a woman, anyway...

Minshall was in a subdued mood, as he examined the damage that the filthy water in the yard had done to his expensive boots. 'I'm not sure what you're suggesting, Sergeant. Anyway, I didn't find this one, did I? I merely saw there was a crowd gathered here, so wondered what was going on.'

Sparrow grunted petulantly. He still blamed Minshall in return – perhaps unfairly, it had to be said – for the embarrassment of Thursday night. Sparrow was aware that his name was now being bandied about in the Met as a laughingstock, especially by that damned Irish troublemaker from Piccadilly Station, Inspector Murphy. But Sparrow was determined to have the last laugh on his colleagues. He was going to catch Silver and his boy-thief accomplice, wherever they were hiding, and make Murphy and the rest of them eat their words.

But, even more urgently, he was going to catch this evil devil who was strangling young women on the streets of Wapping in broad daylight...

*

Silver had got up early that day and gone to the new public baths in Whitechapel, which were a welcome addition to the East End's public amenities, given that few people in the East End had running water in their homes, and even fewer had hot water and their own bathrooms. In that grand red brick building it was possible to enjoy the luxury of a steamy hot shower, and then swim in a clean swimming pool if you wanted. It cost a whole shilling to use the facilities - a lot of money with his original ten pounds from Elisa dwindling rapidly - but it was worth it to Silver for the chance to rid himself of the bugs from the Steams' lodging house, and for the sensation of feeling truly human again. Afterwards, he did feel as if he had sloughed off a whole evil layer of himself, like a snake shedding old skin, and had emerged as a new and cleansed man again.

It was on his return to Wapping, with his skin still tingling and pink from the jet of hot water in the baths, that he saw a procession of people moving eastwards down Ratcliffe Highway towards Shadwell. His curiosity was aroused despite his situation, and he followed them discreetly for a while, wanting to discover the object of their interest.

The procession soon joined with others to form a motley crowd at the gate to an evil-smelling tanner's yard in Albion Street.

Silver, with his significant advantage of height over the general population, could see with ease over the heads of his fellow spectators into the tanner's yard where a group of uniformed peelers was gathered around a sunken lime tank.

Standing a little in front of them was a nondescript man of forty, with mousy brown hair and thick moustache, and dressed in a suit badly in need of the attentions of a flat iron. He had the uncomfortable look of a bank clerk who had walked into a factory yard by mistake and was now severely regretting his error of judgement. A gangly police constable with a lumpish unprepossessing face stood taking notes at his side, together with a grizzled older man who looked more like he truly belonged in this place. The older man's frock coat was stained with white from the lime solution in the pit, while his rabbit-skin stovepipe hat was wafting about so much in the blustery wind that it seemed in imminent danger of carrying itself and its wearer into the evil-looking pit, if he wasn't careful.

But, despite his initial interest in these three principal characters in the tanner's yard, Silver's attention soon shifted inevitably to the object laid out at their feet. It appeared to be the body of a young woman, yet a woman who seemed to have been drained unexpectedly of all colour. *Had she been found in that lime pit?* Silver wondered. Did that explain her deathly white appearance?

But then he felt the colour fading from his own face as he suddenly spotted the woman's silver-buckled shoes and the trace of red colour remaining in her petticoat, and realized who she was...

This was the pretty girl he had seen at the Millwall ferry terminal last evening, the one who had gone off in Daniel Strode's carriage, and who he had later seen at the house in Pennington Street not far from here...

Silver's mind was churning with alarm, but his alarm turned almost to panic when he caught sight of a fourth man, standing a little apart from the body and the three other men grouped in deep discussion about it. This other man was an individual with golden hair, and Silver immediately began to back away through the crowd when he realized it was the very same man who had followed Elisa on her burglary expedition on Thursday night. The man he suspected of being a police informer...

But in his sudden desperation to be gone, Silver moved a little too quickly and the yellow-haired man, perhaps attracted by Silver's sudden movement among the crowd, happened to see him.

The man stared at him for a second, then started running towards him, barging straight into the crowd, and yelling for someone to stop him. Worse still, some of the peelers in the tanner's yard were indeed taking up his call and following him.

Silver ran for his life back towards Ratcliffe Highway. His only hope lay in getting across the highway into Wapping and then disappearing into the maze of back alleys down by the river that he was beginning to know quite well by now.

He ran straight across Ratcliffe Highway without breaking his stride, avoiding a horse-bus, and a brewery dray loaded with heavy beer barrels, by a whisker.

He could still hear his pursuers right behind him, though, as well as the curses of the angry dray driver. Yet his suicidal spurt across that busy main road had won him a precious few seconds' respite, because Yellow Hair and his accompanying peeler friends didn't seem so cavalier with their lives and had taken a little more time carefully threading their way between the heavy carts and buses. With these valuable few seconds gained, and with the natural speed of his long legs, Silver managed to increase the clear distance between him and his pursuers by a few more yards and was able to turn off into a side street without being seen by his pursuers. Or at least he hoped so anyway. He found himself eventually – almost inevitably, it seemed - in New Gravel Lane near the Hostel for Women.

Amy McLennan was standing at the gateway to the women's hostel, her familiar blue woollen shawl wrapped tightly around her, as Silver approached at a gallop, breathing hard.

Her eyes opened wide. 'What's wrong, Mr Wade?'

'Police are chasing me,' he admitted ruefully, skidding to a halt.

He was about to run on, but Amy checked him with a slender white arm.

'Quick. In 'ere.' She led him by the hand into the inner yard, and then to a door on the south side. Inside was a storeroom for horse tackle: wrinkled old leather saddles and worn harnesses, dusty with age. There was a large square bin inside, formed with wooden slat walls and filled with musty old horse blankets. With surprising strength she heaved some of the blankets out to make space for him, then almost pressed him down inside the bin, and threw the blankets back over him.

Through a knothole in the warped timber of the outer wall of the storeroom, Silver was able to see the yard, if not to breathe easily, with the weight of all these stiff old blankets on top of him and their heavy horsy smell invading his lungs.

Amy quickly retreated to the yard where she picked up a broom and began innocently sweeping the dusty cobbles.

From his convenient vantage point, Silver saw Yellow Hair arrive first. He burst into the stable yard on his own and practically grabbed Amy by her arm.

She wrestled herself free and pointed the business end of the broom at him. 'Ere, wot do ye think yer doin'?' she demanded, outraged, using it like a weapon to keep him at bay.

Yellow Hair retreated a safe distance from the end of the broom and glanced around the yard quizzically, looking for anything out of the ordinary. Hardly out of breath at all, he had the air of a persistent hound on the scent of a fox. 'Did you see a man run in here, girl? A tall bearded man. Handsome sort of cove.'

Amy seemed genuinely resentful and not merely acting the part. 'I ain't seen any man, 'andsome or otherwise.' She threatened Yellow Hair again with the broom, and he was forced to skip back a step or two as if he was doing a jig.

Two police constables arrived in the wake of Yellow Hair, then the moustachioed man, who Silver now realized must be a senior detective of some sort, rather than the bank clerk he had first appeared to be from his staid appearance. The man was in as poor a physical condition as a bank clerk, though, it seemed, his lungs heaving far worse than any of his uniformed colleagues after his quarter-mile run from Albion Street.

'What are you doing with that girl, Mr Minshall? Dancing with her?' the detective asked Yellow Hair sarcastically, as he tried to force some air back into his lungs.

Silver almost jumped inside his dusty hiding place when he heard the name of the yellow-haired man. Minshall wasn't a common family name, so this could only be the snooping young turnkey from Newgate, the one old Gardiner had been so sorely afraid of, on the night of the escape. And with good reason it seemed...

Minshall gave Amy a threatening look and she finally desisted with the broom. 'I'm almost sure Silver ran in here, Sergeant. And this girl must have seen him if she's been here for some time.'

The police detective was finally getting his wheezing breath under some sort of control again. 'Are you sure it was actually Silver you saw, Mr Minshall?'

'I'm positive.' Minshall turned to the two constables for support, but neither seemed as sure in their identification of the fugitive as Minshall. One, a good-looking fair-haired lad, shook his head, saying he hadn't got a good look at the man running away, while the other, the same lumpish-faced constable Silver had seen back at the tanner's yard, was equally unforthcoming. 'He was tall and bearded, Sarge, that's all I can say.'

Minshall was rapidly losing his patience. 'That was definitely Silver I saw, Sergeant Sparrow. I promise you I'd recognize him anywhere. And he could be hiding in this very hostel.'

Silver blinked again on hearing that name. *Sparrow!* Where had he heard that name before? Then he remembered Elisa's father telling him in Newgate about the policeman who had arrested him at Gravesend.

So this ordinary-looking man with the coarse hair and moustache had to be none other than the ruthless police detective who had caught

Elisa's father and got him condemned to death. The one Elisa had later sworn vengeance against...

*

Sergeant Sparrow debated for a few seconds, before apparently deciding that Minshall might have a case. He barked a peremptory order to his two constables to begin searching the hostel from top to bottom.

'Who are you lookin' for?' Amy asked in apparent bewilderment. 'And who is this man Silver you're talkin' about?'

'Never you mind about his name, girl,' Sparrow said, repeating his order to his men. 'We're looking for a fugitive; that's all you need to know! And we are going to search this hostel for him...'

'Not 'im,' Amy protested, pointing at Minshall as he moved forward to join the peelers in their search of the premises. 'He's no copper. So 'e can't come in. I want that man out of 'ere. 'E 'urt my arm, the brute.'

Sparrow accepted that, apparently not wishing to provoke the ire of this feisty young lady further. 'You'd better go and look elsewhere, Mr Minshall. Silver might have run further on towards the river...assuming it was him anyway.'

Minshall glowered. 'It was.'

But Minshall did finally leave under protest, if muttering strongly under his breath.

Silver stayed put in his musty hiding place, while Amy followed the two policemen to the main entrance into the hostel and tried her best to get in front of them. 'And you two 'ad better knock before you enter any of the rooms. There's only women 'ere, no men,' Silver heard her say.

More policemen arrived to aid the search which went on for half an hour or more, with much bad tempered protesting from the women residents of the hostel. Eventually a crowd of angry women, mostly young, some half-dressed, had gathered in the yard to make their resentful feelings plain. Silver almost enjoyed seeing the discomfort of Sergeant Sparrow as he was threatened and jostled by the women.

'Bleedin' cheek,' one forthright girl with no front teeth was saying. 'A bobby comin' into my room without so much as a by your leave...'

Sparrow was standing his ground remarkably well, though, so was obviously made of stern stuff. He turned to the fair-haired constable and pointed to Silver's hiding place. 'Kennally, have you looked in that door over there? It looks like a storeroom.'

Constable Kennally reluctantly obliged, although he looked as if he would much rather get as far away from this place as possible before these noisy and clamorous girls had the trousers off him. He opened the door of the storeroom and poked around in desultory fashion, while Silver held his breath. Eventually Silver sensed him standing over the bin where he was hiding, and felt his body becoming rigid with tension at the thought of discovery. As the bobby removed a few of the blankets from the top of the pile covering him, Silver thought that the beating of his heart must surely give him away.

But then a fresh commotion erupted outside in the yard, which luckily caused Kennally to stop abruptly with his search and return to the courtyard to see what had happened.

Silver put his eye to the knothole again. A young woman, the top half of her breasts nearly bare, was standing up to Sparrow, complaining loudly. ''Ere! That constable of yours just touched my arse, the ugly devil,' she spat out. 'I wouldn't 'ave minded the pretty one touchin' my backside, but not 'im.'

The lumpish-faced constable gave a hapless grin. 'I never touched her, Sarge.'

Sparrow finally admitted defeat as Constable Kennally told him that he'd found nothing in the storeroom. 'Let's go, then. It seems that Mr Minshall got it wrong and Silver's not here.' Under his breath he added morosely, 'And even if he is, he's welcome to it...'

But the good-looking Constable Kennally now spoke up, nodding at Amy, standing quietly at the edge of all this female mayhem. 'You know, Sarge, I'm almost sure that's the girl I saw last week being attacked by those two villainous sailors in Ratcliffe Highway. You remember – the one who was helped by a tall man who Mr Minshall told me he thought might have been Silver.'

Sergeant Sparrow gave the constable a weary look before forcing his way through the crowd of clamorous women to confront Amy. 'So, what of it, my girl? Did two sailors accost you in Ratcliffe Highway last Monday night?'

Silver didn't know where Amy had acquired her acting skills, but a *grande dame* on the stage at Drury Lane could never have lied half as convincingly as this slip of a girl. 'They did not.'

Sparrow squinted at her. 'Are you sure?'

'Sure. In fact I'm as sure as my name's Amy McLennan...'

*

An hour or more had passed before Amy came to the storeroom to tell Silver that the coast was clear. 'It's all right, Mr Wade. They've gone.'

He struggled to his feet, as she helped remove the heavy blankets. 'Just as well. I was beginning to think that being taken by the police might not be so bad after all. I just had a bath this morning and now I stink of horse again.'

'Oh, don't make such a fuss! You smell fine,' Amy said complacently.

Out in the yard, now quiet again after all the hostel residents had dispersed to their particular tasks for the day, Silver went warily to the main gateway and peered up and down New Gravel Lane. He didn't put it past Sparrow that he would have left a man behind to secretly watch the hostel.

Ginny Faber appeared from a doorway at the back of the yard with her arm in a sling. She smiled gratefully at Silver.

'How's the arm, Mrs Faber?' he asked her.

'Fine, thanks to you, sir. A real doctor couldn't 'ave done a better job.' She fell silent under Amy's reproving glance, and moved away. 'Got to get on with my work, sir,' she said, excusing herself.

'Don't lift anything with that arm for at least three days,' Silver warned her before she left, aware that Amy was paying him close attention. Finally he returned her curious look.

'So, Mr Wade, wot 'ave you really done,' she inquired, 'that so many peelers should want to nab yer?'

He shrugged. 'I told you. I'm wanted for debt, that's all.'

Amy made a wry face. ''Ave you 'eard that there's been another girl found murdered this mornin', not a quarter mile from here?' Her dark eyes became serious. 'Yer'll 'ave to give me your word that it's nothin' to do with you.'

'I haven't killed anyone, Amy. I promise. Nor even stolen anything.'

She nodded thoughtfully, and seemed to accept that assurance without question. Yet Silver could still almost see the gears and cogs of her brain working. 'That policeman was talkin' about a fugitive called Silver, not you, Mr Wade…' Then clear understanding dawned in Amy's eyes as she apparently remembered the significance of that name "Silver".

This time her acting skills let her down completely because her jaw fell abruptly as she clearly realized the dismal truth.

The silence between them was both tense and deeply embarrassing.

What do I do now? he asked himself helplessly. *She knows who I really am…*

*

Mrs Steams folded her arms across her huge bosom. 'I'm sorry about my 'usband, Mr Wade. The man 'as the brains of an ass.' She giggled. 'Or 'e would 'ave, if he tried 'arder, anyways.'

After leaving Amy, Silver had hidden down by the river in an old tavern for most of the day. No one asked questions in a place like that, provided you spent money on grog anyway.

Eventually he'd had to make a move, though. With darkness falling, he had crept through dismal fogbound alleyways to his lodging house in Gun Alley. The news from his landlady wasn't reassuring, though.

'What about your husband?' Silver tried to remain calm, but could feel an imaginary noose tightening around his neck.

Mrs Steams leaned forward conspiratorially to show off the deep valley between her immense breasts. Silver could smell the Dutch gin on her breath, powerful enough to knock a horse over.

'A couple of peelers were 'ere this evening, Mr Wade. Wanted to know whevver we 'ad any new lodgers recently. Young and very tall lodgers.' She licked her lips. ''Andsome even.'

She pressed herself against Silver in the narrow corridor outside his room. 'Well, I wouldn't 'ave told them anythin', myself. Bastard peelers. But my 'usband 'asn't the brains 'e was born wiv, and 'e gave them your name, Mr Wade, afore I could stop 'im. So they said they would be back tonight to talk to you. I 'ope that's not too much inconwenience...'

CHAPTER 15

Sunday 18th October 1857

Silver crept into her backyard and knocked gently at the kitchen door. 'Elisa,' he called softly.

A bolt was slid open almost immediately, as if she had been standing on the other side of the door waiting for him to knock. 'I thought you agreed not to come here any more, Jonathan,' she whispered severely through the crack in the door.

'I know, but this is urgent. I came to warn you.'

She opened the door wider. 'About what?'

'About a turnkey called Minshall. And a policeman called Sparrow.'

She finally opened the door fully, standing silhouetted against the low gaslight from the kitchen, with her head surrounded by a halo of luminescence like a medieval image of the Madonna. 'Then you'd better come in after all,' she said with a sigh.

*

He sat at her kitchen table while she brought him some fish stew, the remnants of her own supper. He had wanted to decline her offer of food, almost as a matter of pride, but he found he had a ravenous hunger by now and couldn't resist the aroma coming from the pot.

Elisa was still the mistress of deception and metamorphosis, it appeared, because tonight she seemed yet again an entirely different version of Elisa Saltash from any he'd encountered previously. Tonight he could recognize no trace of the wealthy local businesswoman Miss Elisa Smith, nor of the poor locksmith's daughter from Pershore, nor even of the bold jewel thief dressed in men's trousers. Wearing a cream lace bodice and chocolate brown skirt, her shoulders wrapped in a bright yellow crocheted shawl, she had the comforting image of an innocent young country girl. Her thick russet-tinted hair was down, plaited behind, and glowing in the firelight.

The fire burned brightly in the hearth to warm the room, while outside the icy fog pressed against the black windows like a malevolent spirit. The warmth and comfort of his situation should have improved Silver's mood after a tense and trying day, but in fact the homeliness of the scene was sending him into a deep reflective melancholy. No man could truly appreciate the simple pleasures of home and hearth, of a warm kitchen and a crackling coal fire, of a pretty woman ministering patiently to his needs, until they'd had all this taken away from them. Paradoxically, despite his present state of comfort, he had never felt more of a fugitive than he did tonight. Truly it seemed now as if, outside these four walls, the whole world was against him, and there was no one else to turn to for comfort or sanctuary, except for this enigmatic girl. Yet, in truth, she seemed to be in as much trouble as him – perhaps even more.

Yet Elisa seemed unperturbed by the seriousness of her own difficult situation, as Silver began explaining about going to Whitechapel this morning, and how he had happened to follow that crowd of curious sightseers along Ratcliffe Highway.

'*Another* dead woman?' Elisa asked uncomfortably, when she heard this disturbing news.

'Yes.' Silver frowned. 'You mean you hadn't heard?' Somehow he expected Elisa to know everything that was going on in this neighbourhood, almost before it happened.

'I haven't been over the doors today,' she explained, 'nor have I seen anyone to talk to.'

For the first time Silver had an inkling that Elisa perhaps led a lonely life for someone so young. Still, loneliness was not the commonest problem in the East End, nor perhaps the worst. With families living four or more to a room, keeping a roof over your head and finding food to fill your belly were much commoner problems for the poor and destitute.

'And where exactly was this woman's body found?' Elisa went on.

'In a tanner's yard in Albion Street.'

Her eyes widened. 'Warren's Yard, you mean?'

Silver was surprised by her change of tone. 'Yes, I think that was the name of the place.'

Elisa bit her lip. 'Then that's an unfortunate complication.'

'Why?'

She half-smiled in embarrassment, as she sat down at the table beside him. 'Because I *own* that tanner's yard, that's why.'

*

After this unexpected revelation, Silver continued his story and told her of the chase that had ensued, and how he had learned the identities of his pursuers.

Elisa's mind was working rapidly. 'So it was this turnkey Minshall who was following me on Thursday night?'

'Yes, exactly. And Minshall is now working with this Sergeant Sparrow, so they must be on *your* trail as well as mine, Elisa. For all I know, that might have been Sparrow who nearly caught you in Berkeley Square, escaping from Sir Digby Carfax's house.'

'Sparrow is based at Shadwell Station, not the West End, so I think that unlikely,' she observed tartly. 'But how could Minshall have recognized me on Thursday night? I've never seen the man before, as far as I know.'

'Well he's certainly seen you, *and* dressed as a man.' Silver had a thought. 'Did you ever wear male costume when visiting the prison before the night of the escape?'

Elisa looked worried for the first time. 'Yes, of course. It was far safer for me to go there to visit Mr Gardiner and my father dressed as a dirty boy in breeches.'

'Then that must be where Minshall knows you from. He must have seen you at Newgate and remembered your face. That's the only way he could have recognized you so easily on Thursday.'

Elisa tried to reassure herself. 'They still can't know where I live, or that I'm really a woman. Otherwise they would have been here already.'

Silver saw that she had a copy of yesterday's *Morning Post* on a sideboard, and his attention was instantly attracted by an article on the front page. He reached across for the newspaper and read it through quickly. 'It says here that Sir Digby Carfax has offered a reward of *five hundred pounds* for the recovery of that necklace you stole, the *Tears of the Prophet*,' he said, almost accusingly. 'That makes *you* a far more attractive catch for Minshall and Sparrow than me now.'

'Yes, I saw the story too, Jonathan,' she snapped. 'I am well able to read, despite only being a woman.'

'Minshall and Sparrow must know you're the one who has that necklace. And with a reward like that on offer, they won't give up chasing you...'

'They still don't know who I am,' she pointed out sharply. 'Or even what sex. I shall simply have to lay low and confine myself to being a woman for the present.'

'You have to give up thieving altogether, Elisa,' Silver lectured her sternly. 'Isn't that necklace enough booty for you? Isn't it time you retired from the thieving game before you get caught?'

Elisa gave that suggestion some serious thought as she sat opposite him. With her face in meditative mood, the glow of the firelight picked out her fine bone structure and delicate features. In that womanly guise, and with that soft lambent lighting illuminating her sweet face, no one could possibly mistake her for a man tonight, Silver decided, so it was a complete mystery to him how she managed to play a young man so convincingly when she chose. 'Yes, perhaps it is time to retire from the thieving business,' she agreed finally, 'but only after I sell that necklace on. I can't sell it on the open market, of course. I can only make enough money from something this well known if I can deliver it to Amsterdam, to a street called *Herengracht*. There is a jeweller residing there called Jacob Koog who has a client – a Middle Eastern gentleman - anxious to take possession of the *Tears of the Prophet...*'

'You stole that necklace to order, didn't you?' Silver accused her in amazement.

Elisa was puzzled by his accusation. 'Of course I did! Why else would I do it? I never steal things at random any more – it wouldn't be worth my while. How else could I work profitably in this business unless I had a partner I could trust? Meneer Koog and I have had a mutually beneficial relationship for the past three years since I first met him on a visit to London.' Elisa almost blushed as she remembered the occasion. 'Actually he caught me in a hotel in the Strand trying to steal his wallet. But he forgave me that little faux pas and we soon became business partners and fast friends. In the past, though, Jacob always travelled to London to meet me to pick up the goods. But he is now incapacitated with arthritis – he is an old man of seventy – so this time I will have to get the object to him in Amsterdam somehow. Assuming this deal can be arranged, though, I might even make enough money from this one sale to be able to finally afford my first China clipper...'

'A China clipper will be of little value to you if you're incarcerated for the rest of your natural life, Elisa,' Silver pointed out icily. 'You should be taking the threat of this man Sparrow more seriously.'

Elisa glowered at him in return. 'Sparrow should be more afraid of *me* than I of him. And that slimy serpent Minshall should watch his back too. I'll pay them both in kind for the death of my father. It was all their doing, between them.'

Silver shook his head in disbelief. This slip of a girl was as much a fugitive from the law as he was, yet she wasn't at all alarmed by the prospect. She seemed in fact to revel in adversity.

Elisa spoke up again. 'So it was that young girl Amy McLennan who helped you escape from the clutches of Sparrow and Minshall?'

Silver was surprised yet again. 'You know Amy too?'

'I do – a little. I supply the hostel for women where she works with certain essential supplies. Liam usually delivers our goods there himself, and he is very taken with sweet Amy, I've noticed, on the occasions when I've accompanied him to the hostel. It almost gives me call to feel jealous sometimes,' she added with a smile, 'when I see the lovelorn way he looks at her. But I forgive her paying close attention to my beau: she is a bright girl for one so young; in fact, she almost seems to run that place.' Elisa hesitated. 'I do actually wonder sometimes if she's quite what she appears, though. She says she is from Bermondsey, and yet her accent doesn't sound to me like she comes from south of the river. And she is a little too self-possessed for a girl in her position...'

Silver couldn't help smiling at that. 'You think Amy is a fraud? That's good coming from a queen of fakery like you, Elisa.'

'Perhaps it takes a queen of fakery to spot a clever fraud, Dr Silver,' she claimed mysteriously.

'Yes, perhaps it does. Yet I still can't believe that Amy is anything other than she appears to be.'

'Perhaps you're right,' Elisa finally conceded. 'In my line of business, I tend to be overly suspicious of people I meet.'

'And is there anyone in this neighbourhood that you're not suspicious of?' he asked her wonderingly.

'Probably not.' She smiled faintly at him. 'And what do *you* think of Amy, Jonathan? Does she attract you as much as she does young Liam?'

Silver was about to answer that as evasively as he could when he remembered something unfortunate about Amy, and something potentially far more serious than any juvenile attachment he might have formed for her. 'Amy did help me willingly this morning, but I suspect she might have regretted her generous impulse later. You see, I believe she's worked out who I really am...'

Elisa frowned, before relaxing her face again. 'Then that's a pity, if it's true. But you don't need to worry too much for the present, I think.' She smiled condescendingly at him. 'If she really is the simple serving girl she appears to be, then I doubt that she'll willingly betray a big handsome brute like you to the peelers. In any case, working girls like Amy won't have anything to do with the police from choice; they distrust the peelers far too much for that.'

'What, not even for the chance of a hundred pounds reward?'

Elisa wavered slightly at that reminder of the large reward on his head. 'Ah...there is that, I suppose.'

'And there was worse news for me still after my close shave at the Hostel for Women, I'm afraid to say...' Silver admitted, with a wry face. 'When I finally got back to my lodgings, I found another problem. The police had been there this afternoon looking for new lodgers matching my description, and the owner, a hopeless sot of a man called Steams, obligingly gave them my assumed name, Wade...'

Elisa jumped immediately to her feet in alarm at that news, and began pacing the floor in troubled fashion. 'Then you can't go back to Gun Alley, Jonathan. You'd be better staying somewhere out on the Isle of Dogs where you're working. Or - even better still - getting on a ship as soon as you can, before the peelers close the net around you.' She stopped pacing the stone-flagged floor and regarded him doubtfully. 'But being the stubborn man you are, you won't take that obvious course, though, will you? You're still determined to pursue this man Strode to the bitter end, aren't you? The man who you believe killed your wife…'

Silver grimaced. 'That's something else I haven't told you, Elisa. That young woman who was found dead in your tanner's yard today…'

'What of her?'

'I'd seen her before – in fact only yesterday evening at the ferry pier on the Isle of Dogs. I even gave her a lift in the yard directors' carriage back to the Napier shipyard, and then saw her get into another private carriage at the shipyard gates. *Daniel Strode's carriage…*'

Even Elisa felt the need to sit down again at that news. 'So you think that Strode not only killed your wife, but that he's also killing these other young women too?'

Silver bit his lip. 'I have no evidence at all connecting Strode with the first young woman who was killed, yet what you say seems a possibility.' He laughed harshly. 'But I can hardly go to the police with my suspicions, can I…?'

*

The fire was dying down as Silver moved his Oxford chair closer to the hearth to make as much of the warmth as he could.

Elisa slid her rocking chair closer to the embers too. 'Tell me about your wife, and the night she died, Jonathan.'

He looked up in surprise at the question. 'Why?'

Elisa shrugged her shoulders. 'I'm curious about her. And perhaps it might be of some help to you to talk about what happened.'

Outside the fog was freezing hard against cold hard surfaces of brick and cobble, and coating the rooftop slates in thick white rime, but huddled by this fire, and with Elisa sitting intimately by his side, Silver felt at ease for the first time tonight. He wondered though, in response to Elisa's question, how he could possibly encapsulate a woman as complex as Marianne in only a few short sentences. 'My wife was a rather mysterious woman,' he finally admitted. 'I never really felt I understood her properly, even though I loved her deeply.'

'Can you truly love someone you don't really know?' Elisa challenged him.

'Perhaps not.' Silver shrugged but didn't attempt to respond further to her question, which was both profound, and a difficult one to answer without being drawn into deep emotional waters. Instead he elected to carry on with his story. 'I think Marianne had been distracted by something in those last few weeks before she died. Perhaps she was even unhappy with me, I'm not sure. I think she was beginning to admit to herself, perhaps, that marriage to a dull medical man might not have been the wisest choice for her after all.'

'And were you unhappy too?'

'Yes, but not with her. I was unhappy with what was going on at my hospital, St Barts, and with the refusal of the other surgeons there to maintain a clean regime in the wards. I was particularly distraught on the day Marianne died because I had to saw off a young boy's leg when it turned gangrenous. And I'm sure the only reason why that boy's limb had become infected was because of our failure to clean and disinfect the wards properly.'

Elisa said nothing but gave a token nod of understanding.

'I went home that day in a foul mood, let myself in the front door, and found Marianne collapsed on the stairs with a knife stuck in her heart. I thought at first she must have fallen and accidentally stabbed herself, because the knife looked like nothing more than a paper knife...'

Elisa was wide-eyed and pensive. 'Yet she was still alive when you got there?'

'Yes, but only just. She was trying desperately to say something to me, but I managed to pick out only one word from among all the incomprehensible sounds.'

Elisa was intrigued. 'What word?'

Silver shrugged in slight embarrassment. 'She whispered the word...*Leviathan.*'

Elisa frowned, almost disappointed. 'Only that? But why did that make you think of Daniel Strode in particular? Surely not just the fact that he was working on the building of the new *Leviathan?* There are thousands of men working on that ship.'

'Yet he is the only one of those men who had known Marianne intimately in the past and wanted to marry her.'

Elisa continued to look doubtful. 'Still...'

'I also didn't make anything of that single word initially,' Silver argued defensively. 'I even began to doubt that Marianne had said the word at all, and that I must have simply misheard her. It was only later, after the trial, that I remembered Marianne reading an article in the newspaper one evening about the fact that this man Daniel Strode was heavily involved in the design of that ship. I recalled then that he had once asked her to marry him, and that she had turned him down because of his aggressive and domineering manner, and his violent temper.' Silver caught Elisa's still questioning expression. 'I know it's a flimsy connection at best, but I have nothing better to explain what Marianne meant.'

Elisa rolled her eyes. '"Flimsy" is correct. Because even your basic notion doesn't make any sense, does it? If I had just been stabbed and could only get a few last words out, I would have pronounced the name of my murderer. But Marianne didn't say "Strode", did she - she said *"Leviathan"*...'

Silver agreed begrudgingly with her judgement, but was still compelled to argue further. 'But that would mean she was murdered *by* "Leviathan." That makes even less sense than my interpretation.'

'You said the knife was a paper knife – was there anything special about it?' Elisa asked, after a long pause.

Silver didn't have to think; he'd seen the precise shape and decoration of that knife recurring in his dreams ever since. 'It was a decorative silver paper knife. That's why I thought at first that she might have stabbed herself accidentally with her own paper knife. Yet I'm sure I'd never seen that blade before, so it couldn't have belonged to Marianne herself. Apparently it was of Russian manufacture – the handle was decorated with the Cyrillic version of the letter T...'

'Which means it belonged to the murderer,' Elisa declared sharply. 'Which also means the murder must have been improvised at short notice, since a decorative paper knife would not usually be the weapon of choice of an assassin...'

'That's also what the police thought...except that they believed *me* to be the assassin,' Silver added dryly. 'The police made some enquiries with a silver expert in Bond Street who said the knife was made in St Petersburg by a famous silversmith called Timofeyev. So the police claimed that the knife must have been mine, because of my service during the Crimean campaign.'

'Ah, so they thought you'd acquired it somehow as a war souvenir?'

Silver met her frank gaze without embarrassment. 'Yes, I believe they did. But it's not true - I was only in the Crimea for a few weeks and barely saw a Russian there at all, alive or dead. Most of the time I was working at a hospital on the Ottoman side of the Black Sea.'

Elisa pulled her rocking chair closer to him, the wooden runners scratching on the bare stone floor. 'Where did you actually meet Marianne?'

'It was at that very hospital in Turkey during the Crimean campaign. I was a volunteer surgeon seconded to the army for a year...'

'At Scutari?'

'You've heard of it?'

'I read the newspapers,' she answered impatiently. 'Was it really as terrible as they said?'

'Much worse than you could ever imagine.' Silver didn't feel like elaborating further.

Elisa wrinkled her brow. 'Was Marianne a nurse there, then?'

Silver wondered how to answer that question honestly. 'Well, let's say she was certainly working at Scutari in some official capacity, and that she did habitually wear a nurse's uniform. But I have my doubts whether she was a normal volunteer nurse. I believe she was there at the hospital for some other reason too, but I never managed to discover the truth from her about that. Like most women, she was very good at being evasive when she wanted to be.' He felt a brief stab in his heart as he remembered how perfect in every way his wife had been – including her ability to avoid answering a straight question when it didn't suit her. 'I told you there was something mysterious about Marianne. And what she was really doing in Turkey was just one of the many mysteries about her...'

*

Silver was half-dozing now as fatigue took hold of him and his leaden eyelids began to droop.

Elisa was sleepy too, yet still wanted to talk some more. 'What about your life before Marianne, Jonathan? Tell me something about that.'

So he did tell her his life story in brief fashion, anecdotes about growing up in Dorset, about his father's cabinet-making business, memories of medical school in Edinburgh, more about the Crimea and his work at St Barts, and even about his meeting in Vienna with that inspiring young Hungarian doctor called Semmelweiss who'd had his own theories of how infectious disease was spread. In the end, this "brief" account of his life took their conversation past midnight.

'Yet you've still missed something from your career, haven't you?' she queried when he finally fell silent.

Silver retraced his life sleepily in his mind. 'Yes, you're right. After medical school, I was a surgeon in the Royal Navy for five years, and sailed all over the world. It's surprising I omitted that.'

Her eyes were shining. 'Where did you sail to? Tell me!'

'Oh, I had a lazy year in the Mediterranean, based at the port of Mahon on the Isle of Minorca. Then two rather more exciting years with the West Indies squadron, out of Jamaica and the Leeward Islands, with voyages as far as West Africa...'

'Doing what?'

Silver shrugged. 'Mainly blockading American slavers.'

Elisa was scathing. 'Then that's typical of this nation's hypocrisy, isn't it? To free slaves elsewhere in the world, while most of our own population lives and works in conditions as bad as any black slave.'

'You mean, like the workers in your own tanner's yard?' Silver pointed out acidly.

She flushed at that. 'I don't have to defend myself to you, Jonathan.

But in fact I have doubled the wages of the workers in that yard since I bought it. My manager Ernest Harvey thought I was insane doing such a thing, but productivity has actually more than doubled since I did it, so he is coming around to my way of thinking. In the end it can only benefit an employer to treat his workforce humanely. '

'But why should they work for you at all, Elisa?' he mocked her. 'Why should they not take over the factory and run it themselves? Why do they need you?'

'Why? Because no business will ever work without strong and independent management, nor without some impulse to improve efficiency and make a profit.' She held up her hand impatiently. 'But let's not talk about me any more. I freely admit I am a thief and a hypocrite, and totally shameless in my inconsistencies and double standards. Let's rather talk about you and your noble naval career. Where else did you serve Her Majesty?'

Silver thought back again. 'After the West Indies, I was sent with a squadron to the Far East and the coast of Canton in China. That's a wonderful place, full of strange sights and sounds.'

She had a faraway look in her eyes. 'I believe you. The East is certainly one place I wish I could go and see for myself.'

'What prevents you?'

She smiled sheepishly at that. 'A young woman on her own? No chaperone? What chance would I have in a man's world?'

Silver wasn't sure whether she was being ironic or not, but he suspected the former. 'This is eighteen fifty-seven, not seventeen hundred, Elisa. In China there are many powerful and wealthy businesswomen already. I believe you would manage very well out there.'

She narrowed her eyes, as if trying to dissect his words for hidden meaning. 'I do want to see the world someday. What's the most beautiful place you've ever seen? The single place you die to return to. The place you thought about on your last night in Newgate, when you were due to hang in the morning?'

Silver reflected for a moment. 'I wouldn't put it that highly. But there is one place that I remember with special affection. In 'forty-seven, my squadron was sent to the new colony of Hong Kong to aid the colonists after an outbreak of sweating sickness. It's only a bare rocky island at the moment, with a few hundred people living on it, but certainly the most beautiful harbour in all the world. That's what the name Hong Kong means – *Fragrant Harbour*. And one of the safest too, as protection against the fierce typhoons that assault that coast...'

'Typhoons?'

'Yes, great storms, like the West Indies hurricanes, only worse in severity perhaps. Sometimes the wind can be so strong that it uproots whole houses, and the rain so heavy that it washes away entire mountainsides. Initially the English colonists settled a protected valley on the north shore called Happy Valley, but had to give it up because the low-lying marshes were so infected with malaria. So, by the time my squadron arrived, the merchants had all moved their houses to the lower slopes of the island below Victoria Peak and were already planting fine gardens of orchid trees and figs and cassias. It's from this safe island home that they conduct their lucrative trade with the wealthy Chinese merchants on the Pearl River, for silk and tea and gold, in return for opium and machinery. Climb to the top of the mountain above the town and I swear you can see all the way from the blue of the Pearl River to the green water of the South China Sea.' Silver sighed tiredly. 'That's where I'd like to go back to, if I ever had the chance. And build myself a fine house with a white portico and a marble floor, and teak furniture. And the best view of the harbour, of course.'

Elisa's eyes were like glowing pools of light. 'Perhaps we should go together, then, Jonathan. I could run my fleet of clippers from the East, and you could practice your skills as a surgeon. Imagine how happy and contented we could be in such a place.'

Silver hardly believed she was being serious. 'It's a pleasant dream.'

Her face stiffened slowly as her glow of happiness faded. 'But you won't go anywhere until you deal with this man Strode, will you?'

Silver returned her thoughtful look. 'And you won't go anywhere until you pay Sparrow and Minshall back for their sins, will you, Elisa...?'

CHAPTER 16

In the last two days Sergeant Sparrow had discovered from a friend of the dead girl who had come forward – a Miss Anne Kelmscott - something of the background of the unfortunate Miss Jane Penfold. The most striking fact about Miss Penfold, as far as Sparrow was concerned anyway, was that she too had been a governess, just like the first murdered woman, Miss Livingstone. That seemed far too much of an unhappy coincidence for Sparrow not to suspect the worst – that some evil individual was deliberately targeting this particular class of young woman.

The friend of Miss Penfold who had come forward – Miss Kelmscott - was also coincidentally a governess, if a much plainer one than her friend Jane. Plain or not, Miss Kelmscott had proved invaluable in enlightening Sparrow about Miss Penfold's situation. And the more he had found out about that situation, the more disturbingly similar it seemed to that of Miss Charlotte Livingstone.

Miss Penfold too had been a governess of limited means, if living in Somers Town rather than Islington. She had, like Miss Livingstone, also recently left a longstanding post last summer – but in Miss Penfold's case, with a family in Harrogate, Yorkshire rather than in Hampstead. One further point of departure was the fact that Miss Penfold had been an orphan, a fact which Sparrow had selfishly been rather glad of, since it spared him the heartrending ordeal of having to face yet another bereaved and devastated parent like Mrs Adelie Livingstone.

Yet, all in all, the parallels to Miss Livingstone's situation were deeply unsettling…

Miss Kelmscott was unaware that Jane had any special gentleman friends, yet Sparrow doubted that a girl as pretty as Miss Penfold would not have found some male admirers in the course of her young life. On the other hand, it seemed unlikely to Sparrow that Miss Kelmscott herself, given her plain face and squat figure, had much personal knowledge of affairs of the heart, therefore he suspected that she might perhaps be merely unaware of her much prettier friend's romantic entanglements.

Miss Penfold had unfortunately left no handbag behind at the scene with helpful clues inside, as Miss Livingstone had. Nor had she been with child, as the unfortunate Charlotte had been, which was one more important difference between the two cases. Yet Miss Penfold had been an undoubtedly beautiful girl like Charlotte Livingstone, and Sparrow knew that such unspoilt beauty attracted men, whether encouraged or not.

Apart from learning these more obvious facts from Miss Penfold's friend, though, Sparrow had made no great progress at all in the investigation. There were no direct witnesses to the second crime, nor had anyone come forward to explain what a pretty and genteel governess might have been doing in an insalubrious neighbourhood like Albion Street in the East End on a Sunday morning.

Assistant Commissioner Grindrod had been bombarding Sparrow with telegrams from Whitehall since Sunday, and had now ordered him to put all his efforts into catching the fiend who was murdering these young women, rather than to recapturing the missing Dr Jonathan Silver.

Inspector Carew, the chief uniformed officer at Shadwell Station, was also pressing him to come up with some results in the investigation of the murders of these two young women as quickly as possible. Sparrow had scarcely needed to be told that, though, considering the public outcry over the murders. Yet he hadn't entirely forgotten about Dr Silver, of course, nor given up all hope of recapturing him. Of the fugitive doctor, though, there had been no signs or reports either since that disappointing chase last Sunday (assuming that the person they'd been chasing then had actually been Silver – Sparrow was still not *entirely* convinced that the turnkey Minshall had been right in his identification.)

From a report by one of the Shadwell constables, though – Constable Rankine - there seemed a possibility that Silver might have been staying for the last week in a vermin-infested lodging house in Gun Alley near the Wapping waterfront, and using a false name. The description of this lodger certainly matched Silver in some respects, particularly his unusual height. But this lodger had soon disappeared on Sunday night when he'd heard the police wanted to talk to him, and he didn't seem likely to return voluntarily to Gun Alley any time soon, given all this unwanted attention from the law. (And if the man really *was* Silver, then it was doubly unlikely that he would still be in the vicinity, of course.) The landlady in Gun Alley – a gin-soaked baggage called Mrs Steams - had said her tall lodger had been using the name Wade, but denied any further knowledge of him, apart from believing the man to be a seaman home on shore leave. Nevertheless, Sparrow was now planning to print a new set of handbills giving that name as a possible alias for the fugitive doctor, together with an image of Silver that might be closer to his present appearance.

With regard to the recovery of the missing necklace - the *Tears of the Prophet* - that matter had now been taken entirely out of Sparrow's hands. (Not that it had ever really been in them, since the crime had fallen well outside Sparrow's East End patch.)

The bad news for Sparrow, though, was that control of the missing necklace case had been given by Grindrod to his arch enemy, Inspector Pierce Murphy of the Piccadilly station, and Murphy would no doubt take the opportunity to humiliate Sparrow at every possible turn. If Murphy were to recover the necklace, that would be rubbing salt into Sparrow's wounds with a vengeance. Sparrow knew that even his own men were mocking him behind his back now after that disastrous affair at Sir Digby Carfax's house in Berkeley Square last week. And that included Frank Remmert, who had even been part of that sad debacle himself, damn him!

Sparrow realized that he would have to pull off some sort of spectacular success soon on one of his cases, if he wanted to recover his reputation within the detective force of the Met rapidly. Somehow, even though the theft of that necklace wasn't officially his case, Sparrow had to find that boy-thief who'd apparently been helping Silver...

*

On this miserable Tuesday afternoon, with a persistent cold drizzle weeping from an iron-grey sky, Sparrow had been nosing around the Wapping waterfront by himself, following his instincts in looking for signs of Silver, or anything to do with the two murdered girls. After a fruitless second visit to Mrs Steams in her filthy lodging house, which had added nothing to his knowledge of the world, except perhaps in showing the efficacy of gin in adding a network of fine purple veins to a woman's nose, Sparrow's wanderings took him to a chandler's store just off Old Gravel Lane. A heavily freckled young man was working behind the counter - as plain a young man as Frank Remmert, which was saying something. This young man and Frank would certainly make a spectacularly ugly pair of human bookends, Sparrow decided uncharitably.

The young man looked up from the massive ledger into which he was making fine copperplate entries with a quill pen.

Sparrow introduced himself, then the man returned the favour with a much warier look on his face after discovering that he was talking to a police detective.

'So, what can I do for you, Sergeant?' Liam Flintham inquired politely.

'I'm looking for a Miss Elisa Smith, Mr Flintham. I believe she lives here...'

*

Sitting in the warm kitchen at the back of the chandler's shop, Sergeant Sparrow watched the water dripping from a lead gutter outside with metronomic regularity. His day had brightened up considerably, though, despite the fading light outside, and the persistent cold rain spattering off the cobbles in the backyard. Sparrow's mood had improved because Miss Elisa Smith had turned out to be a very pretty girl indeed, and Charlie Sparrow always had time for pretty girls. Not only that, this one apparently had money too...

Sparrow wondered irately why there'd been no girls like this on offer when he'd been courting fifteen or twenty years ago. Edie, despite her buxom figure and apple cheeks, wouldn't have stood a chance if Sparrow had ever come across a girl with both looks and a substantial dowry, like Miss Elisa Smith's.

He examined her again discreetly as she served him with a cup of perfect China tea. Not quite in Mrs Sophie Rolfe's league perhaps, he had to admit. Not the same perfection of feature or complexion, yet still, nonetheless, a girl to set a man's heart pulsing - and probably other parts of his anatomy too. Her hair was a fine dark colour with just a hint of red, her eyes were green – yes, definitely green and not some subtle shade of blue – and she had a pert waist and a nice swelling bosom that looked entirely the work of nature.

Sparrow could hear the enticing rustle of cotton petticoats as she walked about the stone-flagged floor. 'Can I bring you something to eat, Sergeant, to go with your tea? Some cold roast beef, or a nice piece of Stilton cheese?'

Sparrow, despite his good mood, was minded to be slightly suspicious at such generosity. The police didn't normally get treated with such hospitality, so Sparrow did wonder if Miss Smith might be trying to divert his attention from something with this act of kindness. But he let that uncharitable thought soon pass; surely Miss Smith was simply a pleasant young woman, who welcomed anyone's company on such a wet and miserable Tuesday afternoon as this. He smiled warmly at her. 'No, thank you, Miss Smith. The offer of tea is more than kind enough.' He cleared his throat and got to the point of his visit. 'Mr Harvey, the manager of the tanner's yard where this unfortunate woman was found dead, tells me that you're the owner of that yard.'

She sat on a wooden bench at a discreet distance away from him. 'I am.'

'How long have you owned it, may I ask? Is it a family business?'

'No, it's not. I acquired it only recently from a Mr Warren, who wished to sell up and retire to Brighton, after many years of running the business.'

'I can hardly blame him for that,' Sparrow said, thinking aloud. He doubted that it would have been a difficult choice for Mr Warren to make – staying in a miserable street in the East End that stank like purgatory, or instead retiring to enjoy the bracing salt air and Regency fashion of the English south coast.

Miss Smith smiled faintly. 'Nor I, Sergeant, at Mr Warren's time of life.'

Sparrow wondered why anyone, at *any* time of life, would want to run a tanner's yard, when there were so many other more attractive businesses for the rich to invest in. 'It's an unusual sort of business for a young woman to be taking an interest in, though, isn't it?' he suggested.

Her smile broadened a little. 'Perhaps it is. But I saw it as an opportunity.'

Sparrow was enjoying her smile so much, and the remarkable fresh pinkness of her cheeks, that he quite forgot where he was for a moment. Her smile faded to slight puzzlement before he managed to find another word. 'You're very young, Miss Smith, to have these responsibilities.'

Miss Smith sighed gently. 'My parents are dead, Sergeant, so I have no other choice but to carry on alone. Fortunately my father left me well provided for, and I am only trying to carry on with his good work.'

'Very commendable.'

She assessed him with a shrewd look. 'Do you know anything yet about the murdered girl who was found in my yard, Sergeant?'

'Very little so far, I'm afraid. Her name was Jane Penfold – we do know that much. She was twenty-one years old, according to our information, and an orphan from Somers Town. She had worked as a governess to a family in Harrogate, Yorkshire until recently. Then last summer she returned to Somers Town where she was born and since then had been trying to find a new post as a governess in London. That's virtually all I have discovered about her so far.'

'So you have no clue as to why she ended up in the lime tank in my tanner's yard?'

'No, not yet,' he admitted. 'But Miss Penfold was a very attractive young woman so I have little doubt there was a gentleman involved with her in some intimate way.'

Miss Smith gasped. 'You mean a gentleman killed her in a crime of passion? Is that what you're saying?'

Sparrow put up his hand in mild protest. 'I wouldn't go that far at present. But I'm sure that a liaison with a gentleman was the likeliest reason for her being in Wapping on Sunday. I simply can't think of any other obvious reasons why a genteel young lady would be in this part of the East End. And perhaps this man was not such a gentlemanly person as Miss Penfold imagined.'

Miss Smith had fallen silent and seemed reluctant to say more. But Sparrow felt he had to ask more questions while he was here. 'You never heard of this Miss Penfold before?'

Miss Smith looked up sharply. 'No, never.'

'Or of Miss Livingstone, the other woman who was murdered, several days before?'

Miss Smith shook her head emphatically, and something about the shape of her head and her pretty features suddenly jarred something unexpectedly in Sparrow's memory. He frowned curiously. 'Have we ever met before, Miss Smith? I don't mean to be forward, but your face does seem genuinely familiar to me for some reason.'

Miss Smith smiled amiably. 'I've lived here in Wapping for three years, so it wouldn't be too surprising if you'd seen me before.'

'Yes, I suppose that might be it. But where do you hail from originally, may I ask?'

'My father came originally from the Midlands, from Worcestershire. But he died several years ago.'

'I see.' Yet Sparrow was still quietly convinced that he knew her face from somewhere more particular than from simply encountering her in the street at some time. Even her voice sounded vaguely familiar to him now, which couldn't be explained by merely seeing someone fleetingly in the street.

She seemed to sense his lingering doubt, and smiled distractingly. 'I'm sure I would have remembered if we'd met before, Sergeant. An amiable and handsome man like you.'

Sparrow wasn't sure, but thought he detected a hint of insincerity, and even perhaps latent hostility, in that last sentence. But perhaps she was merely tiring of his questions, that was all. Nevertheless, he asked her one more. 'Have you ever met a man called Wade, Miss Smith? A seaman who has been living in a lodging house close by?'

Miss Smith held his gaze with admirable directness. 'No, I don't believe so...'

*

Sparrow didn't leave the shop immediately but stopped to have a few words on the way out with the ugly young man at the counter. In the cobbled lane in front of the shop, a couple of ragged boys were loading up a cart with goods, while Mr Flintham kept a wary eye from inside the shop on their progress.

'Have you worked for Miss Smith for long, Mr Flintham?'

Liam looked up from his dusty ledger, and adjusted his reading glasses. 'A year, or thereabouts.'

Sparrow walked about the shop inspecting the merchandise, then glanced through the leaded glass panes of the bay window facing the street. 'You look like you're getting ready to make a delivery. Isn't it a bit late in the day for delivering? Where are those goods destined?'

'For Millwall, on the Isle of Dogs. At the moment I make a delivery almost every day to the shipyard there – sometimes two a day.' Liam inspected the streaming rain and the rising wind outside with worry. 'And I have to get them there without fail, whether it's fair weather or foul. The yard is working around the clock, and they're always running out of basic supplies for the workforce. Tonight I'm taking barrels of flour and sugar for their canteen, and it looks like I'm going to get wet through.'

Sparrow sniffed. 'That's the yard that's building the Great Ship, isn't it?'

'It is. You should see it up close, Sergeant. It really is an immense undertaking. It makes you proud to be English to see the stupendous things we can build here in this country now.'

Sparrow nodded in agreement. 'Yes, I'll have to go out to the Isle of Dogs and see it for myself. The launch is only a few weeks away, I hear.'

'That's right...'

At this moment, Miss Smith appeared abruptly from the back of the shop and said warningly, 'I think you'd better stop chattering with the sergeant here, Liam, and get the delivery cart on its way before the weather gets even worse.' She directed a firm look in Sparrow's direction. 'Was there anything else you wanted to ask, Sergeant, before you go?'

She seemed even more familiar to him now, for some reason, speaking in that admonitory tone of voice, and Sparrow racked his brains to try and remember where he knew her from. But just as the mists seemed to be clearing, they closed in again tantalisingly.

'No, I don't think so, Miss Smith. But you will be here if I need to talk to you again, won't you...?'

*

As he waited in the coach yard of the Hostel for Women to talk to Amy McLennan, Sparrow kicked his heels in frustration at the wet cobbles beneath his feet. With the coming of darkness, the rain had finally stopped. Yet the wind was rising rapidly, and the roofs and eaves still continued to drip moisture all around him, so that the weather conditions seemed quite as wet and dismal as ever.

Ginny Faber finally returned from the kitchen where Sparrow had dispatched her a few minutes ago to fetch Amy. Sparrow knew Ginny's name from his previous visit here when they had been searching for Dr Silver, and had recognized then that she was one of the unofficial leaders of this little community. The inner coach yard of the Hostel for Women was a deal quieter than it had been two days before, but Sparrow was aware that a number of low-class big-bosomed young women were watching him intently from the galleries above, and stirring bad-temperedly at his every word. They looked in a mood to start throwing things, if he wasn't careful with his language.

'Amy will be with you presently, Sergeant,' Ginny announced perfunctorily.

Sparrow had noticed the sling on Ginny's arm previously, but was now minded to ask her about it. 'How did you hurt your arm, Mrs Faber?'

Ginny wasn't in a cooperative mood. 'What's it to you, Sergeant?' she asked belligerently.

'Just answer me, woman, will you?' Sparrow muttered irately, prompting an echo of similar muttering from the slatternly women watching from the first floor galleries.

Ginny simmered resentfully, but answered anyway. 'I fell down some stairs on Saturday night and pulled it out of its socket, if you really want to know.'

Sparrow detected a hint of evasion in her eyes and was even more interested. 'That must have been very painful.'

'It were. I nearly shit a brick with the pain.'

Sparrow coughed. 'Yes, I'm sure you did. Did a doctor fix it for you properly?'

'No, it were Mr...err...'

Amy suddenly appeared at Sparrow's side, all of a bustle. 'Ginny, why don't you stop jawin' and get on with your work.'

In her confusion, Ginny almost bobbed to her. 'Yes, Miss...err...Amy.'

For such a sweet young thing, it was odd how Amy McLennan seemed to run this place with authority, and even boss around much older women than herself, Sparrow thought.

'You wanted to see me, Sergeant?' she said coolly.

'Yes, indeed I did.' Sparrow watched her as she picked up her broom, and began cleaning the yard, sweeping the deep muddy puddles left by this afternoon's rain into the gutters.

Sparrow followed her on her circuitous journey around the yard. 'Why did you lie to me about being attacked by those two sailors last week, Amy?'

She stopped brushing for a moment, and swept back a loose straggle of hair from her fair brow. 'I didn't lie. It weren't me.'

'My young constable Kennally swears it was you, and he doesn't usually make mistakes where pretty girls are concerned. And he said that you were rescued by a man. Was this man using the name "Wade" by any chance, Amy?' Sparrow held his temper with difficulty at her continued obstinacy. 'Are you protecting this Mr Wade? Did you hide him on Sunday when he came running in here with my boys in pursuit?'

Amy began brushing vigorously again. 'You don't listen, do you, Sergeant? There was no man. There was no rescue.'

Sparrow put on the grimmest face he could. 'I promise you I will make big trouble for you, Miss Amy, and for this place, if I think you're playing games with me. And if you're protecting a fugitive and a murderer, then you can go to prison too.'

She didn't even pause in her brushing.

'Do you know where this Mr Wade is now?' Sparrow persisted.

Amy looked up, puzzled. 'No, I don't know any Mr Wade, Sergeant. Really I don't!'

Despite her innocent expression, Sparrow would have bet a five-pound note that she was lying...

CHAPTER 17

Thursday 22nd October 1857

For a few brief minutes, the drab clouds over the river had lifted and a shaft of watery sunlight now illuminated the great ship, like an Old Testament image of the Ark, with the flood waters rising all round it. And for once, Silver could see the ironwork of the great hull of the *Leviathan* displayed in all its wondrous detail - a vast expanse of rivets and plates and angles - to add even more interest to its fantastic dimensions and brooding presence.

Silver stood up and straightened his back with difficulty, after an hour of working bent double to the saw and drill, making final adjustments to the last few timber baulks on the slipway. But it was high up on that hull, towering above his head, where the truly exciting work was being done, as the last few deck plates were riveted into place, and the last blades of the giant paddles stitched to their vast wheels. The gargantuan hull was still festooned with rigging, access staircases and dizzying walkways as workers continued to swarm all over their improbable creation like an army of ants constructing a monumental anthill.

Billy Faber straightened up beside him, his more youthful back taking the strain of constant bending easier than Silver's. 'God Almighty, but she's a fantastic sight, isn't she, Mr Wade? I 'ope my mum can come and see the Great Ship launched. She'll never see the likes of this again, not if she lives to be a 'undred.'

'Amen to that,' agreed Silver, standing in equal awe at this vast heart-moving spectacle. Working on this ship for so many years had made many of the long-term workers at the yard blasé and even disrespectful about the scale and majesty of this undertaking. But Silver and his small gang of carpenters – Billy Faber, Jimmy Flynn, and their foreman Matthew Spurrell – had certainly never succumbed to that dull and accepting attitude, perhaps because they were newer arrivals at the yard, and still envious of those lucky enough to be working on the hull of the *Leviathan* itself.

Silver was about to get back to his task, when he saw John Harkness approaching down the slope of the stern slipway, with blueprint drawings under his arm. Silver quickly looked around for Spurrell, but his foreman was nowhere in sight, a situation that was unfortunately becoming increasingly common. Silver suspected the foreman had a secret drinking problem because he would often disappear for minutes at a time like this, only to reappear later with a flushed face and the smell of cheap liquor on his sour breath. Silver had done his best to cover for him, but it was becoming a trying business to do so. Yet the last thing Silver wanted was for Spurrell to face the sack because that would expose him even more to the attentions of his workmates, especially if he was asked to replace Spurrell, which wasn't outside the bounds of possibility.

Harkness came over directly to Silver as usual and didn't even inquire about Spurrell's absence. Instead he took off his stovepipe hat so that he could crane his neck and look admiringly up at the ship. He whistled softly to himself. 'This is the only place to really appreciate the size of this monster.' He lowered his gaze and replaced his hat, before turning to Silver with a smile. 'Stuck in my office most of the day, I sometimes forget the scale of this thing that we are creating here, Wade. From down here on the slipways, she looks twice the ship she does from the drawing office...' – his smile broadened – 'and yet she looks vast enough even from there.'

Harkness inspected the bottom section of the stern slipway with approval. 'It seems as if you're almost done here, Wade...although I'm sure there will be more work for you and your men in the fitting out of the ship,' he reassured him quickly. 'So don't worry about being laid off – we can always find work for a man of your quality and skill. This afternoon, we're planning to jack up the two iron cradles under the keel of the *Leviathan*, ready for the launch.'

Silver was surprised they were doing this so long before the launch. 'Does that mean she'll only be supported on the cradles, sir? That means the bows and stern of the ship will be sticking out unsupported over a length of more than a hundred feet at each end. Can the hull really span an unsupported distance like that, for a week or more, without the plates buckling?'

Harkness appraised him with one of those familiar shrewd looks, and Silver cursed himself again for asking what appeared to be an intelligent question.

'Mr Brunel has designed the hull for just this situation, otherwise we could hardly launch the ship sideways in this fashion, could we? And if the ship can support this situation for a single minute, then it can equally do so for days, or even weeks.' Harkness seemed obscurely disappointed with his protégé this time rather than impressed, so Silver was relieved to see that his question perhaps hadn't been quite so clever after all.

Harkness was about to say something more to Silver when Daniel Strode suddenly put in an appearance at the foot of the same slipway. Strode was a rare visitor to the ship itself, so Silver hadn't seen him close up since that encounter in the drawing office a week ago. Yet Silver was surprised – even shocked - at the change in the man in such a short period, a degree of physical change which seemed so obvious that he thought it must be apparent to everyone. The natural confidence and arrogance that Silver had observed in Strode last week had vanished completely. The man seemed nervous and distracted now, and almost shrunken in appearance, with black circles of worry under his eyes, and a stumbling gait to boot. If Silver was being charitable, then it was possible, perhaps, to ascribe Strode's changed appearance merely to the pressure of getting the Great Ship finished.

Yet there was an alternative explanation too. Could this change in him be the mark of a murderer finally tormented by a guilty conscience?

Strode did indeed have the look of a man who might have killed two women in horrible circumstances in the last weeks, and was now having trouble living with the consequences.

Silver was relieved to see that Strode didn't seem to be intending to speak with Harkness, and was merely there on the stern slipway to make some on-site checks of the blades of the giant paddles. Harkness too seemed equally relieved to be avoiding further contact with the man, as he nodded in Strode's direction. 'I used to be good friends with that man, you know, Wade.'

Silver's interest quickened at this chance to learn more of Strode's background. 'Really, sir?'

'Yes. In fact I've known him since we were boys together. We were at school in Hampstead, back in the days when the old Iron Duke was Prime Minister.'

'But you had a falling out, sir?' Silver tried a careful question.

Harkness sighed. 'Yes, we did. I had thought him a man of good character, and a friend, until quite recently. But I discovered regrettably that he is a man of loose morals, a seducer of women and a betrayer of friendships.'

Silver would have liked to ask more but could hardly do so with Billy Faber and Jimmy Flynn standing within earshot. 'Is Mr Strode a married man, sir?'

Harkness smiled bleakly. 'No, not him. But I believe he tells his many mistresses and conquests that he is. To stop them becoming too possessive, I imagine.' He flushed bright red as he apparently realized that he'd spoken much too openly and intimately to a man well below his own social class. 'Please excuse me, Wade. My personal problems with Mr Strode should not be your concern. Please accept my apologies and kindly forget all that I just said.'

'Of course, sir,' Silver agreed hurriedly, casting down his eyes in suitably deferential fashion.

Before Silver could get back to his work, Harkness added, in a more conciliatory voice, 'I commend you for your work, Wade. Mr Brunel is extremely pleased that the slipway has been finished in time.'

'Then perhaps you should commend Mr Spurrell too,' Silver suggested diplomatically…

*

After Harkness had left on his further rounds, Billy smiled across at Silver. 'Wot was all that about, then?'

Silver shrugged. 'Who knows?'

Billy became more serious. 'I saw my mum last night. Most nights she sleeps at the hostel where she works, but last night she came home to see me. She told me how you fixed her arm last Saturday after it popped out of its socket. Thanks, Mr Wade. You're a gent.'

'It was nothing. I did a little bit of doctoring in the navy, and I've seen a few dislocated arms, that's all.'

Billy was a trusting boy, and didn't question that explanation of Silver's medical skills, which was a reasonable enough one, anyway. 'By the way, I meant to ask you. Have you changed lodgings, Mr Wade? You don't walk home at night with me any more, I've noticed.'

'Yes, Billy, I have changed lodgings since Monday. I found somewhere nearer the yard, to save all that walking.' Courtesy of a further loan from Elisa last Sunday, Silver had indeed found a room at The Ship Inn, but he hadn't divulged that to anyone in the yard. It was an expensive room, and one normally beyond the wages of a ship's carpenter to enjoy, so he didn't want to arouse any further curiosity about his personal affairs and finances from his workmates. And a further reason for keeping it from his workmates was that he was renting the room under the name Williams, in case any peelers came around asking about a "Mr Wade". Silver had no doubt that his former landlady Mrs Steams, for all her professed dislike of the police, would have been happy to snitch on him and tell the peelers all she knew about her recent lodger.

Yet, despite the change of alias, Silver didn't feel safe in his new lodgings, or at the yard, either. Nowhere in London was safe with

Sergeant Sparrow, and that man Minshall, close on his trail. It would only be a matter of time, Silver thought, before Sparrow would extend his search for him beyond Wapping to Shadwell, Limehouse and then the Isle of Dogs. One further complication in Silver's life was that the buxom maidservant Alice who worked at The Ship Inn – the one lusted after by Jude Crabtree - already knew him by the name Wade from his occasional earlier visits there, and yet had overheard the landlord Mr Lancelot Grimes addressing him more recently as Williams. Alice wasn't the brightest girl in the world so hadn't made an issue of it, yet perhaps it was only a matter of time before she caught sight of a wanted poster with the name Wade on it and put two and two together.

On the more positive side, he told himself, very few people in the Napier yard knew him by name – Wade, that is – apart from Jimmy and Billy and a handful of his other regular workmates.

And *Harkness* now, of course, which was perhaps more of a potential problem. There was far more chance of a man like Harkness reading the newspapers and becoming aware that the fugitive Dr Silver might be using the name Wade, than of Jimmy or Billy doing so...

Jimmy Flynn appeared at Silver's side and nudged him with a wink. 'Look, Mr Wade. There's Billy's sweetheart come to check up on him.'

Silver glanced up to where Jimmy was indicating and saw to his alarm that it was Amy McLennan he was referring to. What was *she* doing here? She'd never been to the Napier yard before as far as he knew, so her sudden unexpected appearance here was unsettling to say the least. Silver surmised that her visit here was probably more to do with him rather than Billy.

Billy had flushed bright red at Jimmy's comment. 'She ain't my sweetheart, Jim, although I wish she was. She told me she's twenty-two, and therefore far too old for me.'

'Aw, don't give up, Billy, just because she's bigger than you, and six years older,' Jimmy mocked him. 'That's a big healthy-looking girl all right. I wouldn't mind a taste of that myself.'

Silver was still wondering how a simple working girl like Amy had managed to get into the yard at all. It certainly wasn't possible to gain routine access to the shipyard without a pass from the gatekeeper, and you didn't get those unless you had a very good reason for being here. But when Silver spotted whom Amy was talking to, he realized resignedly who'd probably been instrumental in helping her get past the gatekeeper. Her companion was Liam Flintham, of all people. And from his shy and awkward behaviour around young Amy, he did indeed seem almost as captivated with her feminine charms as he was with those of Miss Elisa Smith...

Silver pretended not to be concerned by her presence, and got back to work, advising Billy and Jimmy to do the same. Yet he still kept a wary eye on her from time to time, worried by this slightly ominous development. He was already convinced from their last meeting at the hostel on Sunday that Amy now knew his real identity. And, despite the fact that she had helped him escape the peelers that day, he was far from sure that she would continue to protect his secret.

Had she come here deliberately to track him down so she could point him out to the peelers? *Was that reward of £100 for his capture simply more than a poor girl like Amy could resist?*

He could only hope not, but there was nothing he could do about it now except pray that Amy was as noble a girl as she seemed to be. With that, he deliberately turned his back on her, anxious to avoid meeting her eye...

*

Silver found that he couldn't avoid Amy however because she chose to seek him out deliberately, as soon as Billy and Jimmy had disappeared for their dinner break.

She was looking remarkably pretty in a white cotton dress decorated with pale blue flowers, and with that rare gleam of October sunshine lighting up the river behind her and highlighting her rich dark hair. 'Are you avoidin' me, Mr Wade?' she challenged him.

He glanced up. 'No, of course not.'

Her eyes were hurt. 'It would be a shame if you did. Because I've dun nothin' to justify it.'

Silver straightened up and exchanged a long direct look with her. She seemed to be telling him in coded language that he could trust her - that she wasn't going to turn him in for that hundred pounds.

'What are you doing here, Amy?' he asked her, slightly sheepishly.

'Liam said 'e was deliverin' 'ere today after 'e'd been to the hostel. So 'e invited me along to 'elp him unload. I wanted the chance to see the ship up close.' She raised her eyes in awe. 'I've never seen anythin' like it. It's bigger than a cathedral.'

Silver was puzzled by this girl. 'The people who run the hostel where you work must be very understanding employers. It seems like you can take time off whenever you want to. Who actually is in charge of the hostel?'

Amy appeared confused. 'In charge? No one really. We all take turns to do wot we 'ave to.'

'Someone must be giving orders, and paying wages and bills. Does your rich patron ever visit the home and see her handiwork? What's her name anyway?'

Amy shifted her feet uneasily. 'You mean Lady Rachel Grosvenor?'

Silver nodded in understanding. 'Ah, she's your patron, is she? Yes,

I've heard of her. She's one of the wealthiest heiresses in England – inherited a banking fortune from her late grandfather - but wants to use her money to improve the lot of the poor of the East End.'

'That sounds like 'er,' Amy agreed reluctantly.

'Have you met her?'

Amy was still curiously defensive. 'Once. She came to the 'ostel just the once.'

'Some people would say she's mad to waste her money on low women,' Silver suggested provocatively.

'Well, if she's mad, then I wish she would bite a few other rich folk and make 'em equally mad,' Amy responded tartly...

*

Silver watched Amy retrace her steps up the slipway to rejoin Liam. He waved a greeting to Liam but didn't go over to speak to him.

He wondered if he'd been wise to goad Amy like that when he now depended so much on her continued silence to keep his secret. Yet he had provoked her deliberately because he wanted to find out more about her. He had to concede that Elisa had been right about her - there was something about Amy McLennan that didn't quite add up, something about her that didn't ring absolutely true...

He also saw Daniel Strode finally leaving to return to the drawing office, still looking like a man under a deep cloud.

Strode was an enigma too, if a much more dangerous one than Amy McLennan could ever be.

Silver remembered Elisa's counsel to give up trying to prove anything against Strode. It seemed increasingly like good advice to him now. The difficulties of proving anything against Strode did seem insurmountable when he was a fugitive himself and could be taken by the peelers at any time. Perhaps he should, as Elisa had also advised, simply get hold of what money he could, find a ship, and flee the country forever.

If he were caught now, no one would ever believe his wild stories about a respectable man like Daniel Strode. Without evidence, he might as well accuse the Queen or Prince Albert of murder.

Yet his conscience troubled him deeply over the thought of just cutting and running. If he did nothing, or merely fled the country, then more innocent young women might die at that man's hands.

How was he going to stop Daniel Strode from killing again...?

CHAPTER 18

Saturday 24th October 1857

Sergeant Sparrow could see why his host hadn't chosen to stand too near the ringside tonight. If he had, Mr Tyrell would have got his fine frock coat and top hat liberally spattered by now with the blood of the two bare-knuckle fighters in the ring.

The Lamb and Flag was a notorious public house in Rose Street, just off St Martins Lane, where illegal prize-fights were held in a large converted stable at the rear, and heavily wagered over. The fights were of such savagery that the dingy establishment was known informally in the area as the "Bucket of Blood." Many of the regular patrons of this entertainment were supposedly "gentlemen" but Sparrow hadn't seen much sign of any gentlemanly behaviour so far among the spectators this evening. In fact the two boxers currently attempting to bludgeon each other into submission in the ring were by far the most gentlemanly people in this smoky place, because they at least carried themselves with a certain degree of physical decorum and mutual respect.

This in marked contrast to the lewd, drunken and louche behaviour among the baying audience who had as much decorum as a pack of ravenous wolves. Sparrow had been disgusted to see that there were even women among the spectators – painted and blowsy women on the whole, but women nevertheless – who seemed in quite as much of a bloodthirsty frenzy as the men.

Sparrow glanced sideways at his companion for the evening, Mr Martin Tyrell, and wasn't reassured that he had made the right decision coming here tonight.

On his way home to Lambeth this Saturday night, Sparrow had called at the address in Vincent Square that the delightful Mrs Sophie Rolfe had given him for one of her murdered sister's former suitors. In the absence of any progress this week in tracking down the murderer of the two young governesses, Sparrow had returned briefly to the matter of Jonathan Silver. Since Vincent Square was only a short way across the river from his home in Lambeth, he had decided to take the opportunity to talk to one of the men who had apparently known Marianne Silver intimately before her marriage, and perhaps even after it.

Despite Grindrod's opinion that he was wasting his time, Sparrow had obtained from him a copy of the full transcript of Silver's trial which he had then dutifully read at home in the evenings this week - much to Edie's chagrin (who didn't like her husband bringing his work home, when he was at home little enough anyway.) Yet the more Sparrow had read of the deliberations at Newgate's Criminal Court in September, the more uneasy he had become about the verdict...

Sparrow had got to Vincent Square at 6 p.m. this Saturday evening just as Tyrell had been about to leave for a night's entertainment in Covent Garden. When Sparrow had insisted he delay his departure to answer a few questions, Tyrell had said he was already late for his appointment and therefore suggested Sparrow should accompany him in his cab to Covent Garden.

And almost before he'd realized it, Sparrow had found himself in the Lamb and Flag watching an illegal prize-fight, and with illegal wagers for colossal sums being placed all around him. Sparrow had no interest whatsoever in disrupting the activities at the Lamb and Flag – the Met tended to look the other way when it came to such things, knowing how unpopular it would be to prosecute them – but it would nevertheless be embarrassing if he was discovered to have been here, and on official duty. Tyrell was clearly enjoying his guest's discomfiture, though, so Sparrow guessed the invitation had probably been made with that malicious intent in mind. He'd clearly been invited along to entertain Tyrell and his snooty and aristocratic pals with his lower middle-class vulgarities, rather than because Tyrell felt any compelling urge to answer questions about the life of Marianne Silver.

Yet, even understanding that he was being belittled in this way, Sparrow had still thought it worthwhile putting up with a little humiliation from Tyrell and his friends, in return for getting some information about Marianne Silver. Sparrow was certainly running out of further direct leads to her missing husband, the presumptive murderer. Even assuming that this had been Dr Silver who had been using the alias "Wade" in that Wapping lodging house, that information hadn't helped track him down so far. Silver had disappeared completely from sight this week, despite an intensive further check of every lodging house in Wapping and Shadwell, so Sparrow was privately convinced that he must have left the area. Even the persistent Minshall hadn't been able to drum up any further sightings of him or his boy-thief accomplice, so Sparrow had an uneasy feeling that Silver had perhaps outwitted the law and managed finally to escape on a ship somewhere. The only slight hope of preventing that (assuming it hadn't already happened) remained with that girl Amy McLennan and the Hostel for Women where she worked. Sparrow thought there was a chance that young Amy might know where Silver (or Wade, if he was still using that alias) might be hiding. He had therefore dispatched Frank Remmert this week to keep an informal eye on Miss McLennan in the hope of her giving something away, although so far that surveillance had turned up nothing at all apart from the fact that Frank had fallen badly for the young woman's decorous looks.

Nor had Sparrow made any progress in finding the "Daniel" who had written that cryptic invitation to Miss Charlotte Livingstone. Sparrow had no doubts at all that the same person was responsible for the deaths of both governesses so was anxious to find any possible direct connection between the two. Miss Jane Penfold, the second victim, was however even more of a cipher than Miss Livingstone, so Sparrow thought he would have to return to concentrating his investigation on the first victim's life, which seemed likely to be more productive. He reminded himself again that he should go out to Hampstead and talk personally to Miss Livingstone's previous employers when he had the opportunity, as this might perhaps yield some clue to the identity of the mysterious "Daniel".

Sparrow had briefly toyed with Grindrod's notion that Silver might have some involvement in the murder of the two governesses. He had been there at the discovery of Miss Penfold's body after all - assuming Minshall had been right, anyway, and that the tall labouring man they'd been chasing last Sunday had really been Jonathan Silver. Yet Sparrow's instincts still told him that a second murderer was at loose in Wapping, apart from the elusive Dr Silver.

Sparrow was also considering visiting again the young woman who owned the tanner's yard where Miss Penfold's body had been found. Something did not ring quite true about Miss Elisa Smith, Sparrow had decided, and he thought it might be worthwhile investigating her background prior to her arrival in Wapping three years ago. She still reminded him tantalisingly of someone, but, so far, he hadn't been able to remember who...

*

'So would you care to wager on the outcome of the next fight, Sergeant?' Tyrell asked blithely, after the first bout had ended with one boxer being carried out of the ring in such a bloodied state that he seemed to have been hit by a steam locomotive travelling at fifty miles per hour.

Sparrow still didn't like the man's patronising manner so decided to fight back a little. 'Aren't you concerned, sir, that I might report the illegal activities being carried out on these premises?' Sparrow glanced around menacingly, to make his point. The big old former stable was fitted out with a raised square dais in the middle, forming the ring, while the former stalls all around had been converted into drinking booths at which groups of drunken patrons argued and spat and swore. Most of the crowd of three hundred or so, however, were gathered on the bloodied stone cobbles around the ring. A circle of gasoliers burned brightly above the dais so that the boxers were bathed in an intense white down light that highlighted their impressive musculature, but also revealed their terrible facial injuries.

Tyrell had an oily smile almost permanently stencilled on his lips. 'Hardly, Sergeant. I know for a fact that among the audience here tonight are three members of Parliament, two from the House of Lords, plus several prominent businessmen. Oh, and a youthful member of the Royal Family too. If you did report tonight's event, I would guarantee that you would be directing traffic on the Strand by this time tomorrow. Therefore I beg you to reconsider, before doing something so precipitate.' Tyrell was clearly enjoying himself, Sparrow could see. On the surface Tyrell remained outwardly amiable and respectful to his guest, but was clearly sniggering to himself in private. His three companions – all well-dressed toffs in silk waist-coated finery, and of a similar age and prosperity to Tyrell - weren't so adept at keeping a straight face, though, and barely made any attempt to hide their amusement at this clod of a policeman in their midst.

Sparrow kept his temper, and his dignity, with difficulty. He did wonder, though, why these wealthy and underemployed people were clearly of the opinion that being in the police force was such a demeaning job. No doubt they would come squealing to us soon enough if any crime was committed against them, he thought with irritation. Only yesterday, Sparrow had been called to Great Scotland Yard to suffer a direct haranguing from Sir Digby Carfax and his wife about the theft of his necklace, the *Tears of the Prophet*. The meeting had been Inspector Murphy's idea, of course – one more chance to see his old rival suffer. But if the purpose of such a humiliation had been to make Sparrow redouble his efforts, the effort had backfired because it had made Sparrow lose any interest at all in ever seeing that necklace returned to this irritating old man and his spoilt young bitch of a wife. In fact it had left Sparrow with a sneaking admiration for the young thief who had pulled off such a daring coup with skill and tenacity.

Sparrow turned his attention again to the ring where a fresh pair of fighters had climbed between the ropes, after attendants had first hosed the bloody ring down with water, and then sprinkled fresh sawdust. One of the new bare-knuckle fighters was a Cornishman, the other a Negro, and both were similarly decked out in tight silk drawers. Certainly the more lascivious of the women in the audience were moving closer for a better look at these two well-formed male bodies. The Cornishman was the smaller of the two, shorter and leaner, but with a shrewd face, and a hardened tin-miner toughness in his body. The Negro was four inches taller and had a magnificent body made up of sculpted slabs of muscle, but seemed a dullard judging from his bovine expression and rolling eyes. Under those tight silk drawers his manhood seemed enormous, and one or two of the more forward women spectators seemed determined to feel it for themselves to test its authenticity. Sparrow had heard that black men were well endowed in the reproductive department, and this particular African did seem to live up to the reputation of his race.

Edie, to her slight discredit, Sparrow thought, had an almost pathological fear and loathing of black men. Their woolly hair and thick lips, and those pink palms on otherwise jet black hands, made her skin creep, so she said. Not that she saw many black men in Lambeth, it was true, but earlier in their married life, when they were still living in Wapping, there had been a few visiting black sailors in the area to send a shudder of revulsion through her whenever they had passed by her door.

On the whole Sparrow thought it was unchristian of his wife to think that way. It was true that Africans were ugly – this boxer in the ring was as ugly as any heathen Sparrow had ever seen – but they were still flesh and blood like us, weren't they? And if the truth be told, then a black man's physique could be beautiful, even if his face wasn't. Come to think of it, most white people weren't exactly oil paintings either.

Tyrell studied the physiques of the two fighters in detail as he whispered conspiratorially in Sparrow's ear. 'As you can see, this next contest is about brains against brawn, Sergeant.'

'And which is which?' Sparrow asked innocently.

Tyrell's smile broadened a little. 'Very amusing, Sergeant.' He studied Sparrow's face in detail, as if weighing him up for a fight of his own. 'I tell you what; I'll be extremely generous to you concerning our proposed little wager. I'll let *you* choose between the two, and then I'll take the other one. I can't say fairer than that, can I?'

Sparrow grunted. 'I can't possibly accept your wager, sir. I couldn't even do it if it was legal. I'm on duty tonight. I came here to ask you about Marianne Silver, but so far you've told me nothing.'

'I promise I will answer all your questions about Marianne as truthfully as I can, Sergeant. But only if you first oblige me with a token wager to make our evening interesting. Come on! Five guineas! No more.'

That was more than Sparrow earned in a week – or even a fortnight, come to think of it.

'I can't, sir,' Sparrow refused again, to another round of sniggers from Tyrell's camp followers.

'One guinea, then,' Tyrell persisted. 'Surely even a police detective can afford one miserable guinea?'

Sparrow felt his face burning and finally let himself be persuaded under this man's goading. Edie would kill him if he lost, though, so he was determined to make the right choice.

'Then I'll go for the blackamoor,' he said, placing a guinea – his only one, as it happened - on the table in front of Tyrell.

Tyrell's friends fell about even more at that, laughing raucously in a most ungentlemanly way.

Still deeply resentful, Sparrow watched the fight get under way. Round one turned out to be a fairly even affair as far as Sparrow could tell. The Cornishman was quicker with his hands, flicking lots of mean little punches into the black man's face, but the Negro wasn't outclassed, and his return punches, when he occasionally landed one, were fearsome in their ferocity.

During the first interval, Sparrow pressed Tyrell yet again. 'Now keep your side of the bargain, sir. Tell me something about Mrs Silver. Something that might explain to me better why her husband killed her...'

'What do you want to know about her?' Tyrell assessed Sparrow shrewdly. 'Ah, I see. *That's* what this is all about! You still harbour some doubts about whether you got the right man, don't you, Sergeant?'

'Is that a genuine possibility, do you think?' Sparrow asked, studying his companion with equal frankness. Tyrell was about the same age as himself but there, any resemblance ended. The business financier was a greying, clean-shaven and well-fleshed individual in his early forties – and an unmarried man apparently, judging from his boisterous manner and the lack of a wedding ring. It seemed that Tyrell had made his fortune investing in the railway boom of the early forties, but, unlike many others, Tyrell had known precisely the right time to get out of railway stocks and move his money elsewhere before the bust came.

Looking at the Negro and the Cornishman preparing for the second round, Sparrow had a sudden longing to see the decadent-looking Mr Tyrell standing up in the ring with either one of these fighters that he apparently despised so much. Hopefully, in this delicious imagined spectacle, Tyrell would stay on his feet long enough to be beaten to a pulp, and to have his fine front teeth removed with one final blow...

Tyrell fortunately didn't guess what Sparrow was thinking, as he answered his question with a dismissive shrug. 'No, I doubt that the police have got it wrong this time, even given the limited imagination of you sturdy fellows. For the life of me, I cannot imagine that it could have been anyone else but her husband who was responsible for Marianne's sad death. Marianne was an extraordinarily beautiful woman, and such beauty does inspire strong emotions – love and jealousy, and possibly even murderous intent. But those kind of strong emotions are far more likely to be stirred in a jealous and possessive husband, than in anyone else. Especially if Marianne had taken other lovers - which she probably had, given her dull dog of a husband...' Tyrell sighed, as he took off his fine silk-lined top hat and inspected the rim as if looking for invisible flaws.

Sparrow became aware how shabby his own battered top hat must look alongside the ones these "gentlemen" were wearing. And how muddy and worn his cracked leather boots were, compared to their immaculately polished black shoes. But he ignored the urge to beat a hasty retreat from these awful people, and instead put another question about Mrs Silver's interesting life. 'She fell out with her father at one time, I believe?'

Tyrell looked vaguely impressed that Sparrow should know such a thing. 'Yes, she was a bold and independent spirit when young. I know she travelled abroad for several years on her own, and that she ended up working in Turkey of all places during the recent war.'

'Did you actually know Dr Silver at all, sir? And, if so, what did you think of him? Was he really such a dull dog as you make him out to be?' Sparrow hurried his question as the bell rang for the second round.

'I did know him...' Tyrell said absently, quickly losing interest in his conversation with Sparrow, now that the fight was underway again. 'And yes, he was far too dull for Marianne, I fear,' he said out of the corner of his mouth. 'She was thoroughly bored with married life, I think. At least, when she returned to London as a married woman, she seemed an entirely different person from that rebellious free-spirited young girl of seven years before.'

'How about *you* and Mrs Silver, sir? What was the exact nature of your relationship with her?'

Tyrell reluctantly turned his head away from the action in the ring again and narrowed his eyes in Sparrow's general direction. 'What do you mean by that, Sergeant?'

Sparrow gritted his teeth. 'Were you and she ever lovers, sir?'

Tyrell laughed at his guest's unexpected boldness. 'When she was a young unmarried lady, I did certainly pay her a lot of attention, Sergeant. But that's as much as I'm prepared to say on the matter. A lady has the right of privacy in such matters, which I intend to honour. And especially since this particular lady can no longer defend her own reputation…'

That equivocal answer still didn't satisfy Sparrow completely. Had the man been Marianne Silver's lover, or not? Sparrow thought the answer was probably no, yet wasn't completely sure. At the very least, though, she'd known him well as a young girl, and that probably flirtatious relationship might well have continued even after Marianne returned to London as a married woman.

Round two of the fight was increasingly brutal and bloody. The black man was now getting on top over the Cornishman, his superior size and strength beginning to show. Tyrell's friends became more subdued as they saw the white man take a vicious pummelling.

'So you do really believe that Dr Silver killed her?' Sparrow pressed him again, although it felt like he was talking to himself, with Tyrell's attention clearly caught up in all this violent and distracting action taking place in the ring immediately above their heads.

The Negro caught the Cornishman with a right cross of sickening force, and the white man's nose almost exploded. Tyrell stepped back quickly to avoid the jet of gore spraying in his direction, but not quite quickly enough, Sparrow was glad to see. 'Damnation!' he swore, as he noticed a spot of blood on his fine navy-blue cravat, before regarding Sparrow again with icy distaste. 'The evidence against Dr Silver seemed clear enough. He was more or less caught in the act, wasn't he?'

'Not quite,' Sparrow corrected him. 'He was seen by a maidservant withdrawing the knife from his wife's chest, and then looking as if he was about to plunge the knife into her body again...'

Round two had ended by now with the Cornishman needing help to get to his corner. 'And just how much more evidence would you say was necessary?' Tyrell commented dryly.

Round three began after a minute, giving the Cornishman a little time to recover his strength and poise. With his breath back, he certainly started Round Three better, and showed greater guile and skill than the giant Negro. Yet Sparrow was still convinced that he had made the right choice with his wager. The black man's superior strength would tell in the end – brawn winning over brain in this case, at least according to Tyrell's simplistic analysis of the bout anyway. It was fortunate that brawn didn't always win over brain in all aspects of life, otherwise mankind would still no doubt be living in caves. Yet Sparrow thought that Tyrell's analysis of the fight was at fault anyway - what was going on in the ring here seemed rather more complex than a simple confrontation between intellect and brute strength.

Given the way that the Cornishman had perked up in Round Three, the crowd were now baying for him to drop the Negro. But the simple fact was that he didn't have a big enough punch in his armoury to achieve this feat - he might as well have tried to drop an oak tree with a single punch. The black boxer took everything the Cornishman had left in his dwindling repertory of punches, uppercuts and below belt fouls, and came back as implacable and strong as ever.

At this point something changed, though. Sparrow could tell something was wrong with the black man: his attention seemed distracted by someone in the crowd, and the whites of his eyes rolled like a packhorse in distress. What followed was an almost comically bad piece of acting. The Negro took the softest of blows on the chin from the exhausted Cornishman, but suddenly fell backwards as if he'd been felled with an axe. The crowd didn't care about the quality of this acting, though – perhaps they didn't even notice - but instead whistled their approbation. One of the women at the side of the ring even punched the black man on the ground between the ropes, and Sparrow was amused to see the man flinch, despite supposedly being unconscious.

Or, that is, he would have been amused, if he hadn't remembered that he had a guinea of his own money riding on this disgraceful sham of a bout.

Even Tyrell was embarrassed by this poorly acted farce. 'Don't worry, Sergeant. Even I can't take your money after a disgraceful ending like that.' He frowned and excused himself. 'Be assured I knew nothing of this.' He handed Sparrow his guinea back, plus a freshly minted one to join it.

Sparrow quickly pocketed the two guineas before Tyrell could change his mind, and thought of another question. 'Do you know a Captain Robert Caitlin, sir? An army captain in the Thirteenth Light Dragoons.'

Tyrell seemed thoroughly out of sorts now. 'I do. Robert was at Balaklava.'

'So I've been told. I wondered if you would know how to contact him. I was told he was staying with relatives at Colby House in Kensington Gore, but has since left without telling them where exactly he was going.'

'I do see young Robert on occasion,' Tyrell admitted. 'In fact he has been here at the Lamb and Flag recently, milking his heroic reputation for all its worth. So many of our society ladies seem determined to sleep with the survivors of the Charge of the Light Brigade that the poor devils must be exhausted by now.' He recovered his good humour a little. 'If I do see him, I shall ask him to contact you, Sergeant. Where is the best place for him to reach you?'

'If he sent a note to Shadwell Police Station, and let me know his current address, then that would be perfectly acceptable.'

Tyrell nodded almost imperceptibly. Sparrow decided that Tyrell was now mightily bored with his policeman guest, the novelty long worn off, and only wanted to see the back of him. But Sparrow wasn't quite ready to oblige yet. 'Captain Caitlin and Mrs Silver were friendly in the Crimea, I hear,' he suggested.

Tyrell seemed wary. 'I believe Robert did encounter her there at the base hospital in Scutari after he was badly wounded, and that she helped nurse him back to health. But you would have to ask him the details of their acquaintanceship. I am not privy to what went on between them.'

The black boxer had by now got to his feet and was being escorted from the former stable house to a chorus of catcalls and jeers, particularly from the looser, more slatternly, women.

'When was the last time you saw Mrs Silver?' Sparrow asked.

Tyrell tried to think. 'Late in June, I think, riding in Rotten Row in Hyde Park. And she did look extremely desirable in her jet black riding habit. Her father had recently died, of course, so she was in mourning.'

Sparrow blinked. 'Riding? With who?'

Tyrell seemed deliberately evasive now. 'With a gentleman.'

'And did you recognize this gentleman?'

Tyrell sighed. 'As a matter of fact, I did. I know him slightly - a Foreign Office official called Charles Ferrar, with a mighty high opinion of himself.' Tyrell was still fretting about that spot of blood on his cravat, so his mind still seemed partly elsewhere. 'I was *not* Marianne's lover, Sergeant,' he finally admitted, 'much as I would have liked to be. If she had a lover after her marriage, then I believe it could have been this man Ferrar, despite the fact that he's older than I am.'

'How would you know that, sir?'

Tyrell laughed cynically. 'I saw the way she looked at him in Rotten Row. I may not understand much about ladies, Sergeant, but I think I do recognize when one might be in love...'

*

Tyrell escorted Sparrow out of the Lamb and Flag into Rose Street where he shook his hand with surprising warmth. 'You're a good sport, Sergeant. Thank you for joining me and my group of friends tonight, and for providing us with a little gentle amusement at your expense.'

Sparrow decided not to venture a reply to that, polite or otherwise. In preparation to leave, he turned up the collar of his greatcoat against the bite of the cold wind. Above his head, a gaslight sputtered in the gusting air, causing their elongated shadows to dance around on the cobbles like spirits.

Tyrell had one last question of his own. 'If I might inquire, Sergeant, who gave you my name in connection with this business of Marianne Silver's death?'

Sparrow wasn't sure if he should answer that honestly, but did in the end merely to study Tyrell's reaction. 'It was Mrs Silver's sister. '

'Ah, I see. The beautiful Sophie.'

Sparrow frowned. 'What do you mean by that, sir?'

Tyrell looked uncomfortable. 'It means that I believe the beautiful Sophie is practising what magicians call the art of misdirection or distraction.'

'You think she has things of her own to hide in connection with the death of her sister?'

'Sisters are not always sisterly,' Tyrell pointed out dryly. 'The tales I could tell you about my own dear sisters, for example, would put Goneril and Regan to shame.'

Sparrow frowned. 'What would Mrs Rolfe have to hide, sir?'

Tyrell shrugged expansively. 'Perhaps the fact that she loved her brother-in-law.'

Sparrow narrowed his eyes suspiciously. 'Who told you that, sir?'

'Actually it was Marianne herself who let me in on that little family secret, on one of the last occasions I saw her. A private soiree at the Lovelock house in Piccadilly at the end of May, not long before her father died. I didn't take her comment seriously at the time, but perhaps I should have. Although Marianne herself didn't seem too putout by the notion of her sister being her love rival, I have to say.'

Sparrow wondered if Tyrell was practising a little magician's distraction of his own. 'Sophie had only recently got married herself, then,' he argued.

'Yes, but to whom exactly? To a man she hardly knew – in fact, a mysterious man who *nobody* had ever heard of, only a year before. This man arrived in the capital last year and swept the beautiful Sophie Lovelock off her feet in a few short weeks.'

'So you're suggesting that Mrs Rolfe got married more on impulse than anything? In the hope perhaps of forgetting her obsession with her brother-in-law?'

'Precisely. It's a classic case. Take it from me, Sergeant, despite the fact that she'd just acquired a husband of her own, I suspect that Sophie Lovelock still secretly longed for her sister's husband, and perhaps still does. She wouldn't testify against him at the trial, would she?'

'She didn't support him either, though,' Sparrow countered.

'That doesn't mean I'm not right, Sergeant,' Tyrell said smugly.

But, even if that were true, could Sophie really have killed her sister? Sparrow wondered. Yet she had admitted herself that she possessed a front door key to the Silvers' house in Russell Square so was one of the few people who could have gained admittance without ringing the front doorbell. And she was also one of the few people who would have had the element of complete surprise on her side...

*

Jonathan Silver lay crouched in the backyard of Elisa's home, wondering whether to knock at her backdoor or not.

He was taking a huge risk returning to Wapping on a Saturday night, he knew, but he had to try and escape the encircling trap that seemed to be closing in on him from all sides.

He could see a light inside the house so knew she had to be home. Although whether she would be happy to see him was another matter. She had been decidedly cool and offhand when she'd seen him off before dawn last Monday morning, and he doubted whether she would have missed him since.

But he raised his hand to strike the brass knocker anyway, wondering what he would say to her if and when she answered. Before his hand could even make contact with the woodwork, though, he found himself flat on his back on the hard stone cobbles with a dagger held at his throat by some unknown person.

He waited for a killing blow to come from the silhouetted figure pinning him down, but none came. Instead a voice – *her* voice. 'What the devil are you doing back here, Jonathan? '

Silver found himself diverted for a moment with this girl straddling him in such an intimate fashion, and made no move to get from under her.

Neither did Elisa seem willing to move immediately, it seemed, as she breathed heavily into his face. 'On Monday, you said you weren't coming back here ever, Jonathan. I could have killed you, you numskull! I thought it had to be Minshall or that devil Sparrow.' She sat up a little, but still remained perched on top of him. 'Sparrow was here on Tuesday, you know, asking questions. I was almost tempted to slit his throat there and then, and make a run for it. But I couldn't quite bring myself to do it.'

'Why not?' Silver was still never entirely sure when Elisa was being serious. He truly found it difficult to read the mind of this strange and unpredictable girl, whose moods could vary from womanly tenderness to steely determination in an instant.

'I couldn't do it because Liam was here. I could hardly disappoint young Liam by having the love of his life, Miss Elisa Smith, slit some policeman's throat right in front of his eyes. Could I...?' she added dryly.

She finally climbed off Silver, to his regret, hid the knife under her skirts, and helped him to his feet. Then she opened the back door and let him into the warm kitchen, where she turned up the gaslight until she could see his face clearly.

'So why have you come back, Jonathan? Have you killed this man

Strode yet? And are you ready to leave England for good?' she asked him eagerly.

Silver made a wry face. 'I haven't killed Strode, and now I've given up all hope of ever proving anything against him concerning Marianne's death. He can go on and murder every governess in the damned country now, for all I care. I intend to flee the country and save my own skin.'

'So flee,' she said succinctly.

Silver hesitated. 'I need to get hold of my own money first. I will need that money if I want to start a new life abroad with a new identity.'

Elisa shrugged impatiently. 'Forget your own money – you can't possess enough to make it worth the risk of approaching your bank. I will give you enough money to leave – a hundred pounds in gold - if that's what you really wish. But I don't believe you're serious about going. Deep down, you still want to deal with this man Strode – get some "justice" for yourself, whatever you think that is - and you won't leave until you do. You really are a stupid and naïve man, Dr Silver.'

Silver flushed at the contempt in her voice. 'If you say so. But there is one last favour I need from you, Elisa - some more of your father's clothes. Did he have any finer clothes here perhaps? Gentleman's clothes?'

She squinted at him suspiciously. 'Why would you need a gentleman's clothes?'

Silver wavered for a moment. 'Because I intend to meet a lady in Chancery Lane tomorrow, and I need to look the part again...'

CHAPTER 19

Sunday 25th October 1857

Tonight, for the first time in many months, Jonathan Silver felt a little like his old self again, as he paraded up and down Piccadilly.

Dressed in a fine worsted frock coat, felt top hat, black silk cravat and expensive leather shoes, he once again bore some passing resemblance to that wealthy young surgeon of a few months previously. Yet, regarding his own image in the darkened window of a Piccadilly mansion, he realized that this resemblance between his former and his present self was only a comforting illusion at best. In reality something profound and irreversible had happened to him over these last months, so that, no matter what the future might bring, he could never again be that rather superficial and naïve young man he'd once been. Elisa was quite correct in her judgement of him. Despite the testing rigors of his past life – medical school, service in the navy, army surgeon in the Crimea, and practising doctor at St Barts Hospital in London – Silver was forced to admit to himself that he had remained until recently an innocent, largely untouched by the world and its evils. Yet being a fugitive from justice, and a husband to a murdered wife, had changed all that forever, finally eradicating in him those last traces of innocence and optimism about the state of the world and humankind.

He had been parading up and down outside the Lovelock family home in Piccadilly for more than an hour now. He had kept on the move for fear of arousing suspicion, or - worse still - attracting the attention of a patrolling bobby. Fortunately he wasn't getting wet tonight as the weather had turned relatively benign for late October, with the night air cold and dry and cloudless for once, if still as sooty and smoky as ever. On the south side of Piccadilly, the plane trees of Green Park, lit by hissing gaslight, seemed decorated with smudges of charcoal rather than with the golden tints of autumn.

Piccadilly was one of London's grandest avenues, a street filled from end to end with the mansions and institutions of the rich and powerful – Apsley House, Devonshire House, Burlington House, and the home of the Royal Academy among them. The Lovelock home was one of the more modest houses on this great street, but then Marianne and Sophie's father had only been a railway engineer, after all, not a fine lord or a Royal Academician, or a national hero like the Duke of Wellington. Yet George Lovelock, despite his modest working class origins, had still been able to purchase himself a house on one of the most prestigious streets in London, which said something about the man and his career, and perhaps about social mobility in modern England too. And, even though of narrow frontage, the Lovelock family home was nevertheless a fine King George II house and, more importantly, a place that held many happy memories for Jonathan Silver.

Sophie was presently inside her late father's house, Silver knew, because he had seen her enter at six o'clock, having followed her here in a cab from her own married home in Took's Court. His original intention had been to try and see her privately at her own home, but he had been forced to change that plan at short notice when, on arriving in her secluded street off Chancery Lane, he'd seen her leaving for the evening in a hackney cab, on her own. The chance of seeing Sophie alone, without her husband, was too much of an opportunity for Silver not to take, so he had followed her cab in one of his own, despite the risks of travelling up west where he had more chance of being recognized dressed like this.

Silver had guessed immediately where Sophie was bound on this Sunday evening: she had to be visiting her widowed mother. The Lovelock family had long been in the habit of meeting every Sunday evening after church, to enjoy simple card games, play music together, and make conversation. And Sophie, despite the privations and sorrows of the last months – losing both a father and then a sister in quick succession - was still apparently continuing this family custom. Silver was only sorry that he hadn't been able to catch up with Sophie's cab before she entered the Lovelock house – his own cab from Chancery Lane had been delayed a little by a collision between a cart and a horse-bus in the Strand - so he'd been forced to wait outside for her to reappear, perhaps for hours...

And so it turned out. At eight o'clock, with no sign of Sophie returning to her own home yet, Silver briefly took a turn up Piccadilly as far as Regent Street. The newspaper sellers around the circus were bawling out the latest news from India in broad cockney vernacular. *"Read all about it! Mutineers defeated at Agra! Sir Colin Campbell close to Lucknow...!"*

Silver could only hope that General Sir Colin Campbell was bringing a vast army with him, otherwise the relief of the long siege at Lucknow might not be as assured as the *Times* correspondent William Howard Russell seemed to expect.

A headline closer to home brought Silver back to earth quickly. '*East End murderer still at large! Read all about it...!*' Pulling down the brim of his top hat low over his eyes, Silver moved on quickly.

He soon returned to watching the Lovelock home, but this time, after receiving a suspicious look from a uniformed doorman at a nearby mansion, preferred to wait on the opposite side of the road at the edge of Green Park. The night was getting colder, his breath forming in clouds, and he had to beat his hands together frequently to keep warm. At nine o'clock he was in the middle of just such violent exercise when a square of light finally opened in the doorway of the Lovelock residence. Then Sophie appeared, wearing a velvet cloak over her blue dress and crinoline, and kissed her mama a fond farewell on the doorstep. Silver was shocked at the appearance of Marianne's beautiful mother, who seemed to have shrunk from healthy well-formed middle age into doddering old age in a matter of months.

Sophie was leaving on her own, Silver was glad to see, and had obviously arranged beforehand for a cab to call for her at this time, because a two-wheeler appeared almost by magic at the kerb as soon as she showed her face at the door.

Careful of her voluminous skirts, she stepped up daintily into the back of the cab. Silver realized this departure was happening much faster than he'd anticipated, and raced across the cobbled width of Piccadilly, dodging other cabs and speeding carriages, as he tried to get to the other kerb before the cab pulled away.

For a moment it didn't look as if he would make it, and that all he would get for his pains tonight would be to see Sophie's cab fast disappearing into the distance. But the cabby fortunately chose to turn around in order to head east back along Piccadilly, and this manoeuvre provided Silver with the chance to almost catch up with his quarry. Yet, as if the driver was goading him, the cab accelerated away at high speed from him again before he could attract Sophie's attention inside.

Despite the stares of passers-by, Silver was forced to run alongside. Luckily the cab was reduced to a crawl again as it came to the busy junction with Bond Street, and Silver had the opportunity to catch it again and to tap lightly on the window.

A startled face appeared at the glass. 'Jonathan!' she said, open-mouthed...

*

Silver sat alongside her in the back of the cab as they began to move again and turned south down St James's Street. The elderly cabby, a grizzled man with impressive silver whiskers, had let Silver join his passenger in the back at her request, but didn't seem happy about doing so, grumbling incomprehensibly into his beard.

Silver ignored the cabby's mumblings from outside, and took her hand and kissed the back of it.

'Where have you been hiding, Jonathan?' she asked in a whisper.

Silver smiled ruefully. 'I'd better not say – you wouldn't believe me anyway.' He paused to take in her beautiful features. 'You look wonderful, Sophie,' he said truthfully. A little suffering had added both extra maturity and a startling new beauty to her child's face, Silver decided. Or was it perhaps married life that had caused this subtle change?

Sophie still appeared breathless with surprise. 'How can you tell in the light of a single oil lamp, Jonathan? I could be wrinkled like a crone for all you know.'

'I saw you at the door with your mother. The light was bright enough there; thanks to your father, your house must have the brightest gaslight in London.'

'You weren't there by accident, were you?' she stated slightly accusingly.

'No,' he admitted. 'I followed you here tonight from Took's Court. I need your help.'

She didn't respond to that immediately but instead studied him closely in return. 'You too look remarkably well considering what you've been through, Jonathan. The fugitive life must be an agreeable one to you.'

'Hardly,' he denied moodily. 'In fact I wouldn't recommend it to my worst enemy.'

She coloured instantly. 'Sorry. That was a thoughtless thing to say...'

*

She leaned back in her seat, keeping her voice low so the cabby wouldn't be able to discern any of her words. 'I imagined you would already be far away by now.'

'It probably would have been the wisest thing to do,' conceded Silver. 'But I decided not to flee the country immediately. I wanted to find out instead who really killed Marianne.'

'What hope do you have of that?' She turned away slightly, avoiding his eyes.

'None at all now,' he admitted ruefully. He noted the expression on her face and said dispiritedly, 'You don't really think I did such a wicked thing, do you?'

She turned her face to him again, but her eyes were still lowered.

'No, I never believed you could do such a terrible thing. Nor does Mama.'

Silver was relieved by that. 'Then if I didn't do it, Sophie, it has to be someone else who murdered your sister. Someone who probably knew Marianne intimately.'

'I understand that, Jonathan. But how can you possibly hope to ever discover the truth, in your perilous situation?'

'I can't, Sophie: that's the simple answer.' They had passed St James's Place by now, and turned east again, into Pall Mall. 'Have you told the police anything about me?' he inquired of her, as the rapid turning of the vehicle brought their shoulders into brief contact on the back seat of the cab.

Sophie straightened herself in her seat as the cab lurched on. 'About you, nothing important. But I did speak with a detective from the police force, and told him you were innocent and that he should try investigating other gentlemen in Marianne's life.' She hesitated, her eyes suddenly distraught. 'I should warn you, Jonathan. I believe there was perhaps a chance that Marianne was seeing these other gentlemen socially, and may even have been unfaithful to you.'

'I doubt that, Sophie,' Silver denied quickly, but inside he secretly wondered if it could be true. He had known that Marianne was unhappy and perhaps bored with her married life, even becoming secretive and withdrawn at times. But even so, he had still believed her to be faithful. 'Who was this detective?' he went on.

'His name was Sparrow. Sergeant Sparrow from Shadwell Station in the East End. He looked a very ordinary little man, like a lawyer's clerk, but I suspect he is actually very astute. He is close on your trail, Jonathan, so be very careful of the man.'

Silver swore under his breath. That man Sparrow again! He seemed to be everywhere...

'So who were these gentlemen that Marianne was seeing socially? Do I know them?'

'Possibly. I'm not sure if you ever met them. One of them is a wealthy middle-aged financier called Martin Tyrell.'

Silver shrugged angrily. 'I did meet Mr Tyrell on a couple of occasions, and thought him a thoroughly unpleasant rogue. I'm sure Marianne never cared for Tyrell at all: she had far too much good taste and judgement ever to involve herself seriously with such a man. Who else was there?'

Sophie stirred, embarrassed. 'There was also Robert Caitlin, a young captain in the Thirteenth Light Dragoons. I know for a fact that Marianne met him on at least one occasion last summer, possibly more.'

Silver was less dogmatic this time. 'I know Captain Caitlin too. In fact I saved his life in the Crimea, or certainly his leg at least.'

Sophie was still pink with embarrassment. 'Perhaps he wasn't as grateful to you as he should have been.'

'Perhaps so. But, to be fair, I believe he did know Marianne intimately before I ever met her, and it was me who stole her away from him, if anything. In fact, as I recall, I only met Marianne because of Caitlin. She came into my ward one day to visit Caitlin when he was recuperating, which is how I came to be introduced to her.'

Sophie was puzzled. 'You didn't see Marianne every day at the hospital? I always thought she was working as a nurse in your ward. At least, that is the impression that Marianne gave me.'

Silver picked his words with care. 'No, you must have misunderstood her. She never actually worked with me. She worked elsewhere in the hospital. '

Although doing *what* was a good question. Whatever had been Marianne's prime reason for being at Scutari, Silver had long suspected that it had precious little to do with her nursing duties. But perhaps this wasn't the right thing to say to Sophie, Silver decided reluctantly, who'd obviously heard an entirely different version of her sister's experiences at Scutari.

*

They had passed the Haymarket and were now in a dark stretch of the road before Trafalgar Square when Sophie leaned over with a sigh, locked her eyes with his, and then kissed him tenderly on the lips.

Silver was so taken by surprise by this unexpectedly forward behaviour that he didn't even try to resist her, kissing her with equal tenderness in return. In his present state, he was no longer a man in any mood for self-denial, even if this felt entirely wrong and unbecoming. He had always known instinctively that Sophie was strongly attracted to him, and there was no doubt that he had felt something for her in return that wasn't entirely brotherly in nature. But having never met each other until after his marriage to Marianne, by which time the die had been firmly cast, they had always behaved to each other strictly within the bounds of brother-sister propriety.

Yet Silver had to admit to himself that he had been obscurely disappointed when Sophie had chosen to marry so quickly, and to someone she hardly knew. He had half-suspected that Sophie had married Edward Rolfe in a deliberate move to distance herself from him.

Marianne had certainly had her doubts about the wisdom of Sophie's marriage too, and had spent some time trying to discover the intimate details of Edward Rolfe's past life. Strangely, according to Marianne, Edward didn't seem to have much of a past life at all...

Sophie finally released him from her embrace, breathing heavily. There was an awkward silence, before she said, 'You should certainly leave the country at once, Jonathan. There is no chance of justice ever being done now.'

'You're right, of course; I am planning to leave very soon. And that's the reason why I came to see you tonight. I have a bank account with Coutts Bank in Threadneedle Street, with nearly five thousand pounds in it. I need to close that account and transfer the money to a bank in Zurich, Switzerland, where the law here can never find it. It will enable me to start a new life abroad.'

Her eyes widened. 'Where did you get that amount of money from?'

'It was left to me in a trust fund by my father when he died. The money came from the sale of his factory; my father had reluctantly sold up not long before his death, when it became clear to him that I was not suited by inclination or ability to taking over the running of the factory from him. But I have never touched a penny of that money until now.'

Sophie was curious. 'Is the account in your own name?'

'Yes, it is. But I daren't go to the bank openly with this Sergeant Sparrow chasing me. And I don't trust my own lawyer to do it; the man let me down badly during the trial.'

'You want me to go to Threadneedle Street as a proxy for you? Is that it?'

'If you would. You're the only person that I can truly trust with this delicate task.'

She leaned her head against his shoulder. 'Then I'll gladly do it. I've been looking for some opportunity of making amends to you for my lack of moral support during the trial.'

The cab had traversed Trafalgar Square by now and was in the dense late evening traffic in the Strand. 'You owe me nothing, Sophie,' he said uncomfortably.

After he had passed a note to her with all the relevant bank details, and the password she would need to act as his proxy, she smiled sadly at him, as if silently acknowledging the fact that they might never meet again. 'Was there no other reason for coming to see me tonight, apart from asking me to do this favour for you?' she asked wistfully.

'There was one other thing. It concerns another of Marianne's gentlemen friends - one you never mentioned just now.'

'And who is that?'

Silver hesitated fractionally. 'A man called Daniel Strode. Do you remember that gentleman's name?'

'Yes, I do remember Mr Strode. Not a very gentlemanly person, as I recall.' Sophie had a thought. 'Sergeant Sparrow seemed interested in him too, for some obscure reason.'

'Did he?' Silver was intrigued. 'Then I wonder if he's interested in Mr Strode for the same reasons that I am.' Silver doubted that, though: it seemed too much to hope that the police might already have their own suspicions of Daniel Strode.

'And what is your business with Mr Strode?' There was a nervous catch in Sophie's voice.

Silver's voice faltered. 'Sophie, I think Strode could be the guilty party. I believe *he* might have killed Marianne.'

She blanched at that. 'Why would you think it was him? He was an unpleasant and ill-tempered man, it's true, but his courtship of Marianne ended long ago. Unlike Mr Tyrell and Captain Caitlin, who were still apparently actively pursuing Marianne even last summer.'

'I don't know why he would murder her after all this time. But perhaps there was more jealousy and vindictiveness to Strode's feelings than anyone ever imagined.' Silver hesitated again. 'The man is extremely dangerous in my opinion.'

'Why do you say that?'

Silver took her hand. 'Because two other young women have been recently murdered in Wapping in the East End. You must have read about it. I believe Strode might have killed them too.'

Sophie was reeling at this unpleasant revelation. 'Then give your evidence to the police, Jonathan. Through an intermediary, I mean. *I* could be your intermediary, if you wish.'

Silver grimaced. 'Do you really think Sparrow would listen to you?'

'He might.' She coloured again. 'I believe he looks on me favourably. Perhaps I could try and arrange a secret meeting between you and Sergeant Sparrow where you could tell him what you know.'

'No, that would be asking too much of you. And, anyway, I couldn't trust Sparrow not to spring a trap on me. Until a few days ago I would have liked to see the police taking a close interest in Strode, but it's too late now. The police are closing in on me instead, and much faster than I care for. If this Sergeant Sparrow suspects you've been taking to me, and thinks you know where I'm hiding, he'll never rest until he gets the information out of you. That's why I can't tell you where I'm going - I can't take the risk of you giving me away. I have to get away from England before I'm taken by the peelers again. I can't face the thought of being recaptured and returned to Newgate to hang.'

The cab came to the top of Villiers Street where Silver rapped on the back of the cab to gain the driver's attention. 'Let me off here, Sophie. I shall take the paddle steamer from Westminster stairs.'

Sophie kissed him again, even more forcefully than before. 'Then take care, Jonathan.' She was breathless with worry. 'Is there nowhere I can contact you, if I need to? No other person through whom I can get a message to you...?'

'No,' he stated bleakly. 'Not for the present anyway.'

Silver was about to step out of the cab when Sophie pulled him back abruptly. 'Wait, Jonathan! I nearly forgot. A man called at Took's Court last night briefly to see me. This gentleman left something behind - deliberately, I think. I believe he intended for me to give it to you.'

Silver frowned. 'Why would you believe it was for me?'

'Because he left it in an envelope with your name written on the front.'

'That would seem fairly conclusive, then,' Silver agreed dryly. 'Tell me more about this visitor.'

Sophie wrinkled her brow. 'He was a rather elderly man, although well-mannered. He gave me the impression of having spent many years abroad; he was sunburned and his skin and hair was a little coarsened by the effects of a tropical climate. He said he was a friend of Marianne's, recently returned from the Continent. He was very secretive and strange in his manner. He asked if I had any way of contacting you. I said not, but I could see he didn't believe me completely. He made a particular point of asking me not to mention his visit to anyone, not even to Edward. I had to promise him in the end in order to satisfy him.'

'What was this strange visitor's name?'

'His name was Charles Ferrar. I didn't trust Mr Ferrar entirely at first, of course. But he knew a lot of personal details about Marianne – things only a close acquaintance could possibly know - therefore I'm sure he was genuine. After he departed, I found this letter with your name on it, left on the mantelpiece. I'm afraid I looked inside because I had no idea that I would actually be able to deliver it to you.'

'What was inside?'

'Luckily I put it in my handbag so you can see for yourself. Strangely there was no message, though, only a ticket.' Sophie reached down inside her bag and pulled out a small rectangle of cardboard.

'What's the ticket for?' Silver asked, surprised.

'That's the strangest thing. It's for the Alhambra Music Hall in Leicester Square, of all places. Row H seat 27 in the main auditorium, for the evening of the fourth of November.'

Silver was mystified. 'That's a full ten days away.'

'I believe he wanted to give you sufficient notice to be there. This man clearly wants to talk to you about something.'

'It could be a police trap, perhaps instigated by the clever Sergeant Sparrow,' Silver thought aloud.

'It could indeed. But I don't think so; I believe the gentleman was genuine, and that he might have some useful information about Marianne to tell you.' Sophie touched his hand gently. 'Yet if you have any sense, Jonathan, you will be long gone from this country by then...'

CHAPTER 20

Wednesday 28th October 1857

Mist coiled its way up from the river like an army of serpents, filling the grimy cobbled lanes of Wapping with an impenetrable creeping wall of white.

Silver was exhausted after three more hard days on the slipway at the yard, yet had still made the risky journey back to Wapping tonight. This time he'd come with a more definite purpose in mind than on his last speculative visit to Elisa four days ago, when he'd come simply in the hope of borrowing some better clothes in which to see Sophie, and for yet more money to tide him over in his expensive lodgings at The Ship Inn. Tonight, by contrast, he had come to Wapping in order to plan his final departure from England...

He had by now reached the painful conclusion that he had no hope of ever finding Marianne's real murderer by himself, be it Daniel Strode or another unknown party, and that it was now finally time for him to flee the country before the net closed around him again. And tonight, in a public house called the King George Tavern, he'd found plenty of opportunities for doing so in talking to the many seafaring men who patronized this particular noisy, smoke-filled, ale-drenched establishment. In the end, Silver had made a deal with a Captain Christy Blackburn of the three-masted barque *Tradewinds*. Captain Blackburn was a one-eyed rogue from Deptford who looked like he'd gladly sell his grandmother for a five pound note, but he was exactly the man Silver needed as part of his plan. Blackburn's ship, the *Tradewinds,* was due to set sail with the tide in sixteen days on Friday 13th November, bound for Bahia in Brazil, Buenos Aires and Valparaiso. Fighting to be heard above the chink of glasses, profane curses and drunken raucous laughter in the King George Tavern, Silver had agreed with Blackburn to take one of the three passenger berths available on the vessel.

Silver had freely given his name to Blackburn as Wade, but didn't trust the good captain at all, despite the ten gold sovereigns he'd put down on the ale-stained table, and the promise of fifty more on the day of sailing. He knew well that Captain Blackburn suspected him to be a fugitive, and that the rogue would, given half a chance, betray him to the police for the reward money. If that betrayal did happen, then Silver would have been quietly delighted, because that was exactly what he was hoping for. Silver's arrangement with Captain Blackburn was no more than an elaborate red herring designed to lead the police (and hopefully Sergeant Sparrow) in entirely the wrong direction...

In reality Silver had no intention of sailing with the *Tradewinds,* but had a completely different escape route in mind for the 13th November. On that day, Silver planned instead to take the steam packet from Gravesend Pier, bound for Rotterdam. From there, he had two alternatives in mind now that the thought of a new life on the island of Hong Kong beckoned so enticingly. One was to take a train to the port of Trieste in the Austro-Hungarian Empire, via Switzerland, and from there travel by ship to Port Said, and eventually overland to the port of Suez on the Red Sea. Or instead, if different circumstances arose, he would possibly take a ship direct from Rotterdam to the Cape, and thence direct to the East Indies...

The 13th was still more than a fortnight away, though, and even Silver had to wonder to himself why he hadn't tried for an earlier date to flee when the net was tightening around him inexorably all the time. The truth was that he was finding it hard to take that final irrevocable step and abandon England forever when, by doing so, he would be giving up any hope of ever clearing his name. Yet there was another less obvious reason for his vacillation too – the fact that he wanted desperately to see the Great Ship launched, and floating free and proud in the murky water of the Thames. The future of the *Leviathan* seemed connected to his own well being in some strange way, and he felt as proprietary about the fate of that giant vessel as its true creator, Mr Brunel, even to the extent of delaying his departure and risking recapture in order to see her launched for himself.

And Elisa? What of her? There still seemed a small chance that Elisa would accompany him when he eventually left from Gravesend, although Silver was far from convinced that she had been truly serious when talking about leaving England forever, and making a new life in the Far East. As ever, it was difficult to know with an enigmatic and unpredictable girl like Elisa.

Yet, come with him or not, she couldn't possibly remain in London. It was only a matter of time now before the law caught up with her too, and when they did, the legal establishment would make a vengeful example of her. Silver didn't doubt that they would gaol her for at least twenty years for the theft of something as important as that necklace, and from someone as important as Sir Digby Carfax, baronet. And at the end of her prison term, they would probably then transport her to that God-forsaken hole, Australia, to end her days living in the bush among aborigines and convict hard cases...

Silver still felt a residual guilt, though, that because of his decision to flee the country Strode might escape punishment for all his sins. It was true that Silver wavered more these days in his definite assumption of Daniel Strode's culpability, particularly after hearing Elisa's opinion that Marianne could not possibly have been referring to Strode when she'd said that word *Leviathan* with her dying breath. Yet Strode did seem inextricably linked to the death of Miss Jane Penfold at the very least. Silver remembered that girl's sweet young face as she waited at the ferry pier on the Isle of Dogs. Had he by his inaction condemned that young girl to die in that horrid way? – strangled apparently, and left to decompose in a lime pit in a stinking tanner's yard...

Silver had considered his choices repeatedly over the last few days. Should he have accepted Sophie's offer last Sunday and asked her to try and arrange a secret meeting with Sparrow? There was still time to let Sparrow know about Strode having a liaison with that girl Jane Penfold on the night she died. That might at least save another girl from suffering the same fate…

Yet he could hardly do that – it was just too risky. It would have made it clear to Sparrow beyond doubt that he had been in contact with Sophie, and Sparrow would soon have wormed everything out of her, including the fact that he had asked her to transfer the assets in his private bank account to a bank overseas.

Silver had also briefly considered approaching Strode's driver at the yard. He at least must know about his master's meeting with Miss Penfold, and perhaps suspect something worse than a mere sexual liaison by his master with a young girl. But the man hadn't come forward voluntarily so far, therefore must be being well paid to keep his silence.

Silver had also thought of taking an even more extreme step. *Could he perhaps waylay Strode somewhere, and beat the truth out of him?* Yet what if he had got everything wrong and the man was somehow innocent of murder? After all, he knew of no connection between the first murdered girl and Strode. And all he actually knew of Jane Penfold was that she had accepted a ride in Strode's carriage on one fogbound evening.

Had that really been Strode with her in that house in Pennington Street at all? Silver had seen Jane and Strode's driver together that night. But never Strode himself...

*

On the way back from the King George Tavern, Silver passed Elisa's back door and once again crept into that now familiar backyard. He wanted to break the news of his impending departure to her, and to find out whether she really wanted to come with him and start a new life in the East.

He still wasn't entirely sure what his own feelings were for this enigmatic girl. She was of course an entirely different sort of woman from any he'd ever had a relationship with before – sensual, unpredictable, even dangerous - yet that difference made her an intoxicating and alluring companion. Visiting her was fast becoming an addictive habit with him, something he needed in order to provide relief from his fugitive and threatened existence.

Yet his heart sank when he saw that her house was dark and cold-looking.

Had she herself already fled without waiting for him to come back?

Silver felt something close to despair at the thought that she might be gone for good. It occurred to him for the first time how much this girl had meant to him over the last three weeks since that memorable night she'd broken him out of Newgate and given him a new lease on life...

*

In his disappointed state, it was going to be a long walk back to the Isle of Dogs in this miserable cold fog, but he would have to begin.

How he needed the company of a friend tonight! As he made his way up the fogbound alleyways, he felt like the loneliest and bitterest man on earth.

He avoided Old Gravel Lane as usual, but even New Gravel Lane was a dangerous route to traverse now, especially late at night and on his own. It would only take one inquisitive peeler to take an interest in him, and he was sunk forever.

Keeping away from the streetlights – in Wapping still mostly smoky oil lamps - he moved past the Black Horse public house with all its muffled raucous noise and its sounds of drunken revelry and tuneless fiddle music.

A little higher up the street he came to the Hostel for Women. No sign of Amy tonight on the street, which probably wasn't a bad thing. She was, regrettably, someone best avoided now.

He was congratulating himself on escaping notice and reaching one of the quieter back lanes at the top of New Gravel Lane when he was suddenly sent reeling by a vicious unseen hand, and ended up on his chest in the gutter. He heard a familiar voice say behind him with a glow of satisfaction, 'Tie his hands tight, Joey. We've got him! The infamous

Dr Silver...!'

*

They were an ugly pair.

Silver remembered them all too well from a fortnight ago, and their looks hadn't improved in the meantime. Now his senses were returning, he found he was lying on his back on the wet muddy ground in this dismal back alley, trussed up securely with ropes. The cobbles bit painfully into his back, while the ropes did similar damage to his wrists and legs. Being sailors, his two attackers unfortunately knew only too well how to tie a sound knot, so there would be no breaking free from these ropes without help.

The taller one, Joey, was a burly and pockmarked man with bad teeth and wiry hair. His companion, Jack, was similar in all respects to Joey except that he was six inches shorter. Jack, for all his shorter stature, seemed to be the one in charge, though, and the one of slightly superior intellect. Not that that was saying much: Silver guessed that neither of these two probably spent much of their shore leave in London patronising Michael Faraday's lectures at the Royal Institution, or watching the opera at Covent Garden.

Both were still carrying the scars of their previous encounter with him, Silver noticed worriedly, even though it had been more than two weeks ago. Joey was in the worse state of the two, his jaw still a multi-coloured canvas of rich assorted bruising, and his nose a pulpy mess from where Silver had hit him with a lantern.

'I'm jus' goin' to give him a bit of his own medicine,' Joey decided with grim satisfaction.

Jack held up a fist like a swollen ham. 'No, you don't, Joey, me old son.'

Joey was belligerent in his frustration. 'Why the fuck not?'

'Cos I says so. Mr Minshall says we 'ave to bring 'im in one piece. Or else he won't pay us 'alf the reward, and that's just been put up to two hundred and fifty pounds! If we makes a mess of 'im, the peelers 'll want to know 'ow it 'appened.'

Joey did his best to think with his limited equipment for that purpose. 'Well, if that's right, then we could take 'im to the police ourselves. What do we need Minshall for?'

Jack ran his hands roughly through his spiky hair. 'Except *we're* wanted too by the law, you numbskull. Stop thinking, Joey – it's much too difficult for you - and go and find Minshall. He said he would be at the White Rose tonight.'

Joey glowered. 'All right. But I'm gonna take one kick at this bastard first. Don't worry. Ain't nobody goin' to see this one.' With that he fired a vicious boot into Silver's left side that felt to him like it had broken a rib.

Joey left, still grumbling about only getting half the police reward, while Silver writhed on the ground, his ribs on fire.

Jack bent over him in philosophical mood. 'Well, that's your own fault. That's what you get for takin' on two sailor boys, Doc. 'Ow do you feel about 'angin'? I'll make sure to come and watch you, my friend. It'll be nice to see your eyeballs pop out, and your tongue turn black as you scramble for air.'

Jack straightened up triumphantly, but then suddenly quivered as something struck him with a resounding smack from behind. Then the drunken wharf rat fell sideways on the cobbles like a felled tree.

'Serves 'im right.' Amy McLennan stood over the sailor with a broken brick in her hand, watching him carefully for signs of deceit. But Jack wasn't feigning; he was out like a light.

Silver looked up at her and said woozily, 'That's quite a punch you have for a girl.'

'With a brick to help, anyway.' Amy seemed calm and self-possessed as she dropped the brick and bent down to him. 'Let me untie you, Mr Wade. It's time I returned a few favours.'

'You did that already,' he reminded her, 'when you hid me from the law ten days ago. How did you happen to know where I was?'

'I saw you by chance from my window as you were passin'. And with those two men followin' on your 'eels, I knew you was in big trouble. It was only when I got closer that I recognized this one, though. I'm glad it was 'im. Blackguard!'

*

Silver sat in the kitchen of the hostel while Ginny Faber cleaned his face with a wet cloth, and applied lineament to his scrapes and cuts.

Amy examined Ginny's handiwork. 'No permanent damage to that 'andsome face of yours, Mr Wade, you'll be glad to 'ear.'

Silver shrugged uncomfortably. 'Why do you keep calling me Wade, Amy? You know that's not my real name, don't you?'

She nodded reluctantly. 'Yes, I do know your real name isn't Wade. It's Jonathan Silver.'

'How long have you known?' he asked her. 'Was it that day I came running in here with the police behind me?'

Amy shrugged. 'Yes, that was when I suddenly realized who you were. I'd had my suspicions earlier that you were on the run from the law, but I had never seen a picture of the infamous Dr Silver at the time.'

Silver looked across at Ginny who seemed uncomfortable at this unexpected turn in the conversation. 'You two don't mind helping a murderer, then?'

Amy glanced at Ginny, then, after a long sigh, said, 'You'd better leave us alone, Ginny, there's a good woman.'

Silver, even in his woozy state, had noticed a distinct change in Amy's voice as she gave that firm and unmistakable order. After Ginny had withdrawn discreetly from the kitchen without a murmur of complaint at being ordered about by this slip of a girl, Amy went on, still in that unfamiliar voice, 'My sister Cynthia believes you innocent, Dr Silver. She went to your trial every day at the Newgate Courthouse. Perhaps you remember her – a striking young lady with fair hair and a penchant for blue bonnets.'

Silver did remember her. Despite the tribulations of the trial, he couldn't help noticing the young woman in blue who'd come to the public gallery every day and who, when the verdict came after this three-day farce, had seemed as overcome with the unfairness of it as he had himself. 'That lady is your sister? Is she from Bermondsey too then?' he asked sarcastically.

Amy's voice was changing subtly all the while she was speaking. By now her voice had metamorphosed fully into a refined and genteel upper class accent. 'I have a confession of my own to make, Dr Silver.'

Silver already had an inkling of what was coming but was determined not to make her confession easy for her.

Amy took a deep breath. 'My name isn't really Amy McLennan. It's Rachel Grosvenor.'

Silver wasn't sure what to say. 'Well, Miss Rachel...'

Amy interrupted. 'Actually it's *Lady* Rachel, if you want to be strictly correct, Doctor...'

*

It was astonishing how quickly he came to accept her in this new light. In retrospect he did wonder how he could ever have been taken in by her act. She had far too much beauty, self-possession and poise ever to have been merely a simple maidservant from Bermondsey. Elisa had been absolutely right about her.

She was now every inch the aristocratic young lady. Yet she had lost something in his eyes too – the unspoilt innocence, the simplicity, the naïve goodness of a pretty servant girl. That unspoilt girl he had liked so much, Amy, was now gone forever, he realized sadly.

Silver remembered something she had said on the night they had met on Ratcliffe Highway when she had been accosted by those two wharf rats Jack and Joey. '"*Gentlemen is much bigger blackguards than wot blackguards is, in my opinion*"?' he quoted accusingly at her. 'Where did that come from? It sounds too real to have been invented.'

She gave a sheepish shrug. 'I heard a flower seller girl in Covent Garden say it.' She still looked just like the Amy he knew as she said defensively, 'It made me laugh, the solemn way she said it. So I simply repeated it just the way that little flower seller had said it...'

'Why all this playacting, Lady Rachel?' he asked her abrasively. 'What is the point of it?'

She appraised him coolly in return, still looking disconcertingly like Amy, but with a new level of sophistication in her voice and her manner. 'I propose you continue to call me Amy, Doctor, while I call you Jonathan.' She relaxed a little and gave him a tentative smile. 'As it happens, Amelia is truly my own middle name, and my own family and friends have always called me "Amy", not Rachel. So it seems only fair for the same degree of familiarity between us, after everything we've been through together.'

Silver couldn't help smiling faintly in return. 'Agreed. "Amy" it shall remain.'

'I could ask you the same about *your* playacting, Jonathan,' she went on, still apparently stung by his criticism despite her smile.

'My *playacting*, if you can call it such, was done with the intention of keeping my head out of a hangman's noose. That seems a rather more important reason than any game you might have been playing here, err...Amy.'

She pursed her lips in annoyance. 'I'm afraid I don't agree. I have excellent reasons for performing this bit of playacting, as you choose to call it. I wanted to do my best to help the poor women of the East End. It's a national disgrace that this is the richest country in the world, head of the greatest empire the world has ever seen, and yet we allow so many of our fellow citizens, particularly women and children, to live in squalor and disease and degradation.' She flared angrily. 'I have read about your work to try and stop the spread of typhus and cholera among the poor, Jonathan, so please don't pretend that you don't share some of my concerns at least.'

He rolled his eyes ironically. 'Whether I did or not is of no concern now. I'm a fugitive from justice now, a convicted murderer.'

She conceded that point with a slight inclination of her head. 'Having visited the East End, I was determined to try and help the local women – the girls who have to work the streets, the ones forced into the workhouse by poverty, the older ones suffering violence at the hands of their men folk. I thought the best solution would be to set up a hostel for women in trouble, a refuge for them from the outside world. But I also wanted to be a part of it, and to help with my own two hands, not merely to pay the bills. In any case, in order to truly help the women of the East End, I needed to understand their problems intimately, to feel like one of them. To *become* one of them...'

'So how did you achieve this miracle?' he asked sarcastically.

'Transforming wealthy Lady Rachel Grosvenor into sweet Amy McLennan?'

'Surprisingly it was not that much of a transformation,' she said curtly, not liking his tone. 'I met Ginny through the Whitechapel Workhouse, and she agreed to help me. She taught me how to behave and talk like a working girl...'

Ginny had reappeared at the door of the kitchen. 'You did a good job then, Ginny,' Silver complimented her. 'I was completely fooled by your mistress here.'

Ginny was embarrassed, and went over to the sink to wash dishes, even though it was eleven o'clock at night by now.

'This arrangement wasn't meant to deceive *you*, Jonathan,' Amy chided him. 'And it wasn't really deceit at all. I *became* Amy McLennan while I was here. The servant girl Amy is genuinely me, and I am genuinely her. I didn't feel as if I was playing a part like an actress; I was only being myself, but in a different world, that's all. If I had been born in Bermondsey, then I would have been exactly like Amy McLennan.'

Silver tried to sit up straight. 'I believe you, if that helps.' He studied her pretty face. 'So what now? Are you going to give me up to the police?'

'I am not. I would hardly have saved you from those two ruffians merely to give you up again. But I would suggest you do go voluntarily to the police and surrender yourself. My sister believed you innocent based on the evidence. Other people might believe your story now too.'

Silver breathed in. 'The judge and the jury at my trial didn't, and their voices were the ones that mattered, unfortunately.' He tried to make his point more forcefully. 'The law will hang me, Amy, if I give myself up. I cannot prove I didn't kill my wife; if I could, I would have done it already. And I think the police will also do their best to blame me for the recent murders of these two young women in this area too, given half a chance. That would make their lives so much simpler.'

Amy made a wry face. 'Then what will you do, Jonathan?'

Silver sighed. 'Try and escape the country. It's all I can do now...'

CHAPTER 21

'I suppose, Sergeant, you will want to ask me something about the Charge? Everyone else does.'

If he were being frank, Sergeant Sparrow would indeed have liked to ask young Captain Robert Caitlin of the 13th Light Dragoons about that famous charge of three years before. But he quickly denied it. 'No, of course not, Captain. I'm only here to ask you about Mrs Marianne Silver.'

'Well, that's a refreshing change at least,' Caitlin responded coolly.

Sparrow was obscurely disappointed, though, at missing out on this golden opportunity to speak with one of the survivors about the heroic, and horrific, events of that day. He was curious to know what it had felt like to make that wild and reckless charge into the valley of death. All Englishmen - whether Tory or Whig, rich or poor, high church or low church, upper class or labouring class - wanted to know whether they would have been capable of doing the same thing in those terrible circumstances. Given such a suicidal order, what would they have done? Obey it without question, or turn tail and run like a Frenchie?

Captain Caitlin had been one of those Englishmen who had apparently obeyed that insane order unflinchingly during the Battle of Balaklava. 658 British cavalrymen, of whom he was one, had ridden for more than a mile under heavy fire to attack Russian artillery positions. And under that blistering hail of lead and fire and shrapnel, enough of them had somehow improbably survived to reach their destination, to kill those tormenting Russian gunners, and then retreat in good order, having lost 110 dead, 180 wounded or taken prisoner, and 475 horses killed.

'You did meet Mrs Silver during your time in the Crimea, though, I believe?' Sparrow suggested warily, not wishing to inquire too deeply into Caitlin's war experiences when the man seemed so reluctant to talk about them.

'I did indeed. But not at Balaklava, of course. That was no place for a woman – even a woman like Marianne. Or for a man, come to think of it,' Caitlin added bleakly.

Sparrow could not help but imagine the carnage and confusion of that October day three years ago as Caitlin and his companions had ridden into the full fury of the Russian guns. *What was going through their heads during this madness?* Everyone must have known the order was a grave error, yet no one among them could be the first to turn around and break ranks. And so they had ridden on, the cavalrymen of the British Army's Light Brigade, bound by their rigid code of obedience (or stupidity, some might say) to be duly scythed down by the Russian artillery at point-blank range. In his mind's eye, Sparrow could see it all. Men falling all around them, limbs and heads blown off, smoke and gunpowder billowing, blood spurting from awful wounds, horses wide-eyed with fear, the screams of the dying and the maimed filling the air behind them, the stench of death everywhere...

Yet Sparrow had recently read a piece by William Howard Russell in *The Times* in which he said that the Charge, for all its insanity, had been a key incident in helping Britain to ultimate victory in that war. A few days after the Charge, ten thousand British troops had held fast against forty thousand Russians at the battle of Inkerman, so the sacrifice of the Light Brigade had by no means been pointless. The Charge had first distracted, and then put out of action, an active Russian battery of eight guns, which would have caused countless more British deaths at Inkerman, and later in the campaign. The uncomfortable truth, Sparrow reflected, was that wars regularly involved large-scale blunders. The only difference this time was that the cannon fodder had been lionized into figures of almost mythological stature. In the public mind the cavalrymen of the Light Brigade were now British heroes to match the Greeks at Thermopylae or Hannibal's army at Zama.

Yet Captain Caitlin fell a little short, in Sparrow's humble opinion, when compared to his idea of an Ajax or Achilles. In fact, Captain Robert Caitlin was such a nondescript and polite-looking young man that he didn't look like he had enough gumption to resist a rough cove pushing past him in the queue for the omnibus, never mind half the Russian Army. *Could this slightly built fair-haired boy genuinely be a man who had ridden with the six hundred against those Russian guns?*

Sparrow realized Caitlin was still talking...

'...Although, saying that about Balaklava, the hospital at Scutari had worse conditions than anything I ever saw at the front.'

Sparrow thought he was probably exaggerating with that comment, even though he had heard that conditions in the Turkish hospital had been dire. 'You were wounded at the Charge, I take it,' Sparrow went on. 'Is that how you came to be nursed by Mrs Silver at Scutari?'

Caitlin seemed puzzled by the question. 'Where did you hear that she nursed me, Sergeant...?'

It was late Friday morning in the London Coffee House on Ludgate Hill, a venue which Caitlin had suggested for their meeting, and one to which Sergeant Sparrow had been only too happy to agree. He didn't often get the chance to visit such places on a police detective's weekly wage. Caitlin had even offered to buy his policeman guest a mug of fine Jamaican coffee. The aroma of fine coffee permeated the oak-timbered room as the waiters rushed to tables with their orders. The place was certainly well patronized with customers: well-fed bankers slurping their coffee and baked confections with relish; withered and desiccated lawyers with pince-nez and wobbling Adam's apples, looking down their long noses at the menu; salesmen and dealers in flash outfits mentally calculating the percentages on their latest deals with sly grins of satisfaction; gentlemen idlers with languid smiles and all the time in the world.

The clothing of the customers matched their professions - or even their lack of one - in impeccable detail. Black morning dress suits and top hats for the lawyers and bankers; frock coats, old-fashioned tailcoats and colourful waistcoats for the dealers; cloaks and canes and beaver hats for the city idlers.

Sparrow was equally confused in return by Caitlin's comment. 'You didn't meet Mrs Silver there during your convalescence? Wasn't she your nurse, then?'

'No, Marianne was never my nurse; in fact I doubt that she ever did any serious nursing duties at all, even when she was at Scutari.' Caitlin tried to resolve Sergeant Sparrow's obvious confusion. 'To clarify, Sergeant, I actually first met Marianne at Calamity Bay in the Crimea in September '54, just before the Battle of Alma. It was there that I fell badly for her.'

Sparrow was surprised. 'You mean she was actually at the war front in the Crimea? What was she doing there?'

'I'm not sure, to be frank. I was never sure about anything that Marianne did, in all honesty.' Caitlin adopted a conspiratorial expression and lowered his voice. 'But, if you were to press me on the point, I believe she was working for the government in some secret capacity. That's what I suspected anyway. Later, after I'd been wounded at the Charge, I was repatriated across the Black Sea to the hospital at Scutari where I ran into Marianne again. She came to see me as soon as I was in a fit enough state again to receive visitors.'

'But she never nursed you?'

'No, not at all.' Caitlin frowned, then qualified himself. 'Well, it's true she was wearing a nurse's uniform when she visited me in my ward, and she may have offered me water and helped me wash. But whatever Marianne was really doing there in that hospital, she was certainly no nurse. I was in no state at the time, though, to concern myself much about what she was doing there. I was simply overjoyed to see her.'

Sparrow's mind was reflecting rapidly on this unexpected information. 'Did you know Dr Silver at Scutari too?'

'Everyone at Scutari knew Dr Silver. People talk about Miss Nightingale's work for the troops in the Crimea, and also the generous help of that kind coloured lady, Miss Seacole. But Silver was there at Scutari long before either of them, working wonders with only the meanest resources. In fact it was he who painstakingly removed the shrapnel from my guts and put my shattered leg back together again. It's thanks to him I can still walk.'

'So you were grateful to him?'

Indeed.' Caitlin made a wry face. 'That was, until he happened to meet Marianne. After that, she only had eyes for him.'

'Ah! So you became jealous of Dr Silver?'

'I did,' Caitlin admitted without rancour, 'despite what he'd done for me.'

Sparrow sipped his coffee thoughtfully, enjoying the unusual richness of the taste. This coffee drinking lark could become a habit with him, if he didn't watch out. 'Mrs Silver seems to have been a remarkable woman.'

Caitlin became melancholy at the thought. 'More than that, Sergeant. For me, she was the most beautiful, and the most mysterious, woman in the world.'

'Mysterious?' That seemed an odd choice of word to Sparrow.

'Yes, there was always an element of mystery about her – and joy...and wonder.'

Sparrow let that intoxicating image fill his mind for a moment. 'You saw her this summer when you returned to England?'

'I did. I wrote to her persistently until she finally gave in and agreed to see me.'

'In private?'

'Not exactly. Actually we met *here*, Sergeant, in this very coffee house, at the end of June. In fact, as I recall, she might even have sat in the very same seat you're occupying now.'

'Why did you persevere with your attentions? She was a married woman by this time.'

'I only wanted to see her again. I lived in slight hopes that she might have become bored and disenchanted with her life in London.'

'And did she return your feelings in any way?'

Caitlin shook his head ruefully. 'No, not at all. In fact the only reason she had agreed to see me was apparently to ask me some questions about my time at Scutari. She wanted to know in particular about a foreign correspondent I'd met there who worked for one of the European news agencies - Reuters, I think. The journalist was a Frenchman called Chevreul.'

'What was her interest in this M'sieur Chevreul?' This conversation was taking Sparrow into unexpected territory.

'I'm not sure, to be honest. But I couldn't help her much anyway. All that really concerned me that day was her final rejection of me. She made it absolutely clear that there was no hope that she would ever renew her feelings for me. She loved her husband deeply, or so she claimed.'

Sparrow sniffed. 'Did she sound genuine to you?'

'Unfortunately she did.'

Sparrow narrowed his eyes. 'Do you think Dr Silver killed her?'

Caitlin sighed. 'I don't know, Sergeant. The evidence suggested clearly that he did it. But if you're asking my opinion, based on what I know of the man, I would have said it was unlikely.'

Sparrow pounced on that. 'May I ask where you were on the second of July when Mrs Silver was murdered, Captain?'

Caitlin blinked. 'Oh, you suspect *me*, Sergeant? I should have seen that coming, perhaps. But I'm afraid I was attending a medical inspection in Aldershot on the second of July, to see if I was fit enough to return to active duty. I have a dozen witnesses who can put me in Aldershot at the time Marianne died.'

'And were you fit enough to return to duty? *Are* you fit enough?'

'No, not quite yet. But soon perhaps. In any event I would be the last man to murder Marianne. Even if I couldn't possess her, I would be quite incapable of destroying that much God-given beauty.'

Sparrow decided he would nevertheless ask Grindrod to find someone to check Caitlin's story. Another thought now occurred to him, following his conversation with Martin Tyrell the previous Saturday. 'Do you happen to know a man called Charles Ferrar?' he asked bluntly.

Caitlin had to think for a moment. 'Yes, I have met Mr Ferrar. He's a government official – with the Foreign Office, I believe. I also came across him at Calamity Bay in the Crimea, as I remember. He was certainly acting as a political officer of some sort there. In fact, I had a feeling that Marianne knew him rather well, even though I only ever saw them together a few times at most.'

'Could he have been her lover too?' Sparrow demanded.

That notion hadn't occurred to Caitlin before, Sparrow could tell. 'Ferrar is old enough to have been Marianne's father,' Caitlin protested. 'But it's possible,' he admitted begrudgingly, '...before Dr Silver and I came on the scene anyway.'

'Do you know if Ferrar is here in England now?' Sparrow pressed him.

'I don't know. But if one wanted to locate him, then I would suggest trying the Foreign Office. They must know his present whereabouts.' Caitlin's eyes widened. 'Is he another suspect, then? It seems, Sergeant, that the police no longer truly believe that Dr Silver killed his wife, do they?'

'Not at all, Captain,' Sparrow denied half-heartedly. 'That's very far from the truth.'

'But *you*, Sergeant,' Caitlin said shrewdly. '*You* clearly don't believe in his guilt any more, do you...?'

*

Late afternoon at the Napier shipyard in Millwall, and tensions were running increasingly high as the work to get the ship ready for next Tuesday's launch intensified.

Jonathan Silver could feel the pressure building among the men, as if the very air above their heads was growing ever heavier and more oppressive. This afternoon the sky had fittingly turned into a threatening black maelstrom of cloud that felt like a biblical curse about to descend on humankind, punishing them for their hubris in trying to build such a giant vessel.

Silver had returned to the yard from his brief sojourn to Wapping, and for the last two days had kept as low a profile as possible, working hard on building a timber viewing platform for visitors on the day of the launch, but otherwise doing his best to become invisible. He was still nursing the injury to his ribs given to him on Wednesday night by those two wharf rats Joey and Jack, but thankfully he didn't think the ribs were broken, only bruised. The mental pressure on him was of course even worse than for the others in the yard, since, as well as the unrelenting work, he also had to live with the constant threat of discovery or denunciation by one of his workmates. Yet, for the moment, he felt safer here in the yard than outside on the streets. Here, among the hundreds of men working on the Great Ship, he was hopefully only one more anonymous face among this vast workforce. Outside the walls of this yard, on his own, he was a marked man.

So he intended to stay on here at the yard and hopefully avoid discovery for another two weeks until he could slip away over the river to Kent on the night of the 12th November, and take the early morning steam packet the following day from Gravesend, bound for Rotterdam.

In his new task, Silver still spent most of his working day with Jimmy Flynn and Billy Faber, who had also been delegated by the foreman Spurrell to work on the viewing gallery on the landward side of the ship. Silver worried, though, that one of these two might turn out in the end to be the instrument of his downfall. That would be ironic if it happened because these two young men were now the closest thing he had to friends. Yet he could hardly blame either of them if they did ultimately discover the truth and turn him in for the reward. The police had recently raised that reward for his recapture to two hundred and fifty pounds, and that sort of money could transform the life of someone like Jimmy or Billy. Yet the favourable thing as far as Silver was concerned was that Jimmy and Billy worked almost every hour that God sent, so had little opportunity for seeing wanted bills on police station notice boards, or for reading the newspapers.

Billy's mother, of course, now knew the truth about him, but Silver was sure that Ginny would never betray him deliberately, thanks to the tight hold of her mistress, Lady Rachel.

It still irritated Silver a little that he had been taken in so completely by that young lady, but then she had made a highly convincing servant girl from Bermondsey. Even a local lad like Billy had been taken in absolutely by her. In fact Billy still believed that Amy was an ordinary working girl, and continued to spend half his working day talking and daydreaming about her. Silver could now understand why his mother had quietly tried to persuade Billy to look elsewhere for a girl; it was certainly an unlikely match between an apprentice shipyard carpenter and an heiress worth half a million pounds...

Silver looked up to see John Harkness and Matthew Spurrell approaching him with grim looks written on their countenances, so he held his breath for a moment as he wondered whether he had finally been recognized. In his constant state of worry, Silver had tense moments like this every day when he thought he'd been finally unmasked as a murderer and fugitive. But this uncomfortable moment, like all previous ones to date, proved to be a false alarm, and not that final damning denunciation.

Harkness had actually been less troublesome to Silver of late, becoming cooler and more offhand with him, and resuming an apparently closer relationship with Spurrell, who had in turn become more careful about his illicit drinking at work. Silver didn't understand the reasons for his slight fall from grace with Harkness – perhaps it had to do with the fact that he was no longer working on the slipway itself - but he was glad of it anyway, and for the resumed anonymity it gave him.

But now Silver noticed an even more unwelcome visitor in the shape of Daniel Strode. Since last week, Silver had effectively given up any hope of ever proving anything against Strode, and now only wanted to avoid the man completely. Yet, perversely, the man now seemed to appear in the yard with more regularity than ever before, presumably because of the imminent launch. Today Strode was in the company of a well-dressed young woman who Silver assumed must be a relative of one of the directors on a tour of the yard. He kept his eyes determinedly down to his work and tried to ignore them as they passed. All he saw of the woman as she swished by was the hem of a green chenille dress and a flash of cotton petticoat.

On the odd occasions that Silver had seen Strode over the last few days, it had seemed to him that Strode was a man much recovered in spirits compared to his nervous and drawn appearance of a week earlier. If Strode's conscience had been troubling him then, he now seemed like a man who had put such trifling concerns behind him.

Today Strode was almost in cheerful mood as he and his lady companion joined John Harkness a little way down the slipway. Strode spoke up in an unusually friendly fashion to him. 'John, have you met Miss Smith before by any chance - Miss Elisa Smith...?'

Silver's head jerked up in surprise on hearing that name.

'...Miss Smith owns a chandler's store in Wapping,' Strode was saying, 'that delivers many of our supplies to the yard. And she has many other thriving businesses in the East End, I'm told, so Miss Smith is a very modern young lady indeed.'

Silver studied the group in alarm, hoping improbably that this might be *another* Miss Elisa Smith. But it was indeed Elisa, if such a sumptuously dressed and flirtatious version of her that he did have to check his eyes for a moment to be sure.

Silver could tell that Harkness was immediately interested in this effervescent Miss Smith, even admiring her figure with undisguised frankness. In doing so, though, Harkness also happened to catch Silver looking at them closely, and frowned back in response.

Silver hurriedly diverted his eyes, and began driving six-inch nails with ferocious power into the timber joists at his feet. Yet he couldn't help sneaking another look at Elisa because she did look extremely fine, dressed in that demure fashion, even with the rising wind buffeting her figure and lifting her green skirts.

What was she doing here? Silver asked himself, his mind racing. *And with Strode of all people?*

Logic told him that she must have come here with some ulterior motive in mind. And the way she was dressed suggested she might have come prepared to impress Strode, rather than vice-versa.

She was certainly flirting openly with Strode - outrageously even - as she played the coquettish female. She looked up at the baleful sky. 'We seem to be in for a storm, gentlemen. I fear I shall get very wet returning home.'

Harkness simpered at her. 'I sincerely hope not, Miss Smith. Have you not come here in a closed carriage?'

'Unfortunately not. Mr Strode has however offered to take me home in his beautiful barouche, and I must say that I am tempted by his kind offer.'

'Are you indeed?' Harkness said huffily.

Heavy drops of rain began to fall at this point, and Elisa, after raising her umbrella, scattered with the two men for the shelter of the nearby offices. She didn't even seem aware of Silver's existence as she passed, but then she could hardly acknowledge him openly of course. Even though he knew she must be playing some sort of a deceitful game with Strode, it still hurt him to see her apparently enjoying the man's company in this intimate way.

Yet, on balance, he found that he was actually *happy* that she had come here today, even if she hadn't acknowledged his existence by a single look or turn of her head. He really must be in love with this girl, he decided, for her mere presence to have such a disconcerting effect on him as this...

As he watched Strode take her arm and lead her up the stairs to the drawing office, he wondered what she could be hoping to achieve by this bold action. He could think of no other conceivable reason for her soliciting the company of Strode than that she was trying to entrap him. And the corollary of that was she must be doing it in order to help him prove his innocence. Perhaps she still believed, despite what he'd told her to the contrary, that he would never really flee the country until he had found some proof of Strode's complicity in Marianne's death.

Silver was left with some encouragement from these conclusions, both from the fact that Elisa must genuinely care about his future, but also from the possibility that she might actually succeed in her plan. Perhaps a woman's guile could unearth the darkest secrets of this man's soul, and find the evidence to prove Strode a murderer?

Yet it could also rebound on her and expose her to mortal danger...

*

After leaving his assignation at the London Coffee House, Sergeant Sparrow had taken a horse-bus out of the city, north through Camden Town and Buckhurst Hill to the village of Hampstead. Although, saying that, Hampstead was becoming more of a town than a village these days, with fine new shops in the high street and a rash of new red-brick villas being built on its outskirts.

Sparrow was too deep in thought, though, as his horse-bus threaded its way up Buckhurst Hill, to give much consequence to the rapid growth of the settlement of Hampstead. Instead he was turning over in his mind what Captain Caitlin had said at the end of their chat today. The young hero of the Charge had made a valid point about Sparrow's own judgement of this case: the more Sparrow learned about the death of Marianne Silver, the less he did indeed trust the verdict that her husband had killed her. And the root of those suspicions lay with the character of the victim herself. Marianne Silver had not been an ordinary doctor's wife by any stretch of the imagination: she had both a mysterious past, possibly as an agent of some sort for Her Majesty's Government, as well as being the type of woman whose beauty excited strange passions in all sorts of men. In fact there seemed a whole raft of potentially jealous men with a much better motive for killing Mrs Marianne Silver than her husband. Spurned lovers like Martin Tyrell and Robert Caitlin, for example - or possibly this man Charles Ferrar (whoever he might actually be.) And there had also been that other man who Mrs Sophie Rolfe had mentioned – another rejected suitor of Marianne's called Daniel Strode. Sparrow had almost forgotten about him, but not quite.

Dr Silver did sound to Sparrow a boring prig of a man, and one overly obsessed with his work rather than with his beautiful wife. But he didn't seem the murderous type, if Charlie Sparrow was any judge of character. So could Dr Silver have been telling the truth all the time, with that ridiculous story at his trial – about finding his wife dying on the staircase? Could he really have just pulled the knife *out* of his wife's chest, rather than plunging it in...?

Sparrow got off the bus at the bottom of Hampstead High Street and decided to take a circuitous route through a corner of the heath to reach his destination. He didn't have many opportunities to escape from the city's filthy air to the cleaner air out here in the country, so it was important to prolong these occasions when they came. Here in Hampstead it was still possible to see nature untainted by drab coats of soot and smoke, to find leaves of a rich natural autumn colour, and to appreciate a clear afternoon sky washed with shades of russet and pink.

Looking back towards distant London from his higher vantage point on the heath, he could see the smoke and murk draped over the familiar city skyline all the way from the Abbey and the new Houses of Parliament out to St Pauls. Over to the east, above Wapping and Shadwell and the Isle of Dogs, a vast swirl of iron-grey cloud was threatening a severe storm, but to the west a trace of lightness remained. A moving shaft of autumn sunshine even penetrated the gloom briefly, lifting the murk and revealing the steeples of Wren's churches in succession, one by one. Sparrow thought he could even make out the rooftops of Lambeth on the other side of the river from Westminster, and imagine Edie beating the dust out of her carpets in the back yard of his own home.

Or then again, knowing Edie's lax domestic habits, perhaps not...

Reluctantly, he went on his way, seeking out the address he had written down in his notebook. The house he was searching for - that of Mr George Harkness in Downshire Hill - proved to be a new and impressive red brick gothic pile.

As it turned out, Mr George Harkness was not at home, but his good wife, the lady of the house, was at home, and willing to talk to him in her front parlour - after a fashion anyway.

Mrs Harkness was a well-preserved woman of forty, even if the agent of preservation appeared to Sergeant Sparrow to have been salt-brine. She had a prickly and superior manner, and clearly delighted in putting her social inferiors in their place.

Perhaps she did it for everyone she considered her inferiors, or perhaps she reserved special venom for plainclothes police detectives: Sparrow reserved judgement on that point for the moment.

Mrs Harkness had offered her visitor some refreshment but Sparrow had decided to decline, not wishing to have this woman inspecting and reviewing his table manners. 'Ma'am, I came here to ask about Miss Charlotte Livingstone,' he announced rather nervously.

Mrs Harkness's face remained implacable. 'Yes, I wondered when the Metropolitan police would finally appear. Terrible business, no doubt, but, sorry to say, I always had my doubts about the moral character of Miss Livingstone.'

'What sort of doubts?' Sparrow found himself unexpectedly defending the girl.

Mrs Harkness was trussed up in a gown of green bombazine that seemed polished to a metallic sheen. 'I detected in her a certain weakness of character. A tendency to flirt, for example, without provocation.'

'With whom, ma'am?'

'With almost any gentleman visitor we had, I'm sorry to say.'

'And was that many?'

Mrs Harkness sniffed coldly. 'Err...not many exactly. But perhaps still too many for a young woman with her social weaknesses and easily impressed nature.'

Sparrow ground his teeth together at this disparaging remark addressed at a dead girl. 'Was she a good governess to your children, ma'am? She did work for you for three years after all.'

Mrs Harkness looked down her long nose at him. 'She was adequate.

My daughters are both amiable girls and liked Miss Livingstone well enough, despite her moral failings and intellectual limitations.'

Sparrow looked at the poker in the grate and idly wondered about resorting to murder himself. 'Did Miss Livingstone ever meet any gentleman here with the Christian name Daniel?'

Her brow puckered into a frown. '*Daniel?* Let me see. No, I think not,' she finally concluded.

'Are you sure about that, ma'am? It's very important.'

Mrs Harkness thought again. 'Well, there was John's friend, who came here several times last summer, and showed an unexpected interest in Miss Livingstone. I believe his name might have been Daniel, although he could only have met Miss Livingstone two or three times at most.'

Sparrow's ears pricked up. 'John? Who is John?'

'Mr John Harkness. My husband's younger brother.'

'And what was this friend's last name?'

'I'm trying to recall,' she answered irritably. 'Ah, now I remember. His name was Strode, Mr Daniel Strode.'

Sparrow almost physically jumped when he heard that name and remembered its significance to his other pressing case. 'Then Miss Livingstone did know a "Daniel",' Sparrow pointed out icily.

'Indeed,' Mrs Harkness agreed haughtily. 'A man in the engineering profession, I believe, but gentlemanly enough for all that. He told us that he was working on the design of the engines for the Great Ship being built on the Thames. John is working on that great venture too, of course...'

'Do you have a new governess for your children now, ma'am?' Sparrow interrupted her, as he had a sudden intuition.

'Of course. A Miss Anne Kelmscott. She joined us a month or so after Miss Livingstone left of her own volition.'

Sparrow sighed explosively as he realized the full implication of that name. Miss Anne Kelmscott was the friend of Miss Jane Penfold, who had come forward to give the police information about her late acquaintance. Sparrow had never thought to ask Miss Kelmscott where *she* worked, which in hindsight now appeared an unforgivable omission. 'Did you interview any other women last summer as possible replacements for Miss Livingstone, besides Miss Kelmscott?'

'Several, although I don't remember all their names.'

'Was one of them perhaps a friend of Miss Kelmscott's, ma'am? Do you remember that much at least?'

Mrs Harkness didn't like his abrasive tone, but Sparrow was past caring.

'I think so,' she said. 'I believe her friend's name was Jane something or other. She came here for interview the same day as Miss Kelmscott. But Miss Kelmscott herself was the more accomplished and suitable of the two.'

Miss Kelmscott was certainly much the plainer of the two, Sparrow knew, which might have been a more pertinent reason behind Mrs Harkness's decision to employ her. Miss Kelmscott herself clearly didn't know the name of her predecessor in her post, though, or she would surely have said something to Sparrow about this coincidence between the two victims. 'Could Mr Daniel Strode have been here on the day you interviewed these young women for the post?' Sparrow asked.

Mrs Harkness appeared disconcerted for the first time by his abrupt manner. 'Well, John was certainly here that day, I remember. And Mr Strode may well have been with him. They were very close friends last summer, always in each other's company. Although I believe there has been an unfortunate falling out between them since then, according to my husband.'

Sparrow nodded grimly, and thought that it was about time that he had words with this Mr Daniel Strode...

CHAPTER 22

Tuesday 3rd November 1857

When he saw the crowds streaming along the dirt road from Limehouse to the Isle of Dogs, Sergeant Sparrow realized he had picked an unfortunate day to finally visit the Napier shipyard. Damnation! He should have read a newspaper over the weekend, then he would have realized that the launch of the Great Ship was going to be today of all days! It was at this point that he turned to Frank Remmert sitting alongside him in the police growler and gave him a sour look because Frank had obviously been fully aware of what was due to happen today and hadn't thought it worth mentioning to him...

'Anything wrong, Sarge?' Remmert asked, puzzled.

Sparrow rolled his eyes at that but said nothing. There was no point in turning back now, so he let the driver carry on to the yard despite the vast multitude of people blocking their way. Instead of haranguing Remmert over his failure to warn him about today's big event, Sparrow concentrated his attention instead on the immense black hull of the Great Ship as the growler gradually grew ever closer to its destination. The scale of this vessel did truly defy belief. Sparrow had witnessed it slowly taking shape from a distance, of course – but then, seen across the flat marshes of the Isle of Dogs, it was hardly something that could be missed, even from several miles away. Yet it was not until you got this close that you could really appreciate its immense size and imposing shape. Sparrow was not a man easily impressed, but to see this vast human creation soaring into the sky like some temple to the Gods was a peculiarly humbling experience for a man such as himself, whose lot in life tended to lie towards the humbler and more sordid end of the human spectrum of activities.

Despite the grim weather, a multitude of Londoners had descended on the Isle of Dogs to witness the spectacle of the *Leviathan* finally moving, so that the slow movement of this endless line of people on the road resembled the Children of Israel fleeing Egypt for the Promised Land. Although perhaps the fleeing Israelites did not use such ripe and coarse language as did the colourful people of the East End of London...

Frank Remmert turned out, to Sparrow's surprise, to be remarkably knowledgeable about the details of today's launch. When Sparrow made some remark about the Great Ship causing such a huge splash in the Thames that it might sink the smaller boats about it, Remmert looked at him with an amused eye. 'Don't worry, Sarge. The engineer, Mr Brunel, is not that stupid. He's not going to just drop the *Leviathan* into the water like a rowboat. Instead he's going to ease her slowly down the inclined slipways until she's within reach of the water. Then they wait for tonight's high tide to float her off. That's why they have to try and do this today; they won't get another spring tide as high as this one for many a month.'

'Can they really move a thing that size at all, though?' Sparrow wondered, glancing up at the vast hull, towering above the distant brick walls of the shipyard.

'Well, we'll see. I have heard that Brunel hasn't had time to test any of his equipment beforehand, so anything could happen today.'

'If it doesn't move, Brunel will be a laughing stock,' Sparrow said. And the mood of this mob of spectators, while currently cheerful and good humoured, might suddenly turn nasty if things didn't go according to plan...

It took the police growler two hours in the end to make a journey that would have normally taken less than a quarter of that time, even on the rutted muddy roads of the Isle of Dogs. Finally the driver was able to thread his vehicle, now liberally splashed with mud, through the last of the crowds thronging at the gates of the shipyard.

From the entrance, though, Sparrow was forced to go on foot, wrestling his way through the swelling mob inside the yard to reach the main door of the company offices. Somewhere on the way he managed to lose Frank Remmert, but he gave up trying to find him again for the present in all this brouhaha. Sparrow was confident that he was fully capable of finding this Mr Daniel Strode on his own, and asking the man a few pertinent questions. He was already quietly convinced that this gentleman was none other than the mysterious "Daniel" who had written that note to Miss Livingstone last September, inviting her to meet in Regents Park. And being a regular visitor to the home of Mr George Harkness in Hampstead, there seemed a strong possibility that he had also encountered the second dead governess, Miss Penfold, in the same house on the day she had come to be interviewed.

Most tantalisingly of all, Daniel Strode was also a link to the Silver case because he had, according to Marianne's sister Sophie, been a rejected suitor of the murdered woman.

So...the man had possible links with *three* separate murdered women. It could of course all be a sad coincidence, yet Charlie Sparrow had a policeman's doubtful maxim concerning coincidences. Twice - *possibly*...three times - *never.*

Therefore this Mr Strode had some explaining to do...

After making inquiries of a young desk clerk, Sparrow was shown through to the main drawing office, and a wood-panelled room at the end furnished with drawing boards and plan chests, and all the other paraphernalia of the engineering profession. At Sparrow's entry, a man stood up from behind the oak desk by the leaded casement window and came to meet him. Through the dusty panes behind, Sparrow could see preparations on the hull of the Great Ship going on at frantic speed.

'Mr Strode? Mr Daniel Strode?' Sparrow began.

'Yes.' Daniel Strode did turn out to be an impressive looking man, six feet tall, mutton chop whiskers, a saturnine if puzzled face, hooked nose like an eagle's. His black frock coat was immaculate, and his boots were polished to such a shine that they could have served as a shaving mirror in an emergency. He didn't look like a man who would tolerate fools gladly, peering down his beak of a nose at his unexpected visitor. Yet he turned distinctly pale when Sparrow tipped his hat and introduced himself as a police detective.

Strode didn't offer to shake hands. 'What can I do for you, Sergeant? I hope it isn't anything that will take too long -' he glanced behind him at the window – 'I have to attend to the launch in five minutes.'

'This may take somewhat longer than that, sir,' Sparrow warned him without regret. 'Could I ask you, sir - did you happen to know a young woman called Miss Charlotte Livingstone? A single young lady from Islington.'

Strode wasn't very good at masking his feelings. His cheeks turned white and bloodless, and Sparrow thought for a moment he might be about to faint. Yet he soon recovered, his penetrating blue eyes sparking into life. 'I did know Miss Livingstone.' He put his head in his hands, twisting his mane of black hair. When he finally looked up, he seemed twenty years older. 'Oh, God!'

'You know that Miss Livingstone is dead, don't you, sir?'

Strode's face sank yet again. 'Yes, I know.' He glanced up hurriedly. 'I didn't kill her, if that's what you believe. I loved Miss Livingstone. She was carrying my child. She told me that on the last night we were together.'

'Did you also know a Miss Penfold too, sir? A Miss Jane Penfold?

Was she also carrying your child?'

Strode's head jerked up. 'Don't be impertinent, Sergeant. But I did also know Miss Penfold, it's true,' he conceded.

In the biblical sense, it went without saying...

'I have killed no one, Sergeant. And I am fully prepared to answer all your questions about these two young women, and help you catch whoever did this terrible thing to them. I admit I should have come forward voluntarily before now, but the truth is I was afraid. I didn't understand what was going on; I still don't. But someone is trying deliberately to implicate me in these murders...'

And doing an excellent job of it, Sparrow felt like interrupting.

'...I didn't suspect this at first when I heard that Miss Livingstone had been found dead. But after the murder of Miss Penfold, I became convinced of it.'

He was a remarkably convincing actor, Sparrow decided - exactly the right mixture of contrition, fear and puzzlement. But he didn't believe a word of it nonetheless. Sparrow decided to let Strode talk some more; such well-bred gentlemen often gave away far more than they intended at confessional times like these.

But Strode surprisingly recovered his poise, so Sparrow realized he was up against a wilier adversary than he'd initially thought. 'I will talk with you, Sergeant,' Strode said, straightening his back. 'But now is not the time. I have to assist Mr Brunel with the arrangements for the launch. Thousands of people are waiting on this launch so this must take precedence. Will you allow me to get on with my work for the next two hours, and then I promise I will return and answer any questions you may have.'

Sparrow debated over that. He could hardly arrest the man on the present evidence, and there was no way he could take him back to Shadwell Station for questioning anyway until the launch of the *Leviathan* was complete and the roads relatively clear again.

Sparrow stood aside with reluctance. 'All right, sir. You may go on with your work, and try and launch your Great Ship. But don't try leaving the yard afterwards, except with me, sir. Is that clear...?'

*

Silver was making a last minute check of the surface of the iron rails on the slipways when he happened to look up and spotted Sergeant Sparrow fighting his way through the crowds. Crouching down instantly out of sight, his heart beating suddenly faster, he watched Sparrow enter the main door of the company offices. Fortunately the police detective seemed to be on his own, but nevertheless it was an ominous sign.

Had someone in the yard finally given him away? *Had he survived all this time only to be given away at the death?*

Yet he only had to look at the artless faces of Jimmy Flynn and Billy Faber working alongside him to know that those two certainly hadn't been the instrument of his betrayal at least.

'Everything looks fine here, Billy,' he announced to the youngster. 'Let's move to a safe place now at the top of the slipways, before they lower this ship on top of us.' In his mind Silver was frantically calculating his possible courses of action, although no one could ever have known it from his quiet external demeanour. Being a fugitive had gifted him with new and unexpected abilities, including that of being able to hide his feelings completely from the world.

Should he try and escape from the yard now? he wondered. Or was it best to stay concealed among this dense crowd of spectators, and try and get away unseen among the throng leaving at the end of today's launch. In the end he decided on the latter course. The police wouldn't be able to move freely inside the yard any more than he could, therefore this might give him some valuable breathing space.

Then he had another, possibly better, thought: perhaps there was no need to run. Perhaps, after the launch, he could find himself a secure hiding place somewhere in the yard where the police would never find him. After his weeks at the Napier yard, he knew of many secret nooks and crannies where a man might secrete himself away for days without discovery.

Matthew Spurrell, Silver's foreman, certainly knew of many hiding places of his own in this yard too, because he now suddenly appeared from nowhere. Silver hadn't seen him for the last hour or more and feared the worst from him being gone so long, a fear that was soon confirmed by Spurrell's dishevelled dress, bloodshot eyes and breath stinking of gin. If one of the bosses caught Spurrell in this state, Silver knew he would be sacked on the spot.

Although he had more pressing problems of his own, Silver felt some responsibility for the man, so managed to persuade Spurrell to join him and the others in watching the launch from a safe vantage point. He deliberately chose a place where both Spurrell and himself might be reasonably safe from accidental discovery, near the giant stern checking drum. These checking drums were essentially the brakes of the whole launching venture, Silver knew. Should the *Leviathan* start sliding down the slipway out of control, the brakes on these giant drums would be used to slow or halt her progress. To resist these huge braking forces, the drums were mounted on a ten feet deep slab of concrete, which in turn rested on heavy timber piles driven deep into the dense London clay.

This close to the ship, the vast iron hull blocked out most of the horizon from view, and even most of the weak autumn daylight filtering down between the gantries and staging. Silver had seen the Great Pyramid at Giza on a visit to Egypt with the Royal Navy, but this was a grander spectacle by far because this was a living, moving thing - something which would one day sail the seven seas, from the stormy grey waters of the North Atlantic, to the palm-green shores of the South Pacific.

The weather was in ugly mood, though, not matching the festive spirits of the boisterous crowd at all. The sky was slate grey, streaked with black, and growing ever more malevolent in appearance. All colour had seeped away from the scene under that forbidding sky, so that the riverside now looked more like a sepia daguerreotype brought to life than the real world.

The length of river below the *Leviathan* was so dense with boat traffic that Silver reckoned he could have walked across the Thames to Deptford at this moment. Nearest the middle section of the ship were anchored three huge Essex barges equipped with manual winches attached back to the giant vessel. Further away, towards the Deptford bank, were even larger barges, heavy with ballast, that carried the capstans for the steam winches operating on the shore at the bow and stern of the *Leviathan*. Among all this density of river traffic, there hardly seemed room for the river to flow at all. As a consequence the surface of the river was so heavy and black that the Thames seemed more like a listless stream of coal slurry than a living stretch of water.

Silver, scanning the crowds in the main part of the yard, caught a flash of colour among all the greyness and the sepia tones, before realizing that he was looking at a man's hair. *Yellow hair...!*

This was an even more disturbing development than the arrival of Sergeant Sparrow. Now Silver had *two* people here hunting him in the yard. And of the two, that man Minshall was possibly the more to be feared. That young turnkey from Newgate had the look of a man who would never give up on his self-appointed task when there was a chance of a reward at the end...

Surely someone must have betrayed him if both Sparrow and Minshall had found their way here to the Napier shipyard? Or could they merely be here for the launch, like everyone else? Silver clung with tenacity to that comforting possibility but in his heart didn't believe it for a moment.

Then Silver's attention was distracted, like everyone else's, by the appearance of the man of the moment. The crowd's eyes followed the diminutive figure of the engineer as he made his way stoically from the company offices through the throng of sightseers, whose presence, Silver thought worriedly, must be making this event a nightmare for him.

Soon the enthusiastic crowd blocked his way entirely, and Brunel was forced to make a detour past the stern braking drum. Silver had not left the yard for the last three days but neither had Brunel from all appearances. The most famous engineer in the country looked like a respectable carpenter's foreman in his dusty clothes and muddied boots - only the stovepipe hat and the cigar clenched between his teeth marking him out as someone special from the crowd.

As he came by, he recognized Silver and made a point of making a further short detour to give his shoulder a brief slap of congratulation at finishing the slipway. Silver felt as if God had given him a pat on the back. The gesture of approval from such a man made his heart sing, despite the risk that Minshall or Sparrow might recognize him from this brief encounter. Silver saw that his two young companions were both mightily impressed by him being singled out for personal congratulation in this way - Billy, in particular, pursing his lips in appreciation. Silver hoped that Brunel hadn't seen the drunken Matthew Spurrell skulking in the shadows behind him, though, or the foreman's career at the Napier yard was likely to be over permanently.

Silver's attention was diverted again for a second by events in the specially reserved gallery near the stern of the ship, the viewing platform that he and the other carpenters had built over the last week to house important guests. Today it was decked out in bunting and flags like a ride at the fair, and occupied by a set of richly dressed gentlemen and ladies. The bunting, and the velvet, silk and lace of the dresses of the ladies, were almost the only real splash of colour to be seen at that end of the yard. Among this colourful miniature of society, one particular gentleman was holding court in a most forthright manner.

'Who's that popinjay?' Silver asked his companions.

Neither Billy nor Jimmy knew, but Spurrell spoke up from behind in a slurred voice. 'That's Mr John Scott Russell, the bastard. I don't know how he's –' he burped loudly – 'got the nerve to show up today as if all this is *his* damned work.'

This then was the bankrupt shipbuilder who had caused Brunel so many problems over the last few years, the man who'd spent all the Eastern Steam Navigation Company's money laying down barely a quarter of the required iron tonnage for the ship. He was supposedly a broken man, but Silver couldn't see much signs of it from the man's light-hearted and charming manner with all the well-dressed gentlemen and ladies on the visitors' platform. Silver would have had this man marked down as a rogue instantly from his appearance and manner – he'd seen enough of such smooth-talking cozeners over the years - but apparently Brunel's judgement had let him down in this case as he had been taken in initially by the man's promises and fake sincerity. Silver wondered how Brunel could even bear to have the man so close to him now without going over and knocking him to the ground. Brunel had worked himself nearly to death over the last two years trying to complete the Great Ship and make up to the company for the activities of this devious individual.

Brunel simply ignored Russell however, and went straight up to the dais at the bows of the ship from which he was going to direct the launch operations. It was going to be no easy matter, though, to make himself heard above the hubbub of the increasingly raucous crowd, or to impose order on all those around him.

It truly seemed half of London was here, watching and waiting for this moment of high drama. Silver even recognized buxom Alice among them, the serving girl from The Ship Inn, with a gaggle of admirers all around her, including the ever-attentive Jude Crabtree.

While Brunel was trying to get silence among the crowd, Liam Flintham forced his way through the nearby sightseers and came up to Silver. 'Jonathan, have you seen Miss Smith anywhere?'

Silver glanced around uneasily – *surely Elisa wasn't here too...?* 'No, I haven't seen her today.'

Liam was simmering with anger, an unusual situation for someone as generally amiable in mood as him. 'I think she's here somewhere with that man Strode. She's throwing herself at him without any propriety at all. She can't want a man like him, can she? I don't understand her,' he added desperately.

'Nor I,' Silver replied carefully. 'But then who can understand women?' That last sentiment was an entirely honest one, coming directly from his own heart: he certainly didn't understand Elisa Saltash at all.

He hadn't had the opportunity for a single private word with Elisa since that Saturday night ten days ago when he had called to borrow some decent clothes in which to see Sophie. But when she had appeared subsequently at the yard in Strode's company, he had assumed that she must be trying to help trap the man into betraying his guilt. But doubts had later intruded into this complacent thinking: perhaps she really was simply an amoral creature pursuing her own ends, whatever those might be. Yet, when he remembered how much help she had willingly given him over the last weeks, and the way she had shared her dreams with him about the future, he had felt some shame at his suspicions. The truth was he didn't like Elisa going anywhere near Daniel Strode, even if her motives were intended to help him...

Liam still had something more to say. 'Jonathan, Miss Smith has let me close the shop for a few days because I've got to go home to Maldon to see to my sister Siobhan. My dear sister has taken a turn for the worse with her consumption. So can you watch out for Miss Smith's welfare until then? I should be back on Thursday...'

Silver didn't quite know what Liam expected him to do, but he was in any event intending to look out for Elisa's welfare so he didn't choose to argue with this strange request.

Twelve-thirty arrived, and the first attempt to move the ship began. Silver knew Brunel was normally a meticulous planner, but here his hand had been forced by his directors so he was improvising as he went. No one therefore quite knew what would happen when the blocks holding the cradles were released and the various giant winches and hydraulic rams set to work.

Now that the crowd had fallen reasonably quiet, Brunel took up his position on the control stand on the dais. The crowd were craning their necks to watch his every move and signal, as an eerie silence fell over this vast gathering and the giant vessel towering above them.

From beneath the giant hull, came the thudding of sledgehammers as gangs of men knocked away the mammoth wedges securing the cradles. Nothing stopped the cradles and the ship sliding down the iron slipway now except friction between the cradles and the iron rails.

John Harkness was standing by as Brunel's chief assistant to pass on his orders to the gangs in charge of the checking drums and the steam winches of the bow and stern overhauls.

As soon as the wedges to the cradles were clear, Brunel ordered the checking drum cables to be slackened off, and then a white flag was broken out to signal the man in charge of the winches on the moored barges for his gang to take up the strain.

Then, with a further signal from Brunel, Harkness started up the steam winches at bow and stern. When the slack in the cables was taken up, the white flags were waved as a signal to heave hard.

For ten interminable minutes, the crowd watched expectantly, listening to the rumbling noise, like a prolonged roll of drums, as the straining chain purchases awoke strange reverberations in the hull. It felt as if the Engineer was trying to breathe life into his sleeping monster, like a modern Prometheus.

Yet, for all the noise and strain, there was not a glimmer of the ship moving. Seeing that the power of the winches and tackles was insufficient, Brunel now ordered Harkness to bring the powerful hydraulic rams into action.

The effect of adding this huge motive force to the vessel proved dramatic, to say the least. Silver could feel the ground tremble underfoot, and heard the crowd gasp in amazement.

Then a woman in the crowd screamed as the giant iron hull suddenly moved. With amazing rapidity, the bow cradle slid three feet down the slipway rails, where it was halted in its progress by the gang manning the forward checking drum. This swift movement of the vessel so terrified the men on the winches on the moored barges directly below the ship, though, that some of them, fearful for their lives with twelve thousand tons of iron bearing down on them, dived into the filthy river and swam for their lives.

At this point, Silver glanced to his side and saw that Billy had disappeared momentarily somewhere for a better view.

A woman brushed past Silver briefly. Even in his engrossed state, Silver realized it had to be Elisa, dressed in fine grey silk and matching bonnet, despite her face being turned away from his. As she passed, he heard her breathe a message. 'I am meeting Strode in his private room at six after this is over. Be there, please.'

Then she was gone so quickly that he half thought he had imagined the whole thing. She had gone by so rapidly in fact that Silver hadn't had time to warn her that Minshall and Sparrow were in the vicinity, although hopefully neither had any reason to suspect her in her present guise of the coquettish Miss Elisa Smith.

Silver now glanced at the rear checking drum and saw that in the excitement over the movement of the bows, the crew manning the brake at the stern had neglected their charge entirely and were merely standing around and watching the strange goings-on, like all the other amazed spectators. Silver then spotted Billy Faber standing right next to the handles of the giant drum and had a moment of supreme panic.

'Billy, get away from that drum! It's not safe!' he screamed, despite attracting the attention of everyone in the vicinity in his direction. Not sure that Billy had heard him, he began forcing his way through the crowd towards the giant stern drum.

Then the ground reverberated again as the hydraulic rams were pumped to their maximum pressure, and this time it was the stern cradle that suddenly began to slide at high speed. Immediately the handles of the stern checking drum, with the cables tight and no one working the brake, began to spin at fantastic speed, like the pistons of an engine.

Silver was still trying to fight his way through the suddenly panicked crowd to the stern drum when he heard an awful scream, then saw a body flying through the air as if it had been fired from a circus cannon. The body flew high and wide, and landed a good fifty feet away from the checking drum.

Silver forced his way further towards where the body had landed, fearing the worst. By the time he got there, he found the bloodied and mutilated remains of young Billy Faber, lying like a carcase of meat in the centre of a group of stunned and silent onlookers...

*

A minute later, Ginny Faber arrived to sob over the remains of her son.

A quick glance at that body had told Silver there was nothing he could do. The boy's organs must have been ripped apart instantly by the handle of the checking drum; he'd been dead long before he hit the ground.

Silver moved away from the heaving knot of spectators and curious voyeurs, fighting back his tears. He bumped hard into someone and saw that it was Jimmy Flynn. Jimmy was distraught. 'How could he have been so stupid? The useless little bastard! I told him how dangerous it was to go anywhere near the drum!' Jimmy began to hit his fist against his own brow in his anguish. 'Oh, God almighty!'

*

At two, despite the accident, and now with heavy rain falling from a sky like rusting metal, Brunel tried again, desperate to try and get the ship low enough down the slipway to float off in tonight's high tide. Everyone was in a prickly state after the accident, and the mood of the crowd had changed from cheerful and supportive to brooding and ugly.

Brunel had ordered all the midship tackles to be disconnected, and the barges in the river below the ship to disperse, wanting no repeat of the earlier scenes with panicked man diving into the river. From now on he would rely only on the steam winches at the bow and stern, and the hydraulic rams on the landward side of the hull.

But, after a few minutes effort, a gear on the bow winch stripped several teeth, and then the barge carrying the stern purchase for the steam winch began to drag her anchor.

In the failing light of a November afternoon, Brunel finally admitted defeat for the present.

Silver knew exactly how he felt...

CHAPTER 23

Tuesday 3rd November 1857

The crowds had vanished, leaving the Napier yard like a rubbish-strewn graveyard - a graveyard dominated by one giant iron mausoleum. In the eerie silence, the monstrous vessel, now a few feet further down the slipway than previously, had the look of a long abandoned prison hulk rather than the vanguard of a new generation of ships of the future.

The reporters had long gone too, to file their stories and polish their invective - no doubt ridiculing Brunel's pitiful efforts to launch his "Great Ship." The humorous hacks of *Punch* would take particular pleasure in recording Brunel's embarrassment - for some reason they saw the great engineer as a humbug and someone to be mocked mercilessly. Silver had a feeling however that Brunel's name would live far longer than these purveyors of literary poison dressed up as humour.

Immediately after the attempted launch, Silver had controlled his grief and self-recrimination over the death of Billy Faber, and made his way against the outward flow of the crowd to the main buildings. At the back of the drawing office he had climbed up a fire escape stair, and then squeezed his way into the building through a half-open sash window. At four o'clock in the afternoon (measured by the big clock tower in the middle of the yard) there had still been staff working in desultory fashion in the main drawing office, so Silver had hidden first in a storeroom full of drawing supplies and spare parts for drawing boards. There he stayed for almost two hours until the last of the visitors had departed, and the remaining staff too had joined them in their melancholy exodus. Even Brunel had finally joined them and gone home to his wife in Westminster; through the window of the storeroom, Silver had caught sight of Brunel's distinctive carriage leaving through the main gates at five p.m. So Silver calculated there should be no one left in the yard now, apart from the gatekeeper and a few old nightwatchmen. Plus Daniel Strode and Elisa, of course, assuming her plan had come to its expected fruition anyway.

Tonight had been intended to be a night of grand celebration for the workers of the Napier yard, but instead they would have to overcome their bitter disappointment and wait perhaps for several more months before a second attempt could be made to get the ship afloat. Although the failure must be bitter news for the embattled directors of the Eastern Steam Navigation Company, Silver thought it was possibly even worse for Brunel who had battled like a Trojan to achieve this impossible date, before seeing his hopes dashed. And worse, seeing a young boy die because of those hurried and inadequate preparations. If the launch could have been done in private, and with proper planning, Silver was sure that Billy wouldn't have lost his life because the activities inside in the yard would have been much more closely tested and controlled.

Yet, as he waited in hiding, Silver couldn't stop torturing himself with thoughts of what *he* might have done to prevent the accident. Billy hadn't understood the danger of standing too near the handles of that giant braking drum. But *he* had, and he should have warned Billy properly...

Gradually the building grew quieter until finally there were no more sounds of footsteps, or distant voices, or even the squeak of loose floorboards. When Silver was sure everyone was gone, he finally ventured out tentatively from his hiding place in the storeroom, a few minutes before 6 p.m.

Since Elisa was planning to meet Strode in his own room, which was at the opposite end of the building from the storeroom where Silver had secreted himself, he was forced to negotiate the entire length of the main drawing office. Still nervous of discovery, he decided to crawl from table to table through the darkened room rather than show himself.

He was nervous in particular of Sparrow or Minshall still being in the vicinity. It was true he hadn't seen anything of those two gentlemen again after his initial sightings of them today, but he felt nevertheless that there was a distinct possibility that they might not have gone home with the crowd, and might still be here in the yard baiting a trap for him.

Yet all seemed to be quiet as Silver crawled furtively through the dimly lit drawing office towards Strode's room. He wasn't sure where the ghostly light in here was emanating from since all the main gaslights in the drawing office were off. Some of the light, he realized finally, was coming from the gaslights in the yard outside, yet a few rooms in the office were also still lit. Hopefully that didn't mean anyone was working late. Silver was glad to discover, though, that one room did certainly have its gaslights still fully lit.

Daniel Strode's room...

*

Silver moved carefully towards Strode's office. The sturdy wooden door wasn't completely closed, so by listening in at the crack in the door, Silver could hear what was going on inside, if not see.

Silver heard the chink of a decanter being opened. 'Can I offer you a little more wine, Miss Smith?'

'Yes, you may. Although I thought you had agreed to call me "Elisa", Mr Strode.'

'"Elisa" it is, then,' Strode agreed amiably, to the sound of liquid being poured.

Elisa murmured her thanks, then sipped her drink. 'I do hope you're not trying to get me drunk, though, Daniel.'

'Of course not. Why would I do such a thing to a charming young lady as yourself?'

'Why indeed?' Elisa sighed. 'The launch today was a dreadful disappointment,' she suggested, 'compared to what I was expecting anyway.'

Strode sniffed. 'For me too. Yet, to be honest, I foresaw this happening. The ship should never have been launched in this painful fashion. Everyone considers Mr Brunel to be such a genius, but we saw the truth of his reputation today. A man of imagination, it's true, but also vainglorious and dogmatic in his approach. He would never take my advice about the launch. Anyway, this *Leviathan* of his would be nothing without its engines. I designed those paddle engines myself, Elisa – the largest cylinders ever cast - but I have received precious little endorsement or praise for my part in this venture.'

Silver tried to imagine the look on Elisa's face. A secretive smile at this point perhaps? 'You do have a reputation, Mr Strode, but, from what I hear, it is more to do with seducing ladies than with your abilities as a designer of steam engines.'

Strode laughed, but sounded disconcerted. 'Entirely undeserved, I assure you, Elisa. Where did you learn such a thing?'

'Perhaps I'm mistaken. But I did hear there was a policeman here today at the shipyard to talk to you about something.'

Strode sounded annoyed for the first time. 'Yes, an impertinent devil called Sparrow.'

'What did he want with you, Daniel?'

'Nothing important. Let's talk of something more pleasant, Elisa.'

'It wasn't concerning the death of Miss Charlotte Livingstone, was it?'

Strode sounded angry at her continued pressing. 'What did you say?

How do you know that name?' He moved towards her, his voice growing suspicious. 'Who are you, Miss *Smith*? And what is the purpose of these questions?'

'Did you kill Miss Livingstone?' Elisa asked him calmly. 'And Miss Penfold?'

Strode gasped and put his own glass down with a crash. 'I did not.'

'But you knew both of them, I think? My information is that you were with Miss Penfold at a house in Pennington Street in Wapping on the very night she died. Is that true?'

'Yes, but I certainly did not kill her.' Strode laughed humourlessly. 'So you're a blackmailer, Miss Smith, are you? Well, well! Blackmailers come in very pretty packages now, I must say. I don't know where you got your information from, but it's too late anyway for your pathetic attempts at blackmailing an honest gentleman. You'd better leave now before I lose my temper completely. The police already know everything you do so I have nothing to hide. I did not kill either of these two women, I assure you, as I will be able to prove to the police. In fact I didn't even discover that Charlotte was dead until a week after she died. Her name didn't appear in the newspaper accounts until then.'

'And Miss Penfold? When did you hear of her death?' Elisa demanded.

'I did hear of her death rather sooner,' Strode admitted. 'Only a day or so after the event.'

Elisa sounded disbelieving. 'And none of this was to do with you?'

'No, and now you really must leave.' He moved towards her threateningly. 'Or else I might not be responsible for what happens next.'

Silver decided it was finally time to intervene and ask Daniel Strode a few questions of his own. He straightened up from his crouching position only to hear a sudden whistling sound behind him.

Then his head exploded with pain, and all sight and sound vanished completely as if he'd been thrown down a dark and bottomless well...

*

When he came to, he found that he was still lying more or less in the same position outside Daniel Strode's office. Not having a watch, and now being out of sight of the yard's main clock, he wasn't sure how long he had been unconscious.

He eased himself gingerly to his feet, feeling his limbs for injuries. His ribs on the left side were still sore, but that was a relic of his earlier encounter with Minshall's two wharf rat accomplices, Jack and Joey. His head felt as if the top had been sawn off, but otherwise he seemed to have no other injuries of note. Yet the blow to his head had been sufficient that his vision still felt fuzzy and his movements were slow and uncoordinated. That could mean concussion, he thought worriedly.

He was more worried about Elisa, though, and went inside Strode's office, fearing the worst.

A man's body lay slumped on the floor, but there was no sign of Elisa.

The body on the floor was Strode; a quick examination showed that he was still alive but that there was a bloody gash on his head and his breathing was shallow and laboured.

Silver was perplexed. *Who had struck him from behind?* An accomplice of Strode's? Then why was Strode unconscious too?

And, more to the point, *where was Elisa...?*

Silver heard something outside: muffled footsteps on cobbles, a raised voice, then the sounds of a scuffle and a blow. Silver moved back into the drawing office, then, despite his weakened state, ran rapidly over to one of the casement windows looking out over the yard. For once the hull of the Great Ship was silent, a vertical cliff of iron blotting out the sky, lit only by occasional oil lamps to delineate her shape. There were no figures swarming over her hull tonight, but there was one wooden access staircase still fixed to the side of the hull amidships that had been used during the attempted launch today.

Then Silver thought he heard the sounds of someone hurriedly climbing that staircase up to the deck of the *Leviathan.*

In a few seconds, Silver had found his way out of the drawing office and was at the foot of the *Leviathan* too. His hearing hadn't misled him because there was definitely someone on the staircase above – probably more than one person by the sounds of it.

He followed the thumping sounds upwards, trying to keep his own steps as light as possible. There were twelve fights of stairs in all to climb the near hundred feet to deck level.

In all his weeks at the yard, Silver had never stood on the deck of the *Leviathan,* and from up here it seemed quite as high and dizzying a view as that from the top of the Monument to the Great Fire in Pudding Lane. Oil lamps lit the deck at intervals and made him appreciate its incredible size. It was hard to imagine such a gargantuan structure ever floating...

'You shouldn't have followed me up here, Wade.'

The speaker of these words stepped out from the shadows and Silver reacted with shock.

John Harkness...

'Well, Mr Harkness, what are *you* doing here?' Silver kept his voice matter-of-fact and his tone polite.

'I might ask you the same question, Wade.'

Silver improvised rapidly. 'I heard some noises up here – it sounded like someone was chasing someone else - so I came to investigate.'

A gleam of metal in the dim light revealed that Harkness had a weapon in his right hand. When Harkness noticed the direction of Silver's eyes, he raised the weapon into full view to show Silver. 'Look at this wonderful thing, Wade. I'm rather proud to own such a magnificent firearm – a Smith and Wesson cylinder revolver, one of the first imported into this country. Do you know? - I could fire six shots into you with this weapon before you could move even a single yard. Imagine the future of warfare when everyone has weapons like this at their disposal! The carnage of the Crimea will seem like a child's game compared to the wars of the future.'

Silver had never seen anything like this sleek futuristic weapon. It did indeed make the firearms he'd seen in the Crimea look primitive by comparison. 'I trust you won't fire that thing at me, though, Mr Harkness,' Silver argued reasonably. 'That would be a difficult killing to blame on your colleague Daniel Strode, wouldn't it, since he's lying unconscious in his own room at this moment.'

Harkness frowned. 'As you should be too, Wade. You must have the skull of an elephant. I hit you hard enough to kill any normal man.'

Silver gave up any further pretence of ignorance. 'I must have a thick head indeed – in more ways than one,' he added ruefully, 'not to have seen the truth about you before. But excuse me. I have been misleading you a little too, Mr Harkness. My real name is Silver. Jonathan Silver.'

Realization dawned in Harkness's eyes. 'Ah, the escaped wife murderer. Yes, I always thought there was something special about you. It almost makes us two of a kind, Dr Silver.'

'Did you really kill those two young women?' Silver asked, still not wanting to believe it. 'In God's name, why? What harm had they done to you?'

Harkness glowered. 'And what harm had your wife done you, Dr Silver? In fact Charlotte had done me infinite harm. I loved Miss Livingstone, you see, from the first moment I met her at my brother's home. She was only a humble governess without any connections or property, yet I didn't care. I offered her my hand, and everything I own. Yet Strode took her away from me, as he took everything else away from me. Even here in this shipyard, I am really his underling and lackey.'

Silver tried to stay calm even though his heart was racing. 'How did you do it? And how did you know she was betraying you with him?'

'Because I saw a note that she was writing to him. Then I followed her to her first assignation with him, to his sordid love nest in Pennington Street. I watched them meet there regularly for weeks after that. Finally, three weeks ago, I decided I could take this humiliation no longer. So this time, I waited all night for Strode to leave. He was in the habit of sending a cab in the morning to Pennington Street to take her home. As it happens I have my own hackney cab – I find it the safest way to get about London without being seen, especially dressed as a driver. It was how I followed her in the first place to Pennington Street. Who notices one more cab among thousands? Even Charlotte didn't recognise me that morning under my hat and scarf until it was too late.' Harkness hesitated. 'I'm not a cruel man, though, Dr Silver. I didn't prolong her agony. I made her departure from this world short and merciful.'

Silver wondered how Harkness could still look so sane and well-mannered, and yet still come out with such evil and insane thoughts. 'And Miss Penfold? Did Strode steal *her* away from you too?'

'No, on the contrary, you could say that I stole her away from him this time. I wanted to punish him for his unfaithfulness to Charlotte's memory. Only a few days after seeing Charlotte, and he already had the temerity to see another woman.'

'Perhaps he didn't know Charlotte was dead?'

'He almost certainly didn't at the time, but that's hardly the point, is it?' Harkness lined the revolver up on Silver's brow.

'Why not kill *him*, then, rather than these poor women?' Silver asked desperately.

'Oh, I was rather hoping the law would do that for me, after I laid a trail of guilt pointing clearly in his direction. But first, before the law caught up with him, he had to suffer a little, as I've suffered. That was why I placed Miss Penfold's body in a lime pit in a tanner's yard.'

The man was completely mad...

'Where is Miss Smith?' Silver demanded to know, wondering with dismay if this madman had already killed her.

Harkness waved his revolver vaguely in the air behind him. 'She's back there along the deck, but unconscious and greatly the worse for wear after I beat her skull with the butt of this weapon.' He hissed angrily. 'She deserved it! That bitch has given me a deal of grief tonight – forcing me to chase her up here. If she's not already dead, then I believe I'm going to finish the job, and slit her pretty throat before I push her off the top of this ship. It seems a fitting end for this most miserable of days.' He grunted disdainfully. 'My, but she's a feisty one, I'll give her that! Put up far more of a fight than either Charlotte or Miss Penfold. But for this –' he patted the barrel of the revolver soothingly with his left hand – 'I'm not sure I would have succeeded in pacifying her, to be honest. I thought I had broken her arm earlier in our struggle, and yet she still came back at me like a hellcat until I hit her over the head with this weapon. '

'Don't kill her,' Silver pleaded with him. 'She's done nothing to you. Show some compassion for once, man.'

Harkness sighed. 'Unfortunately I have no choice now with her...or with you, come to think of it.' He raised his revolver and aimed the barrel at the centre of Silver's forehead. 'Now it's up to you, Dr Silver. You can either jump from this deck with no holes in you, or you can leave full of holes, and with rather more gore and mess about your person. It's entirely your decision.' He prodded Silver with the barrel of the revolver and forced him back to a gap in the rails. Silver found himself balancing on the edge of the deck with nothing behind him but a black void below.

Then a second figure, wild of eye and streaming blood from her brow, rushed out from the shadows and hit Harkness a savage blow to the back of his neck with a piece of lead piping. Harkness screamed, stumbled forward blindly, then without a further sound toppled over the rail onto the cobbles far below.

Elisa looked down at the broken figure on the ground below and didn't seem regretful of her actions. Silver wondered why she was holding the pipe in her left hand, and why her right hand seemed twisted back in such an unnatural way.

'Like the good doctor here, I have the skull of an elephant too, Mr Harkness,' she said, spitting contemptuously at the twisted body on the cobbles below, before fainting dead away in Silver's arms.

CHAPTER 24

Tuesday 3rd November 1857

Sergeant Sparrow was struggling to make sense of things...

In late evening, he had finally returned to the Napier shipyard to resume his discussion with Mr Strode, only to find unexpected things had been taking place in his absence...

The reasons why it had taken him so long to return were understandable. At one o'clock in the afternoon, in the absence of anyone else of suitable authority in the Napier yard, he had been forced to take charge of the mangled corpse of a young apprentice carpenter called Billy Faber and see that it was transported back to the police mortuary in Whitechapel (where the mortal remains of Miss Charlotte Livingstone and Miss Jane Penfold also currently still resided, encased in blocks of ice, if not for much longer.) Coincidentally it turned out that the dead boy was the son of the woman who worked at the Hostel for Women in New Gravel Lane, Ginny Faber. Although he didn't have to, Sparrow had arranged, as a compassionate service, for her to be taken back in the police growler to Wapping and put into the care of young Amy McLennan (who had been one of the few people in Wapping who had apparently chosen not to attend today's abortive launch of the *Leviathan*.)

Then, before Sparrow could set off back to the Isle of Dogs, a report from the River Police at Wapping New Stairs of a dead body floating in the river had sent him scurrying down Old Gravel Lane, only to find the "corpse" was a piece of driftwood. (A remarkably human-looking piece of driftwood, Sparrow had to concede, but driftwood nonetheless.)

By this time it had proved to be very difficult for Sparrow and Frank Remmert to get back out to the Isle of Dogs, what with the ferries and watermen's boats clogging the river, and a vast chain of humanity streaming away on the only road off the Isle of Dogs, again much resembling the Children of Israel fleeing Egypt.

Sparrow had been forced to let the disappointed crowd dissipate before he could return belatedly to the shipyard in the police growler.

Finally, at seven o'clock in the evening, he had been able to gain access again to the now near-deserted shipyard, only for the night-watchman to show him a genuine corpse this time – the second one of the day in the unlucky Napier Yard - this being the mangled body of a man found at the bottom of the slipway below the silent hull of the ship.

The man had been identified by the gateman as Mr John Harkness, one of the senior engineers at the yard. Sparrow concluded instantly that this must be the brother of the man whose house he had visited in Hampstead only a few days ago, yet it seemed an even more remarkable coincidence that this man should now be found dead.

Now that he recalled, Mrs George Harkness had mentioned that her brother-in-law worked in the same enterprise as Strode, even if she had glossed over that fact quickly. Perhaps she was ashamed of the connection. She would be even more ashamed of the connection now, Sparrow decided tartly, given the sordid and violent nature of her brother-in-law's death.

For a few minutes afterwards, Sparrow had basked in the complacent assumption that this must be another unfortunate accident – that the man must have fallen accidentally from the deck of the *Leviathan*. Yet the gatekeeper knew of no obvious reason why Harkness should have been on the deck of the vessel at night; and a closer examination of the victim's skull had soon revealed to Sparrow the clear signs that he'd more likely been struck with a hard object from behind, rather than gaining that injury in falling from a height.

Then Remmert had found a weapon on the slipway too – a large calibre revolver, but such an amazing and futuristic-looking firearm as Sparrow had never seen before...

Sparrow and Frank Remmert had gone searching for Daniel Strode at this point, only to find him in his room in the drawing office, semi-conscious and seemingly in quite a bad way. A doctor had soon been summoned and Strode's injuries had turned out fortunately not to be life threatening so at least there was only this one additional death of Mr Harkness to explain, rather than two.

Yet, all in all, Sparrow was thoroughly confused about this mysterious chain of events...

At nine o' clock in the evening, Sparrow sat in one of the director's plush offices, where a cheerful coal fire still burned in the grate. Frank Remmert and another constable stood guard at the door, Remmert taking notes at Sparrow's request. Strode, now recovered enough to answer questions, had a bandage applied to his wounded forehead, and, sitting in a green leather armchair, was enjoying a glass of brandy from the directors' drink cabinet.

Sparrow would have liked a brandy too after a long day, but could hardly do that openly when he was on duty. 'Who struck you, Mr Strode?'

Strode looked blank. 'I don't know, Sergeant. Whoever it was hit me from behind. I didn't see a thing.'

Sparrow sniffed suspiciously. 'Have you heard that a colleague of yours has been found dead in the yard? Mr John Harkness. He apparently fell off the deck of the ship.'

Strode was astonished, his surprise bringing some colour back to his pale cheeks. 'John Harkness dead? Fell off the *Leviathan*, you say? You mean he killed himself?'

'No, not exactly. I believe someone hit him over the back of the head.'

'You mean, the same as me?'

'Possibly rather harder than you were hit, I would say,' Sparrow said dryly. 'After all, you're still here to tell the tale.'

Strode was doing a good job of looking baffled, Sparrow thought. 'What is going on, Sergeant? I don't understand any of this.'

'Nor I, sir. What were you still doing here in the yard at this time, Mr Strode? Everyone else had gone home.'

Strode bristled. 'I was waiting for *you* to return, Sergeant. If you remember, you told me not to leave the yard until we could talk.'

'I didn't really expect you to wait quite this long, sir,' Sparrow denied unconvincingly. 'What were you doing tonight, though? There were drinks in your room as if you were entertaining someone.'

Strode became defensive. 'I was entertaining a guest, as it happened, while I waited for you to come back. I was showing a Miss Smith around the drawing office...'

Sparrow started. 'Not Miss *Elisa* Smith?'

Strode jerked guiltily again. 'Ah, you know her, do you, Sergeant? Why doesn't that surprise me? Although I have to say I don't believe "Smith" is her real name at all. That young woman is a blackmailer and a fraud, I suspect, who wanted to exploit my predicament over the death of these two young women. Somehow Miss "Smith" had learned that I had seen Miss Penfold on the night before she was found dead, and it seemed she thought she could profit in some way from this knowledge.'

'Did she indeed? Did she openly ask you for money?'

'No, but she was certainly working up to it before we were interrupted by whoever assaulted me from behind.'

'Why do you think her name is not really "Smith", though?'

Strode looked chastened. 'I happened to see a letter inside her bag addressed to a Miss Elisa *Saltash*. The woman is certainly a cozener, if she's using a false name like that.'

Sparrow gasped. The fog was clearing instantly from his mind as he realized now why Miss Smith's face had seemed so familiar...

Of course, he should have remembered! Jonas Saltash, the man who had tried to escape from Newgate with Dr Silver, had had no surviving sons to carry on the family tradition of thieving. But he did certainly have a daughter, and one who might well have been called Elisa. Sparrow thought he might even have seen her once with her father when she was younger, perhaps thirteen or fourteen...

And he also imagined, being a tall well-built girl, that she could be well capable of impersonating a boy when it suited her. So could this Elisa have followed her late father into the same ignoble profession? And could she be this mysterious youth who seemed to have been aiding and abetting Dr Silver over these past weeks? It all made perfect sense.

Sparrow now wondered whether, when he'd called at her chandler's store in lower Wapping two weeks ago, he might have been within touching distance of the fabulous *Tears of the Prophet* necklace. That would be ironic if it were true...

Sparrow heard Strode say something else but his attention was still focussed on the thought of Miss Elisa "Smith" as thief and ne'er do well. Suddenly, though, he refocused his mind sharply as some of Strode's words penetrated his consciousness.

'Excuse me, sir. Could you repeat that? Are you suggesting that this Miss Smith, or Miss Saltash, might have been in league with Mr Harkness, and that they might together have killed Miss Livingstone and Miss Penfold?'

'Yes, I am indeed. How else could she have known that I had seen Miss Penfold on the night she died, unless she and Harkness were following me? And Harkness could have been the person who struck me tonight, before meeting a similar fate himself at the hand of his own confederate.'

Sparrow was floundering. 'Why would Harkness kill those women?' Or, even more, why would Elisa Saltash help him? Thief she might be, but *murderess*...?

'Jealousy and revenge – those could have been Harkness's motives,' Strode stated complacently. 'Harkness imagined Miss Livingstone had spurned his advances in favour of my own.'

'Was there any truth in that, sir?'

'Perhaps a little,' Strode admitted. 'Harkness and I had been friends once. And he did admit to me that he had a strong fancy for her. But I could hardly help it if Miss Livingstone preferred my company to his, could I?'

Sparrow was beginning to detest this man's smugness and false sincerity. 'That doesn't explain the other girl, though. What was Harkness's connection with Miss Penfold?'

'None directly, as far as I know, although he met her briefly when she came to his brother's house to apply for Miss Livingstone's former post.'

Sparrow snorted loudly. 'Then why would he kill that poor girl and dump her body in a lime pit of all places? That can't have been purely because of jealousy of you.'

Strode nodded sagaciously. 'I suppose it must have been to continue punishing me for stealing Miss Livingstone from him. And perhaps he was trying deliberately to implicate me for his own terrible crimes, and then to blackmail me for life with the threat of exposure.'

Sparrow was sceptical of Strode's theory, although he didn't presently have a better one himself. Harkness was no longer here to give his side of things, of course, but surely no quiet English gent, as Mr Harkness had apparently been, could turn into quite such an evil and debased monster as this. Yet someone had certainly killed those two women, and if it wasn't this man seated in front of him, then Harkness presently seemed the only other reasonable candidate...

'If what you say is true, who do you think killed Harkness tonight?' Sparrow demanded gruffly.

'I don't know for certain, Sergeant. But Miss Smith was the only other person here tonight. So, by process of elimination, she must be the guilty party. Perhaps it was a case of villains falling out.'

Sparrow had a sudden interesting thought and sent Frank Remmert back to the growler for a copy of the wanted poster for Dr Silver. When Remmert returned at the double in less than two minutes, Sparrow unrolled the poster for Strode to examine, taking care to hide the name at the bottom. 'Do you know this man, sir?'

Strode examined the drawing on the poster and frowned. 'It looks like that carpenter Wade who's been working on the slipway for the past few weeks.' He had a thought of his own. 'The man did appear to be a close confidante of Harkness's. At least I saw them often in each other's company.'

'Really?' Sparrow took away his hand that had been concealing the name on the poster. 'His real name is Silver. Jonathan Silver.'

Strode's eyes widened.

'I can see that name means something to you,' Sparrow interjected.

Strode was clearly disconcerted. 'Yes, I know of him. The murderer who escaped from Newgate four weeks ago.'

Sparrow frowned. 'I'm surprised you didn't know what Dr Silver looked like. You knew his wife very well at one time, I believe.'

Strode was clearly shocked that Sparrow seemed to know so much about his private life. 'I did know Marianne, Sergeant, but that was a long time ago, before she married Silver. I never met him before – not until now anyway, it seems.' Strode was obviously calculating rapidly. 'Perhaps Dr Silver was also a confederate with Harkness and Miss Smith in the murder of these two young women. And then they had a falling out, and Silver and his girl killed Harkness to silence him.'

Sparrow wondered whether he would be the next one to be accused by this man of complicity in the murders. 'They were *your* young women, I remind you, sir. You had some moral responsibility for the welfare of these two helpless young women – one of them even expecting your child. Yet you brought them to a dangerous place like Wapping, seduced them, then left them to make their own way home.'

Bright spots of colour flared in Strode's cheeks. 'I did nothing of the sort. I always sent a cab to take them both home. Don't dare blame me for this!'

'Nevertheless I do blame you, sir,' Sparrow said contemptuously.

Frank Remmert moved in to collect the poster from Sparrow's proffered hand. 'What do we do, Sarge?'

'Silver is on the move again, so we should be able to find him more easily now. And he possibly has this girl Elisa Saltash with him now. So what we'll do is rush out a new set of bill posters all over London for their capture. I believe *she* is our pearl thief –' he glanced across at Strode reluctantly – 'and she may also have some questions to answer about the death of John Harkness.'

Despite Strode's accusation, Sparrow didn't for a moment believe that Dr Silver had any part in the death of Miss Livingstone or Miss Penfold. Sparrow had become convinced after his talk with Captain Caitlin that Silver must be innocent of his wife's murder, therefore was unlikely to be perpetrating any more murders along the way for the sake of it. The responsibility for the deaths of Miss Livingstone and Miss Penfold surely had to lie either with Strode or Harkness. And, although Sparrow had by now a deep distaste for Daniel Strode, he would, if he were a betting man, have presently gone for Harkness as the likely murderer of the two young governesses. There was just enough credibility in Strode's blustering manner to suggest he was telling the truth about those two governesses – or what he knew of it anyway...

Another disturbing thought now occurred to Sparrow. *Why had Silver been working here in this shipyard in the first place?* As a hiding place it was scarcely ideal when anybody might have recognized him at any time. Taking that degree of risk for no reason bordered on insanity, and insane was one thing that Dr Silver certainly wasn't. So it made no sense unless there was something important here that he needed to find, no matter what the risk.

A guilty man would have fled the country by now if he could, and Silver must have had plenty of opportunities in the past four weeks to get a thousand leagues from here if he wished. The only reason that Sparrow could envisage why Silver had hung on here was surely the hope of proving his innocence of his wife's murder...

Did he perhaps believe that someone who worked at the Napier yard might have murdered his wife, or at least know something about it? Could that be it? If so, it was an interesting conjecture because this man, Daniel Strode, appeared to be the only person at the Napier shipyard with a direct connection to Silver and his wife...

Sparrow returned to interrogating Strode with a vengeance. 'When was the last time you saw Mrs Marianne Silver, sir?'

Strode was wary. 'Why do you ask?'

Sparrow sniffed balefully. 'Never mind why! Answer the question.'

Strode was jarred by his bluntness. 'I don't know. Five, six, seven years ago perhaps. She was Marianne Lovelock then, not Silver.'

'You never saw her after she was married?'

'Never.' Under pressure Strode was beginning to babble his words a little. 'Err...no, I lie. Once! I saw her once - riding in Rotten Row. A year ago, I think. We might even have had a brief word, now I recall.'

Sparrow was convinced now that he was right in his conjecture: that Jonathan Silver had taken a job at the Napier yard because he believed that Daniel Strode had something to do with his wife's death. But why would Silver think that? What grounds did he have?

Perhaps nothing more than the fact that his wife had known this man, and that Strode was a deeply unpleasant individual, a seducer of innocent women, and a man who betrayed his friends without a qualm...

Remmert was making faces in the background again, a sign that he had something to say.

Sparrow was irritated by the unwanted interruption. 'Yes, Frank, what is it?'

Remmert straightened his tall stovepipe hat, which the gusting wind outside had knocked awry.' I forgot to mention something, Sergeant. When I was searching the room where this gentleman was lying, I happened to find something on the floor outside. Perhaps it's a clue to whoever knocked this gentleman out?'

'What is it?'

'It's a ticket, Sarge.'

Sparrow was losing patience. 'For what?'

Remmert shifted his feet nervously. 'That's the odd thing: it's a ticket for the Alhambra Music Hall in Leicester Square tomorrow night. Row H, seat 27. Someone may just have dropped it accidentally, of course. If it doesn't belong to anyone, I wouldn't mind taking it,' he added hopefully. 'It's a two and sixpenny ticket, and looks like a good bill.'

Sparrow gestured coldly with his fingers. 'Hand it over, Frank.'

Remmert sighed but did as he was told.

'Do you know anything about this ticket, Mr Strode?' Sparrow asked, examining it carefully. 'Is it yours by any chance?'

'Hardly, no.' Strode raised an insulted eyebrow. 'The Alhambra Music Hall? Jugglers and chorus girls.'

'Perhaps Silver dropped it, Sarge, if he was here?' Remmert suggested.

'Why would Dr Silver be going to the Alhambra tomorrow? A fugitive normally has more important things to do with his time.' Sparrow grunted doubtfully at the notion.

But on reflection he thought that it might be worth a visit to check...

*

Silver gave Amy – or more properly, Lady Rachel, as he now belatedly remembered - an apologetic look as she answered his knock at the kitchen door. Then, without waiting for permission, he half-carried Elisa across the threshold of the Hostel for Women, and through to the comfort of the warm snug kitchen at the back.

Elisa was drowsy now, but feeling less agony at least. Silver had found an apothecary's shop in Old Gravel Lane that was still open, and had subsequently administered several drops of laudanum to her to ease the severe pain of her gashed head and her broken right forearm.

'I'm sorry to come here again,' Silver repeated, 'but I couldn't think of anywhere else to bring her. She's broken her forearm and I need to set the bones of the radius and ulna properly before she can sleep.'

Amy was on her own in the kitchen tonight, Silver was glad to see, everyone else at the hostel having apparently retired for the night, even though it was not yet ten o'clock. He was certainly in no mood tonight for confronting any of the other more quarrelsome residents of the hostel, or for facing Ginny Faber in her abject grief at losing her son. Silver had enough problems on his mind without reawakening his personal guilt about what had happened to Billy today.

Amy finally recognized the girl with Silver. 'This is Miss Smith, isn't it, the lady who owns the chandler's store at the bottom of Old Gravel Lane? I didn't know you and she knew each other,' she added suspiciously. It sounded more of a question than a statement but Silver didn't enlighten her as to the whys and wherefores of his strange relationship with Elisa. It would have been hard to explain in a few words anyway.

Amy inspected Elisa warily from head to foot, clearly wondering at her dishevelled appearance; Elisa was still dressed in the fine gown and petticoats she had worn at the launch today, but they were now dirty and torn, and splashed with her own blood after her encounter with the murderous John Harkness.

'We're on the run, Amy, I should warn you,' Silver told her.

Amy pursed her lips wryly. 'I knew that well enough already, Jonathan...'

Three hours earlier, Silver had somehow managed to get Elisa down from the deck of the *Leviathan* without discovery, and then across the deserted shipyard, and through a weed-filled gap in the boundary wall that only a few people knew about. From there he had half-carried her to the river near the Greenwich ferry stairs where he had eventually managed to find a waterman to take them the short way to Wapping, but only by bribing the man with a whole pound...

'I'm in worse trouble now,' he admitted to Amy. 'A man has died out at the Napier shipyard...'

Amy interrupted. 'Yes, of course I know. Poor Billy! His mother is distraught. I have given her a sleeping draught and sent her to bed. The poor woman wept enough today to fill the Thames.'

'No, I don't just mean Billy,' Silver explained patiently. 'A man called Harkness – an engineer - also died at the yard today. He tried to kill me,' he added defensively.

Amy's face fell. 'Why would he do that? More to the point, though, did you kill *him*? Please tell me you didn't kill anybody.'

Silver sighed heavily. 'He fell off the deck of the *Leviathan* - that was all. But he was a wicked and unprincipled man, so it's no great loss to the world.' It seemed best in the circumstances to say as little as possible about the events at the yard; he certainly didn't want to see Elisa take the blame for what had happened. Silver thought about the tangled and unhappy web of circumstance that had led to Elisa becoming the instrument of John Harkness's death. Yet the man had killed at least two helpless women, and had been willing to slit Elisa's throat too, as well as breaking her arm, so Silver had no qualms of conscience about what she had done to him in return. If Elisa hadn't knocked Harkness off the high deck of that ship, he certainly would have.

Amy found a straw mattress and they laid Elisa gently on it on the stone-flagged floor where Amy quickly undressed her, down to her inner petticoat. Then Silver got to work setting Elisa's arm in earnest, after first giving her another liberal dose of laudanum from his bottle.

It was a difficult compound break of the radius and ulna, and Silver had to dredge from his memory all his old half-forgotten skills to effect the repair. Yet, by the time he had finished binding the arm into a makeshift sling, he was sure that he had pieced all the bits of bone together in their correct positions. With luck, and good healing powers, her arm would be as good as new in a few weeks. Elisa, well drugged by now, made not a whit of protest during the whole uncomfortable procedure, even though there must still have been some considerable residual pain.

When he was satisfied that he had done everything he reasonably could, Silver carried Elisa up to bed in a spare room that Amy had made up for her. She was coming out of her extreme drowsy state a little and she grasped his hand with her left arm before he left. 'Where am I?' she asked woozily.

'You're safe. We're in the Hostel for Women in New Gravel Lane.'

She gave a glimmer of a smile. 'Ah, the Hostel for *Troubled* Women. That's me perfectly. *Deeply* troubled.'

'Don't say things like that. Sleep!' he ordered her with mock sternness.

He went to the door, taking the oil lamp with him.

'Don't take the lamp,' she murmured.

He came back to the bed and replaced the lamp on the bedside table. 'What on earth made you do that?'

Her eyes widened. 'Do what?'

'Try and entrap that man Strode.'

'Ah, that. It needed...to be done. You would never...have left until you knew...the truth about Strode, so I...wanted to help.'

'Now we do know the truth. It was Harkness who killed those two governesses, not Strode.'

Elisa's eyes were drooping again. 'Yet Strode could still...have killed your wife.'

'He could have -' Silver sighed in exasperation – 'but I don't think he did. You were right to doubt my theory.'

'No matter. You'll have to flee the country now, Jonathan,' she said, yawning deeply. 'They'll hunt you forever if you stay...here...'

He smoothed the hair back from her tired face and saw that she was already asleep. 'We'll go together,' he promised in a whisper.

Closing the bedroom door quietly behind him, he made his way back downstairs to the kitchen, where he found Amy sitting at the kitchen table, head resting on the surface, a single sputtering candle lighting the room. She woke with a start on his return, embarrassed. 'So tell me. What is your exact relationship with that girl, Jonathan? Is she in as much trouble as you?'

Silver sat down beside her. 'Yes, she is. And we are...*friends*.'

Amy smiled faintly. 'You look more like lovers.'

He let that mild accusation remain unanswered. 'Her real name is

Elisa Saltash, not Smith. It seems only fair that you should know that since you are kindly sheltering us. She's a fugitive from the law too, now.'

Amy straightened up on her kitchen stool. 'It seems we have all been pretending to be something we're not, Jonathan.'

He studied her face in the flickering light of the candle. 'It seems so.'

Sitting by the light of that single candle, Silver told Amy everything that had happened today in more detail. The candle burnt low as he went further back in his life, telling her of even more intimate things: about meeting Marianne, about the hellish world of Scutari, about the night that Marianne died, about his escape from Newgate with Elisa's help...

Amy was tired too but still engrossed in his story. 'I can see why you're attracted to Miss Smith, even if she is a thief.'

'I already owed her so much even before today. And after what she did for me tonight, risking her life for me like that, I don't think I could ever leave her again. Her future is my future now.'

Amy stirred, clearly uncomfortable with his words. 'So it was this man Harkness who killed those two young women, not Daniel Strode?'

Silver nodded. 'So he said. Now Harkness is dead and I...we...shall probably be accused of murdering him too. And I still have no idea who killed my wife. I had thought Strode was the man, but not now.'

'So where do you go from here?'

'I shall try to get passage on a ship abroad, as soon as I can. There is nothing else for it now, but to run.'

'And what about Miss Smith? Miss Saltash rather? Will she go with you?'

'She will have to make her own decision, when she is recovered enough.' Silver was reluctant to ask for further help from Amy, but the need to know the truth about Marianne still burned a hole in his heart. 'There is perhaps one more thing you could do for me. Is there any way you could get hold of a man's evening dress suit in my size?'

'For you? Why?'

'I want to go the music hall. The Alhambra.'

Amy frowned, not sure if he was being merely flippant. 'Why would you want to go there? It's a low class place from what I hear. And an extremely risky place to go in your perilous situation.'

'For some reason, a man I've never met sent me a ticket to attend the performance tomorrow night. A man who may have knowledge of my wife's death, I believe. It may be the last chance I will ever have to find some clue to the identity of my wife's real murderer.'

'Do you have the ticket with you?'

Silver patted the sides of his coarse labourer's trousers.

'Unfortunately not. I did have it in my trouser pocket at work today, but I seemed to have lost it somewhere in all this confusion. Never mind. I remember the seat number. Row H, seat twenty-seven. I should be able to bluff my way past the ushers.'

Silver had come to the conclusion by now that Elisa had been absolutely right to question the intent of Marianne's last dying words. Marianne must indeed have been trying to name her murderer. So the question was not *what* Marianne had meant by *Leviathan*.

But *whom*...

'I *can* find you a dress suit for tomorrow night,' Amy assured him. 'But you would have to come to my brother's house in Fitzroy Square to get it. He is tall like you, and about the same size physically.'

'Won't he mind me taking his clothes?' Silver asked dryly.

Amy smiled. 'Hardly. His house is unoccupied at present apart from a couple of servants. Charles is currently working as first secretary to the Viceroy of India in Calcutta, and presently has his hands more than full putting down the mutiny.' She hesitated, slightly embarrassed. 'I would have to go with you to Fitzroy Square, of course.'

'Then I accept your kind offer.' Silver noted the continuing enigmatic expression on Amy's face. 'What is it?'

'Just one condition for my further help,' Amy declared emphatically.

'What's that?' he asked suspiciously.

'I am coming to the Alhambra with you...'

CHAPTER 25

Wednesday 4th November 1857

Amy McLennan, dressed in lilac silk finery and with her dark hair worn up in formal style, had been completely transformed tonight into the wealthy Lady Rachel Grosvenor.

Jonathan Silver marvelled at this metamorphosis, but still wasn't sure that he didn't prefer the simple servant girl original to this fine lady. It was disconcerting to remember that he had hardly known this young woman more than three weeks, and even more disconcerting to recall the circumstances of their first memorable meeting. Silver almost smiled as he considered what those two wharf rats Joey and Jack might now make of that pretty servant girl they had tried to molest that first night in Ratcliffe Highway.

Still, she had revenged herself on those two with a certain deadly aplomb, and the help of a piece of brick. The smaller one, Jack, must still be nursing his head as a result...

Amy was very like Elisa in some ways, Silver decided – a young woman who liked to break the rules of convention and live with a certain intensity of experience far outside what might normally be considered as suitable or proper for the female sex. Analysing his feelings for her, he had to admit to a strong attraction for her still, one that in any other circumstances he would have yielded too gladly enough. Yet the truth was that it was the poor serving girl from Bermondsey that he'd been more attracted to, rather than the fine wealthy philanthropic lady that she had turned out to be in reality. In fact, in some odd way, he felt almost disappointed in her because of her deceit, which was an absurd reaction, he knew, yet not one that he could resist completely. And because of that feeling of disappointment, he doubted that he could ever feel quite the same level of warmth and affection for the wealthy Lady Rachel Grosvenor that he had for his sweet Amy.

Yet even if Amy had been the sweet servant girl she pretended to be, Silver knew that the direction of his heart was already fixed elsewhere now anyway, and would not be easily diverted again. The fact was that Elisa dominated his life and thoughts now so completely that he couldn't imagine a future with anyone else but her, even if she was an unrepentant thief...

He and Amy were seated tonight in one of the best boxes in the Alhambra music hall, in the third tier above the main stalls. Somehow she had been able to arrange everything in a very short space of time after they had taken a horse-bus from the East End to Oxford Circus. They had walked from there to her brother's house in Fitzroy Square where there were still a couple of loyal family servants in residence, including Amy's own ladies' maid, Sarah, who welcomed her former charge back like a long lost daughter. In particular Amy had found a dress suit from her brother's wardrobe that fitted Silver perfectly – so her brother Charles had indeed to be a close physical match for him as she had said - and a gown of pale lilac silk and crinoline for herself, in which finery Sarah was delighted to help her mistress dress so that she looked more like her old self again. Even more impressively, Amy had also managed to rent one of the best boxes in the upper circle of the house for the evening rather than have Silver occupy Row H, seat 27 as he'd planned.

'You can't possibly sit there in full view in the stalls, Jonathan,' she'd advised him earlier, 'even if the usher would allow you to do so without a ticket. Far better that we're up here in a private box where we can see everything that's going on, and, more particularly, see who comes and occupies the seat next to H twenty-seven...'

Silver had to concede that her plan had merits; he still wasn't sure whether this Mr Ferrar would really turn up, or whether this might not after all turn out to be some sort of complex police trap devised by that devil, Sergeant Sparrow. So it made good sense to tarry a little up here and see if this mysterious Mr Ferrar would really make an appearance.

Silver glanced around the immense auditorium, having to pinch himself a little at the thought of being here. Twenty-four hours ago he had been fighting for his life on the deck of Brunel's great *Leviathan*, and here he was tonight, basking in sybaritic luxury.

He glanced at his companion again with a secret smile. Despite her expectation that the Alhambra was a place of rather low and vulgar entertainment – which it undoubtedly was – Amy seemed to be enjoying herself well enough tonight, Silver was amused to see.

'I've never been to the Alhambra before,' she said with sparkling eyes. 'This is rather grand, isn't it, despite what I've heard about it...'

'It depends on your judgement of what constitutes "grand", I suppose,' Silver said carefully. But he had to agree that the building itself, and even the décor and furnishings, certainly were grand enough.

The Alhambra was a new building, and one modelled on a vast scale, the outside a symphony of white marble and mock Moorish minarets and towers, while inside, on its six viewing levels, it had space for an audience of up to four thousand. The building had begun its life three years ago as the Royal Panopticon of Science and Art, but the public, liking neither the name nor the staid entertainments on offer, had stayed away in their thousands. So it had soon closed and reopened as a circus - and then, even more recently, to much more popular acclaim, as a music hall.

The Alhambra did make a perfect display arena for daring feats of horsemanship, but Londoners generally preferred musical shows and smutty humour these days to performing animals so it was not surprising that the building was succeeding even more as a music hall than it ever had as a circus. The principal attractions in recent months had become female ballet dancers in daringly tight costumes, death-defying acrobats, and boisterous black-faced minstrels. Even Marianne, not usually one for popular entertainment, had been seduced by the Alhambra, and persuaded Silver to bring her here several times last summer. He felt a brief pang in his heart at that memory, and even spied the exact seats they had used on their last visit. Coincidentally, they had been in the very same row, H, as the ticket he'd been sent for tonight's performance.

Tonight's bill was typical of the fare on offer at the Alhambra – more ballet dancers in tutus and flesh-coloured silk tights, and chorus girls in laces and frills – but also a young eighteen-year-old acrobat, Monsieur Jules Leotard, fresh from Paris to perform his death-defying swings across the auditorium on a trapeze.

The young daredevil Monsieur Leotard wasn't due on until eleven o'clock, and it was still only nine. In the meantime, a selection of acts was performing as a warm up for this eagerly awaited event. At the moment a corps de ballet of two hundred girls, all painted to look from a distance as beautiful as possible, were tripping lightly across the stage lit by limelight, wearing the scanty and revealing costumes normally worn by male dancers.

'Shall I order champagne, Jonathan?' Amy asked eagerly, as the ballet dancers trouped off to desultory applause, and a waiter appeared instantly at the door to the box looking for orders.

'Since you're paying for tonight, why not?' Silver agreed absently.

Silver continued to scan the auditorium with care. Above the massed audience on the main floor, forty magnificent gasoliers burned brightly, turning the place as bright as day, while in the pit below an orchestra of sixty musicians were playing the introduction for the next act, a troupe of French dancing girls of apparently a more bawdy type than the previous demure ballet girls.

Not that too much could be heard from the orchestra, it was true, since their musical accompaniment was mostly drowned by the noise of promenading patrons, male and female, who seemed more inclined to lounge about the many little bars on the main floor and fill themselves with liquor, rather than watch the show.

'Jonathan! Jonathan...!' Amy nudged Silver's arm excitedly so that he thought she must have seen something of this gentleman he was due to meet. But it turned out that Amy's excitement was only to do with the happenings on stage as the French dancing girls began to perform. 'I don't believe it! Those young ladies on the stage are showing their bare bottoms to the audience. It's absolutely disgraceful...' Yet her voice sounded more amused than truly complaining.

Silver was too busy concentrating his attention on row H in the main auditorium below to pay much heed to these bold French dancing girls, and only nodded absently in agreement. Seat 27 was still empty, though, as was the next one, H26. Would this man Ferrar really turn up and take seat H26? Or was this a convoluted police trap after all, as he'd feared?

But Amy's fresh gasp of astonishment at the outrageous behaviour on stage did briefly bring his attention back to the present performance, where, as she had said, the French chorus girls were indeed doing a risqué dance that involved much kicking, squealing and jumping, but also occasionally lifting their short frilled skirts with abandon to reveal glimpses of their bare behinds.

Amy, for all her professed shock, was still studying the chorus line with rapt attention. 'I believe I've heard of this dance, Jonathan. It's called *Le cancan* and it originated in the working class saloons of Paris. But it was always a man's dance as far as I knew. I've never heard of it being performed by a line of chorus girls before.' She gasped again at the sight of one particularly buxom girl, lost in wild abandon. 'And without drawers too – I still can't believe the brazenness of these girls.'

The audience clearly liked their brazenness, though, from their whoops of excitement, which quite matched that of the dancers themselves.

Silver was amused by Amy's avid interest in the bawdy antics of these well-built chorus girls, almost as if she was imagining herself doing similarly outrageous things on that stage. It seemed beautiful women would always mentally compare themselves to other beautiful women, no matter how different their personal situations might be...

*

Silver was becoming restless at the continued failure of anyone to take up either seat H27 or the one next to it, H26. Yet he daren't simply go down there and plant himself down in that seat, hoping for the best, when it would make him far more vulnerable to a nasty surprise than up here in this private box. Equally, though, he was reluctant to simply sit here and wait for events to unfold down below.

He got to his feet and stretched his long legs, which were a little numb with cramp from his long sitting in a well-padded chair. He wasn't used to comfortable armchairs like these any more after months of hardship, straw mattresses and hard stone benches. 'I want to walk around a little downstairs to see if I can find this man Ferrar.'

'Shall I come with you?' Amy asked him in alarm.

'No, it's probably better if I go alone. I might possibly need to make a fast exit –' he indicated her extravagant gown and crinoline – 'and you're hardly dressed for speed tonight, even if you do look wonderful.'

Amy twisted her face despite the compliment. 'All right. But please take no risks, Jonathan. The police may have set a trap here after all, and this is probably not the best time or place to be caught.'

Silver nodded, and left the box, taking the first staircase leading down to the main hall below. On the way he passed a whole spectrum of Londoners enjoying the pleasures of this strange place, from splendid ladies and eccentric dandies to very rough fellows and bawdy women. The Alhambra seemed to be a place where the normal social distinctions went by the board. After all his tribulations, Silver found something reassuring and almost uplifting in the sight of this immense and disparate crowd enjoying themselves so exuberantly, even if some of the pleasures being enjoyed were hardly innocent ones.

The lower floors of the Alhambra were certainly populated by many beautiful women, and mostly of the type who were forced to live by their charms. This music hall was undoubtedly a market place and a Royal Exchange for vice, and Silver had to fight off many enticing invitations on his perambulations.

At the main foyer level was a refreshment room known colloquially as the Canteen where forty or fifty of the ballet girls, still in dance costume, were currently in company with their many male admirers. The Alhambra might not be a respectable venue for a young man to frequent, but its life and raucous noise and humour did make Silver feel like a fully reconstituted member of the human race again.

Yet, despite feeling better, he was still having no success in his mission to find this man Ferrar. Although he got many knowing looks and winks of encouragement from the charming ballet girls, he saw no one he recognized, while no one apparently recognized him in return. That hopefully meant there were no police agents on his trail at least, but neither was there any person who might have been the elusive Charles Ferrar.

Silver left the Canteen and moved into the main body of the auditorium where artisans and working men had congregated in numbers for tonight's performance by Monsieur Leotard. The Alhambra was good value even for working people: it cost only a shilling to stand at the bars down here and watch the show, or 2s 6d for a seat like the one for which Silver had been sent a ticket.

In the boxes and balconies above the main auditorium were whole galleries of brazen-faced women, curled and painted, and blazoned in tawdry finery. Higher up still were small private apartments in which a gentleman desirous of sharing a bottle of wine with a recent acquaintance might retire with his planned conquest for the evening. Behind the refreshment bars that ran the whole length of the hall on each side at ground floor level, superbly attired barmaids vended strong liquors at a speed to match the filling of a horse trough. At the long bar, big-bosomed girls were enticing simpletons to buy them free drinks, while sizing up with hungry eyes the chances of more lucrative pickings elsewhere.

Silver could see why this place was now more popular with the masses than either the Theatre Royal in Drury Lane or Her Majesty's Theatre in the Haymarket.

Silver glanced up at Amy's box, and gave her a discreet signal with his downturned thumb, wryly acknowledging his failure so far in his mission. He was about to move on and perhaps return upstairs when he felt a hand on his sleeve.

'Would you be looking for seat H twenty-seven, sir?' the man asked respectfully.

Silver glanced around nervously, wondering whether the trap was about to be sprung on him. But, regardless, he answered truthfully in the end. 'I am indeed.'

The man offered his hand, which was a reassuring sign. 'My name is Charles Ferrar, Dr Silver...'

*

They moved to as quiet a place as they could find in this bedlam, in a carpeted and gas lit alcove near the main foyer, which was provided with comfortable Ottoman settees. Silver examined his new acquaintance with restrained curiosity as they sat down facing each other. Ferrar wasn't exactly what Silver had been expecting from Sophie's description; he was indeed a man burned brown by years of harsh sun, but he was hardly elderly, being a broad-shouldered and vigorous gentleman of fifty-five, if not a handsome one. Despite the man's gentlemanly manners, Silver sensed that he was in the presence here of someone of steely substance and resolve.

'It's a privilege to meet you, Dr Silver,' Ferrar said.

Silver regarded him suspiciously – it seemed an odd thing to say in the circumstances. 'Not many people would care to join you in that assertion, sir,' he said bleakly.

Ferrar smiled, stretching the crows' feet around his faded blue eyes. 'Well, I do think it, nevertheless. And thank you for coming tonight, and for trusting me. I know it can't be easy in your difficult situation. I wasn't even sure if your beautiful sister-in-law would be able to deliver my covet invitation.'

'Well, she did, and you have me here at your service, sir.' Silver pointed out curtly. 'The question I have in return is: why did you want to meet me, and why *here* of all places?'

Ferrar appeared nervous for the first time as a pair of beautiful ballet girls passed the alcove, giggling. 'A public place like this suits me, Dr Silver, because I am in as much jeopardy as you. Perhaps even more.' Ferrar relaxed his voice a little. 'I have to apologize to you for your ordeal over the past months. I have known from the start that you probably never killed your wife.'

'And how the devil did you know such a thing when the police certainly didn't?'

Ferrar looked intensely uncomfortable. 'Because I have a very good idea who really did kill her...'

*

Silver was outraged by the admission.

'Then why did you not go to the police, sir?' he demanded through gritted teeth.

Ferrar sighed tiredly, suddenly looking much more like the elderly man whom Sophie had described. 'Because, to be frank, Doctor, I have no conclusive proof of my suspicions. Also I am forced by circumstance to have to consider much bigger stakes than merely the life and happiness of one man, Dr Silver – even the life and happiness of a decent individual like your good self. I work for the security and prosperity of Her Majesty's whole realm...'

'Doing *what*?' Silver asked with little grace.

'I work for the Foreign Office, Dr Silver. As did your late wife too, for several years. In fact Marianne worked directly for me for five years in total. She was one of my leading agents in the field, and probably the most accomplished woman agent in Europe, if truth be told.'

Silver gasped. 'Marianne was a government agent – a spy?'

Ferrar nodded. 'She was.'

'And did this have some bearing on her death? Is that what you're finally telling me?'

'It is indeed.' Ferrar hesitated. 'I'm reluctant to go into the details of Marianne's career as an agent, unless you want me to. I don't wish to sully your memory of your wife unnecessarily. But if you do want to know the truth about her, then I will answer your questions as honestly and frankly as I can. But tell me something first...'

'What thing?'

'Marianne said something to you as she was dying, did she not?' Ferrar asked. 'I spoke to your lawyer, Mr Walker, about it, but for some reason he seemed reluctant to tell me what he knew.'

Silver smiled grimly. 'That's because Nathanial never truly believed that Marianne had said that word to me. Not to put too fine a point on it, he actually thought I was guilty.'

'But I believe you, Dr Silver,' Ferrar insisted. 'So what was this word that Marianne said to you with her final breath?'

Silver felt a strange reluctance now to say the word out loud, but finally gave in to Ferrar's curiosity. 'Marianne was trying to say more, but the only word I could make out with any certainty was the word "Leviathan"...'

Ferrar breathed out slowly. 'Yes, I do believe that is exactly what she said.' He looked Silver directly in the eyes. 'Do you want to know the whole truth about her? I warn you that it may disturb you, and alter your view of your late wife entirely. And perhaps not for the better.'

Silver was in no mood for half-truths now. 'Of course I want to know the truth. So what was Marianne really doing in Scutari three years ago?'

Ferrar nodded knowingly. 'Ah, I see you had some suspicions of the truth already, and that this tale is not an entirely unexpected one for you. Very well, I'll tell you more, but first I must go back a little further than three years. For a whole year before the war in the Crimea, Marianne was working in Russia - in St Petersburg actually – as our chief agent. She could pass herself off as a Russian – you knew that she could speak the language perfectly, of course - and because of her beauty, all sorts of doors were open to her.'

Silver felt the blood drain from his face. 'She was sleeping with someone?'

'Yes –' Ferrar lowered his voice – 'with several different high-ranking people, frankly. But in particular with a senior diplomat at the court of the Tsar.' Ferrar saw the look on Silver's face. 'Please don't judge her too harshly. What she did was done entirely for the service of her country. Marianne was never a whore for money; she did only what she had to do in order to accomplish her mission...'

'So you say,' Silver interrupted harshly.

'It's the truth,' Ferrar maintained stoutly. He waited until another drunken couple had passed the alcove – a painted blonde trollop and a man who looked like an undertaker on a night out. 'Marianne was the reason why we understood Russian intentions in the Crimea so well, even though our own later military operations were badly bungled and undid much of Marianne's good work. Nevertheless she must have saved countless numbers of British lives by her self-sacrifice.'

Silver felt a strange stirring of pride mixed with resentment at what his wife had done. 'So what was she doing at Scutari? There were surely no Russians to spy on there, were there?'

'That's not entirely correct, unfortunately. Marianne was indeed still working for me at Scutari, after her return from Russia. We had information from another source that a Russian agent was operating in the area, a spy working for the Tsar...'

'Who was he? Anyone I would know?' Silver butted in sarcastically.

'Since you were at Scutari yourself, then perhaps you would indeed recognize this individual if you saw him. His real name is Dimitri Alexandreevich Turgenov, although he uses many other names and guises. We had the cooperation of the hospital in trying to trap this man, which is why Marianne was allowed to wear a nurse's uniform as a cover for her espionage activities. She did do some nursing duties too, I believe, to blend in.'

Silver smiled faintly. 'Not very well, I would say. Marianne was no natural nurse. It was probably her one shortcoming.'

'Perhaps so,' Ferrar agreed with a sad and downcast smile of his own.

It was obvious to Silver from that downcast look that Ferrar must have had some strong personal feelings for Marianne too, despite the vast age difference between them. *Was there no one who'd been able to resist her?* Silver should have felt angry and betrayed by now at these shocking discoveries about his late wife, yet in truth he didn't. Marianne had always been a mysterious free spirit; he'd known that much from the start. And the fact was that, from all the men she must have met in her interesting life, from all those she'd made love to or flirted with or seduced, she had chosen only to marry *him*, and none other. So, no matter how many other men there had been in her life, her feelings for *him* must have transcended all others in some subtle way...

'Wouldn't a Russian be easy to find in an English army hospital?' he asked Ferrar bluntly.

Ferrar shook his head. 'Not this Russian. As an agent, he was the equal of Marianne in many respects. He was educated in England and France, and was perfectly adept at playing either an Englishman or a Frenchman when it suited him. In addition, no one knew what Turgenov looked like. Yet he had been the Tsar's most successful agent in Europe over the previous ten years. His exploits may have cost the lives of hundreds of our own men in the Crimea, just as Marianne's might have saved them.'

Silver was sombre. 'Marianne didn't succeed in catching him?'

'No, but her mission wasn't a complete failure. She did discover after the event that Turgenov had been posing during the Crimean campaign as a French journalist called Chevreul, and had even come to Scutari in that guise to determine the scale of our military losses. But unfortunately Turgenov/Chevreul escaped from Scutari before Marianne could unravel the truth and have him arrested. She never did discover even what this man Turgenov really looked like. As Monsieur Chevreul, he made sure that he was never photographed, and always kept his features well hidden under a bushy black beard.'

Silver was still puzzled. 'I don't believe I ever encountered this Monsieur Chevreul while I was at Scutari,' he said, before the truth finally came to him with a start. 'Ah...! So you think this man might have come to London later and had something to do with Marianne's death...?'

'Yes, I do. You see, in the Russian secret service, Turgenov has a code name.'

'What is it?' Silver asked expectantly.

Ferrar leaned closer to whisper. 'His code name is *Leviafan*...'

*

Amy appeared suddenly at Silver's side as he and Ferrar returned to the crowded main foyer. She gave Ferrar a penetrating look, then whispered warningly in Silver's ear, 'Jonathan, I've seen that man Sparrow. He was in the main auditorium watching row H.'

That man again! Silver thought that this relentless police detective must have some personal connection to the Devil, for he seemed to know everything he was doing, even before he did it himself. This certainly hadn't been a police trap tonight at the Alhambra, *so how had Sparrow worked out where he would be...?*

Silver cast nervous glances around him, but finally introduced Amy to Ferrar using her real name. 'This is Lady Rachel Grosvenor, Mr Ferrar.'

Ferrar looked both bewildered and impressed by the identity of Silver's titled companion for the evening, and graciously kissed the back of her offered gloved hand. 'Lady Rachel.' He frowned at her questioningly. 'I do believe I know your father, the fourth Earl...'

'Lots of people do, Mr Ferrar,' she agreed coldly. Clearly Amy's relationship with her father was not of the warmest kind, Silver judged from that response.

Ferrar turned to Silver again. 'You understand that I can't go directly to the police and tell them what I've told you, Dr Silver, much as I'd like to. If Turgenov is still here in London, as I suspect, then my political masters will want to make use of this situation for their own ends, rather than necessarily doing the honourable thing. Some factions in the government may even want to protect the man from the law in the hope that he might be persuaded to become a double agent for Her Majesty's Government.' Ferrar looked almost embarrassed to have made such an admission. 'In any event I have no absolute proof that Turgenov was the man behind Marianne's death, only suspicions so far. Frankly I haven't had time to pursue the matter further, what with all my other pressing commitments. Political rivalries are growing again in mainland Europe, and we are desperate not to be enmeshed in another conflict like the Crimea.' He seemed almost to be making a plea for Silver's understanding. 'I have only been back in England for a few weeks as it is, and tomorrow I have to return to Munich yet again on more urgent government business.'

Silver stirred angrily. 'I think you know exactly where this man Turgenov is, don't you, Mr Ferrar? And even what false identity he might be using?'

Ferrar was lost for an adequate reply to that accusation, but Silver could see the answer written plainly in the man's uneasy and downcast eyes.

Silver could see now that Ferrar was actually going to be of little direct help to him in trying to prove his innocence of Marianne's death. 'Thank you at least for telling me this much, Mr Ferrar,' he said curtly before motioning to Amy. 'It seems we'd better leave now, Lady Rachel,' he continued formally, 'even though we will be missing Monsieur Leotard's exploits on the high trapeze.'

Ferrar offered him his hand which Silver accepted, despite his barely concealed anger. 'Good luck, Dr Silver. I'm sure you will persevere. You've done extremely well so far staying one step ahead of the...' Ferrar's jaw suddenly sagged in disbelief, and Silver thought he must have seen something unexpected in the busy foyer behind them so he turned his head that way too. But then Ferrar lurched forward abruptly as if shot and Silver had to move promptly to catch him. When Ferrar's head slumped forward in his arms, Silver saw the shaft of a dagger protruding from his lower back, severing the spine.

Silver lowered the already lifeless body to the ground and looked around him in disbelief. A top-hatted figure was moving rapidly away through the dense crowds thronging the foyer.

Then a fat woman screamed as she saw the dead man on the ground, and the pool of blood spreading inexorably across the woven carpet.

At the entrance to the main auditorium behind them, Silver now saw the moustachioed figure of Sergeant Sparrow trying to force his way through the doorway into the foyer to see what all the commotion was about.

Silver grabbed Amy's hand and they ran in the opposite direction, towards the exit into Leicester Square.

But where to from here?

CHAPTER 26

Wednesday 4th November 1857

A two-wheeler cab took them to Took's Court at Silver's request. A light cold rain was falling in the quiet confines of Sophie's street near Chancery Lane, splashing the cobbles and dripping slowly from eaves. Overhead, a streetlight hissed noisily as the cabby pulled his wet steaming horse to a halt outside Sophie's front door.

Clutching her shivering arms to herself in the back of the cab, Amy was deeply troubled. 'You should have given yourself up to the police tonight, Jonathan.'

He looked at her sarcastically. 'Do *you* want me to hang now as well?'

Amy shook her head. 'Of course not. But tonight's events must show the police that there was more to the death of your wife than they ever imagined.'

Silver bit back a sharp response. This was grossly unfair of him to be angry at her of all people, but he was nearing the limits of his patience and his endurance. 'With Ferrar dead, I have no proof that Marianne was ever an agent of the crown, and certainly none at all that this tenuous fact might have anything to do with her death. No doubt the police will blame me for Ferrar's death too...'

'I can be your witness against that,' she pointed out hurriedly.

'Assuming they would believe you, which I doubt, when you've clearly been aiding and abetting me all along. That hardly makes you a reliable independent witness on my behalf. More likely the police will simply add Ferrar's name to my tally of putative victims, which probably already includes that man Harkness too.' His voice became angrier. 'I am sick and tired of trying to prove my innocence to these useless representatives of the law. They'll never listen! I shall have to resolve this matter myself now, in my own way.'

Amy's eyes widened. 'What do you mean? I hope you don't intend to do anything foolish, Jonathan.'

'The only foolish thing I ever did was to assume that I would be able to obtain justice from the English legal system,' Silver said contemptuously.

Amy was silent for a moment, then glanced through the window of the cab. 'Why have you come here of all places, Jonathan? You can't surely expect to find the answer to the mystery here at your sister-in-law's house, can you?'

Silver stared out of the cab at the falling rain, and the dimly lit windows of Sophie's house. 'I don't know for sure. Perhaps. For some reason I think Sophie is the key to what happened at the Alhambra tonight...'

Amy looked puzzled by this assertion, as well she might. 'This isn't a safe place to hide, Jonathan, if that's what you intend,' she warned him. 'That bloodhound, Sergeant Sparrow, may well guess that you would come here. We should better return to the hostel in Wapping, where I can try and find a better place for you and Miss Saltash to hide before you flee the country.' She had a thought. 'Perhaps my brother's house in Fitzroy Square would do. Sarah and the other servants would keep our secret, I'm sure.'

'You've helped me so much in the last few weeks, and you're still helping me. But I don't know why; there seems nothing in this for you.' Silver was puzzled by this wealthy girl's loyalty to him when she really knew so little about him.

She turned her face away briefly, a catch in her voice. 'I don't know why either, but let's say that I support people when I believe they've been falsely accused.' She turned her head again to look him frankly in the eyes. 'If you're not going to think about yourself, then please consider Miss Saltash. If that man Sparrow catches Elisa, she will go to prison for many years, or even be transported. You don't want that, do you?'

'No, of course not.' It was all too tempting to agree with her and tell the cabby to go on to Wapping.

Except that he couldn't. Not when he was now convinced beyond doubt that he knew who had killed Charles Ferrar tonight.

And who had also killed Marianne...

*

Sophie had fortunately not yet retired for the night.

After having their urgent knock answered by a servant girl (fortunately a new girl in Sophie's employ who didn't know Silver at all by sight) Sophie came to the front door herself to confirm who her unexpected visitors might be.

She was clearly taken aback by Silver's arrival at her front door at this time of night, and also by his appearance, dressed immaculately in a full evening dress suit. Yet she was even more disconcerted by the presence of the well-dressed young lady with him. Nevertheless Sophie regained her composure, and, after quickly telling her new maidservant Agnes that she would deal with this herself, led her visitors upstairs to her own sitting room on the first floor. On the way up the stairs, Sophie told Silver in a private whisper that she had managed to effectuate the transfer of his funds at Coutts Bank to that Swiss bank in Zurich as he'd requested during their clandestine meeting ten days before. She clearly assumed that this was the reason for him coming here tonight, so she seemed put-out by his muted reaction to this announcement, when she had obviously been expecting more of a positive response.

Once safely ensconced behind closed doors in her sitting room, Silver belatedly introduced his companion, an introduction that drew a small formal bow from Sophie, but no smile of welcome. Although Sophie's attention was mostly fixed on Silver, he saw her eyes straying frequently back to his companion, Lady Rachel Grosvenor, as if perplexed about what she was doing here.

'Why have you come here, Jonathan?' Sophie began breathlessly, immediately after these introductions had been made. 'I thought it must be to do with this matter of your account at Coutts, but it seems not. You're risking your life by coming here openly. The police may be watching this house, waiting for you to show yourself.'

'I'm sorry to impose myself on you again, Sophie, but I had to take the risk. I went to the Alhambra music hall tonight to keep that appointment that you told me about.'

Sophie was intrigued despite her worries. 'Did you? That explains your attire, I suppose. And was Mr Ferrar there?'

'He was.' Silver wasn't sure how to break this news gently so simply blurted it out. 'But someone murdered him tonight in the foyer of the theatre – right in front of my eyes...'

Sophie recoiled in shock. 'Who? Who would do such a dreadful thing?' she stammered.

Silver had no chance to answer this, though, because, after the briefest of knocks, the door was flung open abruptly and Sophie's husband Edward rushed into the room. He was dressed similarly to Silver, in evening clothes, but without a hat. His hair was wet and plastered to his skull, and he was breathing heavily as if he'd just ran up the stairs. 'My God! I thought from Agnes's description that it must be you, Jonathan, who'd called tonight. But I still didn't truly believe it until I saw you in the flesh. It's a bold move, though, to come here so openly, isn't it? Perhaps even an insane one...' He relented a little in his harsh tone. 'I think we should perhaps have a bit of privacy to talk,' he suggested, and quickly locked the door behind him, leaving the key in the lock.

Sophie looked thoroughly alarmed by the manner of her husband's sudden entry. 'Oh, you're back from the club, dearest. I didn't hear your cab return.'

Edward seemed equally distracted by the mundane nature of her question. 'Err...no...that is, I walked; it's not far. Hardly more than two miles.'

'Why did you walk in the rain? You're soaked,' Sophie complained, her mind instantly reverting from the drama of the moment to the domestic responsibilities of a dutiful wife.

'No matter, it's only water. It will do me no permanent harm.' Rolfe had finally got his breath back, and now regarded his wife's visitors more with an expression of bemused surprise than shock. 'You look well, Jonathan, all things being considered. Prison life obviously agreed with you after a fashion.'

'Hanging wouldn't have agreed with me much, though, Edward,' Silver commented acidly.

'Is this lady with you, Jonathan?' Rolfe asked complacently.

'She is.' Silver introduced her, and Rolfe gave her a stiff little bow in return. 'Charmed, Lady Rachel.'

Rolfe seemed oddly more taken aback by the presence of Lady Rachel Grosvenor here in his house than by that of his fugitive brother-in-law. Rolfe addressed Silver again. 'It is a pleasure seeing you again, Jonathan, but you really shouldn't be here, I'm afraid. While I sympathize with your plight, you are abusing Sophie's generous nature by imposing yourself on her in this way.'

'Yes, I apologize for that. Yet I had to come and see her; there was something extremely important I had to tell her.' Silver first had a question for Edward Rolfe himself, though. 'Tell me something, Edward. I seem to recall that you speak rather good Russian, don't you?'

Rolfe frowned as he walked over to the fire and turned his back to it. 'You know I speak fluent Russian, Jonathan. You've even heard me speak it. But then in my role as an arts connoisseur, I do travel frequently to St Petersburg to purchase Russian works of art so it is a language I have long studied.'

Sophie was bewildered by this odd choice of subject between her husband and her fugitive brother-in-law at a time like this. 'What was it you were about to tell me, Jonathan?' she asked, her eyes shifting rapidly between the two men. 'About who murdered poor Mr Ferrar.'

Silver grimaced at Sophie. 'There's something else I should do first, Sophie. I should introduce you properly to this gentleman by the fire.'

Sophie blinked in surprise. 'Why would you need to introduce

Edward, my own husband, to me?'

Silver came and stood beside her. 'Why indeed? Yet I have to, nevertheless, because I don't think you know the name he was born with... ' Silver took a deep breath. 'His actual name, unless I'm very much mistaken, is Dimitri Alexandreevich Turgenov. He's an agent working for the Russian government...'

Sophie blanched. 'Edward, tell him this is nonsense.'

Rolfe shook his head ruefully. 'I'm afraid it's not *complete* nonsense, dearest. My real name is indeed Dimitri Alexandreevich Turgenov. But I am no longer working for the Russian government, Jonathan; those days are behind me now.'

Silver felt something approaching relief at this frank admission when he had expected denial and subterfuge. 'So, Edward, when did Marianne realize that you were in reality a Russian government agent with the code name of *Leviathan?* In fact the very man she had been chasing for so many years?'

Rolfe, warming himself against the crackling fire, seemed to have recovered his composure completely. Silver could see little sign of guilt or regret in the man, only a certain air of melancholy acceptance at being found out. 'Oh, she never did - not until the last few seconds of her life anyway,' he qualified himself. 'More to the point, how did you come to this radical conclusion about my identity, Jonathan?'

'It came to me tonight after I had met a certain Mr Ferrar at the Alhambra music hall.' Silver paused. 'I can see you're not surprised by that statement, but then you were there yourself tonight, Edward, weren't you?'

Rolfe smiled in an almost embarrassed manner. 'Actually I have a great partiality for the vulgarities and low humour of the English music hall, I must confess.'

Silver pressed on. 'It could only have been *you* tonight who killed Charles Ferrar in the foyer of the Alhambra. After all, the only people who knew about that invitation for me to meet Ferrar were Sophie, myself and Lady Rachel here. Oh, and anyone who Sophie might inadvertently have told, of course.' He glanced bleakly at Sophie and got direct confirmation of his suspicions in her distraught look. 'Ferrar asked you not to tell anyone about his coming here, Sophie, not even your husband. In fact I think he meant *particularly* your husband...' Silver turned angrily towards Rolfe again '...because he probably had a good inkling who you really are, Edward. But Ferrar didn't want to tell me directly of his suspicions, for some reason.'

'Ferrar probably had thoughts of using me as an agent of Her Majesty's Government,' Rolfe suggested icily. 'A double agent to spy on my own country. But I would never have accepted such a dishonourable proposal – not even to save my life, or even to keep you, Sophie.'

Silver continued relentlessly. 'You realized at once it would be a disaster if Ferrar were to tell me about Marianne's past life as a government spy in Russia, because I might then eventually work out who you really are.'

Rolfe seemed resigned now to this cruel exposure in front of his wife, his eyes dulled and his voice reduced to no more than a whisper. 'Go on. It's interesting seeing your mind finally working again, Jonathan. I wonder that it took you so long to come to the truth, frankly...'

Sophie had gone deathly white as she realized the full implications of what Silver was saying. 'You didn't kill my sister, Edward! Please God, tell me you didn't do that wicked thing!'

For the first time there was a real catch in Rolfe's voice, a hint of true regret. 'I had to, Sophie. Your sister was a dangerous agent herself, who had caused my country much damage in her career as a spy. I came here to England originally under orders – reluctantly, I may tell you - to take revenge on her for her actions against my country.'

'So it was no accident that you met me, Edward?' Sophie was shaking now, though whether with rage or revulsion it was hard to tell.

'No, it was no accident,' Rolfe admitted. 'But my feelings for you are the one genuine thing about Edward Rolfe, Sophie. Initially I found it an amusing idea to seduce the sister of my greatest enemy. But I did fall for you wholeheartedly in the end. I had no need to marry you, Sophie, in order to perpetrate my plan but I did nevertheless. Finally, in these past six months, I had become so contented with my life here in England with you that all I wanted to do was forget this ill-advised mission to take revenge on your sister. I found it so easy to make vast sums of money here too – every investment I made came up tenfold in a matter of months – so I truly had decided to stay, and ignore my orders entirely...'

Silver felt as bewildered as Sophie by these admissions. 'Then, in God's name, why didn't you, Edward?'

Rolfe couldn't look his wife in the face now. 'Because Sophie's father became suspicious of my background and sent some nosy bloodhound of a lawyer, a Mr Body, to investigate my affairs. So, when I got wind of it from a friendly source, I first had to kill this snooping lawyer...' – he lowered his voice to a whisper – '...and then sadly Mr Lovelock too...'

Sophie gasped in horror. *'You killed Papa too...?'*

Rolfe pleaded with her. 'I did it as painlessly and humanely as I could, Sophie, to prevent his suffering. Yet it was still the worst thing I've ever had to do because I was very fond of your father. He had unfortunately already received some sort of interim report from this Mr Body before I had time to deal with this legal bloodhound, so your father finally confronted me in his study and demanded to know the truth about my past.' He grimaced at the loathing and disgust in his wife's eyes. 'I was cornered and fighting for my very life, Sophie. They would have hanged me if I was exposed as a Russian spy. I could simply have run, I suppose, but by this time I couldn't bear the thought of losing you, and this new life I had in England. And, to be frank, the life of a wealthy English gentleman suited me after all these years of wandering. I'd seen enough of wars and killing and pestilential places.'

Silver grunted angrily. 'So just a few more deaths, and then you would be free to live the life of a privileged English gentleman forever.'

Rolfe was still unmoved. 'I can understand your distaste, Jonathan, but that is the truth of the matter nonetheless.'

'It is *not* the truth!' Silver exclaimed. 'The truth is that evil men like you enjoy killing...please don't try to justify yourself as the victim in all this!'

Sophie stared at her husband in horror. 'And then you killed Marianne too! My own dear sister! How could you kill her when you profess that you love me so tenderly? What monstrous hypocrisy is this?'

'As I said, I was given no choice...'

'No choice but *murder*?' Sophie admonished him with revulsion.

'...I was at the Lovelock House again with your mother that day in July. I had offered to go through your father's papers because I suspected he still had that written report somewhere from that snooping lawyer he'd sent to investigate me. From your mother, I discovered that Marianne had called earlier that day with perhaps the same thing in mind, and had left only a few minutes before taking some papers with her. I suspected instantly that she must have found that lawyer's report among her father's papers and taken it home to read. So I followed her immediately to her home in Russell Square.' He turned to Silver. 'Fortunately I had taken the precaution in the past of making a copy of your front door key, Jonathan. Sophie kept one here for emergencies, and I thought it might be useful at some time, which was rather perspicacious of me. I knew I had to hurry because you usually returned home at about seven and she would surely tell you at once about her diverting discovery. If that happened, then I was certainly finished...

'I got to Russell Square with only minutes to spare. I had picked up a paper knife from Mr Lovelock's desk to use as a makeshift weapon. Ironically it was a knife that I had given him as a present when he expressed admiration of it one day on a visit to our house here in Took's Court. Fortunately no one else knew of this, not even you, Sophie, so it never came out in the trial. The police came to the conclusion, because of its Russian origin, that it had to be *your* paper knife, Jonathan, although I swear I never deliberately intended to implicate you. I merely used the first thing to hand – it turned out to be a matter of serendipity on my behalf, and cruel fate for you.' Rolfe's face clouded at the memory. 'I still have nightmares about the moment when Marianne came down the stairs. Some people will tell you that they can kill with impunity, or even enjoyment. But I am not one of those who can take a human life without genuine regret. She was smiling at me as she came down the stairs, so obviously hadn't read the lawyer's report yet, as it happened. But then my face must have given me away – it's difficult to hide your feelings when you have murder on your mind. I saw in that instant that she had just realized who I really was.'

Silver gasped aloud as he remembered again the horror of his homecoming that day.

Rolfe seemed to know what he was thinking. 'I left again by the front door only a few seconds before you arrived home that evening, Jonathan. In fact, as I made my exit, I saw you get out of your cab on the far side of the square. You obviously preferred to walk across the park on a fine summer evening rather than being dropped directly at your front door. In my business, the outcome of things often does turn on such unpredictable matters of chance. Yet if you had but turned your head as you were walking across the park, you would still have seen me, and my plan would have been foiled. But fortunately for me, you were sunk deep in thought as ever - about some interesting medical matter, no doubt - so you never did turn your head...'

'You stabbed my sister to death,' Sophie sobbed, sliding to the floor in her deep distress. 'My poor dear sister...'

Rolfe hung his head. 'I had to: Marianne would have soon reported me to her former masters at the Foreign Office, and I would have been exposed. I wanted to stay here with you, Sophie. That's why I had to do anything to protect my anonymity.' He straightened up, his eyes glistening. 'Now it's all over and I will have to leave you anyway. I have killed four people to try and keep my dark secret, and it was all done in vain...'

'Tonight's murder was even more pointless than the others, Edward,' Silver said quietly. 'If Ferrar knew who you really are, then his superiors probably already know too.'

Rolfe held up his hands helplessly. 'I know that now, Jonathan...'

Rolfe was interrupted in his expression of regret by a heavy banging at the front door, then the sounds of a commotion in the hall below. This noisy exchange was followed further by the tramp of heavy boots on the curving staircase.

A furious banging erupted at the door. '*Open in the name of the police! Dr Silver...! This is Sergeant Sparrow of the Metropolitan Police... I repeat! Mrs*

Rolfe...! If you are in there, then open the door in the name of the police!'

Sophie was sunk in too deep a pit of despair to make any move to open the locked door, but Silver was seriously tempted to obey that order from Sergeant Sparrow, no longer in any mood to run from the law. But Rolfe moved equally quickly from his station by the fire and grabbed Amy, placing a knife drawn from his pocket to her white throat. 'Touch that door, Jonathan, and I swear I'll cut this pretty lady's throat from ear to ear. I don't want to kill again, but I've hardly got anything to lose now, have I?' He dragged a protesting Amy over to the sash window, and jerked it open with his knife hand.

With the knife removed from her throat for one brief second, Amy tried to break free from Rolfe's grip. But he recovered quickly, grabbing her by the hair to prevent her escape. He glanced out of the window to assess his chances of escape, then, when Amy tried to bite his hand, dashed her head cruelly against the wall. He paused for one last moment at the window, regarding the sobbing figure of his wife on the floor with apparently genuine regret. Before Silver could get to him, though, Rolfe had jumped athletically through the window, shinned down the drainpipe, and vanished into the dense shrubbery at the back of the house.

The police were now battering at the door with their shoulders and boots, but making little headway yet apparently against the heavy teak panelling. Silver thought about unlocking the door and letting them in at once, yet the ferocious violence of their assault hardly reassured him that he might get a fair hearing from these gentlemen of the law for the first time.

Sophie still lay sobbing uncontrollably on the floor and Silver went over initially to see to her first. But when he saw that Amy too had collapsed on the floor, and was clutching at her throat and in even worse apparent distress than Sophie, he rushed instead to her side.

Somehow Sophie recovered quickly from her own despair to come to Silver's assistance. 'What's wrong with Lady Rachel?'

Silver was working frantically to loosen the bodice of Amy's gown. 'She's lost consciousness already. She's swallowed her tongue, and it's blocking her air passages,' Silver told Sophie. 'She can't breathe like this. Damn! I can't get my fingers down her slender throat. Help me with her before her heart gives out!'

Sophie was wide-eyed as the door quivered again with yet another savage blow to the far side from a couple of heavy police shoulders. 'You have to go now, Jonathan, if you don't want to be caught here. The police will no doubt call a doctor to look after your friend.'

Silver glanced at Sophie's distraught face, as he forced Amy's head back as far as he could, and tried to free her tongue. 'She'll be long dead by that time unless I can clear her airways. Can you loosen her stays a little so that I can free her chest to inhale...*quickly*...! Her heart's going to give out under the strain...'

The police had given up using their shoulders on the door for the moment, but Silver was sure the pause was just a temporary one and that they'd probably gone looking for some tool, or something heavy to use as a makeshift battering ram, to break the sturdy door down.

Sophie expertly loosened Amy's stays with her nimble fingers. Then Silver finally managed to hook the tip of his little finger around the back of Amy's tongue. Suddenly it seemed he was back in Newgate Prison, trying furiously to restore the life of that old turnkey John Gardiner...

But this time the outcome was different. Amy coughed, at first hesitantly, then explosively, as she took her first proper breath in five minutes and her heart started to beat rapidly again. She came back to life like a drowning woman reaching the surface of the ocean, gulping desperately for air, just as the police resumed their bombardment on the other side of the door. As Silver had suspected, they were now using an axe to break the door down so they would be through in a matter of seconds rather than minutes...

Sophie tugged fearfully at Silver's sleeve. 'She's all right now, Jonathan. You can go now with a clear conscience. I can take care of this lady's welfare now, and deal with Sergeant Sparrow.' She pointed out a hatch in the wood-panelled wall opposite the window. 'That's a dumb waiter that I had installed recently for delivering food here directly from the kitchen in the basement. A man should be able to fit in there, just.' As Jonathan got to his feet, she looked up at his immense height worriedly. 'A man of normal dimensions anyway. Get in if you can, and I shall lower you down to the basement. There won't be anyone down in the kitchen this time of night. If you remember, there is a way out from the kitchen through the alleyway at the side. The police hopefully won't know about that private side entrance yet.'

The door was beginning to splinter as Silver shoehorned his body with difficulty into the confined space.

Sophie held his hand for a second, tearful but regaining control of herself again. 'That is, unless you do want to give yourself up to Sergeant Sparrow now. Perhaps you should...'

Silver considered that possibility, but rejected it quickly. He couldn't simply let himself be taken by the police here. There were too many other things to consider now apart from his own fate, even if he could finally manage to convince the police that he hadn't killed his wife. And chief among those other considerations was Elisa, who was certainly wanted by the police, and who had no hope of escaping prison if she was caught. He couldn't abandon her after all she'd done for him. There were tears in Sophie's eyes as she released the brake on the mechanism and began to lower him tentatively down the shaft. He could only wonder at her self-possession in these terrible circumstances. He'd just destroyed the foundations of her whole world and yet she still wanted to help him escape. Women were indeed remarkable and resilient creatures...

He called back up the shaft to her. 'Please see that Lady Rachel is taken immediately to St Barts to be checked, Sophie. She may have sustained some head injury from that fall too. Take her at once by cab if you can. Ask for Dr Benjamin; he's the best man to take care of her...'

CHAPTER 27

Thursday 5th November 1857

Silver got back to Wapping as dawn was breaking and made his way through hushed cobbled streets to the hostel in New Gravel Lane. The lamplighter had started on his early morning rounds, extinguishing the oil lights along his route one by one, while the midden men were also out in force taking away the accumulated night soil of these mean streets.

Silver had walked the whole way, swapping his fine clothes near London Bridge with the grubbier ones of a surprised and grateful street sweeper of about the same size.

He hoped Amy would be all right but was still ill at ease with himself over leaving her like that, when he hadn't known the full extent of her injuries. Yet she had seemed to be breathing normally again, and returning to full consciousness.

Sophie's plan for his escape had worked perfectly. He had been able to make a clean exit from the private kitchen entrance of Sophie's house in Took's Court without anyone apparently noticing him. Silver thought that Sergeant Sparrow must be getting thoroughly tired by now of him always slipping through his fingers like water. Yet Silver still believed that he had made the right choice in not giving himself up. The problem was that Edward Rolfe – Silver still couldn't quite bring himself to think of his brother-in-law as this sinister figure Dimitri Alexandreevich Turgenov – had also slipped through the police's net as far as he knew, so Silver daren't give himself up when he still had no irrefutable proof of his innocence...

For a while he waited in the street outside the hostel, reluctant to go in, in case the police had thought ahead and were waiting for him.

When he did finally pluck up the courage, after seeing no signs of anything untoward happening in or around the hostel, he marched into the coach yard with a self-confident swagger he certainly didn't feel. There he found Ginny Faber cleaning the cobbled yard with a broom, while a couple of the younger hostel girls – pitifully thin and neglected creatures of fifteen or sixteen - fetched water from the yard standpipe, and coal from the cellar.

Ginny was still obviously devastated by the loss of her son, but she gamely fought her quivering lip as she recognized him.

'Mr Wade...'Ginny was well aware of his real identity by now, Silver knew, yet it seemed that she too had to keep calling him "Mr Wade", regardless.

'Ginny, I'm truly sorry about Billy,' he apologized. 'I should have warned him not to go near that checking drum, but I forgot.'

'No matter,' she declared bleakly. 'What's done is done. And at least Billy is at peace now and won't 'ave to go through all the trials and tribulations of this 'ard life. You should 'ave seen 'im when he was a baby, though – the prettiest little thing you hever saw...'

Silver forced himself to curtail her reminiscences about Billy. 'Can I see Miss Smith, Ginny?'

Ginny straightened up. 'She's gone, sir. Gone yesterday evening, as far as I remember.'

'Gone where?'

'She didn't say, sir, and I didn't choose to inquire.'

Silver's face fell as he wondered if she'd gone for good.

'You could try her shop,' Ginny suggested artlessly. 'Miss Smith might have gone back there...'

*

At eight o'clock, a strange fiery sun was rising above the misty river, perhaps a portent of further bad weather to come. Silver reconnoitred the alleyway carefully, before slipping the familiar catch on Elisa's back gate and creeping up to her back door.

He knocked quietly but got no answer.

Then he tried calling her name softly, which again drew no response, so he followed this up by throwing a pebble at her bedroom window. Even that didn't work, though, so Silver became desperate. He noticed that one window pane on the first floor had been broken, which gave him some cause for concern about Elisa. *Perhaps she hadn't come back here at all?* It was a risky thing to do now that Sparrow might have worked out who she really was, and where she'd been living.

As a last resort, he tried the door.

It was unlocked, so someone was probably inside...

The light was dim in the kitchen despite the broad daylight outside. This interior dimness was partly due to the closeness of the surrounding buildings in the alleyway, and partly because of the smallness of the windows. Silver moved across the kitchen warily, deciding not to call out further when he didn't know who or what might be waiting for him. In the gloom he saw the outline of Elisa's bathtub propped up incongruously against a wall, and couldn't help but remember her stepping out of that swan-shaped vessel like some Greek nymph...

He moved on tentatively towards the door giving entry to the stone corridor leading to the shop in the front of the building. That door too was unlocked and he pushed it open slowly.

He went down the corridor to the door at the back of the shop as quietly as he could. The door was partly open and he pushed it open further to reveal a figure tied to a chair. Even with the interior of the shop dim and unlit, he saw at once that the figure facing him in the chair was Elisa, but with her mouth cruelly gagged and her eyes imploring him with some urgent message of warning. Her right arm was still bandaged, he noticed, but no longer in a sling.

He stepped across the room in two strides to untie her, but as he did so, he felt a massive blow to the side of his head that sent him reeling...

*

The knock to his head had been even worse than the one that Harkness had given him in the shipyard drawing office on Tuesday night.

Silver felt light-headed with pain, and not quite sure where he was. But thoughts soon coalesced again into some semblance of reality as he remembered how he'd come to be here. His head was splitting with the agony – it felt as if someone had driven a railway sleeper spike into the side of his skull. His mouth seemed filled with bits of sawdust and the sour taste of his own blood.

He found he was trussed to the chair next to Elisa. His mouth wasn't gagged like hers, though, and he was still alert enough to wonder why that should be.

He heard footsteps dragging on the wooden floor behind him, but his neck felt as it was clamped in an iron collar so that he couldn't turn it more than a few degrees to see who it was. Eventually, however, a face came into his line of sight.

Even in the dim light of a grey November morning, the man's yellow hair and dandy clothes made him instantly recognizable. Silver felt his heart sink as he realized the extent of his troubles.

'You know me, sir, I think?' the man introduced himself to Silver with quiet, and almost feminine, pride.

Silver nodded wearily. 'Your name is Minshall. You're a turnkey at Newgate.'

Minshall smiled appreciatively. 'Where you'll shortly be returning, no doubt.' He leaned his face towards Silver and breathed deliberately over him. 'I've been chasing you these many weeks, Dr Silver, and now, as a reward for my persistence, I actually have both you and your accomplice. I find this situation a very satisfying and just outcome for all my hard work, don't you agree? After all these days and nights of scouring the miserable streets of Wapping, it is ironic that this lady accomplice of yours should be the one to lead me to you.' He tapped his nose conspiratorially. 'Though I admit in the end it was down to sheer luck. I just happened to spot this young lady at the launch of the Great Ship on Tuesday, and, despite all that feminine finery she was wearing, I recognized her at once as your pretty boy accomplice...'

'No doubt you preferred her dressed as a boy, sir,' Silver said offensively.

Minshall flushed. 'A tradesman in the yard was only too happy to identify the young lady in question, and from there it was an easy matter to find her lair, and to discover her real identity. At the risk of belittling your reputation, I have to tell you that this young lady is now worth twice to me what you are. And perhaps a lot more besides, if I can find that pearl necklace she nabbed three weeks ago. So perhaps I am not as disappointed to discover her real sex as you imagine...'

'She has a broken arm,' Silver pleaded. 'There's no need to tie her up like that. She can't run anywhere. '

'I beg to differ. She was hard enough to better as it was, even just using her left arm.' Minshall felt a bruise on his cheek. 'A regular wildcat.'

At least Minshall was on his own, Silver reflected, and didn't have his two evil wharf rat henchmen, Joey and Jack, along to support him. Clearly Minshall was no longer in a mood to share the rewards of his long search. Silver guessed it was pointless trying to plead further with the man, although he did wonder if he could possibly buy him off with a bribe of some sort. Yet what could he use to tempt this man and get him to look the other way? It would have to be something worth far more than the joint sum of the rewards on their heads. And Minshall would be the type to expect cash on the nail; a promissory note wasn't going to be much help in this case.

For the next fifteen minutes Minshall searched the house from top to bottom.

When he returned, clearly empty-handed, he wasn't in quite such a complacent and self-congratulatory mood as previously. 'Well, no matter. The necklace must be here somewhere. I'm sure Miss Smith – sorry, Miss *Saltash* – will tell me where she's hidden the damned thing.'

With ill grace, he tore the gag viciously off her mouth. 'Well, my pretty thief? Where have you hidden this pearl necklace – the *Tears of the Prophet?*'

'Go to hell, Mr Minshall,' Elisa said succinctly.

Minshall turned to Silver in exasperation. 'That's not entirely a helpful attitude, is it? Look, Dr Silver, I'll be very fair. If she tells me where the necklace is, I might even be prepared to let the two of you go.'

Silver wondered if this was a serious offer but didn't have time to respond before Elisa spat out, 'Don't trust him, Jonathan. The man is a weasel and a sodomite!'

Minshall lashed her hard across the face with the back of his hand. 'That's not a respectful way to talk about me, Miss Saltash...'

Minshall was about to strike her again even harder when he was interrupted by a key turning in the front door of the shop.

Liam Flintham stood there in the entrance, his face grim, his eyes questioning, as he took in the unexpected scene before him...

*

'What's going on here? Who are you?' Liam demanded of Minshall. Silver had never seen Liam looking so deathly serious.

'Never you mind. This is legal police business, so you'd better not stand in my way.' Minshall struck Elisa again across the face, drawing blood from her lip this time. 'Now, Miss Saltash, I intend to keep doing that until something breaks. And you won't look quite so pretty without your front teeth, and with a broken hook for a nose, I promise you...'

'Stop that now!' Liam demanded angrily, moving to free her.

Minshall took in Liam's bony and unimpressive build, and pushed him contemptuously aside. 'Leave now, or you'll be in big trouble. This woman is a wanted felon and I'm taking her in.'

Liam's face was quivering with rage as Minshall struck Elisa viciously again. 'You'll do nothing more to her, you bastard.' With that he stepped forward, pulled a wicked-looking knife from beneath his flapping greatcoat and sliced Minshall's throat neatly from ear to ear...

*

There was blood everywhere in the shop; the place was a charnel house.

Silver was an experienced surgeon yet he could have sworn that he had never seen a man leak as much blood as James Minshall had when dying. Minshall lay there now on the floor of the shop, undeniably dead, swimming in a swelling pool of his own dark crimson tide. Silver was fighting not to lose all control of himself at this grim turn of events; the last few moments had been the stuff of nightmares and he kept hoping desperately that he would soon wake up from this particular one. But to no avail: the die was cast, and both he and Elisa seemed doomed now....

A dazed Liam had untied Elisa, who was herself having great trouble in controlling her shaking limbs. Despite having the shakes, she had nevertheless untied Silver in turn with her good left hand, cutting warily through the knots with Liam's bloodstained knife.

'That man...wouldn't have got...the better of me...but for my broken arm,' she complained through chattering lips. Her cheeks were both bruised, and one eye was beginning to swell badly.

Silver gritted his teeth, and put his arms around Elisa. 'Breathe deeply,' he advised her, 'and the panic will pass.' It was good advice for himself too, as he stood there inhaling great gulps of air, like a man rescued from a wreck at sea.

Elisa began to recover her wits after taking this advice, yet still regarded the body on the bloodstained floor without pity. 'I'm glad he's dead. It was all his doing that my father died impaled on that wall at Newgate. Our escape would have all gone perfectly if Mr Gardiner hadn't been so scared of this devious man.'

Silver held her again in his arms to calm her, yet his own mind was still reeling as he wondered what to do. No matter what, though, he could see no other outcome now but disaster. They were finished; the law would hang all three of them for this...

Elisa somehow pulled herself together, her mind apparently working more lucidly again. She went over to her employee and held him with her good left arm. 'Listen, Liam, listen carefully. I have to leave for good now...'

'No, don't do that, Miss,' Liam begged in a near panic of his own. 'I'll clean up all this mess, and get rid of the body, and then everything can go back to the way it was.'

'No, Liam,' she explained patiently, putting her left hand gently on his cheek, 'it can never go back to the way it was. My name is not really Elisa Smith; it's Elisa Saltash. And it's true what that man Minshall said – I'm wanted by the law already. So I must take the blame for what happened here today. Understand! If anyone asks you what happened here, tell them you know nothing about it. Or, if you have to, tell them I must have done this.'

'No, Miss!' Liam begged her like a child.

'Why are you telling him to say that?' Silver demanded.

Elisa ignored Silver and continued to speak to Liam as if he were an insecure child. 'Understand, Liam? You go back home to Maldon now and continue looking after your sick sister, Siobhan. If the police come and question you, tell them you've been in Maldon since Tuesday, and that you know nothing of the death of this man Minshall.' She went to the kitchen and returned rapidly with a jangling bag of coins. 'Here! Take this, all of it.'

'What about the shop?' Liam asked dumbly.

'Afterwards it'll be yours, Liam. But for now, stay away. Now go!' she declared urgently, almost shoving him towards the door with her good left arm.

Liam looked at the body on the floor and shuddered as if he'd just noticed his own bloody handiwork. But he did finally accept the bag of coins, and then allowed himself to be pushed through the door and out into the cobbled street. 'Go!' she called again after him, before closing the door firmly behind him.

Silver stared emptily at her. 'Do you think he'll really stay away?'

'I don't know. Perhaps. But the question is more what *we* should do now.' Elisa seemed in despair for the first time in all the weeks he'd known her. 'We seem to be bringing death and disaster with us wherever we go, Jonathan.'

Silver thought back to last night's events and was forced to agree with her. 'It does seem so...' Although it scarcely seemed to matter now, he told her briefly what had happened at the Alhambra last night, and then later at Sophie's house in Took's Court.

Her bruised eyes lit up briefly. 'At least you finally know who killed Marianne. You have your answer.'

'Yes, but I still can't prove my innocence for certain. I'm still a fugitive.' That fond hope he'd formerly entertained of proving his innocence now seemed to Silver hardly worth worrying about after the trauma of what had happened here.

She took his right hand in her left. 'You *will* be able to prove your innocence in time, Jonathan.'

Silver sighed heavily. 'I'm not sure. That man Ferrar and his political masters apparently knew the truth about Marianne's death already – or suspected it anyway – and didn't raise a finger to save me from the hangman. So why should it be different now?'

Elisa squeezed his hand to reassure him. 'The police will eventually catch this man Rolfe – or whatever his name is – and then the law will have to pardon you, no matter what these politicians say or do. And that's why it's doubly important that you don't get linked to what happened here today. I have to take the full blame for this! I am already a known thief -' she glanced down uneasily at Minshall - 'so if I have to be hunted as a murderess too, it's of no great consequence.' She put her left hand on his cheek. 'So this has to be goodbye, Jonathan. You have to go your own way now, and leave me to mine. With the help of your friends, you will finally be able to take your rightful place in the world again.'

Silver was numb. 'And what do you intend to do?'

'Don't worry about me,' she said, her old feistiness returning rapidly. 'I'll give that damned Sergeant Sparrow a merry chase for his money. He won't catch me easily, I promise you.'

'Your arm is broken; you're bruised and beaten, and covered in blood; you're exhausted. What chance would you have of getting away on your own?' he demanded angrily.

She bristled resentfully at that. 'Don't feel sorry for me, Dr Silver. I don't need your damned help. Or your damned pity!'

'I'm anything but sorry for you, Elisa. But I am coming with you to look after you.'

She snorted angrily. 'No, you're not. I don't want you to.'

'Yes, you do.' He leaned forward and kissed her violently on her swollen lips, initially against her strong protests. But then he felt her yielding to his touch. 'Yes, you *do* want me to come with you! And stop arguing with me; I'm sick and tired of it.'

She gazed at him in wonder. 'Why are you doing this? Do you really care for me that much?'

Silver stroked her dishevelled hair. 'Yes, I do. I'd rather take my chances with you than go back to my old life.'

Her eyes were huge and solemn. 'Would you, Jonathan? Really?'

Silver got to work, thinking rapidly. 'The police will be checking all the ports, of course. But if we can find a way through and get safely on a ship, we can still make a new life abroad - *together.*'

Her eyes became hopeful. 'Where? The island of Hong Kong?'

'Don't get too far ahead with your optimistic plans, Elisa,' he cautioned her. 'Let's just try and get on the steam packet to Rotterdam first...'

CHAPTER 28

Monday 9th November 1857

Sparrow was losing his patience with this young lady, despite her decorous looks and well-bred manners.

'Lady Rachel...'

'I have told you, Sergeant. I have no idea where Dr Silver and Miss Smith have gone.'

Sparrow gritted his teeth. 'Her real name is Elisa Saltash, as you well know by now, since you were sheltering her here for a day or more after the incident at the Napier shipyard,' he admonished her.

Lady Rachel inclined her head gracefully. 'I beg your pardon, Sergeant. I have no idea where Dr Silver and Miss *Saltash* have gone.'

After four days without any fresh sightings of Dr Silver or Elisa Saltash, Sergeant Sparrow had been forced to return to the Hostel for Women in Wapping for a fresh talk with this annoying and opinionated young woman, even though he was sure from his many searches of the place that neither of the fugitives was still hiding here. Sparrow had been frankly amazed when he had discovered the real identity of young Amy McLennan, yet he had to be careful now because it seemed she had influential friends in very high places. It turned out that her father was even an Earl and a member of the House of Lords. Sitting alone with her in the kitchen of the hostel, it was hard to believe that, though, because she was dressed again as the servant girl Amy, and looked every inch the simple maid he had once thought her to be.

Sparrow was still kicking himself that Silver had managed to slip through his fingers again last Wednesday. He had been unlucky first not to nab him in the foyer of the Alhambra, but then he'd thought he had him for certain after his inspired guess that Silver would seek shelter with his beautiful sister-in-law Sophie Rolfe. Sparrow hadn't imagined however that his pursuit of Dr Silver to Took's Court would throw up all sorts of new possibilities about who had really killed the good doctor's wife - this lady with the mysterious past, Marianne Silver, nee Lovelock.

Yet this young woman, Lady Rachel Grosvenor – Silver's companion on Wednesday night - seemed almost as much a mystery as Marianne Silver had been. 'I could arrest you, Lady Rachel, you know,' he threatened her. 'You have been aiding and abetting a fugitive.'

'I have been aiding and abetting a falsely accused man, Sergeant,' Lady Rachel declared complacently. 'Dr Silver did not kill his wife, as I think you well know by now. Dr Silver's own brother-in-law, Edward Rolfe, killed Marianne, as well as several other people. I've told you that already several times, yet you seem to refuse to believe it. I heard the man confess his wicked crimes openly and brazenly.'

Sparrow wasn't prepared to be magnanimous. 'There's no evidence of that at the moment, apart from *your* testimony.'

Lady Rachel was scathing. 'There was no real evidence of Dr Silver killing her either, apart from one over-excited maid servant, but that didn't stop the police from accusing him, did it, Sergeant? And you do presumably have Mrs Sophie Rolfe's evidence too, which should corroborate mine. She would hardly lie about her own husband's guilt, would she?'

'She's scarcely an unbiased witness in Dr Silver's defence either, though - any more than you are, Lady Rachel.' Sparrow narrowed his eyes, taking in her dark glossy hair and delicate Latin features. 'Dr Silver has never had problems attracting impressionable young ladies to his cause, it seems.' Sparrow saw her fine cheeks flush at this deliberately provocative statement. 'You played the servant girl extremely well, Lady Rachel. I didn't spot you as a fraud, and I've worked in the East End for years. What sort of sport are you playing here, Lady Rachel? Does it flatter your pride to play games with the lives of these local women?'

Her cheeks burned even redder. 'It's not a game, Sergeant. I wanted to be trusted here, and to do that I had to be one of them, not a wealthy outsider. And that's the way I want it to stay,' she warned him. 'Don't give me away to the women here. Only Ginny knows who I really am.' She almost pleaded with him. So please call me Amy, or Miss McLennan.'

'Very well. Miss McLennan.' Sergeant Sparrow wasn't comfortable with being too intimate with her any more. 'But, even if all you say is true, I still find it difficult to believe that you have no inkling of where your friends are hiding now.'

She put her hand on his sleeve. 'Let them go, Sergeant. You've persecuted an innocent man long enough, surely.'

'That's as may be, Miss. But Miss Saltash is undeniably a thief and a ne'er do well. And she and Silver still have many questions to answer about the death of Mr Harkness at the shipyard, and their part in it. Not to mention the death of this man Charles Ferrar at the Alhambra last week.'

Lady Rachel snorted angrily. 'You forget, Sergeant. I was there in the foyer of the Alhambra when Mr Ferrar was murdered. Dr Silver was standing *facing him*, so could hardly have plunged a dagger into his back at the same time.'

She had a good point, Sparrow was forced to admit. But he was still in no mood to be conciliatory. 'Don't think you've seen the last of me, Miss *Amy*. I will be back in due course.'

'I can hardly doubt that, Sergeant,' Lady Rachel said tartly. 'But you will be welcome here when you do come back, provided you don't give my real identity away to anyone.'

Sparrow relented a little. 'I won't do that. Your hostel does useful work around here in keeping these unfortunate girls off the streets and out of the workhouse.' He hesitated. 'Are you fully recovered now, Miss? You did take a bad knock on the head during that altercation in Took's Court. You nearly choked to death too, according to what I heard from Mrs Rolfe who witnessed it.'

Lady Rachel nodded gratefully. 'I did nearly die, Sergeant, but I'm fully recovered now, thanks to Dr Silver's timely assistance.'

'Yes, the man is a veritable saint, no doubt,' Sparrow agreed sarcastically...

*

Returning to Shadwell station, Sparrow found Frank Remmert waiting in his office, seething with quiet excitement.

'You've got something to tell me again, haven't you, Frank?' Sparrow suggested dryly.

'Yes, Sarge. I have received one possibly useful piece of information. A certain Captain Christy Blackburn, master of the vessel *Tradewinds*, came to Shadwell Station an hour ago and let it be known that a man calling himself Wade has booked passage with his vessel, bound for Bahia in Brazil. His ship, the *Tradewinds*, is due to set sail from the London Dock with the tide this coming Friday, the thirteenth of November.'

Sparrow was wary, despite the promising nature of this information. 'What's this Captain Blackburn like?'

'A rogue, in my opinion, Sarge, who'd slit his old granny's throat for an ounce of tobacco. His only interest was in the reward for Silver, but it is two hundred and fifty pounds now. I wouldn't mind a share of that myself.'

Sparrow finally smiled broadly, and smacked Remmert's shoulder in congratulation. It seemed that this time he might just have his man after all...

*

In the meantime, though, Sparrow kept looking.

Sparrow had scarcely imagined that Elisa Saltash and Silver would be stupid enough to hide in a place as obvious as Elisa's home. Yet Sparrow had gone there anyway last Wednesday, the day after the *Leviathan*'s abortive launch, and sniffed around inside. The shop was all boarded up that day, but Sparrow had forced an entry through a first floor window at the back and made a thorough search of the place. Although the house was still full of her possessions, it seemed clear that Elisa was probably gone for good. Nevertheless Sparrow had had the place watched continuously by one of his officers for the remainder of that Wednesday before deciding it was probably a waste of further police time. At the time, he was sure that Elisa Saltash would be long gone from Wapping, taking that stolen necklace with her, and would never be back. He knew now that she had in fact been hiding in that Hostel for Women, which was one place that had not occurred to him at the time since he hadn't known of any connection between Elisa and that place. But he had been too late to nab her there, so was now trying to discover where else she might have gone into hiding. He had as a precaution sent one of the Shadwell constables to check briefly on Elisa's shop every day since then, but from their daily reports it seemed that the place had indeed been abandoned, and that Elisa was unlikely to ever return there.

But now, five days later, he'd had a second thought and decided it would now be worth a second look inside to see if Elisa might have left some clue as to where she might have fled. There was also a possibility, he now realized belatedly, that the place might have a secret cellar or some other place where a pair of fugitives could possibly hide up for a week or more until they were ready to run.

Sparrow and Frank Remmert walked down Old Gravel Lane on this gloomy November afternoon to check his theory. The place still looked unoccupied from the outside, though, the front door to the chandler's shop locked, with no sign of any lit candle inside.

Frank Remmert peered in through the dusty glass of the front bay window. 'There's something lying on the floor in there, Sarge.' He sniffed the air. 'Something stinks to high heaven as well, doesn't it?'

'Good,' announced Sparrow. 'Then that gives us a reasonable excuse for breaking in the door and checking the cause of the smell.' This time he was happy to go in openly through the front door, rather than make a difficult clandestine entry through a back window as he had before.

He hardly thought that the source of the stink really would be a body, though, but this complacent assumption was soon denied by the physical evidence.

The full force of the smell hit them hard as soon as they broke the door open. Both men were forced to put kerchiefs over their noses as they took in the blackened corpse, the stains on the floor and the buzz of houseflies everywhere.

'Well, they've really gone and done it now,' Frank said, shocked. 'That looks like Mr Minshall, or what's left of him, anyway. I thought you said this man Silver was no murderer after all.'

Sparrow was grim in return. 'Perhaps we forced him into it in the end...'

Sparrow sent Frank immediately to fetch more uniformed officers from Shadwell while he searched the premises. The shop and the living quarters above had clearly been ransacked by someone since his own visit last Wednesday, or else these were the signs of someone leaving in a panicked hurry. So Elisa and her stolen necklace were certainly gone now, if they hadn't been before. And, knowing the attractive power of the female sex, Sparrow suspected that the missing Dr Silver might well be back in her company again after his recent adventures in the West End...

Sparrow cursed his own stupidity in not maintaining a constant watch on these premises as he should have. Back downstairs, though, he found his foot snagged by a piece of paper partly wedged under the bottom of the counter. He pulled the paper free with no great expectations, but his pulse began to race a little when he discovered it to be a timetable.

A timetable for the steam packet sailings from Gravesend to Rotterdam...*and with one particular sailing circled in ink...*

CHAPTER 29

Friday 13th November 1857

A Gravesend jetty in the early morning...

Mist swathed the river in a cloak of dour grey yet this dismal and dank scene seemed to Jonathan Silver to be the gateway to a quite different world. In his mind he imagined tropic islands, frigate birds and flying fish, blue-fringed reefs and coral sand...

'What are you thinking about, Jonathan?' Elisa asked him, with a suggestion of a smile playing across her lips. 'You seem miles away.'

Silver came back to the present. 'I was wondering - where in the shop did you keep that necklace that you stole? Minshall searched the whole place and he was probably an expert at finding secret hiding places.'

She leaned towards him and smiled coyly, glancing down at her skirts. 'Not as secret as *this* place. Actually the pearls were sewn into my drawers, Doctor, so if Mr Minshall had been a little less repulsed by the female body, and a little more willing to carry out an intimate body search, he would no doubt have found them. Mr Minshall had no problems with beating a woman to death, it seems, but did have a great reluctance to look under a woman's skirts.' Her voice fell to a conspiratorial whisper. 'And in case you're wondering, they're still there. Those pearls are our financial future, so I'm keeping them warm and secure until I deliver them to Meneer Koog in *Herengracht* in Amsterdam.'

Silver hadn't told her yet that Sophie had earlier fulfilled her promise to him and arranged for the contents of his own bank account at Coutts to be forwarded to a bank in *Bahnhofstrasse* in Zurich. So the fact was they had more than enough money to start a new life abroad, even without the proceeds of that stolen necklace. Yet Silver was reluctant to tell her such a thing. Knowing Elisa, there would be no imaginable way that she would willingly return that necklace, after all her hard work and daring in purloining it, and, truth to tell, Silver was beginning to side with her view. It seemed she had turned him from the painfully honest man he'd once been into one of more elastic and obliging morals. Yet that all seemed to be a part of the implicit bargain he had made with himself to be with her, and he was even content at the thought of his tacit connivance in that crime.

They stood on the wooden jetty among the line of passengers watching the Rotterdam steam packet manoeuvre towards the berth at the end, paddles churning the water into grey-brown froth. Their bags and trunks stood side by side on the quayside, four for her, two for him. A new and enticing life beckoned.

During the last few days, they had stayed at a riverside inn overlooking the Thames and dared to dream of that life. In that time they had finally – inevitably - become lovers.

Silver had abandoned himself totally to this woman now. Her hold over him was now so powerful and all embracing that he knew that, if he had to, he would even kill to protect her...

He took the time to admire her now, dressed in a burgundy velvet outfit and wearing a delicate feathered chapeau perched on her pretty head. She looked every inch the respectable English lady, even if her right arm was still in a sling, and she needed powder and paint to hide the remnants of the bruises Minshall had given her. 'What will happen to all your businesses?' he asked her curiously. 'The chandler's store? The tanner's yard? Do you simply intend to abandon them?'

'I have left instructions with a lawyer in Chancery Lane to transfer ownership of my businesses to various people. Ernest Harvey will get the tanner's yard. He's a good man, and will make a success of the business.'

'And the chandler's store?'

Elisa looked away briefly in embarrassment. 'I've left that to Liam,' she declared finally, after a long pause.

'Is that wise?' Silver frowned. 'Liam must be unbalanced in the head to do what he did to Minshall.'

'I don't know. I don't think he's insane; he's more of a child who tried to protect me...'

Silver muttered. 'A dangerous child...'

'...He did what he did for love, that's all. He saw me, the object of that love, being struck and threatened, and responded in the only way he knew. It was all my fault. I never meant to lead him on. Yet I was flattered by his attentions so I may have done so inadvertently, even though I understood the harmful effect my presence had on him.' She sighed. 'Poor Liam! What will happen to him?'

'I don't know,' admitted Silver. 'But guilt may eventually force him to give himself away.'

Elisa shook her head sharply, causing her pretty hat to sway alarmingly on her head. 'I hope not. I trust Liam can live with what he did, terrible as it was, and make a new life for himself. Hopefully he will find a good steady wife, and have armies of ginger children to enliven his life...' She smiled at her own remark, but the smile turned into a shiver as a chill autumn blast of wind blew in off the river.

The steam packet was now moored securely fore and aft alongside the jetty and the crew were busy lowering the gangway.

The line of passengers, with their porters carrying their luggage alongside, began to shuffle forward in anticipation of being allowed to board.

Elisa gripped Silver's hand as they inched towards the gangway. 'I have a small confession to make, Jonathan, before we step on that boat.'

Silver was wary of the apologetic tone of her voice, wondering what revelation might be in store. 'Yes, what is it?'

She coughed with fresh embarrassment. 'You remember that first full night you were sleeping in my kitchen? And then you woke up the following morning and found me taking my bath...?'

He smiled at the memory. 'How could I forget such a thing? What is it you want to confess?'

She shrugged sheepishly. 'Only that I had to wait a dreadful long time in that bath for you to wake up. The water was nearly stone cold before you finally stirred. I thought you were going to sleep forever, you lazy bones.'

He laughed. 'You scheming minx!'

She held his gaze now with determination. 'I had to try and think of some way to make you stay. I didn't want you to leave too soon. I had just lost my father and Mr Gardiner, and I couldn't bear the thought of being left alone with all that emptiness and pain.'

Silver squeezed her left hand surreptitiously, touched by this admission from her. 'And yet the cold and haughty way you looked at me then,' he remembered with wonder.

'It's well known that a man will only want what he thinks he can't have,' Elisa declared primly.

He laughed again. 'So does that mean you had plans for me all along?'

She gave that some honest thought. 'No, I'm not quite so calculating a woman as that. But let's say that I do admit to taking a liking for you almost from that first day...' - her slight smile broadened - '...in fact, probably from the moment that you saved me from falling off that roof in Newgate...'

She couldn't finish her sentence, though, as a hand was placed roughly on both their shoulders. 'Not so fast, sir...and you, Miss.' Silver spun around to find Sergeant Sparrow and several young police constables regarding them with expressions of grim satisfaction...

*

They were taken to a waiting room in the ferry building.

There were no handcuffs, no displays of triumph. In fact Sparrow seemed to be as gloomy as his prisoners about finally outsmarting them.

Sparrow sat across the scratched deal table from them on his own. For some reason, he had sent his uniformed constables out of the room and told them to wait outside to be called. One of them was the same plain young constable Silver remembered from the day he'd been chased to the Hostel for Women. But Sparrow clearly wanted first to speak to Silver and Elisa alone and off the record. Silver wondered why; perhaps Sparrow wanted to first establish the truth in his own mind, from all the conflicting evidence he must have heard.

Even in his depressed state, Silver couldn't help noticing that this waiting room was a suitably dismal place for such an interview – ugly green glazed tiles on the lower half of the walls, a thin strip of threadbare jute-backed carpet on the wooden floor, a smoky coal fire that did little to dispel the November damp, a faded picture above the fireplace of the Queen and Prince Albert looking particularly dour. Silver glanced at Elisa at his side: she was clearly desolated at being caught like this, but standing firm and not giving in to self-pity.

Sparrow's attention seemed entirely focussed on Silver for the moment. Sparrow hadn't asked Elisa anything directly at all, apart from making it obvious when he addressed her briefly as "Miss Saltash" that he was now aware of her real identity, as the daughter of the burglar and condemned man Jonas Saltash.

He got Silver to tell his version of what had happened at the Alhambra music hall ten days ago, and then later at his sister-in-law's home in Took's Court.

Sparrow let Silver finish his brief story without interrupting. Finally he cleared his throat. 'So, Dr Silver, you claim that your brother-in-law, Edward Rolfe, was an agent for the Tsar. And that he killed your wife because she was close to unmasking him...'

'And he murdered my father-in-law, George Lovelock, too,' Silver reminded him, 'and made it look like a heart attack.'

Sparrow sniffed doubtfully. 'Unfortunately we cannot find Mr Rolfe to verify any of these accusations of yours.'

Silver shrugged his shoulders. 'It's not surprising. He's probably far away by now. His real name, by the way, is Dimitri Alexandreevich Turgenov. He told me so himself. Mr Ferrar also suspected the man's real identity, I believe.'

'But Mr Ferrar is even more difficult to contact for verification than Mr Rolfe,' Sparrow pointed out ironically, 'seeing as how my name isn't Michael or Gabriel.'

Silver tried not to lose his temper; he suspected this was exactly the uncontrolled state that Sparrow was trying to goad him into, in order to discover the truth. 'You must have spoken to my sister-in-law? And to Lady Rachel Grosvenor, who was also present?'

'I have spoken to both those ladies,' Sparrow admitted. 'But I'm not sure I trust their evidence entirely without some independent confirmation,' he added dryly. 'They both clearly have some vested interest in your welfare therefore could be lying. Regrettably, even well-bred ladies do lie when it suits them...'

'How is Lady Rachel?' Silver interrupted. 'Is she recovered from that blow on her head that she suffered?'

'She's perfectly well, Dr Silver, you'll be glad to hear.'

This was the one welcome piece of news that Silver had heard today and he glanced at Elisa to see her reaction. But she had turned her head away at this moment to look out of the window at the wintry river scene outside. Silver could imagine what bitter and forbidding thoughts must presently be going through her head. *So near and yet so far...*

Sparrow continued strangely to ignore her and speak only to Silver. 'Tell me about the events at the Napier shipyard last week, Dr Silver. What were you doing working there?'

Silver would have preferred not to talk about his former suspicions of Daniel Strode, which had led him in entirely the wrong direction in his hunt for Marianne's killer, and embroiled him in further evil circumstances not of his own making. But he felt there was nothing for it now but to be frank with this man, who was turning out to be a more reasonable person than Silver had expected. 'I suspected Mr Strode of killing my wife,' he confessed wryly, 'even though the link between him and Marianne was a tenuous one at best. So I went to the shipyard hoping to discover some more substantial evidence against him. Later I believed he might have been implicated in the deaths of these two other young women – the murdered governesses, Miss Livingstone and Miss Penfold. I had seen one of those women - Miss Penfold - accept a ride in Strode's carriage on the night she died.'

Sparrow narrowed his eyes disconcertingly. 'And yet it doesn't seem to have been Strode at all, does it? Neither in the case of your wife – if your other evidence is to be believed - nor in the case of Miss Livingstone and Miss Penfold.'

'Harkness confessed directly to me to killing those two women. The man was quite mad, in my opinion.'

Sparrow jumped on that statement, like a bull terrier tearing at a red rag. 'Did you kill Mr Harkness? He didn't commit suicide by any chance, did he?' he suggested artfully.

Silver suspected that Sparrow was trying to trap him rather clumsily with that loaded question since Harkness's injuries could certainly not all have been the result of his fall from the Great Ship. 'I killed the man in self defence,' Silver said uneasily. 'He was going to shoot me. He had an American revolver that he obviously intended to use for that purpose; you must have found it at the scene...'

'No! Dr Silver didn't hit anyone, Sergeant,' Elisa suddenly interrupted, leaning forcefully across the table. 'I hit Harkness over the back of the head with some lead pipe. But the man was certainly intending to kill us both.'

Sparrow finally looked at her with affected surprise, as if he'd just noticed she was in the room. 'You know something, Miss Saltash, you sound exactly like your old man. And you look just like him too, I have to say. - I wonder I didn't recognize it at once.'

Elisa stared at him balefully. 'Leave my father out of this!'

Silver now pushed himself forward impatiently. 'She had suffered a broken arm that evening, Sergeant, as you can readily still see. Harkness broke her arm viciously when they were struggling, and then struck her over the head with the butt of his revolver.' He touched her arm in the sling to reinforce his point. 'She was certainly in no position to have hit anyone with a lead pipe afterwards. Don't believe her; she is just trying to defend me.'

Sparrow weighed that reply up. 'I might even give you both the benefit of the doubt concerning Harkness, who does seem to have been an evil man who preyed on women.' He sighed. 'But what about Minshall? Who slit that young gentleman's throat? Was that also self-defence?' he said accusingly.

'No, it wasn't. I killed him too,' Silver stated baldly. 'He was going to hand us over to you.'

Elisa thumped the table angrily with her left fist. 'Don't believe him, Sergeant. It was I who killed Harkness...*and* Minshall. It was all my doing...'

Sparrow shook his head as the steam whistle of the packet boat sounded a shrill note outside to warn that it was leaving in five minutes. 'Dear, oh dear! You two really are a puzzle.' He got to his feet abruptly and paced the floor for a second, before then saying, rather bizarrely, 'Excuse me for a moment, I need to consult with my constables outside...'

*

Two minutes went by, the clock ticking loudly on the wall in front of them. Elisa hadn't said a word for a while, her head sunk forward in dejected misery. 'Where has he gone?' she finally asked irately.

Silver had a feeling something strange and inexplicable was going on. He jumped to his feet and went to the door, which he opened slightly to peer out in all directions. 'Our bags are still on the quayside,' he announced in a whisper. 'And there's no one here in the waiting room except us. No sign of any policemen. Come, Elisa, let's try and get on that boat.'

He grabbed her good arm but she resisted, staying glued to her seat. 'It's a trick, that's all. That devious man is playing games with us. He wants to humiliate me in particular.'

But Silver forced her to her feet and out of the door anyway, and then propelled her with a firm hand on her backside across the misty jetty to the gangway.

A young purser came hurrying down the gangway to greet them, a passenger list in his hand. 'Are you Mr and Mrs Williams? You'd better get on board, sir, if you don't want to miss the boat. We're casting off in one minute.'

Elisa looked around in bewilderment, but nevertheless moved slowly up the gangway with Silver, both expecting any moment to hear a shout behind for someone to stop them.

But the shout never came...

*

Frank Remmert watched the steam packet pulling away into the river. The mist was thinning and sheets of mother-of-pearl water were appearing through the gloom, reflecting the colours of the rising sun.

'That wasn't them, then?' he asked Sergeant Sparrow conversationally. 'That man certainly looked to me like the pictures of Silver I've seen. And the woman was sporting what looked like the remains of a black eye, as well as having her arm in a sling.'

Sparrow shifted his feet uneasily. 'The height of the man matched, but nothing else. They were a Mr and Mrs John Williams from Canterbury travelling to Berlin on business. As for the lady's black eye and injured arm, she was recently in a coach accident.'

'Why didn't you want me or Constables Kennally and Waddle talking to them then, Sarge?' Remmert asked resentfully.

'No point in upsetting a nice young couple with too many interrogators, Frank, was there?'

Remmert didn't look entirely convinced by his chief's explanation. 'Then why did *you* speak to them for so long?' he inquired brazenly.

'Come on, Frank, enough of these damned pointless questions,' Sparrow urged him hurriedly. 'Let's take that dogcart back to the station. We've got a train to catch back to London Bridge.'

'Inspector Carew won't be happy if Silver has got away,' Remmert observed, 'not after all the time we've put into trying to catch him.'

'Bugger Inspector Carew, Frank! That's what I say to that!' Sparrow said succinctly. But as he clambered up into the back of the muddy cart with Remmert and the other constables, he did wonder ruefully to himself why he had let these two fugitives go. That certainly hadn't been his intention when he'd rushed to Gravesend last night and made secret enquiries about the couple staying at the nearby Saracen's Head Inn.

On the plus side he was sure that Dr Silver was no murderer, or even someone of a criminal disposition - except perhaps for the people he consorted with. Yet the girl – *why on earth was he letting her go?* Of course the truth was that he either had to let both of them go, or none, and in the end he had chosen the former. Yet there was a very good chance that the girl had indeed murdered that unfortunate man Minshall, although, as a hopeful student of human nature, Sparrow preferred to think not. For all her coolness, she didn't have the look of someone who could slit a man's throat as cold-bloodedly as that. Plus the fact was that Minshall's throat had been cut from his left to his right, which implied that the killer had used the knife in his right hand. Sparrow had been relieved to discover that Elisa Saltash had a broken right forearm at the time, which meant she could hardly have wielded that knife herself...

Yet the other circumstantial evidence was clearly against her, though. The man had been killed in her shop, and there were clear signs that she had been there at the time of the killing and got into a fight with Minshall. It was also hard to come up with any obvious alternative suspect. The only other possibility, the store clerk Liam Flintham, had been away in Maldon in Essex at the time, and had witnesses to prove it. Sparrow knew the judges and lawyers of the Newgate Assizes well enough by now to appreciate that, based on that evidence, they would hang this girl for sure if they ever got their prissy hands on her. Sir Digby Carfax had a lot of clout with the judges at the Old Bailey and he would make sure she would hang, as much for her temerity in stealing that necklace from him, as for the murder of Minshall.

There had also been one other consideration in Sparrow's decision to let her and Silver go, if Sparrow was being truthful. It had been at this very pier at Gravesend that Sparrow had arrested her father as he'd tried to flee the country last summer. Afterwards, particularly after what had happened to the man in trying to escape from Newgate, Sparrow had regretted not looking the other way that day and letting Jonas Saltash go. So this was a chance to make some amends for that bad decision. Hanging at Newgate was only for the truly evil in Charlie Sparrow's view, and neither Jonas Saltash nor his daughter qualified remotely for that description.

So given the alternative of letting this girl go scot free, or seeing her hang outside Newgate before a baying mob, he'd gone for the only choice he could make, and still be able to sleep at night. The debit side of that decision was that he'd had to let her leave with Sir Digby Carfax's necklace still presumably in her possession.

And yet – was that also perhaps a benefit...? This was Inspector Murphy's case after all, not his, so that Irish inspector at Piccadilly Station was going to get the blame for any failure to recover the necklace, not him...

Sparrow also remembered the way that elderly rascal of a baronet, Sir Digby Carfax, had spoken to him a few weeks ago – addressing him like he was talking to some pointer dog trained to sniff out his quarry for him. Even worse for Sparrow was the contemptuous way that his silly wife had inspected him like some strange specimen from Regents Park Zoo. So Sparrow was pleased to exact some revenge on this snotty couple – Sir Digby and his supercilious young wife could go hang themselves before he would ever bring their damned necklace back to them...

In his own judgement Sparrow had achieved enough of a result from his own case already. He had identified the murderer of Charlotte Livingstone and Jane Penfold with certainty, and the man, Harkness, had met his own summary form of justice, even if Sparrow still wasn't quite sure whether it had been Elisa Saltash or Dr Silver who had administered the final blow to dispatch him to his maker. Even Inspector Carew had been content with the outcome of that case, although trying to take the credit himself, of course. The important point was that a criminal had been justly punished, and the public spared the expense of a trial, which was all highly satisfactory. And the melancholy Mrs Adelie Livingstone had been saved from having the story of her daughter's sordid death, and of her affair with that man Strode, coming out in a public court.

And what about the murder of Marianne Silver and that man Ferrar? Strictly speaking, this was no more Sparrow's concern than was the stolen necklace. Yet that case also seemed to be solved, even if the perpetrator was still regrettably at large.

A man from the Foreign Office had visited Sparrow yesterday at Shadwell Station (in company with an unusually subdued Assistant Commissioner Grindrod) and told Sparrow unofficially what was going on. The official had revealed their suspicions about the missing Edward Rolfe, otherwise identified as a Russian government agent called Dimitri Alexandreevich Turgenov. The government was quietly hunting for the man, the foreign office official had said, but it was a chase that would be conducted diplomatically in private so as not to cause any fresh confrontation with Imperial Russia. And one day, Sparrow guessed - perhaps on a Munich street in winter, or on a Paris boulevard in the leafy spring - Dimitri Alexandreevich would get his just deserts from some anonymous passer-by when he was least expecting it.

It was also made clear to Sparrow that he should instantly forget everything he had just been told. From that Sparrow assumed that there would be no official measures taken to clear Dr Silver of responsibility for his wife's murder. This seemed to Sergeant Sparrow tantamount to duplicity on the part of Her Majesty's Government, and was one more reason why he had decided to let Dr Silver and his girl go free.

So, all in all, a satisfactory end to the case as far as Charlie Sparrow was concerned.

And yet, if Sergeant Sparrow had understood himself a little better, and recognized the romantic side to his own character buried deep beneath that flinty exterior, he might have realized that he had in fact let Silver and Elisa go for a much simpler reason than all those other convincing arguments he had just made to himself.

Prior to detaining them, Sparrow had spent several minutes closely observing Silver and his girl as they waited on that jetty, talking quietly to each other, and clearly anticipating their new life together. And there had been something particularly sweet about the way she had smiled up at him, and touched his sleeve, and about the manner in which he had responded, that set this couple apart in Sergeant Sparrow's mind from the common run of humanity. It would be a hard man that would destroy something as precious as that in a world as grim and unrelenting as this one...

At one of the station stops on the way back to London Bridge by train, still in a fulsome romantic mood himself, Sparrow impulsively bought a bunch of winter violets from a platform flower seller to take home to a no doubt surprised Edie...

EPILOGUE

January 1858

Lady Rachel Grosvenor had watched earlier in the day as the *Leviathan* had finally been winched down to the river's edge. At first the movement had been almost imperceptible to the eye. But, gradually, the progress of the majestic vessel towards the water, although still only a painstaking inch at a time, had become clear for all to see.

Amy had marvelled at the tiny man on the dais behind the ship who had made this miracle work, who had somehow found the means to move this immense weight of iron on its first tentative journey. Mr Brunel had finally proved his clamorous critics wrong. The journalists from *Punch* and the *Illustrated London News* looked extremely disappointed that nothing had gone wrong this time to provide fuel for their acid pens and acerbic wit. There were no humorous articles to be written when everything had gone to plan, no delicious barbed witticisms to be employed at the engineer's expense, no salacious cartoons to be drawn and laughed over.

Now, in late afternoon, the ship had been lifted by the incoming tide and was floating free and proud in the river. Amy found the sight of this immense vessel both uplifting and intensely moving. To her this triumph of modern technology seemed to prove that there might be no limits to what mankind might achieve in the future if they put their minds to it.

As this momentous day came to its end, even the dirty muddy river seemed in beneficent mood to welcome this iron giant. The sun sparkled on the water revealing unexpected traces of beauty, even here in this drabbest of places. The East London sky was an unfamiliar wintry blue haze, lit by a brilliant setting sun. Even the city, away to the west, looked less grimy than usual, the distant blackened chimneys and soot-covered domes picked out in glittering silver light.

Ginny was standing at her side watching the Great Ship being manoeuvred by barges into a safe mooring place for the night. Amy could imagine what deep morbid thoughts must be going through her mind at this moment, because the sight of that proud vessel could never be an uplifting one for her, given its melancholy connection to the fate of her son. *Poor, dear Ginny*...she deserved so much better from life than it had given her...

'It was nice of Mr Brunel to ask us here as his personal guests of honour to see the launch, wasn't it?' Amy suggested hesitantly. 'I have heard that they don't intend to use the name *Leviathan* after all, though, but to call the vessel the *Great Eastern* in honour of the fact that she is intended for the mail service to the East Indies and Australia.'

Ginny sighed, her voice melancholy, filled with infinite sadness. 'Truly it is a wonderful vessel to see. Yet it still weren't worth my boy's life, Miss.'

Amy put her arm around her and gave her a long tearful hug. 'No, you're quite right, Ginny. Nothing would be worth Billy's young life.'

Wiping the tears from her own eyes, Amy excused herself and went and found a seat on a nearby capstan as dusk began to fall. Making herself as comfortable as she could on the hard iron surface, she felt inside the pocket of her skirt and pulled out the letter she had received only this morning.

'Is that letter from Dr Silver, Miss?' Ginny asked her, finding a similar makeshift seat on a coil of thick rope beside her.

Amy was startled by Ginny's inspired guess. 'Why would you think that, Ginny?'

'Because you've read it about sixteen times today, Miss,' Ginny pointed out dryly. 'Also your face 'as lighted up every time you read it. You liked that young man, didn't you, Miss?'

'Nonsense, Ginny,' she denied half-heartedly. 'He was only an interesting acquaintance, nothing more.'

Amy spread the letter out and scanned its contents again in the failing light, admiring the fine educated hand. By now she had almost memorized its contents, though, so that she scarcely needed the fast fading light to read it at all.

"My dearest Amy (it began)

(I take the bold step of still addressing you as Amy, because you will always be sweet Amy to me, rather than the grand Lady Rachel, even though that pretty servant girl who befriended a man in deep trouble never truly existed.)

I hope I will always have your friendship, even though you are a great and wealthy lady, and I remain a fugitive and convicted murderer...

...As you can probably discern from the Cape Town post office stamp on this letter, we have decided to take the Atlantic route to our new life. We now have a few

days in port before continuing our journey. Strangely, everything in these southern lands is topsy-turvy, and Cape Town basks in high summer even though it is late December. There are strange plants here too – proteas and euphorbias and aloes – and even stranger birds – sunbirds and parrots and bulbuls. As I write this, I am sitting in a garden on the slopes of Table Mountain, under the shade of a palm tree shaped like a woman's petticoats. There is a white-painted Dutch house behind us, and dragonflies filling the air above the lily pond in front. Elisa is beside me, reading one of her learned books (thankfully not about rare jewellery!) and trying not to smile at me. Her arm is now fully recovered, as is her general condition, and she proved it today by racing me up the hill to this garden, beating me by about a mile. From up here, above the growing town, it is almost possible to see where the great oceans of the Atlantic and the Indian are finally conjoined...

...I will miss my homeland, and miss you most of all, sweet Amy, but I have been given much in return...

Tomorrow we sail onwards to our new life. I don't want to tell you exactly where, but it is a place that holds the promise of a long and happy life for us in a true fragrant harbour..."

Amy looked at the riverside scene before her, at the giant ship floating free in the evening dusk with its army of workers clambering all over it, and tried to imagine a very different scene: the blue clarity of the African sky, the brilliant Protea flowers, the sunbirds and dragonflies.

She put the letter away with a sigh. 'Come, Ginny. It's getting cold. Time to go home...'

THE END

ABOUT THE AUTHOR

Gordon Thomson is a civil engineer by profession, a Geordie by birth, and Sunderland supporter (and therefore masochist) by inclination.

His professional engineering career took him all over the world - Africa, the Far East, South America, as well as Holland and the UK - and this experience of exotic places and different cultures is what gave him the urge to try writing.

He has a Japanese wife and two grown up sons, one of whom was born in Holland, so he does claim to be a citizen of the world, if a very English one.

Leviathan, which is set in 1850s' Riverside London, is his first published novel.

Printed in Poland
by Amazon Fulfillment
Poland Sp. z o.o., Wrocław